DARK
FISSURES

Also by Matt Coyle

Yesterday's Echo

Night Tremors

Blood Truth

Wrong Light

Lost Tomorrows

DARK FISSURES

A RICK CAHILL NOVEL

MATT COYLE

OCEANVIEW PUBLISHING
SARASOTA, FLORIDA

ISBN 978-1-60809-268-0

Published in the United States of America by Oceanview Publishing
Sarasota, Florida

www.oceanviewpub.com

10 9 8 7 6 5 4 3 2

PRINTED IN THE UNITED STATES OF AMERICA

For Charles Henry Coyle, Jr.
Father, Veteran, Self-Made Man
Dec. 6, 1924–Oct. 3, 2015

ACKNOWLEDGMENTS

THIS BOOK AND my career have been made better by the people who have touched both of them.

My sincere thanks to:

My agent, the Velvet Hammer, Kimberley Cameron, for her unwavering support and invaluable advice.

Bob and Pat Gussin, Lee Randall, Emily Baar, Lisa Daily, and Michael Fedison at Oceanview Publishing for all the expertise and for being fantastic partners.

Carolyn Wheat, Cathy Worthington, Judy Hamilton, Linda Schroeder, and Grant Goad of the Saturday Writers Group for helping to make this book worthy of submission.

My family, Jan and Gene Wolfchief, Tim and Sue Coyle, Pam and Jorge Helmer, Jennifer and Tom Cunningham for all the support and year-round marketing.

Nancy Denton for an essential early line edit and her continued goodwill.

Jennifer Cunningham for a sharp eye, lots of questions, and a final read.

Bob Buckley for all things lawyerly.

Matt Menotti for information on car dealerships.

Diane Villarino and George Alexander for their expertise on life insurance.

Gina Mattern Corsini for inside real estate info.

Dr. D. P. Lyle for his knowledge of opioids and all things medical.

Pamela Putnam, San Bernardino County Deputy Coroner, for the extensive information on coroner procedures.

Retired FBI Special Agent George Fong for his knowledge regarding FBI field offices.

David Putnam for his bottomless well of knowledge of all things police and his generosity of spirit.

Finally, thanks to two Navy SEALs, one freshly minted, the other retired, who, true to their selfless service to our country, asked not to be singled out by name for their contributions to this book.

Any errors on the law, car sales, life insurance, real estate, medical issues, coroners, the FBI, police procedures, or SEAL conduct are solely the author's.

CHAPTER ONE

A RAINBOW LIGHT bar went off in my rearview mirror. Then the quick whir of a siren. I pulled over onto the side of the road.

Again.

Pre-rush-hour traffic sped by on Torrey Pines Road, the main artery in and out of La Jolla's northern end. I checked the side mirror. The cop exited his cruiser. Tall. Lean. Aviator sunglasses above seacliff cheekbones. I'd seen him once or twice, but he'd never stopped me before.

Others had.

The cop put his hand on the handle of the Sig Sauer P229 pistol in his holster as he approached my car. I put both hands on the steering wheel. In plain sight. Nothing in the car could get me arrested. Or shot.

Except me.

I scanned the outline of the cop's uniform. Pressed and too form-fitted against his body to hide a throw-down gun. Unless he had it tucked between his Sam Browne duty belt and his back. He stopped behind my left ear.

"License and registration." Military cadence with a dollop of contempt hanging off the end. The cop's brass nameplate read Sgt. Buchholz.

"I have to reach into the glove compartment for the registration," I said before I slowly reached across and retrieved the document, keeping my left hand on the steering wheel. I repeated the exercise while taking my license from my wallet.

"Been drinking today, Mr. Cahill?" He called me by my name before he even looked at my driver's license.

"No." The truth. Luckily. I put my hands back on the wheel and stared straight ahead.

"Smoke some marijuana?"

"No." I waited for him to run down a list of drugs legal and illegal, but he stopped at weed.

"What's your business in La Jolla today?"

"Just picked up my mail." I bit down the urge to say none of his damn business and nodded at a stack of letters in a rubber band on the passenger seat. I kept a La Jolla mailing address at a Postal Annex to keep erect the façade that my investigative agency operated out of that town. La Jollans had nice houses and liquid assets, but they had problems just like everybody else. Maybe more. Money caused as many problems as it solved.

"Do you know why I stopped you, Mr. Cahill?"

"No." Because the chief of police put a target on my back.

"You were swerving in and out of traffic and doing forty in a thirty-five-mile-per-hour zone."

"How fast was the guy going who sped past me right before you pulled me over?" I could only take so much.

"Step out of the car, please." He stepped back and kept his right hand on the handle of his gun.

As usual, I had to pay the debt that my lip had borrowed. I slowly got out of the car. Traffic whizzed by, swirling a wind that pulled at me.

The cop ran me through the drunk-driving exercises. He made me walk the inner line of a bike path three feet from whizzing traffic. Cars honked, teenagers hooted. I walked the line. When I'd run through his tricks, the cop had me sit down on the curb while he went back to his car so people could eyeball me as they sped by.

The November sun sliced down between fluffy clouds and bounced off my sunglasses. Not the way I'd planned to spend my afternoon. The Postal Annex that held my mailbox was on La Jolla Boulevard. If I'd just taken the Boulevard out of town going south, I might have avoided Sergeant Buchholz or any of his friends. The cops had a heavier presence in the northern section of La Jolla. The drive home would have been longer, but I probably wouldn't have been sitting on a curb waiting on a warrant check.

But that would be giving in.

Sergeant Buchholz talked into the car radio and checked his computer for warrants, but he already knew me front to back. Everybody did down at the La Jolla Police Department. What they may not have known was why Police Chief Tony Moretti had circled a bull's-eye around me. I did.

And I knew the bull's-eye would grow tighter and tighter.

Sergeant Buchholz finished up in the car and sauntered over to me like he had all the time in the world and like my time was irrelevant. He stood over me and pushed down a pen and a traffic ticket book with a citation flipped to the front.

"Sign at the bottom and appear at the courthouse on the back before the date listed." He curled the right corner of his lips into a smirk. "Of course, your signature is not an admission of guilt. You'll receive a letter in the mail giving you the option of paying the fine ahead of time, in case you don't want to argue your case against me in court."

I stood up and faced Sergeant Buchholz before I took the book and pen from his hand.

I could feel his eyes boring into me behind the sunglasses, daring me to challenge his authority. His power. The power to disrupt a citizen's life just because he could. Or in my case because he, like all the cops at LJPD, had a wink and a nod from their chief to harass me whenever possible. But Buchholz came to it naturally, like a cat toying with a mouse.

I knew the weight of the badge. How it could find a crack in your character and chip away at it until a dark fissure ran through your soul. I'd been stripped of my badge long ago, before the crevasse within could swallow me up. The crack inside Buchholz seemed to be deep and wide.

"You did some good police work here today, Sergeant." I signed the citation and handed the ticket book and pen back to him. "I'm sure this is what you envisioned when you signed up twenty years ago. Harassing citizens on dubious traffic stops. Your chief will be proud. Tell Moretti I said hello."

"Drive home safely, Mr. Cahill. The streets can be a dangerous place." Buchholz pulled my copy of the ticket from the book and handed it to me. "Even in La Jolla."

CHAPTER TWO

I LET THE call go to the answering machine. Again. I looked over at the phone on the kitchen wall from my spot on the couch in the living room. I wondered if I'd miss it. Probably not. Nothing good ever came from answering that phone. I'd miss the wall the phone hung from, along with all the other walls that held up the roof of my house. Well, my house and the bank's. Soon to just be the bank's.

Midnight stared at me from the backyard through the sliding glass door. He didn't paw the glass like he wanted to come inside. Just stared. He'd spent more and more time outside lately. Almost like he knew his days in a spacious backyard were numbered. He was a black Lab, after all, and clairvoyant. Those big brown eyes stared right into your soul.

My cell phone rang in my jeans pocket. I pulled it out and looked at the screen, hoping the bank hadn't cracked the code and found my work number. I'd worked for a big bucks investigative agency in La Jolla when I signed the mortgage papers a couple years ago. Now I worked for my own agency. My phone number had changed.

So had my income.

I didn't recognize the number on the phone's screen. It wasn't the bank's. I'd memorized that one. It wasn't the La Jolla Police Department Chief of Police's, either. I knew that number, too. The chief hadn't called me in a while, but I knew he'd contact me again.

Maybe soon, maybe not. But eventually there'd be a knock on the door and a cop holding a warrant for my arrest.

For murder.

In the meantime, I'd fight the battles right in front of me. Maybe the call on my cell was from a paying client, and I'd get to stave off the foreclosure for another month. I answered the phone.

"Mr. Cahill?" The voice flowed like a mountain stream, holding the Ls for an extra beat. A hint of the South. Musical. Sensual, without effort.

"We can start with Rick."

"I think my husband was murdered." Nothing sensual about that.

"Then you should call the police." I needed the fee, but I knew my limitations. And the law.

"I already did. They ruled Jim's death a suicide." Calm.

"Then I'm not sure what you think I can do for you."

"You can find the truth."

A year ago, somebody else hired me to find the truth. Back when I worked for a man I respected and could pay my mortgage. I found the truth and people lost their lives. I only lost my job. And a couple friends.

"Sometimes the truth is what everyone else thinks it is." I thought about the people who'd died during my quest last year. "And sometimes it's better to let the truth lie."

"That's not good enough for me, Mr. Cahill." A slight scold in the alpine stream's current. "I need to know what happened to my husband. And I thought you would be the man to help me find out. I thought you cared about the truth."

The house phone rang. I walked into the kitchen and looked at the screen. The bank.

Again. I owed it three months' mortgage payments. That was the bank's truth. And mine.

"Meet me at Muldoon's Steakhouse in La Jolla at five. I'll be in the bar."

"I'd rather meet at your office."

"That is my office."

* * *

La Jolla sits on the coast just north of San Diego and is known for its beautiful beaches, stratospheric wealth, and Dr. Seuss. Muldoon's Steak House had been a fixture on Prospect Street, La Jolla's restaurant row, for over forty years. I'd spent seven of those years as its manager with a sliver of ownership that had never amounted to anything but a fractured friendship. Now it got me a table in the bar or dining room whenever I had to meet with a client.

The hostess greeted me by name when I entered the restaurant. I couldn't remember hers, so I just nodded on my way to the bar. Pat, a bartender I'd hired ten years ago, held up a Ballast Point IPA. I shook my head.

"Client?" Pat's eyebrows rose on his moon face.

"Yep."

"Haven't seen you in a while."

Pat was on the Post-it note list of people I considered friends. I could have told him I hadn't been to Muldoon's lately because I hadn't had a client in a while, but kept it to myself. He had his own problems, I guess. Our conversations rarely ventured past the Chargers' or Padres' problems.

I sat at a table in the far corner with my back to the wall. I hadn't bothered to tell the woman on the phone what I looked like. She'd done her research on me, so I figured she'd seen a picture. My face had turned up in a few newspapers and online a couple times over the years. Some for fame, some for blame. Most of which I didn't deserve.

The bar sat empty save for Pat and me. Muldoon's didn't officially open until 5:00 p.m., another five minutes. At 4:58 p.m. a woman walked in. Tall, long red hair, fair-skinned. Levi's hugged her legs and a sky-blue sweater couldn't hide her lean curves. She looked around and spotted me. Recognition in big round eyes colored a shade darker than her sweater, but no smile.

She walked over to me. Long confident strides of an athlete. A sexy athlete. She looked to be around my age, thirty-six. When she pulled up at my table, something about her eyes told me she was slightly older. Not wrinkles or crow's feet. Confidence. Pain. Life.

"Mr. Cahill?" A question that didn't need answering.

I stood up and offered a hand. "Rick."

She shook my hand. "Brianne Colton."

The mellifluous voice from the phone. Light, but resonant. Musical. Her last name rang a dull bell in the back of my mind, but I couldn't place the connection.

"Can I get you something to drink?"

"Are you having anything?"

"Not on the job."

She peered at me, her left eyelid dropping to half-mast. "I'll have a beer. You choose."

When a woman tells me to choose a beer, I usually go for something light and delicate. Light and delicate didn't match my first impression of Brianne Colton.

I looked at Pat. "You can pull that Ballast Point IPA back out of the fridge."

The IPA was bitter and whacked you hard with hops.

"Just one?"

"Yep." Too early to get hit hard with anything.

Pat put the beer on the bar with a glass next to it. "No charge."

I went to the bar, laid down a five-dollar bill, grabbed the beer, and left the glass.

"Thanks."

"Mrs. Colton, let's get a table inside." I arced my arm toward the hallway that led past the hostess station into the dining room.

Brianne Colton walked over and I ushered her down the hallway. The petite hostess whose name I couldn't remember smiled as we neared her.

"Can I get you a table, Mr. Cahill?"

"We're going up to booth four. Thanks. I know the way. You can tell the staff to ignore us."

The arrangement I had with the owner, Turk Muldoon, allowed me to grab a table or booth when the restaurant wasn't busy. I scheduled most of my client meets when the restaurant just opened to avoid a crowd.

And Turk. We'd been best friends once. Now we had a business arrangement.

Muldoon's Steak House was stuck in the 1970s: salad bar, bronze and redwood paneling, dim lighting. Stale atmosphere, but good food. That's the way Turk and his regulars liked it. The ones who hadn't died off, yet.

Muldoon's had once been my working sanctuary. A place where I'd kept busy enough to avoid the shadows from my past. Now, three years after I'd left, I was back. Sifting through other people's shadows for a daily fee.

I led Brianne up an elevated platform to the first leather-clad booth on the left. We sat opposite each other across a polished wood table.

"Why did you order me an IPA?" Brianne asked.

"I'm a gentleman, remember. It was the polite thing to do."

"Yes." She tilted her head and looked at me like I was a jigsaw puzzle. "But why not a light beer or something less robust?"

"Was it a bad choice?"

"No. But why?"

"Lucky guess?" I shrugged my shoulders, but she kept giving me the cypher look. "The way you carry yourself. Your confidence. A bit of athletic arrogance in the way you walk."

"Athletes don't drink light beer?"

"Maybe, but you struck me as someone who doesn't like anything watered down." I pulled a notebook and pen from the inside pocket of my leather jacket. "So, let's start at the beginning. When, where, and how did your husband die? For right now, use the police version of how."

"He died two and a half months ago. At home." She pressed her lips together and shook her head, both eyes set to half-mast. "He was found hanging from a beam in the garage."

"Did you find him?"

"No." She looked down at the table for a five count. When her head came up, tears filled up the bottom of her blue eyes. "My son did."

"I'm sorry. Do you need a moment?"

"No. I'm good." She blinked a few times and the tears evaporated, leaving behind steeled resolve. "That's why I'm sure Jim didn't kill himself."

"Why is that?"

"Jim would never let Cash be the one to discover his body."

"Would he let you?"

She hesitated long enough to put a lie to her response. "No."

"What time of day did your son find him?"

"Around midnight." She looked down at the table again. Sadness for what her son went through or guilt for not being there first? Both?

"Where were you?"

"At my apartment. Jim and I were separated."

"Separated, as in getting a divorce? Or, as in figuring it out?"

"Is that relevant?" She leaned forward and gave me the tight lips and the squint.

"It might be." Her eyes, blue half-moon spotlights, bored into me. I'd looked at worse things in my life. "Losing you might have pushed your husband over the edge. And regarding him not wanting your son to find his body, when you're spiraling down into that type of depression, you don't think past just wanting to make the pain stop."

She relaxed back in her seat. "You sound like you've lived through that kind of depression."

"How long were you and Jim separated?"

"Four months."

"Four months sounds like you'd gotten it figured out and the next thing to do was sign the papers."

"I don't see what this has to do with anything." She gave me the angry eyes again. "I met you here with the understanding that you'd help me get my husband's case reopened and, instead, you're acting just like the police who ruled Jim's death a suicide."

"You asked me to find the truth, Mrs. Colton." I leaned toward her and pushed the bank's late notices to the back of my mind. "And if I agree to take you on as a client, that's what I'm going to do. If you want an investigator who will go through the motions and chase your phantoms for a daily fee, I can give you some phone numbers."

"I want to find the truth, Mr. Cahill." Her jaw cinched tight.

"Even if the truth turns out to be that your husband committed suicide?"

"I have to know the truth."

"Okay, then play along with me a bit longer." I settled back in the booth and scanned the few notes I'd taken. "So, were you two getting a divorce?"

"We'd talked about it but hadn't decided yet." She looked down at the table again.

"But you initiated the separation." My guess was she had decided on divorce, whether she told him or not.

A long enough silence to again answer the question. "Yes. How did you know?"

"Even in today's world of dual incomes, it's unusual for the woman to be the one who moves out of the house when a couple separates." I scribbled a note on the pad. "How often did you see, or talk with, Jim after you left?"

"We talked on the phone a couple times a week about our son. He was about to start his freshman year at UCLA and money was tight."

"When was the last time you saw Jim?"

"Two weeks before he died."

"Had your husband been depressed?"

"My husband went through periods of depression over the years, Mr. Cahill." Brianne tugged at the collar of her sweater like she'd suddenly gotten hot. "But never anywhere near depressed enough to kill himself."

Her hesitation earlier when I'd asked her if her husband would have allowed her to find his body told me that she'd wrestled with the possibility that her husband had committed suicide. But no need to push that point until I learned more facts about the death.

"Is there anything else that makes you think your husband didn't kill himself?"

"Jim had guns all over the house. If he was going to kill himself, he'd use a gun."

"Maybe he didn't want to make a mess."

"He was a neat freak, but would have used a gun." She took a long swig of her beer. "Besides, I'd never seen the rope that . . . that he was hanging from before."

Maybe Brianne Colton wasn't just an estranged wife putting denial between her and the guilt she'd feel if she accepted her husband's death as a suicide. She'd thought it out, and separated or not, no one knows a man better than his wife. But I wasn't ready to jump onboard, yet.

"Did he have any problems at work? Anything other than your marriage that he could have been depressed about?"

"Sure. Work bothered him sometimes. You, of all people, should understand that."

"Why?"

"Jim was a cop. I'm sure you remember what it's like."

"San Diego PD?"

"No. La Jolla."

CHAPTER THREE

LA JOLLA PD. Police Chief Tony Moretti and all his men. The man squeezing me whenever he could and the man convinced I'd committed murder.

"Mrs. Colton . . ."

"Brianne."

"Brianne." She'd be back to "Mrs." after she heard me out. "I can't take your case. I'm sorry I made you come down here. I can give you the contact information of a couple investigators who are very good, better than me. I'm confident either can find out the truth about what happened to your husband."

"I don't want any other private investigators." Her eyes went wide. Vulnerable. "I want you."

"I don't have a very good relationship with the La Jolla Police Department. Somebody else would be able to get more information from them than me."

"That's why I want you, Rick. You're not afraid to stand up to LJPD. You won't take what they say at face value."

She was wrong. I was afraid of LJPD. I might not believe what they'd have to say, I just couldn't afford to have the conversation.

"You think you know me because you read some old newspaper articles or Internet stories, but you don't." I suddenly wished I'd taken Pat up on that beer. And about six others. "The articles, the stories, they're not a hundred percent true. I'm not the man they make me out to be."

"Then what kind of man are you?" Her eyes went half-mast again, blue lasers boring into me, searching for some truth that wasn't there. "I thought you'd understand what I'm going through. Someone murdered your wife eleven years ago and got away with it. Did you just stop caring?"

I felt that pain every day, but it was my pain. Nobody else's and not for public display.

"I can give you the names of a couple good investigators." I tilted my head. "I'm sorry I can't help you, Mrs. Colton."

"I already hired someone else two months ago." Her glare could cut glass. "He copied the police report and charged me five thousand dollars. You're my last hope."

Everybody has problems. Mine could put me in jail for the rest of my life. Brianne Colton's was not believing that her estranged husband had committed suicide. My problem was unsolvable. Hers had probably already been solved. She just didn't like the result.

I wrote the names of two PIs I respected and their phone numbers on my notepad, ripped off the page, and set it down in front of Brianne. "Call either. They'll be thorough and honest."

"I know Dan Coyote." Brianne held the notebook page I'd dropped onto the table in her right hand. "He used to work for LJPD. He'll back their version. Moira MacFarlane does mostly workers' comp cases."

"You did your homework, but it didn't tell you everything. Coyote quit LJPD because he didn't agree with their tactics, especially Moretti's. He'll play it straight. Moira MacFarlane worked with me on the Randall Eddington case last year." The one where people died. But not because of her. The deaths were on me. "She's good."

"Maybe you're right about both of them, but I can't afford to make another five-thousand-dollar mistake. I need someone who's not afraid to take on Chief Moretti and find out what he's covering up." She crumpled the paper in her hand. "Someone I can trust. That's you."

I didn't know why Brianne Colton thought she could trust me. Maybe in today's world of social media and twenty-four-hour news cycles where Andy Warhol's prediction became a biblical utterance, people thought they knew someone they'd never met because of some story on the Internet. The only thing the Internet had ever gotten right about me was my age. But her instincts about Moretti were good.

I'd already caught him in a cover-up once. Back when he was just a detective and before he thought I'd murdered somebody. Well, he probably thought I'd murdered my wife but that was years earlier and way out of his jurisdiction. And he wasn't alone. I'd already been tried and convicted by the press, which made me question Brianne's trust in me even more.

"Why so much trust, Brianne?" I scanned her eyes looking for something I could believe. Or not believe.

"A friend of mine speaks very highly of you."

I couldn't think of many people who would speak highly of me. Bob Reitzmeyer, my old boss at La Jolla Investigations, thought I'd betrayed him, which was close enough to the truth. Turk Muldoon, my former best friend and partner, now avoided me as much as I did him. I worked hard and did a good job for my clients, but most of the time I gave them nothing but bad news. Hard to give a glowing review for the person who confirmed your suspicion and broke your heart by catching your spouse sheet wrestling with someone else.

No. I drew a blank. "Who's that?"

"Kim Parker."

"Kim Parker?" I knew both names, first and last, but they didn't go together.

"Formerly Kim Connelly." She raised her eyebrows and searched my eyes. "She got married a few months ago. I thought you knew."

Kim. The woman whose heart I'd broken and who broke mine. With plenty of help from me. I knew she'd moved in with the real estate king, and the Christmas cards stopped coming last year, but I hadn't expected this. Denial only works until reality hits you in the head. Right then, I could have used a helmet. It must have shown.

"I'm sorry. I thought you knew." Brianne gently rested her hand on top of mine. A gesture of kindness that startled me. I hadn't felt pure kindness, kindness without a hook hiding within, in so long, I didn't trust it.

"How do you know Kim?" I slid my hand out from under Brianne's and picked up my notepad like I'd missed something important that I'd already written down.

"I sing in a local country band that performs all over San Diego. Kim comes to a lot of our shows. About a year ago, we sort of became friends through osmosis, I guess. I sang at her wedding. She's a great gal."

"I know."

"Anyway, she said I could trust you. That you'd find the truth no matter what and you'd do what was right."

I wasn't sure if I knew what was right anymore. I only knew what was wrong. Moretti and his boys in blue were mostly wrong when it came to me. Did they have anyone else on their hit list? Jim Colton? How far would they go to stop an enemy? Murder?

I wasn't ready to go that far. I couldn't let my feelings for Moretti taint the evidence or my gut instinct, which was that Jim Colton, like so many cops and ex-cops, killed himself. He just chose a rope over eating his own gun.

"Jim never trusted Chief Moretti," she said.

Brianne seemed to be reading my mind. If true, I had to give the deceased credit. He must have had good instincts. Except for the suicide part.

"Why do you think Moretti is covering something up?" I leaned forward.

"When I was finally able to pick up Jim's belongings, his cell phone was missing."

"Maybe Jim didn't have it on him because he'd just gotten up the nerve to kill himself and didn't want to risk getting a text or a phone call that might change his mind."

"I checked all over the house and couldn't find it." She shook her head. "Either the police took it or the person who killed him did."

"Did you try to find it with the Find Your Phone feature?"

"Jim didn't have it set up."

"Maybe the cops lost it?" Brianne may have been convinced her husband was murdered, but I wasn't. Not yet. Maybe never.

"Or the killer took it."

"Why would someone kill your husband and stage it as a suicide? Did he have any enemies?"

"I don't know."

"Exactly." No matter how badly I needed the money, I wouldn't take it from Brianne Colton, or anyone else, under false pretenses. "There has to be more than a lost phone and Jim choosing a rope over a gun to kill himself."

"I know Jim was thinking of quitting the force."

"How does that make him a target for murder?"

"Jim wasn't a quitter. He'd been a Navy SEAL. They don't quit because something is difficult." Her eyes softened and she looked at memories over my shoulder. "He would only quit if he was asked to do something dishonorable or his superior was behaving dishonorably and Jim felt he couldn't stop him."

Moretti. Dishonorable. I was surprised Jim Colton had lasted a week on the La Jolla Police Department. But the fact that he had been a SEAL curved the ball a bit. SEALs were the best of the best.

The toughest of the tough, both mentally and physically. If Colton killed himself, something had to have gone way wrong in his life. A pending divorce might have been enough, but I doubted it. And if it hadn't been divorce and there wasn't anything else, Brianne Colton might be right about Jim being murdered.

"What did he do at LJPD?"

"He led the CIT."

Crime Impact Teams are small units in a police force that combat specific crime areas and problems. I briefly worked CIT in Santa Barbara doing parole and probation sweeps before they booted me off the force.

"I didn't know LJPD had a CIT."

"They didn't until Chief Moretti hired Jim to run it three years ago."

"Where was he a cop before La Jolla?"

"He wasn't. He worked for the GRS overseas."

"GRS?" I asked.

"Global Response Staff. A CIA security force."

"Jim worked for the CIA?" Now I was starting to believe.

"No. He was an independent contractor. The CIA uses contractors for most of the security work. CIA agents are in supervisor roles."

"Was he in the Middle East?"

"Yes. His last post was Benghazi."

"Geez. Tough duty." I made a note about Colton's service on my pad. "Was he there during the siege when the ambassador and the others were murdered?"

"Yes. One of the others was Jim's friend." She air quoted "others" and I felt like an ass.

"Jim quit after the attack. He thought the State Department had FUBARed the whole thing and acted dishonorably."

Brianne Colton was definitely a military wife. FUBAR was military slang for Fucked Up Beyond All Repair. My dad had been in the Navy during Vietnam and carried FUBAR into his career as a cop. And his family.

"Could Jim have made any enemies with fellow contractors or the CIA after the shit went down?" I asked.

"He made his feelings known to his supervisors at the CIA that people had died needlessly, but he didn't take it any further." She shook her head. "The independent operators were upset with the State Department, but not each other. They're all former Special Ops guys. They love each other like brothers."

I didn't bother to bring up Cain and Abel.

"Did the medical examiner perform an autopsy?"

"Yes. She determined the cause to be death by strangulation due to hanging." She pressed her lips together and shook her head. "But that doesn't mean someone else didn't put the noose around his neck."

Maybe. Maybe wishful thinking.

"Anything else you can give me?"

"Well, I don't know if this means anything or not." She reached into her buckskin purse and pulled out a manila folder. From the folder, she took a sheet of paper. "This is Jim's last phone bill with all the calls he made in the month of August."

Brianne handed the sheet of paper to me. It was a computer printout with a long list of phone numbers next to dates and times. One phone number three quarters of the way down the bill was circled. The date was August twenty-third, five days before Jim Colton died, either by his own hand or someone else's. Brianne reached over my arm and tapped the circled number. "That's the number to the local FBI office."

CHAPTER FOUR

"THE FBI?" THE case just got interesting. "How do you know?"

"I called the number."

"And?"

"I tried to find out why Jim had called and who he talked to but didn't learn anything." She tucked a long strand of silky hair behind her ear. "I couldn't even get past the operator."

I looked at the duration of the call, seventeen minutes. Why had he called the FBI? Five days before his death.

Brianne said Jim had been contemplating quitting LJPD. Had he found corruption within the department worthy of a call to the FBI? I knew from personal experience LJPD and Chief Moretti were corrupt. Corrupt enough to murder someone to keep things quiet? That, I didn't know. It would be dangerous to find out, but danger as a free man beat life behind bars. Maybe Jim Colton had found the leverage I needed to keep Moretti away from my front door.

I scanned the other phone numbers on the bill. Most of them started with the three San Diego county area codes: 619, 858, and 760. Fourteen calls Jim Colton made in the last two weeks of his life were to a phone number with a 775 area code. One on the day he called the FBI and two on the last day of his life.

I tapped the number and looked at Brianne. "Do you know this number?"

"Yes. That's Oak Rollins's number. He was Jim's best friend."

"Oak?"

"Odell. He and Jim were SEALs together and both worked the detail in Benghazi. Oak was his nickname. If ever you saw him, you'd understand why."

"Did Jim and Oak talk often?"

"Pretty often. Probably every few weeks."

I wondered what they talked about during the last two weeks of Jim Colton's life.

The missing phone. The call to the FBI. Moretti. Just enough to take a look.

"Okay." I folded the printout and put it in the inside pocket of my leather jacket. "I'm going to need a copy of the police report, the autopsy, and a check for twenty-five hundred dollars to start. That'll cover the first week. I'll email you a contract to sign when I get home."

Brianne smiled for the first time since we met a half hour ago. Warm, just a hint of teeth, but her eyes seemed to brighten. In my line of work, I didn't see too many smiles. And none that looked like that. I hadn't quite earned the smile yet. The information she'd given me was just enough to question the finding of suicide in her husband's death. The opportunity to possibly find more dirt on Police Chief Tony Moretti was a bonus. I needed any advantage I could get when that knock finally came to my door.

Brianne slid the file folder across the table to me. I glanced inside and saw the police report and autopsy. Underneath them was a short list of handwritten names and phone numbers. Presumably, Jim's friends. Brianne was smart and thorough. My kind of client. When I looked back up, she was already ripping a check from her checkbook. She handed it to me, and I stuffed it in my pocket without looking at it. I wanted to show her that trust went both ways.

"One last thing." I locked on her eyes.

"Whatever you need."

"I have to talk to your son."

"Why?" Her eyes went wide, forcing up her eyebrows. "He's been through enough. I don't want him to have to relive finding his father."

"He may know something you don't."

"That's why I gave you a list of Jim's friends." Her face flushed and she reached across the table and opened the folder, rustled the papers until she came out with the list. "See?"

"That's very helpful, and I'll talk to all of them." I kept my voice psychiatrist cool. "But I need to talk to your son, as well."

"No." She clasped her hands together and rubbed one thumb with the other. Over and over. "I can't allow that."

"Brianne. Kim said you could trust me, right?" Just uttering Kim's name put a hole in my gut and made me long for a beer, chased by a fifth of tequila. "And she told you I'd find the truth and do the right thing. I need to talk to your son to learn all the truth. I won't ask him anything more than necessary."

"What's necessary?" Thumb rubbing thumb, over and over.

"I won't know until I talk to him, but you have to trust me." I understood Brianne wanting to protect her son. The image of his father hanging in the garage would be forever branded into his psyche. Brianne didn't want me shining a spotlight on it. Fine. But years of dealing with duplicitous people made me wonder if the son might know something his mother wanted kept secret.

Brianne looked at me without saying anything for what seemed like a minute. Her eyes still wide with fear, anxiety, or both. Finally, in a voice just above a whisper, "Okay."

CHAPTER FIVE

I DID THE speed limit on the drive home. Fall had pulled the night down early and headlights stared unblinking at me in the rearview mirror, refusing to reveal the make or model of their car. They were all Crown Victoria police cruisers in my imagination. I didn't know how much longer I could tempt fate. Or Chief Moretti. But without the money to lease real office space, a free table at Muldoon's was the best I could do if I wanted to keep a La Jolla presence and have a chance to pay most of my bills.

The twenty-five hundred from Brianne Colton would help. I'd be able to pay off a month's mortgage and buy a six-pack of beer. Domestic. Brianne had bought me for a week. Finding the truth about her husband's death would likely take longer than that. Probably not long enough to pull me back to even, but at least I had a place to start.

Midnight greeted me at the front door when I got home. The breadwinner had just bought him a few more weeks to enjoy a spacious backyard. Things were looking up. Except for the fine I'd have to pay for the traffic ticket.

I gave Midnight a treat and let him outside. His tail arced up like a scorpion about to strike as he trotted around the yard sniffing out the best spot to pee. Someday, I hoped to feel that kind of joy again.

I went upstairs to a spare bedroom I'd converted into an office. The other spare remained empty, waiting for a reason to be filled up. I sat at my desk and typed in the personal information Brianne Colton had given me onto a standard contract and emailed it to her to sign and send back to me.

I opened the manila folder to read the police report. On top of the report were three "crime scene" photographs. Although the death was later ruled a suicide, crime scene investigators are almost always called when a body is discovered. The photos were three different angles of Jim Colton's body hanging by a rope a foot off the ground. I'd seen death many times before. Back on my cop beat in Santa Barbara's barrio, here in San Diego in my civilian life. And in the morgue staring at my wife's lifeless body. Colton looked peaceful in comparison to most deaths I'd seen, but that wouldn't have mattered to his son. I knew the pain Cash Colton must have felt when he found his father. He'd take that image to his own grave.

The photos would seem to fit the conclusion of death by suspension hanging and a probable suicide. A knocked-over kitchen chair lay on the garage floor to the right of Colton's dangling legs.

The only thing that possibly seemed out of place was the rope tied to the ceiling beams and around Colton's throat. It was a nylon climbing rope. Actually a piece cut from one. Most climbing ropes are at least 150 feet long. I'd used them when I'd gone rock climbing with Turk Muldoon in college. The rope in the photos was at most a quarter of that. Colton must have cut it from a rope he used when he went climbing. Brianne had said she'd never seen the rope before. Odd if her husband was a rock climber. I made a mental note to ask her if Colton ever went climbing.

Climbing ropes have a lot of spring in them so they can take the weight of a climber falling fifty to a hundred feet. Good choice for a hanging in that it could take the drop without fear of breaking. Bad choice in that the rope might stretch from the weight and put your feet back on the ground, at least for a second. Colton had apparently estimated it perfectly.

Unlucky him.

The first thing in the report made me shudder almost as much as the death photos. The reporting detective was Hailey Denton. We had a history and, as with everyone I'd come in contact with at LJPD, it wasn't a good one. For the second time that day, I cursed the fact that Jim Colton had lived in La Jolla and, by his hand or someone else's, had died there.

The report echoed what Brianne told me earlier. Jim Colton's body was discovered hanging from a beam in the garage by his son, Cash, at 12:15 a.m. on August 29. Cash had just returned home from a party at the beach. The fact that Colton had been hanging high enough to have his feet off the ground ruled out accidental death by autoerotic asphyxiation. Maybe a little solace to Brianne and her son.

The coroner determined the method of death to be strangulation by hanging. She'd listed the time of death to be between 9:00 p.m. and 11:00 p.m.

I pulled Jim Colton's last phone bill from the folder. He made three calls on his cell phone the day he died. The first call was placed at 12:31 p.m., the second at 7:17 p.m., and the last at 8:43 p.m. The first call lasted three minutes and the last two a minute each according to Colton's phone bill. If you took the coroner's earliest possible time of death, Jim Colton made a short call to someone roughly twenty minutes before he died.

A call to say good-bye or for a last hope to be talked out of killing himself? Or neither?

I pulled the list of Jim's friends and their phone numbers that Brianne had given me from my jacket pocket. The calls Colton made the day he died matched phone numbers on his friends' list.

The first to Kyle Bates and the last two to Odell Rollins. The man Brianne called "Oak" who she said was Jim's best friend. If you were contemplating suicide and looking for a good-bye or a way out, you'd call your best friend if your wife wasn't that person anymore.

Suicide remained the leading contender. That still left the call to the man named Kyle Bates. I went back to the police report to see if there was mention of the phone calls or the missing cell phone. Nothing.

So, if the police were right and Jim Colton committed suicide, he made a call to his best friend, disposed of his cell phone somewhere where no one could find it in the next twenty minutes to two hours, and then killed himself.

Why?

A question I'd ask Odell "Oak" Rollins, but not over the phone. I wanted to do a face-to-face for that. I've found it's easier to lie on the phone and harder to detect. First I had to find out where Rollins lived. I couldn't afford the subscription to the data-mining website that we used at the agency where I used to work and certainly couldn't call in any favors over there. Hard to believe, but I didn't have any connections at LJPD or even the San Diego Police Department.

So, I used free websites whenever possible or paid for each search individually. I hid the cost in other expenses on clients' expense reports because I didn't want them to know how threadbare my "agency" really was. Luckily, there was a free and easier way.

I called Brianne.

"I've got a gig tonight and I'm running out the door." Brianne rushed her words after I'd told her what I needed. "Can this wait until tomorrow? Or you could come by Chapin's tonight, and I'll give you the addresses between sets. Everything's on my phone."

"What time?"

"We start at eight and our first break is at eight forty-five. I'll reserve a table for you near the stage. Tell the bouncer your name when you get there, and he'll take care of you. Gotta run."

CHAPTER SIX

CHAPIN'S IS A bar/restaurant located in the Gaslamp Quarter in downtown San Diego. Named after the gas lamps that once lined its streets, the area is a mix of historic Victorian buildings nestled among modern high-rises. Old and new, the DNA of San Diego. Constantly reinventing itself while holding onto its historic roots. The eighth-largest city in the country that still thinks it's a small town.

The Gaslamp Quarter had a sordid past, from saloons and bordellos in the late eighteen hundreds to adult movie theaters and "massage" parlors in the middle of the last century. Now a trendy, Millennial hang with diverse live music and great restaurants. Part of the gentrification finalized when the former owner of the Padres upped the team's payroll enough to climb into the World Series in the late '90s and then conned the city into bankrolling a new ballpark only to gut the team after its completion. Another chapter in San Diego's shady dealings that tourists and most locals never see amid the blinding 365-days-a-year sunlight. Nice ballpark, though.

Chapin's long, skinny rectangular bar took up half of a Victorian structure opposite its twin restaurant. I told the bald, Sub-Zero-sized bouncer collecting covers and checking IDs that Brianne had a table for me. He nodded me into the bar. I scanned the crowd looking for Kim Parker and was both disappointed and relieved that she wasn't there.

A small raised stage sat up against an original red brick wall at the far end. Brianne stood on the stage with her back to the cramped crowd sitting at tiny bar tables. She wore the same blue jeans she had on earlier and they still looked good. A buckskin jacket over a turquoise blouse gave off just the right country vibe. It wasn't quite eight and she and the band looked to be talking over the last few details before they began playing. Even though she was the only woman onstage, I would have recognized her from behind. I reminded myself she was my client and sat up front, just to the left of the stage, at an empty table with a reserved sign on it.

Brianne turned around and greeted the crowd to jarring applause. She had a following and they cheered her in the intimate room. She saw me and winked, then turned her attention back to her fans.

"Ya'll ready to have a good time?" Brianne's voice filled out the hint of a southern accent I'd heard earlier at Muldoon's. The crowd answered in full throat on cue.

The band kicked off, guitar, bass, banjo, and drums, and Brianne broke into the Patty Loveless classic "That Kind Of Girl" and I instantly understood her fans' reaction. Big full voice, but sultry in between. The band was good and could keep up, but Brianne was clearly the draw and on a different level. She commanded the stage without effort, like the sun commands the day. She didn't so much sing the songs as live them. You believed every word. I could hear her life's pain in Carrie Underwood's "Jesus Take The Wheel."

I got lost in her performance.

The band took a break after forty-five minutes. Brianne stepped off the stage toward me, and her male bandmates slipped into the crowd. I got up and pulled out a barstool from the high-topped table. "A gentleman," Brianne said as she sat on the stool I'd proffered.

"I can fake it." I sat back down opposite her and caught her eyes flickering in the candlelight. "Get you something to drink?"

"No thanks. I don't like to drink while I'm performing, but I can get you another beer on the house." She pointed to the empty beer bottle on the table. The second one I'd consumed during her performance.

I'd gotten so lost in the music and Brianne's talent that I'd forgotten why I was there. I'd forgotten about everything. Police Chief Moretti, the bank trying to foreclose on me, Jim Colton hanging from a beam in his garage. Maybe this was how normal people felt when they went out for a night on the town.

"I'm good. Thanks." I did want that beer, though. So I could continue my drift into normalness. But that was fantasyland. I didn't belong in normal anymore. And getting lost was dangerous.

Even off the stage on a break from performing, Brianne was different than when I'd met her earlier today. Like a light inside had been turned on and its glow haloed her whole being. She smiled. The beers, the smile, the glow, or all three sent a warm buzz along my spine. I needed to follow Brianne's lead and not drink on the job.

"Heck of a set."

"Thank you." Brianne smiled again, all the way up to her eyes. A blue dazzle. I felt like an average Joe scoring points with the beauty in the bar way out of my league.

Normal.

"How come I don't see you on the CMA Awards on TV?"

"So, you're a flatterer as well as a gentleman."

"No. Just a good judge of talent. I used to book the bands at Muldoon's, so I know a little bit about music. You belong on the radio or on tour, not on a tiny stage in a bar in San Diego."

"I've already done the honky-tonks and bars in Nashville." No more smile. No more dazzle. "I had my chance a long time ago. Country radio isn't looking for a forty-year-old ingénue."

"When were you in Nashville?"

"Before I met Jim. I moved there from Brooksville, Kentucky, when I was eighteen. I didn't know how the world worked yet. Thought I'd get a record deal by the time I was twenty. Instead, I met Jim, got married, and had Cash and . . . no singing career."

I caught eyes watching me over Brianne's shoulder. Jealous eyes. I scanned the crowd and saw most of the men in the room, single or not, giving me the same look. They all wished they were sitting in my seat. I wondered what Jim Colton thought about those looks. Before and after he and Brianne separated.

"A lot of the guys in the room have been eyeballing us. How did Jim feel about all the attention?"

"He never came to any of my shows." Deadpan.

"He didn't approve?"

Brianne leaned forward and propped her elbow on the table, rested her chin in her hand, and studied me. I couldn't tell what she was looking for or what she saw. "Is this pertinent to the case, Rick?"

"Right now, everything is."

The beginning of a case was like mining for gold. You scooped up everything you could find and dumped it into a sieve and shook it until the dirt and dust disappeared leaving only the gold. I liked Brianne Colton. More and more each minute. But the truth was my journey and I followed its path.

"Jim was old-fashioned. He grew up on a farm in a tiny town in Alabama."

"A woman's place is in the home?"

"Yes, but it's not that simple." Her eyes softened and she seemed to be looking back at an earlier time. "He was old-fashioned in a southern gentleman kind of way." She shook her head and came back to the present. "Anyway, to answer your question, no, Jim didn't approve."

"How long have you been performing with the band?"

"A couple years, but I took some time off after Jim . . . after Jim died." She leaned back on the barstool. "This is my first week back."

"Was your performing again the main reason for the separation?"

"Really, Rick, I don't see how this has any bearing on finding the truth about Jim's death." She leaned forward and whispered the last two words. She then pulled her cell phone out of her jeans pocket, tapped the screen a couple times, and pushed it across the table in front of me. "Here's my address book with the addresses for Jim's friends. Isn't that why you came?"

"Yes. Thanks." I picked up the phone. "But you came looking for me, Brianne. I didn't knock on your door begging for a job. You want me to find the truth about Jim's death, you have to trust me. I'm not a psychiatrist trying to heal your pain. I'm here to find the truth. So please answer my questions and never lie to me. Okay?"

She folded her arms across her chest and nodded her head. "Okay."

"So, why the split? The band?"

"Yes." She stared at my shoulder. "But we'd also drifted apart. Jim would be deployed for months and months overseas, come home for a few months, and then be gone again. We lived separate lives for most of our marriage, but we always meshed whenever he'd come back home. The last time he came home three years ago, it was different. He was distant. Morose. I thought things would get better when he quit the GRS and joined the La Jolla Police Department. But they never did."

I took the list of Jim Colton's friends Brianne had given me earlier that day out of my pocket and scrolled through her phone taking pictures of the addresses that matched the names. Plus one more. Cash Colton's address up at UCLA. Brianne was busy acknowledging waves from her fans and didn't seem to notice. I quickly found her cell phone photos and found numerous pictures of a scowling teen with brown hair and blue eyes. Cash Colton. His father's hair and his mother's eyes. I took a picture of one of the photos, shut off the screen on Brianne's phone, and slid it to her across the table.

"Thanks," I said. "A couple questions and then I'll leave you to your fans."

"Okay." She looked away from the crowd and smiled at me.

"Did Jim rock climb or go mountaineering?"

"I don't think so." Pinched eyebrows. "Why?"

"The rope he was hang . . . the rope is the kind used by climbers."

"In all the years I knew him, he never talked about climbing. He may have had to do some on his missions, but he never mentioned it."

"And you told me you'd never seen the rope before, right?"

"Yes."

"Was there more of the rope in the garage or just the one used in his death?"

"Just the one rope. Why?"

"I'm not sure yet."

The band's guitar player walked up behind Brianne. Clean-cut for a musician and granite good looks. He smiled at me and put his hand on Brianne's shoulder. "Bri, it's time to get started again."

Brianne lifted her hand and squeezed the guitar player's. The movement almost involuntary, like a reflex. Something someone in a relationship would do. A romantic relationship. She caught me watching and dropped her hand.

"Be right there, Seth." Brianne looked at me and smiled. Dazzling, but tight around the mouth.

I smiled back and held onto the new piece of information, not sure what to do with it yet.

"You going to stick around or go home now that you got what you needed?"

I wasn't sure if I'd gotten what I'd needed, but I got more than I expected. "I'm going to stick around and listen to some country."

"See you in forty-five." Brianne stood up and took the stage to excited applause from the crowd.

The band started playing and Brianne made every man in the room wish he were a cowboy. I wondered how I'd look in a Stetson. I stuck around for the second set, watching Brianne's interplay with the guitar player. What I'd taken for shared musical kinship in the first set now took on deeper meaning. Brianne went back to back with all the band members during their solos, but her contact with the guitar player now hinted of intimacy.

How long had she been seeing him and did the relationship play any role in Jim Colton's death?

While Brianne performed onstage and commanded the attention of the entire crowd, the truth whispered to me, beckoning.

CHAPTER SEVEN

UCLA, THE UNIVERSITY of California at Los Angeles, is in the middle of some of the choicest zip codes in California, if not the country. A couple of wrong turns could put you on Rodeo Drive in Beverly Hills. Exiting there, you could spend the rest of your day counting Rolls-Royces in Brentwood, to the west, or Bel Air, to the north.

Royce Hall, not related to the Rolls, is the iconic Lombard Romanesque brick building with twin towers and high arches that anchor the UCLA campus. Atop the mesa above mini grassy rolling hills, it was my favorite building while on campus as a scholar-shipped jock almost twenty years earlier. Before I blew out my knee and transferred to UC Santa Barbara to be near the woman who became my wife.

I staked out Royce Hall's main entrance and waited for Cash Colton to exit after attending a lecture on the pedagogical disciplines of early Peruvian cave dwellers. I checked the picture I snapped on my phone last night against the students leaving Royce Hall. Fifty or so students in, I spotted Cash sleepwalking down the entry steps. An early morning class of any kind for college-age students was cause for somnambulism. Toss in cave dwelling and you had Zombie U.

"Cash. Hi." I plopped a friendly hand onto his shoulder when he hit the cement walkway. "I'm a friend of your mom's and just need to talk to you for a minute."

Cash stopped dead stride and eyeballed me. Tall like his mom and wide through the shoulders like his dad, he looked like a young movie star. I could tell, right off, that he hadn't bought the "mom's friend" ploy.

"I've got to get to my next class." He shook off my hand and started walking north.

A lie unless it took him an hour and a quarter to get there. I'd found his class schedule online. A half-truth by me and a lie by him. I'd call it even.

"This will only take a couple minutes." I matched his stride. "It's about your dad."

"You're not a friend of my mom's." He stopped and faced me. Challenging. "You're the private detective she hired."

"Yes, I am." After listening to Brianne sing and talking to her between sets, I felt I'd moved from hired hand to at least acquaintance, but no need for a semantics argument.

"What are you doing here?" Hard scowl. "She told me I had to talk to you when I went home this weekend."

"Change of plans. Give me five minutes, and we'll get it out of the way now so you can do whatever you want with your weekend." Plus, he'd be free to answer questions without his mother hovering over his shoulder.

"My mom know you're here?"

The kid could think on his feet, freshly awakened from zombie sleep or not.

"I don't know." Time to challenge back. "Do you need her to be here or can you handle it yourself?"

He squinted his eyes down on me like his mom had yesterday when she'd tried to figure me out. Only, I don't think she'd contemplated punching me like I thought her son might. I slid my right foot back half a stride and loosened my shoulders just in case.

"Alright, dude." He tossed up his hands. "You got five minutes."

I led him over to a concrete bench, and we sat down as students passed by in all directions.

"I know this is difficult, but please walk me through the day you found your father."

"What do you want to know, man?" His voice rose. "I came home at midnight and found my dad hanging in the garage."

Anger. Maybe to hide the tears.

"When did you last see your dad alive?"

"Why don't you just read the police report?" Lips snarled, chest and chin out.

"I did. But I want to hear it from you. Five minutes and we're done. When did you last see your dad alive?"

"About five o'clock that night." Cash looked down at the ground. The anger evaporated from his voice leaving sadness behind. "Right before I went to the last rager of the summer."

"Did he seem depressed?"

"Yeah. He was depressed. He'd been depressed since my mom moved out."

I thought of Brianne and the guitar player's hand on her shoulder. Too delicate to broach now, if ever.

"Did he ever talk to you about the separation or his depression?"

"If he did, I wouldn't tell some asshole like you."

Back on familiar ground.

"Did your dad ever go rock climbing?"

"Rock climbing?" He jerked his head back. "What the fuck are you talking about?"

"Humor me. Four minutes to go."

"My dad didn't like heights. Why the hell would he go rock climbing?"

Because the rope around Jim Colton's neck was the kind climbers use.

"Your dad was a Navy SEAL. I'm sure he jumped out of airplanes and rappelled down cliffs. How could he be afraid of heights?"

"I don't know, dude, but he was." A scowl, but he went on. "We were in one of those outside elevators in San Francisco one time, and he couldn't look down. He never told his SEAL buddies, but he didn't like heights."

Then why the rock climbing rope? He would have had to have driven to a climbing specialty store to buy it instead of just going to a Home Depot for a regular rope. More expensive, too.

"Had you ever seen, ah, the rope that was . . . had you ever seen the rope before?"

"No."

The image of his father's lifeless body hanging from the rafters must have run through Cash's head. It ran through mine. But still no tears. A gruff façade.

"Did anything seem unusual or stick out to you in the garage? Anything out of place?"

"Yeah, my dad was hanging from the rafters, asshole." He stood up like he'd won the argument and our talk was over.

"Point taken. Now sit back down." I let some command presence from my days as a street cop slip into my voice. "We're not done yet."

Cash remained standing just long enough to convince himself that he was still a tough guy before he sat down. The kid was stuck with an image imprinted in his brain that he'd never be able to erase and a loss he'd never be able to fill. I could cut him some slack, but I doubt he'd appreciate it or that it would get me any closer to the truth.

"Your mom is paying me to investigate your father's death. She already paid some thief five grand to investigate, and all he did was count the money. I know you probably think she can just pull hundred-dollar bills off a money tree in the backyard, but it doesn't work that way. She's getting her money's worth this time. Anything strange or out of place in the garage?"

"No."

"Do you think your dad killed himself?"

"Yes." A slight tremble in the lips. Cash stared down at the ground. "He was hanging there so still. I tried to push him up so his weight wouldn't be on the rope, but I knew he was already . . ."

My dad went to his sister's to die of cirrhosis of the liver. I didn't even have to watch him turn yellow and waste away, much less find his body at the end. I'd seen my wife on the cold steel of a coroner's table. I knew the pain of seeing the body of a loved one hollowed out in death. But I'd had time to prepare myself. Cash Colton hadn't had that remove. I couldn't imagine what it felt like to find your dad hanging at the end of a rope.

"I'm sorry you had to go through that, Cash." I now wished I hadn't gone so hard at him. I gently patted him on the back, but he slid down the bench out of my reach. "Why do you think he did it?"

"'Cause my mom is a whore and broke his heart." Now the sadness escaped, and his eyes filled with tears. He turned away hoping to hide what he couldn't control.

"Why do you say that?" The guitar player?

"Fuck you, man." Tears in his voice now, but he still wouldn't look at me. "This is none of your fucking business."

"Is that why your mom moved out, Cash? Who did your dad think she was fooling around with?"

"Fucking Seth Macklin."

Seth, the guitar player.

"The only reason she's trying to have Dad's death made into a murder is for two million in insurance money." He stood up and glared down at me. "Ask her about that, asshole. That's her money tree."

CHAPTER EIGHT

MY CELL PHONE rang before I even made it out of the UCLA parking garage. I checked the screen. Brianne Colton. That didn't take long. I answered the call.

"I thought you were going to talk to Cash down here this weekend." Voice off the leash and a little higher than when I'd talked to her last night.

"I didn't want to wait that long."

"It would have been nice of you to let me know." A creeping edge squared off her words now.

"I'm not going to be able to alert you to every move I make before I make it, Brianne." I eased my Mustang onto Sunset Boulevard. "I asked you to trust me last night, remember?"

"Yes, and I want to trust you, Rick." Still some serration. "But my son went through an incredibly traumatic experience. He's still recovering. I don't appreciate your ambushing him and undoing all the therapy he's been through."

She had a point, but it was too late now. "Trust goes both ways, Brianne."

"What do you mean by that?" The catch in her voice told me she had an inkling that I knew she'd been holding back information from me.

"You get a check from the life insurance company for Jim's death yet?"

Brief silence. "No."

"Is that because the suicide clause kicked in? Jim had had the policy for less than two years?"

A longer silence this time. "Yes."

"Don't you think that might be pertinent information for me to know?"

"Would you have taken the case if I'd told you?"

"I don't know. But it's not about that. It's about trust and the truth. You told me last night you wouldn't lie to me. Well, I consider holding back information lying."

"Okay, Rick. You've made your point." Soft, like I'd hurt her feelings.

"Two million dollars would go a long way toward resurrecting a promising singing career." I exited off Sunset Boulevard onto the 405 freeway.

"The money would be to put Cash through college and law school."

"But you're the sole beneficiary, right?"

"Yes, but what kind of a mother do you think I am?"

Wasn't sure what kind of mother, but I had an idea about what kind of wife.

"Tell me about the guitar player, Seth Macklin."

"What do you want to know?" A quick cadence.

"Whether you started sleeping with him before or after you moved out of the house you shared with your husband. And son."

"You're not a very nice man." Sadness over anger. "I moved out before anything happened between Seth and me."

"How long?"

"A week."

That didn't take long. "So Jim didn't have any delusions about the two of you getting back together."

"No." A sniffle. "Anything else you'd like to know, Rick? I don't want you to accuse me of lying again for holding back some personal and private information."

"No. Sorry."

"No you're not." She hung up.

I was sorry. I could have kept my peeve to myself and just asked Brianne about the insurance and let the affair lie. It would have been the professional and smart thing to do. I told myself I'd spoken up because of my unrelenting quest for the truth. But there were other ways of finding the truth. I'd felt a connection to Brianne that had been strengthened by seeing her perform. Deep down, I feared that learning the truth about her had knocked her off the pedestal I'd erected.

An hour later I was on Interstate 5, California's cement desert. Populated by never-ending lanes of hot rubber and steel. All in a hurry to get somewhere else at the speed of a glacier. There are hundreds of beautiful places in California, the 5 takes you to all the ones that aren't.

Except for San Diego at the tail end. Los Angeles and San Diego really aren't that different. San Diego is just more condensed and squeezes out most of the ugly that fills the voids between LA's beauty spots.

I'd moved two-tenths of a mile in five minutes when my phone rang again. The screen read Odell Rollins, the last person Jim Colton called before he'd died. I'd called Rollins in the morning on my drive up to UCLA and gotten his voicemail. I answered the call on speaker.

"You left me a message about Jim Colton, Mr. Cahill. What can I do for you?" Crisp and clipped, echoing his military pedigree.

"I'm going to be in Lake Tahoe tomorrow." A lie only if he didn't agree to see me. "I'm hoping we can meet and have a brief chat. I'll buy you lunch or dinner. Whichever you like."

"What's this regarding?"

"Jim Colton's death."

"Brianne hired you?" A hint of contempt. Jim must have told him about the separation and Brianne's new boyfriend.

"Yeah."

"Why don't we just take care of this over the phone. I've got a busy week."

"We could, but I'd rather do it in person. We can skip the food and it will only take about thirty minutes."

"Sorry, Mr. Cahill, I just don't have the time."

"You think your best friend committed suicide?" Maybe the direct approach would work.

Silence. Finally, "That's how the police ruled it."

"I'm not so sure they're right. Meet me tomorrow and we can talk about it."

More silence. Better than a reflex "no."

"Meet me at the Grand Lodge Casino in Incline Village at one tomorrow afternoon."

"How will I know you?"

"Ask for the head of security." He hung up.

CHAPTER NINE

Reno, Nevada, prides itself as being the Biggest Little City In The World. They got half of it right, but Reno does have the only commercial airport within fifty miles of Lake Tahoe. The drive to Incline Village took about forty-five minutes of steady climbing through mountain passes. The six-thousand-foot-high November air had a winter sting to it, but I kept the rental car windows at a crack to smell the pine mountain air.

Lake Tahoe is a vacation destination half the year, split between summer and winter. The mountains that hug the lake have some of the best powder for skiing in the country, and the crystal-clear water ranges from cobalt-blue at its bottomless center to turquoise in the shallows along its shoreline.

In a playground of unmatched beauty, Incline Village is where the adults with the most toys reside. The lake-level villas and mountainside chateaus aren't residences where people live, they're second and third vacation homes.

The Grand Lodge Casino is nestled among pine trees and bumps up against the Incline Village Country Club as part of the main building of the Hyatt Regency Hotel. The Hyatt also features cottages right on the shore of lapping Lake Tahoe. I wished I hadn't scheduled my return flight that evening so I could stay overnight and loll in the view. Mostly, I wished I'd taken my life on a different trajectory so I could afford the price of a cottage for one night.

I arrived at the casino about 12:30 p.m., a half hour early for my meeting with Odell Rollins. A habit from my years of surveillance work. I liked to get the lay of the land before I set up and went to work.

The casino was alpine rustic, exposed A-frame wood ceiling beams and slate brick walls. The gambling floor was small, boutique-ish, with twenty or so gaming tables and two-hundred-plus slot machines, although it did have a sports book and a live poker room. It looked to cater to Incline Village's wealthy biannual residents. Set up to be more a local activity than a way of life. The bigger Tahoe casinos that cater to the full spectrum of gamblers are in the South Shore. That's where whales are comped rooms and degenerate gamblers wager away their life's energy.

The snow season hadn't arrived yet, and the casino floor held just a smattering of well-dressed senior citizens seated at black jack tables and slot machines. The roulette wheel was silent. When the ski season arrived so would a glut of recreational gamblers.

I sat down at the bar in the sports book, ordered a burger, and ignored the inset video poker machine staring up at me. It would have to wait for the barstool's next occupant. I'd dabbled over the years, but the gambling bug never bit me. At least not too hard. I wouldn't let it. I'd seen it melt the resolve and beat down the common sense of my once best friend, Turk Muldoon. It had nearly cost him his restaurant.

Someone tapped me on the shoulder after I'd just swallowed the last bite of my burger. I turned and faced a block of onyx. Although he was about my height at six feet, the fabric in his navy-blue suit could have made up a buy-one-get-one-free for me. And nobody had kicked sand in my face since I was a kid. I'd played football in college and seen dozens of weight room warriors, but I'd never seen a neck like the one holding up the chiseled head of the man standing in front of me. It was more like a thigh than a neck. With his dark skin, boxcar chest, and tree trunk legs, I knew I'd just encountered Odell "Oak" Rollins.

He extended a vise-grip hand and removed all doubt. "Mr. Cahill, Odell Rollins."

I stood up from the barstool and shook his hand. Luckily, no bones broke. "Was it the name tag on my back or the sticker on my forehead that says Private Investigator?"

"Whenever possible, I like to know who's in my casino, Mr. Cahill." No smile, all business. I appeared to be an unwelcomed bit of business.

With my police entanglements and good and bad write-ups in newspapers and the Internet over the years, a quick Google search made me a "whenever possible." My past must have been strike two against me. The first strike being that I'd been hired by the woman who'd left Oak Rollins's best friend and taken up with another man. Back in high school baseball, I'd never been a good two-strike hitter.

I'd done a little of my own research on Odell Rollins. He'd served twenty years in the Navy, the last eighteen as a SEAL. He'd retired with the rank of Chief Petty Officer and gone on to work as a special operator for GRS with Jim Colton in the Middle East. I guessed that his retired military rank still meant something to him.

"Well, I appreciate your taking the time to see me, Chief. And you can call me Rick." I smiled. He didn't.

"Odell is fine." I guessed wrong. Or he just didn't like hearing his former rank coming out of my mouth. "Let's go to my office."

Rollins led me through a door next to the cashier's cage and down a hall that dead-ended into a locked door. He unlocked it and took me into the casino's surveillance room. Eight forty-two-inch flat screens, each televising different games of chance from the casino floor and one each on the cashier's cage and credit area, hung from

the walls. Two men sat in front of a bank of computer monitors
with split screens showing the same live feeds as the TVs. The men
kept their eyes on the screens and said nothing as Rollins walked
through the room to an office in the back. He ushered me to a seat
facing a desk with its own bank of computer monitors on it. I sat in
front of the desk as he sat behind it.

A photo hung from the wall behind Rollins. It must have been
from his time overseas in the Middle East. He and three other men,
all dressed in desert camo, knelt in front of a Humvee holding
M4A1 Carbines. All the men had big victorious smiles. Probably
after a battle or a successful mission. One of the men in the photo
was Jim Colton. Judging by the looks of Rollins and Colton, the
photo was about ten years old.

"How can I help you . . . ah, Rick?" He sat straight and still like a
granite statue; the only things moving were his eyes, which zeroed
down on me like the lens of a camera.

"How long did you know Jim Colton?" I kept my smile on.

"We went through SEAL training together twenty-five years
ago." He kept the granite wall up.

"You two were friends?" Brianne Colton had said Rollins was her
husband's best friend. I'd let Rollins define the relationship for me.

"Yes, we were friends." His eyes softened for an instant. "Jacks
Colton was a good man."

"Jacks?"

"That was his nickname back in SEAL training. It stuck over the
years."

"Why Jacks?"

"Jacks or better. It's from poker. When it was Jim's deal, you had
to have a pair of jacks or better to open."

"Did the name suit his personality?"

"I'm not sure what you mean." Raised eyebrows above a blank wall.

I bet that he did. "Someone who only plays jacks or better wants to get as much information as possible before he'll bet. Was Jim Colton that way in real life? Always learning every angle before he'd commit to something?"

"I'm not a psychologist, Mr. Cahill." No more calling me Rick. A hint of exasperation in his voice. "However, every man forced to make life and death decisions on the battlefield would be wise to gather as much intel as possible before he takes action."

"That makes sense. What about in the rest of his life?"

"I'm not sure what you're getting at." A vein in his anaconda neck pulsed. "Jim Colton was a good sailor and a good man. That's as much as I know and as much as anyone should need to know."

Including some asshole detective digging through Colton's remains and reputation. I understood Rollins's dislike for me and wanting to protect his friend's memory. But my job was to find the truth, no matter who got hurt or pissed off.

"How often did you two talk?"

"A couple times a month." His eyes shifted to the side, then he quickly added, "Sometimes more."

I bet the add-on came because he'd guessed I had Colton's phone records that showed the two of them had talked fourteen times in the last two weeks of Colton's life.

"Why so many calls right before Jim Colton died?"

"We didn't have a set number of calls we made a month, Mr. Cahill." His lips and eyebrows knifed down. "Sometimes we didn't talk for weeks, sometimes we talked every few days. That's how it works with friends."

He made it sound like I was unfamiliar with the concept of having a friend. I knew how it worked. I just hadn't practiced it in a while.

"What did you talk about on the day he died? He called you twice."

"The calls went to voicemail." The stone wall fell, and his eyes went soft and human. Just for an instant. "I wish to hell I'd talked to him."

Each call had registered as a minute on Colton's phone bill, the smallest increment the phone company would record whether the call was three seconds or sixty. Rollins was probably telling the truth.

"Do you still have the messages? What did he say?"

"Just to call him back."

"Did you keep the messages?"

"No."

Maybe ex-SEALs weren't sentimental and didn't need to listen to a recently lost pal every once in a while. Or maybe there was more than just a request for a returned call and Rollins didn't want me to know about it.

"Was it normal for Jim to leave two messages to call him back a few hours apart? Did it seem like there was something important he wanted to talk to you about?"

"Not necessarily. Sometimes he'd get impatient like we all do, Mr. Cahill."

"Do you think he committed suicide?"

Rollins's mouth flattened into a straight line and his eyes did the same. He put his boxing glove–sized hand to his chin and rubbed it. Finally, he shrugged and I thought for a second that the world might spin off its axis. "That's how the police ruled it. I don't have any reason to question their findings."

When it came to the La Jolla Police Department, I could always find a reason. Rollins's expression said more than his words. He wasn't convinced either, but he wouldn't share his doubts with me. I'd gotten under a couple layers of his rawhide skin.

Maybe if I stabbed deeper I'd strike a nerve and he'd spit out some angry truth.

"So you believe your best friend and SEAL team brother who'd fought for you and his country would take his own life?" I laced each word with disdain, digging deeper under his skin.

The vein in Rollins's neck pulsed again and his massive mandible clenched tight enough to crush diamonds. His eyes squeezed down on me. I was glad we were in an office with a desk between us in civilization instead of in a war on opposite sides of a foxhole. He didn't say anything for what seemed like a minute. He finally spoke.

"People do things every day that surprise me, Mr. Cahill. I saw it on the battlefield overseas and I see it here in the casino. Jacks hadn't been himself since Brianne left him. He seemed depressed when we'd talk on the phone. Sometimes the fight just leaves you and there's nowhere to go but home."

He eyed the door like that was my cue to leave and go to my own home. Hopefully, he meant in San Diego and not my final resting place. I wasn't ready for either just yet. "How well do you know Brianne Colton?"

"Well enough." Stone face.

"You don't like her?"

"I liked her just fine until she took up with another man."

"She come across as money hungry to you?" I thought about the life insurance policy with the suicide clause.

"No. She only cared about her singing career."

Maybe.

"Did Jim Colton make any enemies on our side of the battlefield while he was overseas?"

"No. Everybody loved Jacks." Unmovable.

"Even after Benghazi? He didn't piss anybody off up the ranks?"

"We all had concerns about how State handled things that night. Jacks didn't make a stink about it." He stood up, dismissing all earlier subtleties. "I really have to get back to my responsibilities, Mr. Cahill."

I didn't move. "Why did Colton call the FBI five days before he died?"

A slight pause, then raised eyebrows. "I didn't know that he had."

"Really?" I gave him my own pause and eyebrows. No effect. He stood still, chiseled like a face on Mount Rushmore. "He called the local San Diego office one day right after he hung up from a lengthy phone call to your cell number. You sure you don't know why Colton called the FBI?"

"I told you I didn't, Mr. Cahill." He circled his desk and stood in front of my chair, staring black eyes down at me. "If you were more thorough at your job, you'd know that Jacks commanded the CIT unit for the La Jolla Police Department. He could have had any number of reasons to call the FBI, and it's not unusual for CIT and the Feds to discuss strategy and coordination at times."

If I'd scratched a piece of flint in front of his eyes, they would have burned two holes right through me. I wondered if Jim Colton had ever seen that look—directed at him. Best friends don't always stay best friends. Sometimes they become enemies. If I had to choose an enemy, it wouldn't be an ex-SEAL. If an ex-SEAL were my only choice, it wouldn't be Oak Rollins.

I stood up. Rollins kept his twin torches on me, but I didn't challenge him. I'd gotten what I'd needed. An overreaction. To cover a lie. Rollins did know why Jim Colton had called the FBI five days before he died. Of that, I was fairly certain. But I was even more certain that he wouldn't admit it. What I didn't know was why Colton had made the call or how it had affected his and Rollins's friendship. Or if the call had gotten Jim Colton killed.

I extended a hand. "Thanks for your time."

Rollins shook my hand without denting it. He walked over to the office door and opened it. I went through the doorway but stopped and turned back to Rollins.

"Do you know if Jim ever went rock climbing?"

"No."

"Do you know if he owned a rock climbing rope?"

"No."

"How about that he was afraid of heights? Did you know that?"

"No." His eyebrows went up right away this time. No hesitation.

This backed up what Cash Colton told me about his father and put another red flag on the rope that was used to hang Jim Colton. Why would he buy an expensive nylon climbing rope from a specialty store when he could easily buy a cheap twine rope from any Walmart, Target, or Home Depot at the nearest mall?

"Do you ever rock climb?"

"Not since I was a SEAL."

"Would it surprise you to know that the cell phone Jim Colton called you with twice the day he died was never recovered?"

"No." He shook his head. The question hadn't surprised him. "The police probably lost it when they recovered his personal items. Wouldn't be the first time, I'm sure."

Rollins was either trying to bluff me off my hand or he'd worked for the casino too long. He played by house rules. The cops had ruled his best friend's death a suicide, so it was a suicide. You can't beat the house. Still, I wasn't convinced.

"When was the last time you saw Jim before he died?"

"Sometime in June. Good-bye, Mr. Cahill." Oak Rollins closed the door leaving me on the other side.

CHAPTER TEN

I GOT HOME at seven that night. Midnight was happy to see me. That was worth something. My neighbor's fourteen-year-old daughter, Micalah, Midnight's pal and dog watcher, had fed him and taken him outside to play while I was trying to squeeze information from a stone. More like a boulder. I wasn't sure if I'd learned enough to justify the expense of taking a flight to Lake Tahoe instead of just making a call. I'd write it up anyway. I liked Brianne Colton. Maybe too much, but I wasn't running a charity.

I led Midnight up the stairs to my second-floor office, and he took his spot under my desk. I pulled my laptop out of my backpack and went over the notes I'd written on the plane ride home from Reno.

The trip hadn't been a total washout. I came away from my meeting with Oak Rollins thinking he might not believe Jim Colton had committed suicide, that he knew why Colton had called the FBI, and that he didn't know Colton was afraid of heights. I just didn't know why he'd seemingly held back information.

Maybe he was mad at Brianne and wouldn't cooperate with someone she'd hired. Honor, a scarce commodity in the new millennium, was important to brothers in battle. Brianne had broken the code when she moved out of the home that held her son and husband and then took up with another man. But the deeper code was to his fallen brother. If I was right and Rollins didn't believe his best friend committed suicide, he knew there was only one explanation for his death. Murder. Colton hadn't slipped and fallen into a noose hanging a foot over his head.

Yet, Rollins hadn't done anything about it. I'd given him an opportunity to share his doubts about Colton's death, and he'd rode the cops' story line. He and Jim Colton had spilled blood for righteous causes and been each other's family when their real ones were half a world away. How could he sit still when there might be a killer loose who had murdered his friend, his comrade, his brother?

Maybe Rollins wasn't sitting still. Maybe he knew who killed Colton and he had a plan to handle the murderer on his own but he didn't want me getting in the way. But Colton had been dead for ten weeks. How long was Rollins going to wait?

Of course, I could have been all wrong. Maybe Rollins really did believe Colton had taken his own life. And he didn't know why Colton had called the FBI. Maybe Rollins had gotten angry because I'd questioned his veracity. Or because he didn't like me digging around in his friend's grave. Could be that he just didn't like me. The latter had been the answer to a lot of questions over the last ten years.

One last possibility was that Rollins was somehow involved in Jim Colton's death and had something to hide. A long shot, but so was the whole case. He'd seemed genuinely sad when he said he'd wished he'd talked to Colton on the last day of his life. My gut told me Rollins had nothing to do with Colton's death, but my gut had been wrong before.

Right now, whatever Oak Rollins knew or didn't know or believed or didn't believe didn't matter. The more I dug into the Colton case, the less I believed LJPD's conclusion. I knew them to be a shoddy and corrupt police force. If I didn't buy the suicide, I had to find out if the misdetermination of death was due to the former or the latter. One was discouraging, the other frightening.

For all the cities in San Diego County, the county medical examiner is the ultimate determiner of the manner of death: natural, accident, suicide, homicide, or undetermined.

However, it's not as scientific as they make it out on TV. The medical examiner can be swayed one way or the other by the evidence the cops share with him. Or don't share.

I pulled the file Brianne had given me that contained the police report. I hadn't paid attention to the medical examiner's name the first time through, only the results. Now I needed the name. Beverly Lin. Tomorrow I'd try to find out if she'd bent under pressure by Moretti.

I put away the file and scratched Midnight's head. He looked up at me, trust and affection in his eyes. The best look I'd seen all day.

CHAPTER ELEVEN

The San Diego County Medical Examiner's Office is located on the campus of the County of San Diego Operations Center in Kearny Mesa. The ME who performed the autopsy on Jim Colton was Dr. Beverly Lin. She was one of eight pathologists in the Medical Examiner's Office. I met her at the Commons Dining cafeteria in the middle of the sprawling Operations Center.

She sat alone at a table in a white lab coat with name tag.

"Doctor Lin?" I stuck my hand out for a shake. She put down the turkey club she'd just taken a bite of, wiped her hand on her napkin, and shook my hand. "Rick Cahill."

"Please." She put a delicate hand over her mouth as she chewed. "Sit down."

Dr. Lin looked to be late twenties or early thirties. Hard to tell. She had dark brown bangs that framed a round face with prominent cheekbones and a square chin. Separately her features wouldn't figure to go together, but they did. Attractively.

"I appreciate you taking the time to see me on a Saturday."

"I had to be in today anyway. What would you like to know about James Colton's death, Mr. Cahill?" Matter of fact. Not aggressive or defensive. Not what I expected from someone affiliated with LJPD, no matter how loosely.

"You can call me Rick."

"You can call me Bev." A smile.

"Okay, Bev." I gave her an "it's nice to be friends" smile. "How long have you worked for the ME's office?"

"Four years."

"Have you ever dealt with a hanging victim before?"

"I believe Mr. Colton was my third." She lowered her eyes and raised her chin.

"Were the others suicides?"

"Yes. Suspension hanging is not that unusual a way to end one's life. And not as painful as people think. The pressure from the rope on the carotid arteries cuts off blood flow to the brain and causes unconsciousness in as few as ten to twenty seconds. The continued lack of blood to the brain will cause death in less than two minutes. It's the loss of blood flow to the brain that kills you, not loss of oxygen to the lungs like people think. Aside from the first few seconds, it's a very peaceful way to die. You just go to sleep."

"Did you check under Jim Colton's fingernails for fibers from the rope used to hang him?"

"Yes." No smile this time and a slight lean toward me. "There weren't any."

"Do people who hang themselves ever grasp, possibly involuntarily, at the ligature around their neck in those first few seconds after they step off a pedestal and begin to hang?"

"Sometimes, but not in most cases."

"Did it happen in either of the hanging cases you investigated?"

She stared at me a couple beats before she spoke. I'd gotten under her skin. Not what I'd planned. Finally, she said, "There were a few rope fibers underneath the fingernails of one of the victims I investigated."

"Did you find anything else under Colton's nails? Skin? Other fibers?" Jim Colton had been a fit former SEAL and sergeant of a police CIT team. If someone had put a rope around his neck, it wouldn't have been easy.

"No."

"Any scratches or bruises on his body?"

"No, Mr. Cahill." Rick was a distant memory.

"Any punctures, possibly from a hypodermic needle?"

"Not that I found."

"You ran a tox scan, correct?"

"Yes. It's in the report. It doesn't sound as if you read it. If you had, you could have saved yourself the trip over here and left me to enjoy my lunch uninterrupted." I'd now made it to LJPD level. Another place I didn't want to be.

"Dr. Lin, I'm not trying to insult you. I read the report with layman's eyes. You are obviously good at what you do. But I'm working for Jim Colton's family and I'm trying to do a good job for them. I'm just asking the questions that need to be asked so the Coltons can get the answers they need." I figured I had a couple more questions before she stormed away or called security. "Did you check for any fast-acting sedation drugs that could incapacitate someone and then leave little trace?"

If putting a rope around Jim Colton's neck hadn't been his idea and there were no bruises or scratches on his body or skin under his fingernails, he'd have to have been sedated or restrained.

"You do understand how ill-informed that question sounds, don't you, Mr. Cahill?"

"I do, but I'm just doing my job."

"I have work to do." She grabbed her half-eaten sandwich and stood up. I'd been off by one question.

"You seem like someone who tries to get things right, Bev." I stayed seated. "There's something that's just not right about Jim Colton's death."

"I did my job and got it right, Mr. Cahill." Still standing but hadn't yet taken a step.

"I'm sure you did, under the circumstances."

"What circumstances?"

"It looks to me that LJPD wanted Colton's death to be ruled a suicide and not a murder. For whatever reason. Maybe that's what the facts on the surface told them. But they didn't dig very deep. They took everything at face value."

"I look at the evidence surrounding each death independently, Mr. Cahill."

"That's good to know." I pushed an open hand to her former seat, but she remained standing. "But there's evidence that you probably don't know about."

"What do you mean?"

"The rope used to hang Jim Colton was the kind used by rock climbers."

"I gathered that information on my own. So you are wrong about what I know and don't know." The sneer. Finally.

"Did you know that Colton didn't rock climb? That he was afraid of heights?"

She didn't say anything, but I could almost see her brain whirring behind her eyes.

"And the rope around his neck had been cut from a longer piece of rope that wasn't found at the scene." A guess by me, but an educated one. I doubted any manufacturer made climbing ropes as short as the one used to hang Jim Colton.

"That's interesting information, but hardly definitive." But her eyes told me I now had her attention.

"There's also the fact that Colton's cell phone was missing. Not on his body. Not in the house. Not in his car. The cell phone he'd used, at the most, two hours before his death. Did the police make you aware of that fact?"

"No. Have you talked to Detective Denton or anyone else at the La Jolla Police Department about this?" She sat back down.

"No. I wanted to talk to you first." I left out that everybody at LJPD hated me and Chief Moretti wanted to see me in jail. "If you'd had that information, would it have made a difference in your determination?"

She pursed her lips and looked past me for a moment before she spoke. "Possibly. If the detectives investigating the case presented me with that evidence and were pursuing other leads, I might have ruled the death undetermined and given them a little time to come up with new evidence that would give me direction."

"I thought you said you investigated deaths independently."

"I do, but not in a vacuum." She scooted her chair in. Engaged. "I don't have the financial freedom to run any test I like on a whim. If I get a body with ligature markings around the neck that was found hanging in a garage above a knocked-over chair and whose death was caused by anoxia, lack of blood flow to the brain, I'm going to rule suicide unless presented with refuting evidence. If the detectives push for homicide, I may run further tests and ask for a panel review."

"A panel review?"

"Yes. A panel of other pathologists and detectives go over the evidence, talk, sometimes argue, and then we vote on manner of death. Majority rules."

I wondered if Moretti could stack the panel so his majority ruled.

"What would it take for you to call for a panel review?"

"A lot more than just your conjecture." A smile not a sneer. "The detectives would have to present me with new evidence they believed could lead to a homicide determination. And it would have to be more than the choice of rope used in the hanging or a missing cell phone."

"Thank you, Bev." I stood up and put out my hand. "Or is it now Dr. Lin?"

"You can stick with Bev . . . for now." She shook my hand. "I suggest you talk with Detectives Denton and Sizemore. Maybe they'll take your observations into consideration and reopen their investigation."

She was right. I needed to talk to the detectives, but I wasn't ready to face anyone from LJPD yet. Just the thought shot a frozen finger down my spine.

CHAPTER TWELVE

THE HOUSE THAT Jim Colton died in and the one that Brianne Colton had since moved back into was on Soledad Road in La Jolla. An offshoot from Soledad Mountain Road, it sported mostly medium-sized ranch houses that had views of either the mountains in East County, the Pacific Ocean, San Diego Bay and downtown, or combinations of up to all three. About average for La Jolla homes.

The Colton house had the East County view. It sat back from the street shrouded by Torrey pines and an ivy-covered fenced-in front patio. I'd called ahead and Brianne was even less happy to see me than she had been to talk to me on the phone. I stood in the doorway admiring the view of the distant mountains through the windows of the living room.

"Well, come in." Brianne, barefoot in jeans and a blue t-shirt that made her blue eyes pop against her fair skin and auburn hair, shot her hand into the foyer.

Another onetime advocate crossed over to the other side. I had a knack. She led me to the living room and sat down crossed-legged in an overstuffed chair that had an acoustic guitar leaning against it.

"I'm sorry about your son and I'm sorry about being indelicate regarding your relationship with your bandmate." I sat down across from her on a brown leather sofa. "But you hired me to find the truth. That's what I'm going to do until you tell me to stop. Do you want me to stop, Brianne?"

"No." She picked up the guitar and held it in her lap. "Just try not to be such an asshole about it all the time."

"You've heard about the leopard and his spots, right?" I smiled.

"I think there's a decent guy in there underneath all the acid and sarcasm." She strummed a chord. "You just won't let anybody see him because you're afraid you'll get hurt. Again."

"If I become the subject of your next song, make sure I get a writing credit."

"I've written enough sad songs." She didn't smile. "What did you want to talk to me about?"

"I want to see the garage and Jim's office."

"Follow me."

She led me down the hall, through the laundry room into the garage. A three- or four-year-old Ford F-150 pickup sat parked in the middle of the garage floor. Its cab rested under the beam that Jim Colton's body had been found hanging from by his son.

"I need to sell the truck, but I haven't been able to get myself to list it yet." Brianne stared at the truck and let out a long sigh. "Jim loved it."

"Did he usually park it in here or in the driveway?"

"The driveway, where my car is now."

Where the truck must have been the night Colton died. I walked over to a wooden workbench on the left side of the garage. All manner of tools hung from a pegboard on the back of the workbench. The tools were clean and the bench was immaculate. I grabbed a handsaw off its peg and examined the sawtooth blade. Clean. No fibers that could have matched the sawed rope used to hang Jim Colton. A large combination lock gun safe sat next to the workbench.

"Jim's guns still in there?"

"Some of them. There are more in the house. I need to sell them, too."

A gun safe full of guns and Colton supposedly chose to hang himself with a strand of climbing rope cut from a larger coil that nobody could find. LJPD either ignored the circumstantial evidence or hid it and pushed for suicide. Why?

I climbed into the cab of the truck and searched the console and the glove compartment. Brianne watched me through the open driver door.

"What are you looking for?"

"Jim's cell phone. Anything." I didn't find anything interesting. Just the truck's registration and service records.

"I already looked for it there."

I got out of the cab and went around to the back of the truck. The truck bed had a built-in toolbox up against the cab. I jumped up on the bed and went over to the toolbox. It was locked with a padlock.

"You check in here, too?"

"No. I never thought to."

"You have the key?"

"Be right back."

Brianne went into the house and thirty seconds later came out with a key chain full of keys. She tossed it up to me, and I tried a couple keys that looked like they'd fit a padlock. The second one worked. I opened the toolbox and found a well-organized shelf of tools one would use for general fix-it jobs. I pulled the shelf out and underneath found a Sig Sauer P229 pistol in a holster. The regulation firearm for La Jolla cops. Three boxes of ammunition sat next to it. Another chance for Colton to end his life the quick and easy, albeit, messy way.

A large blue backpack was next to the gun and the ammo. I picked it up and opened it. Inside, a rock climbing rope matching the color of the strand used to hang Jim Colton stared up at me. I pulled out the rope and looked at one end. Rough edges of a cut.

CHAPTER THIRTEEN

BRIANNE STARED WIDE-EYED at the rope. "That's the same rope, isn't it?"

"Yep." I held up the slightly frayed end. "Looks like the strand used in the hanging was cut from here."

"I've never seen that rope before. I've never seen Jim with any kind of rope."

"How about the backpack? Ever seen it?"

"Yes. Jim took it with him when he went to the shooting range."

"You ever look inside this toolbox before?"

"No." She shook her head. "I left Jim alone with his toys."

I searched the pockets of the backpack, hoping to get lucky and find Colton's cell phone. Nothing. I put the rope back into the backpack and jumped down from the truck.

"Did Jim ever tell you he was afraid of heights?"

"No." More wide eyes. "He jumped out of airplanes as a SEAL."

"But he was afraid of heights. Your son told me. Jim told him on a trip to San Francisco."

"He never told me. We were married for nineteen years." Gravity and hurt pulled at her eyes and mouth.

"I know."

"Are you trying to make a point, Rick?" She put her hands on her hips.

"Just that there were some things you didn't know about your husband." I held up the backpack. "The rope. His fear of heights. You hadn't seen him for two weeks before he died. Your son and Oak Rollins both said Jim had been depressed."

"So, you're buying LJPD's official story now?" She spread her elbows off her hips like angry wings.

"I'm just saying it looks more probable than just possible now."

"What about the phone call to the FBI?"

"Jim could have called the FBI for any number of work-related things. CIT planning, a joint task force, anything." I echoed Oak Rollins's words and silently cursed myself for not thinking of them on my own.

My distrust of LJPD had tainted my perceptions of this case. I'd let it influence my read on Oak Rollins. I'd seen secrets and deceit when there'd only been anger that I wouldn't let a comrade in arms rest in peace.

"I can refund half your money, Brianne. And you can get on with your new life."

"Go to hell, Cahill. You're full of crap." She wagged a finger in my face. "I bought into your bullshit about pursuing the truth and nothing else. It was all an act."

"The truth is your husband probably committed suicide."

Fear slipped out from behind the anger in Brianne's eyes. Maybe her crusade to prove her husband didn't kill himself hadn't been about money, after all. Maybe it was to assuage the guilt she felt about his suicide. If Jim hadn't killed himself, it couldn't be her fault that he died.

"I don't want a refund. I paid you for a week of work and you still owe me three and a half days." Her hands went back to her hips and she gave me an attitude head roll that would have made a diva R & B singer proud. "You think you can give me my money's worth for the rest of the week, Rick?"

"Yeah."

"Or are you just going to go through the motions like the first private dick I hired." She hit "dick" hard and I got the message.

"I'm going to give you all I have." In truth, there still were a couple angles I could measure. "But if the facts don't change, you'd be smart to start looking at things differently."

"Save the pop psychology. I've already tried that."

"Show me Jim's office."

Brianne led me back into the house and across the hall into an office that was even cleaner than the workbench in the garage. A large hardwood desk against the near wall took up almost a third of the room. The desk had an iMac computer, printer/fax machine, and a landline phone with voice messaging. Pens in a SEAL mug, a yellow legal pad perfectly lined up with the desk blotter. A large brass paperweight topped with a Navy SEAL coin sat in the upper middle of the blotter. No clutter. The desk had a polished sheen.

The back wall of the office was a sliding glass door and mirrored the view from the living room of East County. Another large standing gun safe anchored the corner of the wall. Military and private contractor commendations hung from the other walls. A smattering of SEAL training and in-country photographs broke up the sea of honors.

Honors. Jim Colton had enough for a whole platoon. Would a man like that do the dishonorable thing and take his own life? Not unless it was the only *honorable* thing he could do.

I sat down in a leather executive chair and searched each desk drawer. No cell phone. No suicide note. No smoking gun. I turned on the computer. The screen came on asking for a password. Brianne stood next to me with her arms folded across her chest.

"Use SEAL TEAM, all caps, and the number 5."

I did as told and the computer unlocked to a desktop.

"The police go through his folders and emails looking for a suicide note or a reason?" I asked Brianne.

"Yes. So did I."

"And neither of you found anything."

"Nothing."

"What about anything else? Anything unusual or out of place?"

"What do you mean?" She tilted her head.

"You and the cops both looked for a suicide note or signs of Jim's depression."

"Yes. So?"

"Well, let's take a different tack."

"Such as?" She squinted her eyes down on me.

"You're convinced Jim didn't kill himself. If you're right, that means someone else did. Let's look for reasons why."

"I've been trying to do that. I went through his emails, his messages on this phone, the desk, his clothes, his truck."

"But, as of yet, you haven't found anything suspicious, right?" I said.

"Right."

"How far back did you go on his emails?"

"A couple weeks."

"Is his account still active or did you close it?" I asked.

"Still active. He used Gmail."

"Good." I pulled out a notepad and pen from my jacket pocket and handed it to Brianne. "Write down his user name and password for his Gmail account. Does he have any other email accounts?"

"I don't think so." She wrote on the pad and handed it back to me.

"I'll access the account from my office computer and take a look around. I'll go back further than a couple weeks." I stood up. "Does he have any other electronic devices? An iPad, a laptop?"

"No. He thought all that was a waste of money when he had all he needed on his phone and home computer."

"How about a work laptop?"

"He had one, but he rarely brought it home. At least while I was here."

"Did you come back here that night when the police notified you that Jim was dead?" I asked.

"Cash called me before the police did. I got here maybe five minutes after the police arrived."

"Aside from Jim and the rope you'd never seen, was there anything about the house that seemed out of place? Or just anything at all that wasn't quite right?"

"There was something in here, but you're going to think I'm crazy." She smiled for the first time since I'd been there. It brought me back to watching her onstage and being in awe.

I shook it off. "What was it?"

"Well, you see how clean and organized Jim kept this place. I'd never even seen a single pen out of place." She walked over to a wall with framed photographs and commendations and pulled down two pictures. "These pictures had switched places on the wall."

Brianne handed the photographs to me. The first one was of Oak Rollins standing next to another soldier, arms locked around each other's shoulders. The second looked a lot like the photo I'd seen on Oak Rollins's office wall. Jim Colton and Rollins were kneeling in front of a Humvee next to the two other soldiers in the Rollins photo. One of them was the same soldier in the other photo with Rollins Brianne had shown me. The four men held the same rifles and the lighting was the same as the picture on Rollins's office wall in Lake Tahoe. The only difference was that the photo was taken from slightly farther away than the first one. A blanket was visible on the ground in front of the men and it was covered with thirty or so gold bars.

"That has to be a couple million dollars in gold." I looked at Brianne.

"Jim told me the Army bean counters said it was seven point three."

"So, obviously, they turned it in."

"Of course. By Jim's count he and his unit collected over fifty million dollars in gold and currency from secret hiding places they found clearing houses during his four tours in Iraq."

Clearing houses sounded like something a landscaper would do, but it was dangerous work done on the battlefield and surrounding areas. Soldiers entered homes and structures and made sure no bad guys with guns or explosives were inside.

"Who are the other soldiers in the photos? I've already met Oak Rollins."

"When?"

"Yesterday."

"Was he in town?" Her eyes got bigger than normal.

"No. I'll tell you about it later."

She pinched her lips together. "Are you going to keep everything a secret until I ask about something?"

"No. I'll send you a report at the end of the week. Let's stay focused on the photographs. Who are the other men?"

She shook her head and squinted at me. "The man in both pictures was Doug McCafferty."

"Was?"

"Yes. He died over there. In Iraq."

"How long ago?" I asked.

"About ten years ago. It happened only a few months after these pictures were taken."

"Who's the other guy?"

"Kyle Bates. He lives over in Coronado. He and Doug were pretty close."

"Were Jim and he close? Coronado's only twenty minutes away."

Bates was next on my list to interview. He had been the other man Jim Colton had called on the day he died along with Oak Rollins.

"Not as close as he was with Odell. Jim and Kyle probably got together a couple times a year."

"What's your theory on the photos switching positions on the wall? Could a maid have done it?"

"We didn't have a maid," she said.

"How about Cash?"

"I asked him. He said he hadn't been in Jim's office in weeks and he never touched the pictures."

"Is it possible that Jim switched them after you moved out and you didn't know it?"

"Jim put things in specific places for a reason." She pointed at the plaques. "I helped him hang everything on these walls four years ago. He had made a chart where everything would go. He was as anal as a colonoscopy."

"Don't take offense, but is it possible that the photos weren't moved at all and you misremembered where they were?"

"Yes. That's possible. But I doubt both Cash and I misremembered." She air quoted the last word.

"Okay, then what do you think happened?"

"I have no idea. I just know that someone other than Jim moved them. Maybe the police accidentally knocked them off the wall and replaced them in the wrong spots. I didn't think it was a big deal, but you asked if anything was different in the house."

I wasn't convinced they were moved by someone other than Jim Colton. Maybe he'd looked at the photos when he'd contemplated ending his own life. Looked back at a fallen comrade and wished he could have gone out on the battlefield like Doug McCafferty had. Or just looked back at the highlights of his life when it had tangible meaning. Maybe he put them back in the wrong spots because order wouldn't matter anymore after he went into the garage with the rope.

Or maybe he'd been looking at the pictures at his desk and had been interrupted by his murderer who put the pictures back in the wrong place after he killed Colton.

Another loose end on a case that had a sack full of them.

CHAPTER FOURTEEN

MY PHONE RANG on the drive home. The name on the screen almost made me pull over. Or keep driving until I outran my life.

Alan Rankin. A man I hadn't seen or talked to in almost a year. A high-end criminal lawyer who teetered on the edge of the law and who I'd hoped never to see again. I let the call go to voicemail. I was in the burbs but still in the city of La Jolla. With my luck, I'd get pulled over by a stray patrol car and written up for talking on my cell phone. Plus, I wasn't ready to hear what Rankin had to say.

I might never be.

Midnight greeted me at the front door when I got home. I took him out to the backyard and tossed a tennis ball around. He'd chase it down and snatch it as deftly as any Gold Glove shortstop in Major League Baseball. I usually enjoyed watching Midnight chase the ball as much as he did the chase. Today, anxiety replaced joy.

I checked my phone. Alan Rankin's name still showed as the last incoming call. I hadn't imagined it. It was real. The only call I feared more was one from Chief Moretti. I tossed the ball until Midnight had a good pant going, then sat in a patio chair and stared at the sliver of ocean miles away.

Midnight, tongue hanging out, sat down next to me and leaned his shoulder against me. It would have been a good place to get an early start on a relaxing evening. If I didn't have a call to make. I doubted I'd have many relaxing evenings for a while.

I pulled the phone back out of my pocket. Rankin hadn't left a message, but the call itself was message enough. I hit dial.

"Have you seen today's *La Jolla Lantern?*" Not even a hello.

"No." The *Lantern* was the weekly paper for La Jollans. More local event driven than hard news. I hadn't read one since I left Muldoon's three years ago. They didn't deliver to Bay Ho. That was fine by me.

"Read the article, then meet me at my office at seven."

"What article?"

"You'll know which one." He hung up.

I hung up and Googled the *Lantern* on my phone. Unfortunately, its website still had last week's edition up. Shit. I'd have to drive to The Village and pick up a paper copy. The Village. LJPD headquarters and highest density of patrol cars. If the cops stopped me tonight, I'd be strapped. CCW—carrying a concealed weapon. Which could get me killed. But meeting Alan Rankin without a weapon could get me killed, too.

I went inside and fed Midnight then went upstairs to my bedroom to change. The technology for concealed holsters had changed quite a bit since my days as a street cop in the barrio of Santa Barbara. I pulled my UnderTech compression concealment t-shirt from my bureau and slipped it on. Cool and tight to the body, it had a nylon holster sewn into the fabric of the shirt under the left armpit. I pulled my Ruger SP 101 .357 Magnum from the nylon gun case on the nightstand and slipped it into the holster. Snug to the body. I didn't secure the Velcro strap over the handle. I just wanted to see how the weapon felt in the holster. I hadn't had need to wear it in a while. Tonight was different.

I pulled the gun from the holster and put it back in the case. The concealed weapon was for my meeting with Alan Rankin, not for my drive into La Jolla. If LJPD stopped me, I'd tell them about my licensed weapon in the trunk of my car. Any misunderstandings with a gun on my body could be deadly.

I Googled Alan Rankin, Attorney At Law, to find the address to his office. The only time I'd met him had been at his home. Without an invitation. I had a gun that time, too.

Rankin's office address made me do a double take. The same address as Muldoon's Steak House, just a different suite number. It must have been one of the offices behind and below the restaurant with a view of the ocean. Figured. I wondered how long he'd been there and how I'd never bumped into him all the years I'd worked at Muldoon's. Maybe I had and didn't know it because it hadn't mattered.

Now it did.

* * *

I picked up the latest issue of the *La Jolla Lantern* at a liquor store in a mini-mall in The Village. They have mini-malls in La Jolla, just nicer buildings and cleaner parking lots than most of the rest of San Diego. It was six o'clock. I had an hour to kill and was hungry. I knew where I could get a good meal with an employee discount within walking distance of Rankin's office. I just hoped I'd be early enough to miss Turk.

The hostess took me up to the booth where I'd first talked to Brianne Colton. My table on slow nights like tonight. I ordered a teriyaki sirloin, mid-rare, and a baked Idaho, just butter, from the waiter and plopped the newspaper onto the table. Nothing interesting above the fold. I unfolded the paper and a picture of a sad older couple caught my eye. I didn't have to read their names. Jack and Rita Mae Eddington.

My stomach swallowed itself into a sucking hole.

The caption of the story read: Eddingtons Running Out Of Hope.

The article recapped the story of the Eddingtons' grandson, Randall, who was convicted of murdering his parents and sister and spent seven years in prison. He'd been freed on appeal last December when newly discovered evidence pointed at another suspect. Evidence that I helped uncover. The DA chose not to retry and the remaining Eddingtons were given another shot at a happy life that lasted about five days. Randall disappeared and hadn't been seen since. The article said that the Eddingtons were trying to come to grips with the fact that their grandson, the last remaining heir of their family, was probably dead.

I felt for the Eddingtons. I always had. Especially for Rita Mae, who reminded me of my late grandmother. The Eddingtons had to endure the murders of their son, granddaughter, and daughter-in-law, and then see their grandson go to prison for the crimes. They never gave up hope and used their life's savings to get Randall out of prison only to lose him again. Forever. Jack and Rita Mae's pain must have been unbearable. But the truth would have hurt them even more.

The Eddingtons had hired me to try to find Randall. I'd taken the case pro bono for six months and hadn't found any evidence of Randall. But I hadn't looked very hard.

I read the last sentence of the article and my throat constricted and my face flashed hot. Police Chief Moretti was examining new evidence that could persuade him to consider the disappearance a homicide.

I had my waiter box up my dinner. I'd lost my appetite.

* * *

The glass door to Rankin's office was locked, but I could see a receptionist sitting behind a marble desk inside. I tapped on the glass, and she came to the door and let me in. She was tall, blond, and pretty in a grown-up tomboy sort of way. Looked like she'd once been a bodybuilder, but had let femininity creep back into her curves. She wore black yoga pants, tight to her muscular legs, flip-flops, and a purple hoodie.

I'd never seen a receptionist dressed this casually anywhere but a gym. It was Saturday. Maybe she was Rankin's girlfriend just helping out. Much younger girlfriend.

"Mr. Rankin is ready to see you." Higher voice than I expected. She smiled and went from tomboy to sexy girl next door. "Follow me."

I set my to-go container down on the reception counter and followed the woman over to a door to the right of the reception area. She knocked on the door once.

"Mr. Cahill is here." She didn't wait for a response and opened the door for me to enter.

I walked in and squeezed my left arm against the revolver holstered in my shirt hidden by my jacket. Still there. Alan Rankin, slight and balding, sat behind a massive hardwood desk that dwarfed the one in Jim Colton's office. He was alone and my body unclenched. I'd expected to see the steroid-inflated tough guy I'd sucker-punched at Rankin's house almost a year ago. Right before I'd beaten information out of Rankin.

"Mr. Cahill." His voice, the confident ooze of a man comfortable telling lies in front of juries. He stood and pointed to a leather chair in front of his desk that could cover the cost of one of my mortgage payments.

I took a step toward the chair and something hard exploded into my left ear. I staggered but stabbed my hand inside my coat for the gun and spun just in time to see the flash of a bare foot before it slammed into my nose.

Stars. Night.

Blood streamed from my nose over and around my lips when I came to face-first on the marble floor. Maybe that's why Rankin chose marble over carpet in his office. Easier cleanup. Judging by the viscosity of the blood and the ringing in my ears, I figured I'd only been out a few seconds. Long enough. I groped inside my jacket for the gun I knew wouldn't be there.

"Looking for this?"

I rolled over onto my back and saw Rankin sitting behind his desk holding up my gun. At least it wasn't pointed at me.

"Let's try again." He pointed to the leather chair a couple feet away and set the Ruger .357 Magnum down on his desk.

My head felt like a bowling ball teetering atop a pencil and my ear a cymbal in a heavy metal band drum solo. I wobbled up onto one knee. Blood dripped down onto my jacket. I attempted vertical and the bowling ball listed to the right and the rest of me followed. A pair of strong hands steadied me. The "receptionist." Her weapons back in their flip-flops, she guided me over to the chair. I sat down. I wasn't proud. Not tonight.

"I see you've met Miranda." Rankin smiled at the woman who stood to my left, a leg's length away from me. "She used to fight mixed martial arts. You know, MMA? Never lost a fight. She's been out of the game awhile, but still packs a punch. Or should I say a kick?"

"We even now?" My voice sounded nasal and muted at the same time. I could only hear it out of one ear. I wiped blood and dark crimson from my nose and smeared it onto the arm of the king's ransom leather chair.

"Miranda, get Mr. Cahill a towel." He eyeballed me like I was a hostile witness on the stand. "No, Mr. Cahill, we're not even. You'd better hope we never are."

Miranda went through a door in the back of the office and came out with a sea-foam-colored hand towel and handed it to me.

I wiped a bloody sunset into the middle of the sea foam. "I'm here, Rankin. What do you want?"

"You read the article?" Rankin held up a copy of the *La Jolla Lantern*.

"Yes."

Rankin looked at Miranda as she hovered within striking distance of my face. "Miranda, please wait in the reception area and close the door behind you."

She looked at Rankin then at me and left the office.

"Your conscience ever bother you?" Rankin asked.

"No." A high frequency buzz hummed in my ear and my nose felt like a throbbing fist, but my conscience was just fine. "You're worried about my conscience?"

"I'm worried about your mouth and what your conscience might make it say to the police."

"No need to worry." I knew Rankin was more concerned about the capo of a biker gang in San Quentin than LJPD. Concerned enough to have me killed? Maybe. But Rankin's expertise was cleaning up after other people's murders, not his own. As far as I knew, he hadn't crossed the line you could never uncross.

Yet.

"Moretti says he has new evidence."

"You believe him?" I asked Rankin.

"You're not as dim as I thought you were, Mr. Cahill." Rankin smiled at me like I was supposed to take that as a compliment. "You think Moretti might be laying out a false narrative to put a scare into the killer and see if he panics?"

"Maybe." I tossed the bloody towel onto Rankin's desk. "You'd have a much better idea about new evidence than me."

"I don't know anything about any evidence. New or old. No way that I could." He picked up my gun and pointed the barrel at the ceiling while resting his elbow on the desk. "Just make sure you don't play into Moretti's game and panic. I gave you a pass once. I won't do it again."

"You take care of your business, Rankin. I'll take care of mine." I stood up. "Now give me back my gun."

"I trust this isn't the same gun that you threatened me with last December and then used for something else."

"It's not. Give it to me." I reached my hand across the desk and stared at Rankin. As a cop on the street ten years ago I'd shown command presence. Gun or no gun. Right now I felt naked without it. I held my bluff.

"I like you better without it, Mr. Cahill." He flopped his wrist and let the gun barrel drop down and point at me. His finger curved around the trigger. "You're much more reasonable and not so tough. But gun or no gun, you're still a problem."

"Give me the gun." Sweat pebbled my hairline. The last man who pointed a loaded gun at me ended up dead. That didn't make staring down the wrong end of a gun barrel any easier. Especially unarmed. I didn't think Rankin would shoot me in his own office. Then I thought about the easy cleanup on the marble floor and wasn't so confident.

"If we ever have the misfortune of meeting again, don't bring a weapon or I'll let Miranda give her pretty feet a real workout." Rankin tilted the revolver up, disengaged the cylinder, and spun all five bullets out into his free hand. Then he set the gun down in front of me.

I picked up the gun, holstered it, and left his office.

Miranda stood next to the reception counter. She gently touched my arm as I grabbed the to-go container I'd left there. "Nothing personal."

I stopped and turned toward her. "Maybe not to you."

I left without saying another word.

The walk back to my car felt like a marathon at altitude. I'd left it a couple blocks away in a bank parking lot where I used to park when I managed Muldoon's. Now, that seemed like a decade ago. The bleeding from my nose had slowed to a trickle. Still, the blood wouldn't make way for any air to come in or out. I'd had my nose broken before and I'd had my nose not broken before. They felt about the same. A doctor could tell the difference or I could just wait a few days. I mouth breathed like a gaffed fish. The buzz continued to stream through my left ear and my head throbbed.

People stared and angled away from me on the sidewalk. I kept my head down and edged up along the passing buildings. I stashed my gun in the trunk and checked myself in the rearview mirror when I finally got back to the car. A gargoyle without the grin. My nose had swollen into a potato. Clotted blood caked my nostrils and above my upper lip. Raccoon black and blue had started to circle under my eye slits.

Repercussions. Every ill-conceived action I'd ever taken in my life had resulted in repercussions. This one was more painful than most and had taken eleven months to occur, but the debt for my beatdown of Alan Rankin had finally come due.

And there was still one more debt out there from actions I'd taken later that same night which had yet to be paid. That one would take all of me to pay back.

CHAPTER FIFTEEN

MIDNIGHT, SPIKED NECK hair, growled at me when I came in the front door. He realized his error and sidled up to me, tail low, swishing side to side. I couldn't blame him. I'd barely recognized myself, either. I went into the bathroom and delicately washed the dried blood off my face. Midnight stayed tight to my side, like my disfigurement needed protection. I could have used him an hour ago.

I took an ice pack from the freezer, wrapped it in a thin dishtowel, then grabbed a bottle of Bushmills Irish whiskey and went into the living room and lay down on the sofa. Doggie bag dinner could wait. The chill of the ice pack bit through the dishtowel and doubled the pain in my nose. Gradually, the ice and the whiskey numbed down the pain.

My phone buzzed in my pocket. I considered letting it go to voicemail, but thought better of it. Could be a new client. I'd need one soon. Brianne's name showed on the screen. I answered.

"Rick?" She seemed unsure. "You sound horrible. Did you catch a cold or something since you left my house today?"

"Or something."

"What does that mean?" Her voice competed with road noise through the phone. She must have been driving.

My problems were mine. I'd caused most of them and could live with that. I didn't need anyone to take them on for me or offer advice. Or commiseration. I'd have to see Brianne sometime in the next couple days. Even if the swelling went down and the black and blue faded to yellow, the way I looked would require explaining. I might as well get some of it out of the way now.

"Someone I'd pissed off in the past got even tonight."

"That doesn't sound good. Are you hurt?" Concerned, but calm. Her husband had been a Navy SEAL. Panic wasn't in her makeup. "You sound like you have a broken nose."

"I'll survive." Pretty good diagnosis. "Nothing that will prevent me from working your case."

"I'm not worried about that." She sounded hurt like I'd insulted her. "I'm a pretty good emergency medic. I'm coming over."

"You don't have to do that." Hadn't expected that. Especially after her anger at me today. "I'm fine."

"You don't sound fine. Cut the macho bull crap and stop being such a guy. I've had enough of that for a lifetime." I heard a deep intake of air, a pause, and then an exhale. "Where do you live?"

She either took a hit of weed or was doing breathing exercises. I told her I lived in Bay Ho and gave her my address.

"I'm on I-5. I'll be there in ten minutes." She hung up.

I took the ice off my face and inched up to vertical on the couch. My nose and head objected. I took another slug of the whiskey and wondered what my head would feel like in the morning.

A few minutes later Midnight growled and then someone knocked on my door. I lumbered over and eyed Brianne through the peephole. The brim of a Charger ball cap covered her eyes. I settled Midnight and opened the door to get a better view. Gray sweatshirt over jeans. Cowboy boots. She looked up exposing half-mast blue eyes trailing tiny red saffron threads. She hadn't been doing breathing exercises on the way over. Even my impacted nose couldn't filter out the heavy skunk smell of marijuana.

"You really didn't have to come over."

"Oh my God." Bloodshot eyes wide, but still composed. "You look worse than I thought."

"Thanks." I cleared the door to let her in. "You look like you just came from a reggae concert."

"Funny." Brianne kneeled down to pet Midnight, and he thumped his tail and licked her face. He liked the ladies. Especially the pretty ones. "What's his name?"

"Midnight."

"You are dark and mysterious, aren't you?" She stood up.

"He's black. Midnight. Nothing mysterious about that." I pointed to the couch. "Have a seat. You want some of this?" I held up the Bushmills bottle. "Or are you fine flying redeye?"

She grabbed the bottle, took a tug, and handed it back to me. Still had some country girl to her.

"Thanks for saving me from washing a glass." I followed her to the couch and we both sat down. Midnight came over and laid down against my legs.

"Tilt your head back." She picked up the toweled ice pack I'd left on the floor and gently pressed it against the bridge of my nose. The ice pack covered my eyes closing darkness in around me. "What in the good Lord's name happened to you?"

I released back into the couch and let her play nurse. I didn't want anyone dealing with my problems, but it had been a while since someone had been there to cushion the aftermath. I'd forgotten what someone caring felt like. My stomach turned over. In a good way. The first time in a long time.

"Like I said on the phone. Just an old debt repaid. Nothing to worry about."

"You don't have many friends, do you, Rick?" A trace of sadness in her voice.

"I make new friends every day." I hoisted the whiskey through the dark and found my mouth. "I appreciate your coming by and taking care of me, but you called me earlier for a reason."

"It's not important."

"It's all important, Brianne."

She sighed. "Detective Denton called me today."

"How could that not be important?" I pulled her hand with the ice pack away from my face and straightened up. "What did she say? Are they going to reopen the case?"

"No. She called about you." Her stoned eyes got serious.

Not one single good thing could have come from that call. Plenty of bad ones. "And?"

"She doesn't like you very much."

"The sky is blue. Is that it?"

Brianne shifted on the couch like she couldn't get comfortable. Neither could I.

"She said you have a hero complex and that you don't care who gets hurt when you're on one of your missions because you're convinced you're always right."

Denton was wrong about one thing. I did care who got hurt. "Isn't that why you hired me?"

"I hired you because you don't give up." Brianne grabbed the whiskey bottle off the floor and took another slug. Longer this time. "Detective Denton also said that you're dangerous and that I should be careful."

"Coming over here tonight alone wasn't very careful."

"I don't believe a word Detective Denton said." Brianne edged closer on the couch and laid a hand on mine. Warm. "I came to apologize for being a bitch today and . . ."

Her eyes half-closed, but not from the weed now. I only saw the blue, cool and hot at once. Full lips parted. Blood rushed, but the pain in my face dissolved. Brianne could make all my pain go away tonight. But the morning would eventually come.

I lived by few rules. Not romancing a client was one of them.

I took the bottle from Brianne, threw down a gulp of my own, and leaned back into the couch. Damn rules.

"You had a right to be mad."

"I've made mistakes in my life, Rick, but I have few regrets. Leaving Jim wasn't a mistake. Leaving him for Seth was." Brianne removed her hand from mine and looked down. "Coming here was just a way to forget about that for a while."

"It would have been more than a replacement memory for me, Brianne." I touched her chin and lifted it up so our eyes could meet. "But it would complicate things and right now your husband's death is complicated enough."

"Settle down, cowboy. It was just going to be a roll in the hay." Her eyes didn't seem quite so sure, but that could have been my hero complex talking.

"I thought you already had a hay-rolling partner."

"Not anymore. It had been over for a while. I just made it official tonight."

"Why?" I wanted her to say because of me and I didn't want her to say because of me.

"Lots of reasons." She gave me a smile that said the discussion was over.

"When was the last time, before today, that you talked to Denton? Has she been checking in with you?" Back to the "mission."

"No. This is the first time she's called me since she told me the medical examiner ruled Jim's death a suicide two and a half months ago."

"Somebody told her that I was investigating the death. Did she say anything about the investigation?"

"Not a thing. Just the diatribe about you and the warning to be careful."

"Dr. Lin must have called Denton after I talked to her."

"That can't be good." Brianne looked up from scratching Midnight's head.

"Actually, it might be. I took Lin as a professional, someone who would want to do the job right. Especially if her death determination left some murderer in the wind. Maybe she had second thoughts about her decision and asked Denton about the rope and the missing cell phone."

"Yeah, but you solved the mystery of the climbing rope." She tugged on the Bushmills again. "That's one less thing to point to homicide."

"Just because the rope was in Jim's toolbox doesn't mean he put it there. If he was murdered, the killer could have put it there figuring the police would find it if they were competent."

"So you're back on my side about Jim being murdered?" Brianne raised an eyebrow.

"Not quite, but I'm not convinced that he wasn't either. LJPD didn't look hard enough to find the truth. I'm not stopping until I do."

CHAPTER SIXTEEN

CORONADO IS A step back into the 1950s, at least how I envisioned them. Red vinyl stools at the counter in the diner on the corner, pristine California Craftsman, Spanish revival, and Victorian neighborhoods. And, of course, the iconic Hotel Del Coronado where some still like it hot. Built entirely of wood in 1888, it's still a getaway playground for the rich and famous. The island is also home to the Naval Special Warfare Center where Navy SEALs train.

There's no place to park in Coronado, and you can't afford to own a home there unless you bought one fifty years ago or are part of Dot.com wealth Version 2.0, but the city hums with a vibe of what life should be.

Kyle Bates lived in a California Craftsman a couple streets back from Orange Avenue, Coronado's version of Main Street, USA. A woman answered my knock on the door. Midthirties, dark hair, and tan. She wore a white tennis outfit, complete with racket, and could only be described as stunning.

"You must be Mr. Cahill." She smiled and was the first person who seemed happy to see me since I'd started investigating Jim Colton's death. She hadn't seen me without my sunglasses on, yet.

"Rick."

"Well, come in, Rick. I'm Alyssa." She extended a hand, which I shook. "Kyle is in his study. Down the hall, first door on your right. I'm late for a match." She went out the door after I came in.

I took off my sunglasses after she closed the door behind her. One frightened look avoided.

The living room of the Bates house was classic Craftsman, dark wood floors matched by paneling up the walls. A stone fireplace dominated the left wall. The furniture wasn't quite in the same league as the furniture in Alan Rankin's office, but it hadn't come from a discount warehouse, either. Antique plates with hand-painted military themes hung on the walls. A glass and wrought-iron chandelier that would have been at home in a La Jolla art gallery hung from the ceiling. The kitchen that opened up into the living room was equipped with high-end appliances and modeled to blend with the Craftsman bungalow look.

Internet searches on Bates had turned up security consultant as his profession. Nothing more specific. He'd either found consulting work that paid like a La Jolla lawyer or his wife did more than just play tennis. A lot more.

I went down the hall and peeked into Kyle Bates's study. He sat behind a desk worthy of the rest of the house eyeing a computer screen. Two towering oak bookshelves took up one wall. The other walls looked just like the ones in Jim Colton's office covered with military plaques and photos.

I gently knocked on the opened door.

Bates looked up. Blue eyes, sculpted features, a wedge of straw-blond hair atop his head. "You must be Mr. Cahill."

"Rick."

"Okay, Rick. People call me KB." He stood up, strode around his desk, and shook my hand. Six foot two, ropey muscles, vice grip. Boyish good looks, but I figured him for midforties. "Have a seat."

I sat in a leather chair facing the desk, and he went back to his ergonomic chair behind it.

"What happened to your face, Rick? You look like you came out on the wrong end of a bar fight."

"Something like that." I didn't think telling him a woman had done it would raise his opinion of me.

"Be careful who you insult in a bar. People can surprise you." He flashed a thirty-two-tooth smile that probably won him his drop-dead younger wife. Made me want to punch him. Probably a bad idea.

"Yes, they can. Especially when you're not looking. Anyway, thanks for seeing me on short notice."

"Sure." He leaned back in his chair. "Now you said you wanted to talk about Jacks Colton. What would you like to know?"

"How many years were you in a unit together?"

"Eight."

"So you knew him pretty well?"

"I knew how he'd react on the battlefield. Beyond that, I didn't know him that well."

"How would he react on the battlefield?"

"Like a SEAL." Bates's chin rose an inch.

"Meaning?"

"You never served, did you, Rick?"

"No."

"If you had, you'd know what I mean." Blue eyes turned hard and vised down on me.

This went south even quicker than normal. "That's why I asked."

"Dependable. Lethal."

"Not the kind of man you'd think would commit suicide."

"Sometimes people surprise you." He tilted his head.

"So you think Jacks Colton took his own life?"

"Is this about insurance money? His wife trying to squeeze what's left out of Jacks even after he's dead?"

Now I understood the attitude. Another fan of Brianne Colton. Two for two on Colton's friends who didn't like Brianne. What did they know that I didn't? Right now it didn't matter.

"What insurance money?" Bates claimed not to have known Colton very well, but he knew about the insurance policy.

"The two-million-dollar life insurance policy Jacks took out a while back."

"You seem to know a lot about a man you claim not to know that well." I gave him my version of his smile. It would have looked better without a bent nose and raccoon eyes.

"Jacks asked me about life insurance and I turned him on to my insurance guy."

"And you know most life insurance policies have a clause that absolves it from paying benefits if the policy holder commits suicide in the first two years?"

"Sure. The insurance companies have to protect themselves from some guy paying a couple months of premiums and then eating his gun so he can take care of his family." The smirk again. A disconnect from what had happened to a friend three months ago.

"Colton only had a few more months on the policy to hit two years. You really think he'd kill himself and deprive his family of the payout instead of gutting it out for a while longer?"

"Maybe. Depression can be a strong motivator. Like I said, I didn't know him that well anymore. It's been eight, ten years since we ate sand together in the Middle East."

"Yet, he called you on the day he died." I watched his eyes. They gave away nothing.

"Yeah, I guess he did."

"Why did he call?"

"Just to say hello. Talk about old times."

"Did he seem happy, sad?"

"Honestly, he seemed a little depressed." Bates's eyes dropped to the desk and his lips followed. This from the guy who'd sounded so cavalier about someone eating their gun a minute ago. "After I found out what happened, I wondered if I could have said something that would have changed his mind."

"You're convinced he killed himself?"

"I figured the cops wouldn't rule a suicide about one of their own if they weren't certain." Bates slowly nodded his head. "So, yeah. I'm convinced."

Bates stood up like we were done and led me through the house to the front door. I was struck again by the expensive furnishings. He opened the door, but I stopped short of the threshold.

"What kind of consulting do you do?" I did a one-eighty with my head. "Looks like it pays pretty well."

"The kind that's confidential." The thirty-two-tooth grin. "Enjoy your time with Miss Bowlegs."

"Excuse me?" I'd stepped out onto the porch, but turned around.

"I was just wondering how you were being compensated for your time." He raised an eyebrow like we were sharing a secret. "She can be a very giving person when she wants to be."

"Something you want to tell me, Bates?" My face flushed with anger, not embarrassment. "Or do you just throw innuendos around to be an asshole?"

"Hold on, chief." He held up open hands like he didn't want a problem. But his eyes said he'd welcome one. "You're taking this a little personal."

"She's a client. I take them all personally."

But he was right. I'd overreacted. Nothing had happened when Brianne had come on to me last night. Only because I had to fight myself not to let it. I'd felt special that she'd chosen me. Was I angry now because she'd been slurred or because I was afraid I wasn't so special?

"This isn't an innuendo." The grin. "She came on to me at a party down at the beach. Wanted to do it right behind a sand dune. I was tempted, but you've seen my wife. Couldn't risk losing her for one night of some strange. Would have been fun, though. I'm sure you already know that. Say hello for me."

Bates closed the door in my face.

The clouds were still winning the battle with the sun. I put my sunglasses on anyway so as not to frighten other drivers on the road. I took the main drag out of town that dumped me onto the Coronado Bridge, climbed up to the top of the long curve two hundred feet above the water, and looked down at the dark blue expanse below. Since the bridge was built forty plus years ago, more than two hundred people had taken in the same view right before they jumped to their deaths.

Jim Colton hadn't been one of them. His death had happened quietly in the comfort of his own garage. Talking to Kyle Bates hadn't gotten me any closer to figuring out whether Colton's death had been his choice or someone else's. Bates was on the side of suicide. Oak Rollins leaned that way, too.

The only thing I knew for sure was that I didn't know Brianne Colton very well at all.

CHAPTER SEVENTEEN

ACCORDING TO BRIANNE, Jim Colton's closest friend on the La Jolla Police Department had been Sergeant Hector Ruiz. I didn't want to talk to Ruiz at the Brick House or call and leave my name if he wasn't there. The less Chief Moretti and LJPD thought about me, the better. Brianne called him at home last night and set up today's meeting for me. I left choice of venue up to Ruiz so he'd feel comfortable and maybe open up. He chose Pacific Beach Bar and Grill. I'd expected something in La Jolla, but then it made sense. He didn't want to be seen with me by anyone from LJPD. Whatever it took to get him to talk to me.

I arrived at PB Bar and Grill fifteen minutes early out of habit. Ruiz had a habit of his own. He was already there, mashed into a booth in the back. Brianne had given me a rough description of Ruiz, but I could have found him cold. His physique and demeanor shouted cop or military. Or just plain badass. A squat brick of muscle stretching the seams of jeans and a leather coat that must have measured 60 short. Though sitting, I guessed Ruiz couldn't have been taller than five eight and couldn't have bench-pressed less than 580.

I walked over to the booth and introduced myself even though I knew he'd spotted me the second I came in the bar. I put my card down on the table in front of Ruiz. He didn't look at it. Instead, he eyeballed my black eyes and swollen nose.

"Have a seat." A tenor voice didn't match the baritone body.

I slid onto the bench across from Ruiz. "Thanks for meeting me, Sergeant."

A crew cut flattened the top of Ruiz's round head. He looked to be late thirties. The only fat on his body puffed out his cheeks. His enormous lats shot sharp ridges up through his coat. He had the look of a roided-out power lifter. I'd try not to piss him off.

The waitress arrived right away and dropped menus. Ruiz told her he wasn't eating, but I ordered a burger before she left. A beer would have been a nice accompaniment, but I didn't drink on the job. At least not during the day.

"I don't have much time, Cahill. What can I do for you?"

"You a former Marine?" You could trace a yardstick along his spine, if the pencil didn't break. A military background would have added to his camaraderie with Colton. Plus, I didn't buy his claim that he was short on time. I saw it as a ploy to control the conversation. We both had the same idea.

"I don't see what my military background has to do with anything. Brianne Colton told me you wanted to talk about Jim. I'm here out of respect to her and to him, not to talk about my military career."

Well, at least I'd been right about the military. Ruiz had been the first of Colton's friends to mention Brianne in favorable terms. I wondered what he knew that they didn't. Or vice versa.

"How long you been on LJPD?"

"Long enough to know about your old man." Ruiz gave me interrogation room cop eyes. "And you."

That hadn't taken long. Another fan of the Cahill clan at LJPD. So much for control of the conversation.

"And yet, knowing who I was, you still agreed to meet me." I held his glare to let him know I'd been in the square room with the bright lights on the wrong side of the table and could take it.

Finally, I leaned back against the booth. "I don't know whether Jim Colton was murdered or committed suicide. I don't think you do either. But neither one of us is satisfied with the way LJPD investigated Colton's death. That's why you're here."

"You got something solid or you just pounding your chest for Brianne."

He kept up the glare. More than just the tough-guy cop look. Personal. About Brianne? I checked Ruiz's ring finger. Wedding band, which matched what Brianne had told me about him. Not that a ring had ever stopped anyone. Didn't matter now. She was paying me to find out if her husband had been murdered, not to vet potential suitors.

"I don't have anything solid, yet." I opened a portfolio that contained a copy of the police report of Colton's death and my own file on the case. I slid a picture of the rope I'd found in Colton's truck across the table to Ruiz. "Just a lot of little things that could add up to something solid. You ever see that rope before?"

"No." He looked up at me. Sad eyes. "Where did you get it?"

"Found it in the toolbox of Colton's truck. The strand of rope that Colton was found hanging from looked to have been cut from it."

"How do you know?"

"I saw the crime scene photos. Have you?"

"No." He shook his head. "I never saw the report. Chief Moretti kept it buttoned up."

"SOP?" Standard operating procedure.

"Yeah, by the book . . . but . . ."

"But what?"

"What's in this for you, Cahill?" He pushed brown cop eyes into mine. "You looking to get back at LJPD for kicking your father off the force? Wasn't the Eddington mess last year enough? Or do you just like seeing your name in the paper at LJPD's expense?"

Hatred for the Cahill name was imprinted on LJPD's DNA. Ruiz couldn't get past it.

"I don't like seeing my name anywhere, Ruiz. I've seen it where it didn't belong enough for a lifetime." I leaned across the table to invade his massive space. "And I don't want a thing to do with that corrupt Shit House you work out of."

He'd mentioned my father twice. Once had been too many. My father's legacy was my domain. No one else's.

The waitress arrived with my food before I could do anything stupid. I took a bite of the burger. Ruiz continued to eye me like I was a street punk. I swallowed the bite and the anger. Everyone at LJPD hated me. The sun rose in the east. Just another day. I couldn't control the sun or the hate. Just myself.

"Brianne Colton hired me because she doesn't believe her husband committed suicide. I took the job because I needed the money." I set the burger down on the plate and wiped my hands with a napkin. "I read the police report and thought LJPD got it right. I told Brianne that but she kept me on the case. I dug deeper. Now I'm not so sure. And the fact that you're still sitting here makes me even less sure. What's bothering you about the way Moretti handled the Colton investigation?"

Ruiz eyeballed me some more. Dead cop eyes, but I knew his mind was working behind them. Finally, "I need a beer."

I got the waitress's attention and ordered two IPAs with backups in another five minutes. I didn't drink on the job unless the job demanded it. Today it did.

Ruiz didn't speak again until he'd swallowed half his beer in one gulp. "I've been at the Brick House for seventeen years. Chief Moretti's been there for twenty-five. I know this isn't news to you, Cahill, but Moretti is a world-class asshole."

I nodded my head to something we finally agreed on.

"But the little prick is a cop first. Even with all the politics that goes into being chief, he's still a cop."

He didn't have to tell me. "What's bothering you, Sergeant?"

"In my seventeen years, we've had one cop eat his gun. Ed Reeves, about ten, twelve years ago. The chief at the time took the medical examiner's suicide call as gospel." He swallowed the rest of his beer and wiped his mouth. "Moretti went ballistic and pushed for an investigation. He went to the union when the chief wouldn't budge. The chief finally relented and put Jimmy Riley and Buzz Garrett on the investigation. The best homicide dicks we had back then. They came back with the same finding. Suicide."

"So what's your point?"

"Moretti didn't even like Reeves. In fact, I think he hated him. But he couldn't abide that a cop would take his own life. He needed to be one hundred percent certain there wasn't a cop killer roaming free on the streets."

"But when it came to Jim Colton, he took the medical examiner's word as gold and buttoned the investigation up tight."

"Right."

"Why?"

"I don't know." Ruiz dropped his eyes to his empty beer mug.

Ruiz may not have known why Moretti didn't investigate Colton's death further, but he knew something. His body language wanted to tell me, but his fidelity to the thin blue line wouldn't let him. Or something else wouldn't. Fear? I sensed it would take a lot to physically scare Hector Ruiz. But I also sensed that losing his job as a cop would scare him more than any physical danger.

"Brianne told me that Colton didn't trust Moretti. Do you know why?"

He kept his eyes on the beer mug and stayed mute. I let the silence work on him. It started to work on me instead, but I stayed mute until the waitress arrived with round two. Ruiz hit his beer, then leaned back.

"I've given you enough, Cahill."

"Do you think Jim Colton committed suicide?"

"I don't know."

"You just willing to let the suicide stand?"

"I don't have a choice." Again, he kept his eyes low.

"But I do. The only way to get the case reopened is from the outside." I leaned across the table and waited for Ruiz to look at me. "You've seen I haven't written anything down today. Nothing you tell me goes into the report with your name on it. Why didn't Colton trust Moretti?"

"I've told you what I know." But his eyes told something different. "Thanks for the beer."

"You don't care if there's a cop killer out there somewhere?" I grabbed Ruiz's lead-pipe wrist before he could slide out of the booth. "You think Jim Colton would just let it lie if you were the one found hanging in your garage?"

"Careful, Cahill." He looked down at my hand then back up at me. Smoke building behind his eyes.

I let go of his wrist and pushed the Colton file across the table at him. "You said you haven't seen the police report. It's in there."

Ruiz eyed me and let the smoke build. Finally, he opened the file and started reading. I ordered another round of IPAs. Ruiz finished reading the report by the time the waitress came back with our beers. He slid the file back at me.

"What in that report makes you think Jim didn't commit suicide?" Ruiz asked me. "Nothing sticks out."

"It's what isn't in the police report."

"Such as?"

"Why did he have a rock climbing rope when he was afraid of heights?"

"I didn't know that he was."

"Was Colton a good family man? A good father?" Brianne had told me that Ruiz had two sons that he doted on.

"Yes, but what does that have to do with anything?"

"Why would he commit suicide when the act nullified a life insurance policy worth two million dollars that would have taken care of his family?" I shook my head. "You wouldn't do that to your family."

He seemed to be thinking it over before he finally spoke. "Seventeen years on the job has taught me that you can never know what's in a man's heart."

"Maybe not, but working alongside Jim Colton for three years must have told you something about him. Something good, otherwise you wouldn't have been his friend." I pulled the photo of Colton's body hanging limp in the garage and tapped it. "This was a selfish move. If Colton did this, he had to know his son would be the one to find his body. He could have driven his truck into an embankment or off a cliff. He could have swum out into the ocean and opened his mouth. He could have killed himself a hundred different ways that wouldn't have screamed suicide and wouldn't have allowed his son to find his body. What if it were your son finding you?"

Ruiz looked at the picture of his dead friend. He dropped his eyes for a second and they then came up angry. I'd pushed too hard.

"There's nothing here that would convince Chief Moretti or anyone else to reopen the case." He slid out of the booth and stood up.

"Put it together with what you're not telling me about Moretti."

"Thanks for the beer, Cahill."

I jumped out of the booth and blocked his way. A brick wall in front of a Mack truck. "Give me something, Sergeant. Tell me what I need to know."

I knew if he wanted to, Ruiz could make my wall come tumbling down, but I stood firm. He cocked his head and eyeballed me. I couldn't tell if he was wondering if he should tell me what I wanted to know or take me down. He wasn't in his jurisdiction so he couldn't slap steel bracelets on me just for fun. If we went at it, he might get into a jackpot with his chief. He straightened his head and I braced for a collision. But his eyes went from tough to something else. Sad? Frightened?

"Moretti likes to use CIT for arrests that result in asset forfeitures." Just above a whisper.

"And Jim had a problem with it."

"Yeah."

"Why?"

Ruiz's eyes scanned the room. "Jim didn't think the seizures were always warranted."

"What do you think?"

He cocked his head, pursed his lips, and raised his eyebrows but didn't say anything. He didn't have to. He agreed with his dead friend.

"But what about the judicial procedures people can follow to get their assets back?" I kept my voice low.

"There are other ways to get the assets back."

"What do you mean?"

Ruiz put up his hands. Palms out. "I've told you enough."

"Is that why Jim called the FBI?"

"I don't know anything about that. Good-bye, Cahill." He stepped around me and left the bar.

CHAPTER EIGHTEEN

I POINTED MY Mustang in no particular direction and drove. I didn't see the road, I sensed it. The car made turns on its own as I stayed inside my head.

Moretti.

My nemesis. The man who could put me behind bars forever. Did everything surrounding Jim Colton's death come down to Chief Moretti? Had he been using CIT to run shakedowns and seizures on crooks who couldn't prove their assets hadn't been ill-gotten? Most asset forfeitures come from drug busts. Where were the arrests? The trials? I couldn't remember reading about any big drug busts in La Jolla. Or big arrests of any kind. But LJPD didn't need convictions to keep their 65 percent off the top of seized assets. They just had to make sure no one filed a claim within a year of the seizure.

If Moretti was running a racket, where did the money go? To his department, or was he taking a cut? I didn't have to imagine him using his position to intimidate people to keep them from reclaiming their assets. I'd seen his intimidation up close.

Ruiz had pointed a crooked finger at Moretti for questionable asset seizures. Maybe Moretti decided not to investigate Jim Colton's death because he thought the investigation might splash back on him and reveal his shakedown racket. Maybe Colton had evidence that Moretti had twisted the law beyond recognition.

Moretti wore the badge prouder than most and got off on the power it gave him. He wouldn't give it up easily. Maybe his reasons for not investigating Colton's death went to a darker place than I'd first imagined. I knew Moretti to be a bully, a liar, and an asshole. Murderer? Maybe.

But how did I investigate the Chief of Police when he had the power of the badge and all I had was a past that could put me in jail? And was it worth the risk? I was already in Moretti's crosshairs for Randall Eddington's disappearance. The disappearance for which he'd just told the *La Jolla Lantern* he had new evidence. If my investigation got too close to Moretti, he might arrest me for Randall's murder and let the facts catch up when they could.

All that potential danger to investigate a man's death that very well may have just been a suicide.

I'd taken Brianne Colton's money and promised her that I would put all of me into the investigation of her husband's death. But it hadn't been a suicide pact. If all of me meant a life behind bars, I'd consider our contract null and void and mail her a refund.

My car kept driving and I kept stopping at red lights, signaling turns, and giving pedestrians the right of way. By rote and reflex, without any thought or recognition, my mind drifted to my late father as it often did when I contemplated ethics and morality.

Or lack thereof.

Twenty-six years ago my father had been kicked off the force at LJPD. All that time and I still didn't know exactly what he'd done. I'd asked him once and hadn't gotten an answer. There hadn't been anything in the newspapers. I didn't read them as a ten-year-old kid, but I'd checked through online search engines later in life. To investigate through LJPD would have been too humiliating and probably wouldn't have gotten me any more information than I already had. The rumor was that he'd been a bag man for the mob.

No charges were ever filed. He just quietly walked away from his job and his pension.

And later, his family.

I'd defended his name, my family name, with my fists on school playgrounds, but I had known deep in my heart that he'd done something wrong. Guilt that a bottle couldn't wash away hung off his body like an albatross. Pulling him under and his family with him. Before all that there'd been a code of honor that my father had lived by: A truly guilty man should never go free. Whatever my father's guilt had been, he hadn't gone free. It had chased him into shame and an early grave.

I didn't know my father's crime, but I knew his guilt. It coursed through my veins. And I had earned it on my own. Maybe the guilt of my sins would lead me to my father's end. But would I add to it by letting a murderer walk free?

I finally saw the world outside my windshield and my destination. The cross atop Mount Soledad. The war memorial where my father had taken me as a kid and where I'd often gone on my own as an adult. I'd always felt at peace up there, eight hundred feet above the ocean and the town of La Jolla. The best view in all of San Diego County. Above it all. La Jolla, my job, my past.

I parked below the forty-foot-tall cross and pulled out my phone. I wasn't sure the number I needed to call was even in my contacts. It was. I called it.

"Scott Buehler." A trace of cynicism hung off his voice in just saying his own name. But that was fine with me. I needed a cynic right now. Working for a newspaper in the age of the Internet could make you one. Especially a free newspaper. Free or paid subscription, Buehler was the best reporter in San Diego. Or maybe I just felt that way because he'd been fair to me in print regarding my encounters with the police over the years.

I heard a "Hmm" through the phone after I stated my name. Considering the brick wall I'd built for the press over the years, including Buehler, I took his reaction as positive.

"You still working the crime beat?"

"I'm the lone investigative reporter so I cover all the beats that need investigating." Another hmm. "I know you didn't call me on a Sunday to see how my career is going. What can I do for you, Rick?"

"You know of any big drug busts or any busts by LJPD in the last six months or so involving asset forfeitures?"

"Nothing comes to mind. I don't focus on La Jolla unless events demand it, but if something big had happened I would have heard about it and investigated." A tiny thread of interest dangled from his answer.

"Are busts where nobody is formally charged but assets are seized interesting enough to be investigated by the only investigative reporter at *The Reader*?"

Buehler stayed silent for a few seconds. A long few seconds.

"What's the game, Rick?" The cynicism returned to his voice.

"No game. Just came across some information that I thought needed looking into."

"Why don't you look into it yourself? Last time I checked, you still had a private investigator's license issued by the state of California."

"First of all, I only investigate when I get paid. Secondly, as you know better than anyone, I don't have too many fans down at the Brick House. No one there would be willing to answer my questions." Plus, they'd ask some of their own.

"Exactly."

"Meaning?"

"I'm a newspaper reporter, Rick. Even in the age of Twitter, Snapchat, and Meerkat where every pajamaed Millennial with a cell phone living in his parents' basement thinks he's an investigative journalist, I still need sources. If I start poking around LJPD just to feed your vendetta, I'm going to lose every source I have there."

Not the response I'd expected.

"Do or don't do whatever you like, Buehler." Time to change tactics. "But you said something about being a newspaper reporter and an investigative journalist. I guess those only come into play when there's no risk involved. Maybe I'll just have to find some stoner in his parents' basement who gives a shit."

Buehler didn't say anything, but he didn't hang up either. Probably thinking. Good. Better than a hang-up. Finally, "You better not burn me, Rick."

"I won't."

"Where did you get your information?"

"I'm strictly an unnamed source, right?" I didn't want Moretti to find out that I was behind the investigation.

"Sure."

I looked out my windshield at the town of La Jolla below. The marine layer had burned off leaving cotton candy clouds lolling in the sky. The ocean beyond, cobalt blue in the fall sunshine. Another postcard day in paradise. I couldn't see the Brick House from my vantage point, but I knew it was there. The quaint white brick building that had destroyed my father. And had tried to destroy me. Dry rot in the core, eating its way into the soul of paradise.

"Sergeant Ruiz. Head of the Criminal Impact Team." I'd told Ruiz he wouldn't go into my report, but I hadn't said anything about talking to a reporter. Of course, that was worse. "I don't want to tell you how to do your job, Buehler, but this is going to take finesse. Don't run at it head-on, and don't talk to Chief Moretti until you absolutely have to."

"Thanks for not telling me how to do my job."

"Sorry, I just don't want to put Ruiz in Moretti's doghouse. I can tell he wants the truth to get out, but he won't risk his job to do it." That was my rationalization to give up Ruiz. That down deep he wanted to right a wrong and find out the truth about the death of his friend. Still, I didn't feel good about it.

"I'll do the job the way I see fit, Rick." I heard fingers tapping a keyboard over the phone. "I thought so."

"What?"

"You said Ruiz heads up LJPD CIT, right?" Now the hum in his voice was from excitement.

"Yeah." I knew where he was going and I didn't know whether to be happy or worried.

Buehler was an investigative reporter. He investigated. That's why I called him. But I couldn't just point him at what I wanted investigated and hope he'd stop there.

"The former head of CIT, Sergeant Jim Colton, committed suicide three months ago. Do these supposed asset forfeiture arrests have something to do with that?"

"I don't know." I didn't, but I'd just lost sole control of my investigation. Maybe Buehler would uncover the truth that I hadn't yet been able to. And maybe he'd ask Moretti questions that could lead back to me.

I wanted to know what really happened to Jim Colton. But I didn't want the bulls-eye that Moretti had put on my back to get any bigger.

CHAPTER NINETEEN

THE LIGHTS OF Pacific Beach and Mission Bay below strobed through the shifting gossamer fog. The ocean beyond, invisible, loomed in the darkness. I was into my third beer sitting on the patio when Midnight alerted and I heard a knock on the front door through the open sliding glass door into the living room. A hope that it was Brianne bubbled up inside me. I hadn't talked to her all day. Her visit last night and Bates's crack about her today were layers of the same onion. I wanted to know which one was closer to the core. Then I reminded myself that she was a client and nothing else. The rest shouldn't matter.

Even if it did.

I exited the evening chill into the living room and went to the front door. Midnight beside me, hackles at full battle height. I looked through the peephole and understood why.

Moretti.

LJPD Police Chief Tony Moretti. Out of dress blues in an Italian suit, but still carrying the authority of the badge. And still with the power to put me behind bars.

My stomach turned over and my mouth went cotton. I looked at Midnight. My one call would be to my neighbor to make sure she and her daughter would take care of him.

I settled Midnight and opened the door. He growled when he saw Moretti. Instincts trump command authority.

"Cahill." Jet-black hair still greased back. Eighties porn mustache still pulled down his mouth. Cologne still pulsed from his pores. He hadn't grown any, either. Still huge attitude in a sawed-off body.

The one chance that my living nightmare hadn't yet come true was that he was alone. No boys in blue with steel bracelets ready or Sergeant Ruiz with the CIT team. Moretti had a huge ego, but I doubted he'd try to take me down alone. I might just sleep in my own bed tonight.

"Moretti." I kept the door at my body's width.

"Aren't you going to invite me in?"

"No. That would make this social and we're not friends."

"Let's pretend we are." He smirked. His version of a smile. The only version I'd ever seen. "I have some information that will interest you, but I'm not going to tell it to you standing on the porch."

I let him in. Midnight growled. I quieted him and led him back through the living room and outside. It wouldn't be fair to subject his sensitive olfactory glands to Moretti's gasoline cologne. Wasn't fair to me either. I turned around and found Moretti seated in my recliner. I wondered how much it would cost to steam clean it. Or if I should burn it.

"What happened to your face?" He smiled.

"Get to it, Moretti."

"We found the Volvo." Moretti's dark eyes radared me, searching for a reaction.

"No need to sit." I held steady. "You won't be here long."

"I made myself at home. Comfy chair."

"You said something about a car?"

"Playing dumb, Cahill?" His eyebrows knifed up. "Thought you were too smart to play dumb. Smarter than everybody else." He strung out the "everybody."

"I'm just a citizen trying to live my life, Moretti." I remained standing, frozen in place.

"For now." He chuckled. A hyena closing on the kill. "The Volvo was found in Reno a couple months ago. Found in an abandoned warehouse, like it had been there a while. Same VIN number as the one that belonged to Jack Eddington until it went missing on December twenty-first of last year. You remember Jack, don't you, Cahill? Randall Eddington's grandfather?"

"Sure." This wouldn't have a happy ending for anyone but Moretti.

"Well, I talked to Jack yesterday. He told me you spent six months trying to track down Randall after he disappeared the same night the Volvo did. Funny that you never talked to anyone at LJPD during your investigation. That's where most PIs start when they investigate a missing persons case. The police. Especially since we were already investigating on our own. We could have compared notes. How much did you charge the Eddingtons to search for their grandson, anyway?"

Chocolate chip cookies, which I never ate.

"Is that why you came by? To talk about my old cases?"

"Speaking of your cases, I hear you're leading Brianne Colton on a wild goose chase. Is that your specialty now? Exploiting grieving families? How much are you squeezing out of that poor woman to keep her delusion alive that Jim didn't kill himself?"

"Why do you care? If the Colton suicide is a slam dunk, you have nothing to worry about." I thought of the asset forfeitures, but kept my hole card buried. Wouldn't do me any good now. I prayed someday it could.

"I'm not worried about anything. I just care about a dead cop's wife. We're all family here, Cahill. Everybody in blue. But you weren't a cop long enough to understand that."

"Anything else, Moretti?"

"The DNA evidence the Reno crime scene techs collected has been sent off to their lab. Results should be coming back soon."

"Congratulations. I hope it helps you find Randall." I'd never been in the Eddingtons' Volvo. If all he had was the car, I had nothing to worry about. But I was worried.

"You mean his remains, don't you?"

"I sure hope not. As far as I know, Randall's disappearance is still a missing person investigation."

"As far as you know." The chuckle again. "Well, unfortunately for Randall, things are starting to add up to a murder investigation."

"Sorry to hear that."

"Yeah. We all are." He eyeballed me for a three count. Like a lion waiting to pounce. "Remember that little talk we had down at the Brick House around Christmas last year?"

He pulled a notepad out of the inside pocket of his jacket.

"Yeah." The walls closed in on me.

He made a show of reading the notepad. "According to the notes I took that day, you went down to Windansea Beach at eleven twenty-two on the night of December twenty-first."

"If you say so." I remembered.

"Did you happen to see anything besides the waves that you said you looked at that night?"

This wasn't a bluff. He had something new. My stomach knotted up.

"That was a long time ago. I'm sure I saw a lot of things that I can't remember now. Just like any other night."

"But it wasn't any other night. It was the night Randall Eddington went missing. Did you happen to see him when you were gazing at the ocean?"

"No."

"That's odd." He went silent. Sweating me. I didn't bite. "You may remember that the Volvo Randall's grandfather had lent Randall was seen on a security camera driving in front of Windansea Beach ten minutes before you were seen getting out of your car in the same area by another camera."

"Doesn't seem odd to me. How could I see Randall if his car drove by ten minutes before I even got to the beach? He was probably on his way to his grandparents' condo on La Jolla Boulevard a few blocks away." I waited for the hammer to drop.

"Sure, that makes sense." He scrunched up his mouth and his eyes rolled upward. "But the problem is that Randall's cell phone was found by a guy with a metal detector at Windansea a couple weeks after Randall disappeared. The battery was dead and the guy stuck it in a drawer because it was an iPhone with their new lightning power cord thing and his charger wouldn't work. But here's where it gets good, Rick. This guy just bought a new iPhone with the same kind of charger last week. So he pulls out the phone he found and charges it up. And being a good Samaritan, he wants to get the phone back to its owner. So he calls the only number in the address book, Rita Mae Eddington."

Moretti gives me big eyes and an open mouth like it was time to celebrate.

"I guess I'm happy that Rita Mae got her grandson's phone back. Is that it, Moretti?" But I knew there was more and where it went.

"Well, we now can place the phone right at Windansea and we know from Eddington's phone records that the last call that phone ever made, before Mr. Good Samaritan found it, was on December twenty-first at eleven forty-nine p.m. Cell tower records confirm that the call was placed in the area of Windansea right around the time a man walking his dog thought he heard gunshots. Four minutes later, the security camera caught you returning to your car on Westbourne, a short walk up from the beach."

My face flushed. I couldn't hide it, so I just held Moretti's glare.

"Is this all a coincidence, Rick?" He used my first name and it sounded like a real question, but it was all according to script.

"If what you just told me is true, it would have to be."

"You know whose phone that last call went to?"

"No." Yes. I knew and so did Moretti. What he didn't know was that I made the call.

"Alan Rankin, a high-priced criminal lawyer who'd defended the shot caller for the Raptor biker gang. Do you know him?"

"I've heard of him." I touched my still swollen nose, remembering Rankin's MMA beauty who put her foot through my face.

"Well, I would hope so." The icy chuckle. "I'm sure the Eddingtons gave you Randall's phone records when you were investigating his disappearance. Even a low-rent PI like you would find out who he called on the night he disappeared."

"Time to go, Moretti."

"Anything you want to get off your chest, Cahill?" He stood up. "Now would be the time, before the phone comes back from the lab. You could tell me how Alan Rankin is involved in all of this. Might make for a shorter stay in the state's hotel."

Sweat pebbled my forehead. I went to the front door and opened it. "Time to leave."

Moretti gave me the wolf smile and stopped in front of the door.

"You take care of yourself, Rick. Your secret's safe with me. But the clock is ticking. I'm sure we'll see each other again soon." He walked out the door.

I went back out onto the patio with Midnight. The November night chilled the sweat along my forehead. I stared out at the view. Midnight leaned against me and sighed. I tried to breathe.

Moretti had me in a vise. Each new piece of evidence was another twist tighter. How many more twists did he have? I'd find out with the next knock on the door. But why did he spill tonight? And why tell me *my secret was safe* with him? Was he telling me that he was running the investigation alone? Why?

Moretti hated me. Because of my father. Because of me. He'd never needed an excuse to stick a knife between my ribs and twist it. But as much as he enjoyed making my life miserable, he wasn't stupid. He'd just given me evidence that would be used against me in court after he arrested me.

Why tell me about the call to Alan Rankin on Randall's phone the night he disappeared? Maybe he thought I killed Randall and then called Rankin on Randall's phone. He wanted to play me against Rankin, but why? Wasn't I a big enough prize for him?

CHAPTER TWENTY

I WOKE UP early the next morning. Or, at least, got out of bed early. To wake up, you had to have been asleep. I'm sure I cobbled together a couple hours in between sweat and spin cycles. Just not enough to take on the life I'd built for myself.

Moretti was out there somewhere. Collecting new evidence and building a case. The next knock on the door would be with handcuffs and a murder warrant. Right now there wasn't much I could do about it. Running wasn't an option. Neither was standing still.

I got out of bed and threw on a pair of jeans and a t-shirt, went into my office and turned on my computer. Midnight followed me and laid down under the desk. I still owed Brianne two days of work. Something to do while I hoped Scott Buehler from *The Reader* came up with something on Moretti that would distract him long enough for me to find a way to stay out of prison.

I logged on and pulled up Gmail, using the password Brianne Colton had given me to access her husband's account. I didn't know what I was looking for, but figured I'd know what it was when I saw it. If there was anything to see. Jim Colton had died. That much was certain. How was still in question. At least to me and Brianne Colton. I wasn't convinced her husband had been murdered, but I wasn't ready to sign off on suicide yet, either.

I scrolled through Colton's personal emails, starting two weeks before his death. Brianne had told me she'd already gone through them and hadn't found anything that pointed to suicide or to someone wanting to kill Jim. Still, I wanted to be thorough and I had the time. For now. I checked Colton's inbox first and then his sent file. Luckily he wasn't prolific. Most of the emails were to and from old SEAL and GRS buddies. They were about life in general, the mess in the Middle East, and occasionally old war stories. He never mentioned Moretti or the asset seizure arrests. He did ask Oak Rollins about private security and stated it might be the next move for him.

Colton's emails were terse and mostly devoid of feeling. However, when he mentioned Brianne, I could sense it still hurt. Although it's difficult to discern tone in emails, Colton came across as a bit wistful about Brianne. But not suicidal.

I went back another three months. More of the same. The first couple weeks after Brianne left him, Colton let out some pain to Rollins but nothing about LJPD or Moretti.

I found the first and, so far only, email addressed to Kyle Bates, the SEAL from Colton's unit who I'd interviewed in Coronado. It was sent nineteen days before Colton's death. Oak Rollins was also a recipient. The email read: "I thought I saw Dirt today. I caught him from behind. Same build, same head. Walked just like him. That bull-legged swagger. I almost called out his name, but the guy turned and I saw his face. Not him, of course. Just some guy getting on a yacht. But for a second I really thought it could be Dirt. Brought me back, boys. Gone times."

I checked the return emails from Rollins and Bates but didn't learn anything more about "Dirt." They both thought the sighting was strange and joked that it couldn't have been Dirt because he couldn't sail for shit.

The three of them had all been in the same SEAL unit, but only Colton and Rollins had worked together with GRS. Dirt had to have been an old SEAL buddy. The email didn't feel like an "aha" moment, but the date it was sent scratched at something in my memory. I pulled Colton's file out of a desk drawer and found the cell phone records from the last month of his life. I checked the date of the Dirt email. Colton called Oak Rollins that night for the first time that month. In the next eighteen days, the last of his life, he called Rollins thirteen more times.

Who was Dirt and why did things seem to start moving faster in Jim Colton's life after he mistakenly thought he saw him? And could the man Colton mistook for him have had anything to do with his calling the FBI five days before he died?

I felt for the first time that the case had some momentum. I called Brianne. Straight to voicemail. I needed to talk to her about "Dirt."

I wanted to talk to her because when I wasn't thinking about prison, I thought of her.

I wanted to see her.

CHAPTER TWENTY-ONE

THE STREETS WERE still and mostly empty. The marine layer pressed a low ceiling on the morning, graying out everything but fifty feet ahead. The haze gave me some cover as I drove up Soledad Road into La Jolla. Then again, it would do the same for anyone following me, like one of Moretti's boys in a police cruiser. I pulled up in front of Brianne's house, safe from any rainbow light bars in my rearview mirror. Brianne's 1965 cherry-red Mustang convertible sat in the driveway.

There was a lot to like about Brianne.

I rang the doorbell and waited. A dog barked, more of a howl, inside the house. There hadn't been a dog the last time I was here. Nobody came to the door. I knocked again. The dog howled again.

"George, shush." Brianne's voice through the door. More throaty than usual.

The door opened. Brianne stood slightly stooped holding the collar of a large brindle boxer. Amber hair piled wild atop her head. A little red around sleepy eyes. No makeup. Toned bare legs and feet below a short kimono. I'd awakened her. Half asleep, she looked as good as she had on the stage in performance mode.

Rules. Couldn't break the rules.

"Rick? Why in the Lord's name are you knocking on my door at seven twenty-five in the morning?"

"Country girl like you, I thought you'd be up."

"You see any cows that need milking in here?" She opened the door wider, but kept hold of the Boxer. "I haven't lived on a farm since I was eighteen." She wiped a stray strand of hair from her eyes. "Lord, I'm not even presentable."

I thought of the Sammy Kershaw song "She Don't Know She's Beautiful," but kept it to myself. "Sorry."

"Well, come in then." She stepped back to let me in and the Boxer snarled and held his tail low. "George, that's enough."

"George, huh?" I slowly knelt down and turned slightly to the side. "As in Jones or Strait?"

"Both."

I clicked my tongue and called the dog by name.

"He doesn't like strange men," Brianne said, still holding George's collar.

"Something we have in common." I clicked my tongue again. "Let him go."

Brianne squinted at me then shrugged her shoulders and released the dog's collar. I clicked again and looked down at the ground. George snuffled then walked toward me, tail down with a slight wiggle in it. I stayed partially angled away from him. He tentatively sniffed my hip, but his legs weren't convinced. He had to lean forward because his back legs wouldn't come any closer. I let him sniff. He moved a little closer, sniffed my shoulder, and stuck his tongue in my ear. Ten seconds later I had him on his back, scratching his chest and belly.

"I guess this makes me not so strange." I stood up. George whined and waved a paw at me.

"Maybe not, but you're still a bit different, Rick." Brianne shook her head and a couple strands of red hair washed across her forehead. "Hard candy on the outside and soft nougat on the inside."

"Probably closer to bittersweet."

She laughed and walked into the kitchen. George and I followed. He ran his head under my hand. I gave it a scratch. The kitchen was rustic and had a butcher board island twice the size of mine that doubled as a breakfast table. A large window over the sink would have had a view of the the mountains of East County if it weren't foggy. There was a large fenced-off herb garden to the right of the covered patio in the backyard.

"Coffee? It will take a few minutes." She pushed a button on the coffeemaker on the polished wood countertop. "You probably like yours blacker than a moonless night."

"I only like coffee in ice cream, but thanks anyway. Sorry for dropping by unannounced." Not that sorry.

"It's okay. It's not really that early." She sat down at the island. "I had a gig downtown last night and got home late."

"I thought after you dumped the guitar player, you'd take a break for a while." I took a seat across from her.

"Seth's a professional. He wouldn't let a little breakup get in the way of a payday."

"Good to hear." I doubted it was that easy for him. Hadn't been for Jim Colton. Wouldn't be for me.

George pressed his body against my leg as he walked by, then returned and repeated.

"That's enough, George. Go lie down." Brianne pointed to a doggie bed in the corner of the kitchen. George gave her hurt Boxer eyes and slunk over to his bed.

"Midnight's going to think I've been cheating on him when I get home."

"Sorry."

"Yeah, you can tell it bothered me."

"Well, maybe not as much as me coming on to you the other night." She studied a spot on the place setting in front of her.

I thought of Kyle Bates's story about Brianne coming on to him, but let it lie. For now.

"A beautiful woman who I like very much showing interest in me is a highlight, not a bother. Under any other circum—"

"Okay. Enough said." She smiled and made the rules that much harder to obey. "So, why did you come over this morning?"

"I'll get to that in a second, but tell me about George. Was he here the night Jim died?"

"No. He was at my apartment. I took him with me when Jim and I split."

Brianne got up and poured herself a cup of coffee. "If you don't drink coffee, can I get you some orange juice or water?"

"Sure, I'll take some water." Brianne handed me a bottled water and sat back down with her coffee. "Thanks. I went through some of Jim's emails this morning. Who is Dirt?"

"Was. Doug McCafferty. A SEAL buddy who died in Iraq ten years ago." She sipped her coffee. "He was in the two pictures in Jim's den that I thought were in the wrong spots on the wall. Why?"

"Jim sent an email to Oak Rollins and Kyle Bates nineteen days before he died saying he thought he'd seen Dirt."

"I know. It freaked him out."

"He told you about it?"

"Yes. He saw the man right before we met for lunch that day in Seaport Village."

"How often did you two meet during the separation?" Colton hadn't mentioned the lunch in his email.

"Not that often." A long exhale. "Jim wanted to reconcile."

"And you didn't."

"No." She stared at her coffee.

A bad day for Jim Colton. He thought he saw a ghost and his wife didn't want him anymore. Three weeks later he'd be dead. The lunch with Brianne and her revelation to Jim that they'd never get back together put a different spin on the events that happened afterward. Was this day the beginning of a spiraling depression that ended with him putting a rope around his neck? His emails would say no, but Colton was old school. Kept his emotions to himself. Where they could fester and metastasize. Just like my father. He committed suicide. With a bottle. It just took nine years.

The frequent calls to Oak Rollins could have been to cry on his shoulder about his marriage, or his version of shoulder-crying. But why the call to the FBI? I needed to talk to Rollins again and I needed someone at the FBI to return my calls.

"Jim didn't seem like a guy who got freaked out over anything," I said. "What did he do?"

"You're right. He wasn't like most people. At least most non-SEAL people." She leaned forward. "But seeing this guy really got to him. Jim said his physique was exactly the same as Doug's and that his walk and mannerisms were just like him, too. He said he almost forgot Doug was dead and that he was about to shout his name when the man turned toward him and Jim saw his face and it wasn't Doug. He said it felt like Doug died again right there in front of him."

"And then you two had lunch and you told him you didn't want to get back together." The words felt barbed leaving my mouth. I could have left them unsaid.

Brianne tilted her head and stared at me. Pain, maybe anger in her eyes. Finally, "You know, Rick, there's something hard and cruel in your soul. It's not the only thing there, but it's there."

I hadn't thought about my soul in a long time.

"Sorry. I didn't mean to be cruel."

"Yes, you did." Calm. "You just stated a fact, but you wanted it to hurt a little bit."

She was probably right. I shoveled some of my own pain onto Brianne and others before her. People I cared about. I sympathized with Jim Colton's marital woes even though I'd had much more in common with Brianne in my own long-ago marriage. Maybe I jabbed at her to push off the guilt I still felt about how I'd failed Colleen.

"I am sorry." I was. "Do you want to talk later?"

"No. Let's get it over with." Same hurt, angry eyes.

"I'm just trying to find the truth, Brianne."

"That, I believe." She took a sip of coffee, but her eyes remained on me. "In your own way."

However right or wrong she was about me could wait. I'd gradually come to feel that something was off about Jim Colton's suicide. Nothing definitive, just little pieces here and there that made me doubt. But when I stood back and looked at Colton's death from thirty thousand feet, suicide made the most sense.

"Your husband saw the man he mistook for Doug McCafferty and found out you two weren't getting back together nineteen days before he died. Right afterwards, he started calling Oak Rollins a lot more often than ever before and he seemed sad in his emails." I let out a long exhale, delaying the question I had to ask for as long as possible. "Is it possible that feeling like he'd lost an old friend all over again and realizing you two were never going to get back together could have sent him on a downward tilt that he never recovered from?"

Brianne stared at me. The hurt left her eyes leaving only the anger. "When are you going to make up your damn mind, Rick?"

"What do you mean?"

"Half the time you sound like there's something suspicious about Jim's death and the other half you try to blame me for driving him to suicide."

"I'm not blaming you, Brianne. We're each responsible for our own actions." I knew that better than anyone. "I'm just saying the information about Jim seeing a man who reminded him of a dead buddy and finding out you two were definitely over seems to have affected him deeply. His behavior changed immediately after that day. I'd be stupid not to consider suicide a legitimate possibility without compelling evidence pointing to the contrary."

"You're forgetting his call to the FBI."

"He called the FBI two weeks later. The call was most likely work related." Or it could have been about Chief Moretti and his asset forfeiture arrests, but I didn't want to give Brianne another hook to hang her hopes on. Besides, Moretti's involvement in Colton's death, or anyone else's, seemed less and less likely after what I'd learned today.

"Really? How come he never called them on his private cell phone before?" Her eyes more challenging than angry now.

"You can't be sure of that. You only have one month of phone records."

"Wait here." She jolted up off her stool and dashed out of the kitchen.

George took the opportunity to get out of his bed and amble over to me. I rewarded him by scratching him behind the ear. Brianne returned to the kitchen a minute later with a few sheets of paper gripped in her hand. She slammed the papers on the island in front of me, and George scampered back to his bed.

"I got more records from AT&T since we last talked." She folded her arms tightly against her chest. "I went back four months and didn't find another call to the FBI."

"Why the sudden urge to check phone records?"

"When you quit, I'll have to investigate on my own. The phone records seemed like a good place to start."

"I'm not quitting, Brianne. Just because I have doubts doesn't mean I'm not doing the job. I want to get you an answer once and for all. Did you find anything else in the phone records?"

"No. I checked numbers against the ones on Jim's last bill, looking for odd patterns and I called numbers I didn't recognize. I didn't find anything out of the ordinary. Just in that last month that you already have. All the calls to Oak and the one call to the FBI. Have you gotten anything from the FBI yet about that call?"

"No. I can't even get an agent to talk to me." I'd called three times asking to talk to the agent who took Colton's call and was told each time that the FBI didn't divulge that kind of information.

Brianne's head sagged but her eyes stayed on me, like I was a disappointing child. I didn't blame her. Not finding a way to talk to the agent Colton spoke with on the phone wasn't a good enough answer.

"Finish your coffee and get dressed," I said. "Put on something business sexy, not something you'd wear onstage."

"Why?"

"We're going to see the FBI."

CHAPTER TWENTY-TWO

THE SAN DIEGO FBI office is in Sorrento Valley, a community hard by Interstate 5 that serves as a buffer between La Jolla and Mira Mesa. The building is multi-stories of blue glass with a concrete outline. Official, intimidating, unyielding of its secrets.

I'd prepped Brianne on the drive over. The office opened at 8:15 a.m. The government deals in fractions. We entered through a glass door on the right side of the building at 8:19. A shiny brown marble floor with white veins and the FBI shield took up the foyer. We were immediately greeted by two NFL lineman–sized men in suits with endangered seams. They asked us to empty our pockets into hard plastic bowls and walk through a metal detector. No alarms went off. I wasn't strapped. My Ruger .357 was in the trunk of my car parked at Brianne's house. Brianne had offered to drive and seemed surprised when I accepted the offer. She wouldn't have been if I'd told her about Moretti's tightening noose. The less time driving around in my bulls-eyed car, the better.

We were greeted at the main desk by a thirtyish woman in a blue suit who rivaled Brianne in buttoned-down sexiness. Mocha skin, burgundy lips, and raven hair floating atop her shoulders. I'd hoped for a man. Brianne wore a brown pinstriped suit with a white blouse unbuttoned just low enough to give a glimpse of cleavage. Male or female special agent, Brianne still had a role to play.

"I'm Special Agent Myrna Singh." Her full lips half-rounded to a smile. "How can I help you?"

I introduced myself and Brianne, and stuck out a hand over the desk, high enough so Special Agent Singh would have to stand up to shake it. Once she did, I had her on our level and forced to engage. I shook her hand long enough to keep her standing and kept talking. "I'm investigating the death of Brianne's husband, Sergeant James Colton of the La Jolla Police Department."

I let go of her hand and she dropped it down along her gray slacks. "You didn't show me a badge, Mr. Cahill. Are you a detective with the La Jolla Police Department?"

"No. I'm a private investigator."

She held the half smile, but pressed the hand I'd shook against her slacks like she was trying to wipe my residue off her. She may not have even realized she did it. More of a reflex. Everybody likes a PI.

"I'm sorry, this should be investigated by the local authorities. A suspicious death, unless the victim was a government official or employee, is not under the bureau's jurisdiction. Unless the victim's civil rights were violated."

"Just his breathing rights. We're not here to ask the bureau to investigate Mr. Colton's death. However, we need to talk to the special agent Mr. Colton talked to on the phone on August twenty-fourth at nine forty-seven a.m."

"We can't disclose that kind of information, Mr. Cahill." She gave me a closed-mouth smile and tilted her head like she was talking to a slow child or a dog. "Besides, this was three months ago. We wouldn't even still have it on our phone logs."

"You're the FBI. You keep track of everything." I didn't expect Agent Singh to make it easy for us to get what we needed, but I hadn't expected her to lie to me when she didn't have to. Heat crept up the back of my neck. "I'm sure some Russian hacker has the phone log information and all the FBI's other files. You must have it, too."

"Can't you help us, Agent Singh?" Brianne jumped in before I made things worse. She laid a little extra southern on the accent. I really wished Agent Singh had been a man.

"I'm afraid it's out of our jurisdiction." She gave Brianne the same patronizing smile.

"It entered your jurisdiction when the deceased called this office and spoke to someone for seventeen minutes and then died under suspicious circumstances a few days later." I set my hands on the counter and leaned toward Agent Singh, invading her space. "We'd like to talk to Special Agent in Charge Richmond."

"I'm afraid that's not possible." Singh surprised me by leaning in. Her breath, Dentyne riding coffee. "It's time for you to leave, Mr. Cahill."

I heard the squeak of size fourteen Florsheims on marble and knew the seam-splitters would soon surround me.

"I don't want to have to involve my friend Congressman Peck, Chairman of the Appropriations Committee, Agent Singh." Brianne worked a tsk-tsk smile of her own. "But I will if I have to. He told me to call him if I had a problem. Do we have a problem, Agent Singh?"

The right side of the FBI's offensive line compressed the air on either side of me like I was a safety trying to shoot the gap on a blitz. I waited for vise grips to pinch my arms. The big boys eyeballed Agent Singh.

Brianne pulled her cell phone from her purse, hovered her finger over it, and stared at Agent Singh. "Are you going to call Special Agent Richmond or am I going to call Congressman Peck?"

Singh targeted black eyes on Brianne then me. Finally, she gave a quick nod to the security twins and they walked back over to the metal detector.

"Please have a seat." She pointed to a row of chairs against a large window opposite the front desk. She picked up the handset from under the counter and spoke into it. All I could hear was a bureaucratic hum. A moment later she hung up the phone. "It will be a few minutes. Would you like some coffee?"

Same smile she'd given us when we walked in like nothing had happened. I thought of ordering coffee with cream and two teaspoons of sugar just to be an ass, but wasn't ready to show Brianne that side of my personality yet. Or, maybe, again.

Brianne hadn't mentioned Congressman Peck on the ride over from her house. I leaned my shoulder against hers and whispered, "You really know Congressman Peck?"

Brianne matched my lean and whispered, "The boys and I played at his daughter's high school graduation party out in Poway before Jim died. I only met him the one time."

"So you don't really know him well enough to call and ask a favor."

"Well, the Congressman would like to get to know me a whole lot better. In fact, he tried to when his wife was in the other room and he gave me the check for the birthday gig."

"Our tax dollars at work."

"Well, at least we got a smidgen of a return on our investment today."

We waited for thirty minutes. An hour. An hour and a half. A few special agents with all-American smiles passed by while we waited, but no one spoke to us. I got up and went over to Agent Singh's desk to voice a complaint for the third time when the elevator on the right opened and a bespectacled man exited it and outstretched a hand to me.

"Mr. Cahill?" He grabbed my hand and pumped it. Then looked over at Brianne. "Mrs. Colton? I'm Special Agent Brad Blanton. Special Agent in Charge Richmond will see you now."

Bureaucratic smile. Close-cropped hair. Late thirties. Blue suit. Off the rack. Nothing remarkable about Special Agent Blanton. The kind of guy you looked at every day, but never saw.

Agent Blanton led us into the elevator and up to the third floor, the last stop. The doors opened. More marble. More tax dollars at work. We followed Blanton down a hall to an office protected by two large dark hardwood doors. Blanton knocked and then opened one of the doors.

"Right this way." He gave us a butler arm wave into the office and then closed the door and stood quietly in the back of the room.

A man stood behind a desk that matched the doors. Spit-polished with hard angles and sharp edges. His physique said seven-days-a-week-gym-honed early forties, but his eyes said a decade older. He flashed a perfect smile at us. I had the feeling it could flip to an angry grimace in a blink.

"Please sit down." He pointed to two leather chairs in front of his desk. "I'm Special Agent in Charge Richmond. Sorry to make you wait. I've had meetings all morning."

"Thanks for seeing us." Brianne gave him a southern charmed smile.

"Thank you, Mr. Blanton." Richmond sat down without looking at Blanton.

The door clicked shut behind us on not-so Special Agent Blanton. Richmond eyed me, unimpressed, then looked over Brianne. Impressed. "Now what can I do for you?"

I nodded at Brianne to take the lead. She told Richmond about her husband's death and the phone call he made to the FBI. She explained that we just wanted to talk to the agent that her husband had called or see a transcript of the call.

Richmond steepled his hands in front of him on his desk, and I braced for bureaucratic mumbo jumbo.

"We, of course, liaison with local law enforcement agencies in the region and it wouldn't be uncommon for the sergeant of a CIT unit to call our office and coordinate training opportunities. Sergeant Colton could have called for any number of ordinary reasons."

"Great." I forced a smile. "Then how about we talk to the agent he spoke with or you show us the transcript and find out just how ordinary the conversation was. We're just connecting the dots, Special Agent Richmond."

"It's Special Agent in Charge, Mr. Cahill." He winced a smile. "I worked awfully hard to get here. Might as well enjoy the title."

"I meant no harm, Special Agent in Charge Richmond." I held up my hands like I meant it. And I did. I hadn't meant any harm. After the speech about the title, I wish I had.

"None taken," Richmond said and we all pretended it wasn't a lie.

"Can you help us?"

"Your quest is commendable." Richmond gave us a smile that told me SAC of the San Diego field office wouldn't be the last governmental stop for him. He was destined for great things. Probably politics. That was the only hope I had of us getting what we needed. "But, a conversation with anyone in this office is confidential under the laws of this country."

"Please, Special Agent in Charge Richmond, I need to find the truth about what really happened to my husband." Emotion caught in Brianne's throat. I couldn't tell if it was an act or if she was sincere. Richmond's face said sincerity.

"You can call me Charles, Mrs. Colton. I wish I could help, but you're asking me to break the law. That I will not do. I'm sure Congressman Peck would agree with my decision." He gave Brianne a tight-lipped "I feel your pain" squint. "Have you talked to Police Chief Moretti about this? We could certainly discuss this phone call you're so interested in if he talked to us in an official manner regarding your husband's death."

"Police Chief Moretti won't reopen the case," Brianne said.

Moretti was a loaded gun, cocked and pointed at my head, waiting for an excuse or inevitability to pull the trigger. But he was a politician, too. Just like Special Agent Richmond, looking for the next rung on the government ladder. Their paths surely had crossed. Had Richmond read corrupt megalomaniac in Moretti or had he bought the public persona? Did he care either way? Time to find out.

"The call Jim Colton made to your office on August twenty-fourth was from his personal cell phone," I jumped in, fighting the urge to call Richmond Chuck. "Brianne checked his phone records going back six months. That was the only time he ever called the FBI from his personal phone. What if the call was about Chief Moretti? About some practices Jim couldn't live with anymore?"

"Is there something you'd like to tell me, Mr. Cahill?"

Special Agent Richmond and Brianne both looked at me expectantly. The asset forfeiture arrests were the only arrows I had in my quiver against Moretti's Randall Eddington arsenal. Using it now without determining how much leverage it gave me against Moretti could secure me a room without a view up in the Bay Area. The other side of Marin County. San Quentin.

"No. I'm just wondering out loud. There had to be a reason Jim Colton called this office on his personal cell phone and not his work phone." I avoided Brianne's eyes and looked at Special Agent Richmond. I could lie to law enforcement, no matter the agency. I'd been doing it for over ten years. Brianne was different. She mattered. Not enough to go to prison for, but enough to feel guilty when I lied to her. "Maybe he didn't want his chief to know he called. Doesn't it seem strange to you, Special Agent in Charge Richmond?"

"Not particularly, for the reasons I described earlier." He stood up and smiled at Brianne.

"Mrs. Colton, I really think your best avenue going forward is to deal directly with LJPD and convince Chief Moretti to take another look at your husband's death. As I said before, we'll cooperate with the local police. Otherwise, there's nothing I can do for you. I'm sorry."

Brianne stood up. "I've already tried to get Chief Moretti to reopen the case. Twice. He won't do it. We aren't even asking the FBI to investigate. We'd just like to know who Jim talked to and what was said on that phone call. It's really not much to ask. He was my husband."

"I'm sorry." Solemn frown, then he looked at the door.

Brianne turned to leave. I stayed seated. "Do you really want us to get Congressman Peck involved, Agent Richmond? Or the press? A grieving widow stonewalled by the Feds makes good copy. Might adversely affect one's future ambitions."

Richmond looked down at me. The grimace I'd feared earlier finally pulled angry at his face. "Are you threatening a federal agent, Mr. Cahill?"

Shit.

"Not in any way whatsoever."

"He didn't mean anything, Charles. Come on, Rick. We've taken up enough of the agent's time."

Brianne walked over to my chair. I stood up to leave, but Richmond's voice stopped me. "I'm sure you think it was a good idea to hire Mr. Cahill, Mrs. Colton." He kept his eyes and his grimace pointed at me. "Avenger of the underdog. But the truth is, he was a corrupt cop who is still the main suspect in his wife's murder."

Richmond opened a desk drawer and pulled out a file that no doubt had my name on it and dropped it on the desk for effect. He must have done his homework when he heard I was here with Brianne. He continued with my career highlights. "He was fired from the Santa Barbara Police Department and no other agency in the state would hire him. He makes a living peeping through motel windows and doing odd jobs for questionable characters. Oh, and he's on his way to be foreclosed upon. Again, Mrs. Colton, I suggest you deal directly with the police and not waste your money on this con man."

The FBI had a file on me. I shouldn't have been surprised. But that didn't help fill the sucking hole in my gut. The bank, Moretti, the FBI. The walls were closing in.

Brianne grabbed my arm and pulled me out of Special Agent Richmond's office. Exiting the rest of my problems wouldn't be so easy.

CHAPTER TWENTY-THREE

BRIANNE DIDN'T LOOK at me or say anything on the walk to the car. The November gray hung heavy in the air. She stared at the windshield for a few seconds before she turned on the ignition. I didn't interrupt her silence. She was working out the pluses and minuses of hiring me. And she didn't even know about all the minuses. She exited the parking lot and the silence hung as heavy as the November sky.

"Is what Special Agent Richmond said about you true?"

"Everything but me being a con man."

"A corrupt cop?"

"That's a matter of opinion. I lied to the police during the investigation of my wife's murder and once to protect a partner. They don't take kindly to that. Apparently, someone advised the FBI about it sometime over the past ten, twelve years."

"Why did you lie in your wife's murder investigation?" The words came out haltingly, like they were painful to form in her mouth.

"To protect myself." I'd only told one other person the whole truth. I didn't know Brianne well enough for that, but she deserved some of it. "And someone else. It had nothing to do with Colleen's death. Only my reputation and that of the other person."

"I told the police the truth about everything in my life when they investigated Jim's death. Even the embarrassing parts. That's what you do when you want them to find the truth about why someone you cared about died. What lie did you tell to protect your partner? That was just for his reputation, too, right?"

Brianne's husband had been a cop; surely she knew about the honor of the thin blue line. But I knew the honor could shield the public from the truth and allow some cops to act like crooks. Just as my partner had back on SBPD.

"I've made mistakes in my life, Brianne. Big ones. People have gotten hurt because of some of them. I can't change that. Only learn from it." But I hadn't really learned. I'd just withheld information from the FBI to hold on to the leverage I may need to keep myself out of jail at the expense of possibly finding the truth about Jim Colton's death. "The week you hired me for is over after tomorrow. I can reimburse you the last day of the week and we can call it even."

I was compromised and hurting the case. Brianne didn't know it, but I did. I shouldn't have taken the job in the first place. Only problem was, I didn't have the money to reimburse her. The bank did.

"No. Let's keep things the way they are. Work through tomorrow." Brianne kept her sunglasses pointed at the road. She hadn't looked at me since we left the FBI building. "Let's communicate through emails going forward."

The silence pressed down on me during the remaining drive to my car.

I drove home from Brianne's in the same silence as I'd left in her car. Music or sports talk radio wouldn't fill the void sucking inside me today. I knew who I was. I never tried to fool myself. Sometimes other people, but not myself. The FBI's file on me was accurate and showed who I'd been and still mostly was. And the FBI didn't know the worst of it. Yet.

Neither did Brianne.

Brianne mattered. I didn't want her to, or anyone to, but she did. After only six days, she mattered. Maybe it was seeing her onstage, living the songs she sang that spoke to my heart. Maybe it was loneliness. Maybe it was the reality that I might live the rest of my life behind bars that made me want to suddenly make something of the life I was barely living. I couldn't tell anymore. But Brianne mattered and so did what she thought of me. Five days ago when it didn't matter, she saw me as a hero. Now that it did, she saw me for who I was.

The found-again feeling of caring for someone had made me want to be better. Maybe I could tell Brianne about it in an email.

CHAPTER TWENTY-FOUR

I TURNED DOWN my street and spotted a car parked opposite my home, one house down. The black late model Camaro was occupied. Its windows were too small to get a good look at the driver, but I caught a flash of blond hair. Couldn't tell if it belonged to a man or a woman.

Whoever sat in the car didn't know much about surveillance. My street was atop an embankment that featured just one row of houses. Similar embankments stair-stepped above and below. The spot afforded the driver an easy view of my house, but the Camaro stood out like a lone beacon next to the incline. No other cars were parked on that side of the street. Of course, there could have been an innocent reason for the car to be parked there with a driver waiting in it. But I didn't believe in innocent anymore.

I pulled into my driveway and hustled out of the car, leaving the door open, and jogged up to the front door of my house. Whoever was watching would expect me to come back outside to the car in a minute or so. I ran upstairs with Midnight on my heels and changed out of my sweatshirt and jeans into black slacks and a leather bomber jacket, then put on a Padres cap. Hopefully, just enough of an appearance change to give me the couple seconds I'd need if spotted. I pulled my Ruger .357 Magnum from the nightstand and slipped it into the jacket pocket.

I went downstairs and out into the backyard, leaving Midnight inside. I hopped the chain-link fence that partitioned my backyard and shuffled down the lower embankment to the street below. A hundred yards or so west, I climbed back up a cement drainage channel to my street.

The Camaro was still parked on the street, four houses away from my current vantage point, facing me. I hoped the driver was looking back at my house waiting for me to come back out to my car and not looking in my direction.

The neighborhood was quiet and the street was empty except for me and the Camaro. I walked down the sidewalk, ball cap brim low, and eyed the Camaro through my sunglasses. LJPD's plain wrap detective cars were Crown Vics. The Camaro could have been someone's off-duty personal car, but I doubted it belonged to a cop. Even for LJPD, this was bad surveillance. Had to be an amateur. Maybe a professional hard guy, but an amateur tail. Thus the gun in my pocket.

Two houses from the car, I saw that I'd been right. I caught the profile of Miranda, Alan Rankin's MMA tough girl, looking back at my house. I crossed the street and walked directly at the Camaro on the passenger side. Miranda's head spun toward me just as I made it to the front headlight. I kept walking to the passenger side door. The window was halfway down. I bent down and peeked in, and Miranda pressed the ignition button.

"Keep it in park and your foot on the brake." I took a half step back and half pulled the handle of the .357 out of my pocket. "Unlock the door."

Miranda's eyes went big, and the color grayed out of her face. She pressed the remote door lock, and I whipped the door open and jumped inside.

"Circle down around the cul-de-sac and park in my driveway next to my car." I kept my hand on the butt of the gun in my pocket.

"What are you going to do?" Miranda's voice cracked.

"Nothing more than I have to. Drive."

But I hadn't quite figured it out yet. Right now I could be arrested for kidnapping. When Miranda punched the ignition, I'd reacted on instinct. Grabbing a gun to get your way isn't imprinted at birth. You have to learn it. This was where all the decisions I'd made in my life had taken me.

Too late.

Miranda finished the Sunday drive around the cul-de-sac and parked in my driveway.

"Let's go inside." I kept my hand in my coat pocket and waited for her to open her door before I opened mine.

Miranda got out of the car and slowly walked to the front door of my house. She wore yoga pants, blue this time, and a pink zip-up sweat top that hugged her athletically feminine frame. Red toenail polish camouflaged her most dangerous weapons propelling her flip-flops. I followed a step behind, swinging closed the door to my Mustang I'd left open when I arrived home a couple minutes ago.

"Open the front door, but don't go inside yet."

Miranda opened the door, and Midnight met her with a spiked-haired, dagger-tooth growl. She yelped and jumped backwards, bumping into me.

"Midnight, leave it," I said in a calm but firm voice. "Go lie down."

Midnight disappeared from the doorway.

"Let's go."

Miranda walked into the small foyer and then the living room. Midnight eyed her from his rectangular bed next to the fireplace. He loved company, especially pretty ladies, but he sensed by my body language that Miranda wasn't a friend.

"Stay." I spoke to Midnight, but Miranda stopped walking as if by command. Her body tensed. She pivoted. Her leg swung. I smashed a left hook into her kidney. Her roundhouse kick flailed, and she collapsed to the floor. The momentum sent her flip-flop flying into the foyer.

Midnight lunged from his bed, but my straight-armed open-hand signal stopped him.

"Go lie down." He did, but kept his head high and ears alert.

Miranda lay below me, fetal and gasping for air.

I could have avoided the kick and not hit her. From behind. I could have avoided the altercation altogether. But a part of me, the part that Brianne had referred to as cruel, had welcomed the action. Miranda had sucker-kicked me in Rankin's office. It hadn't been her idea, but a command from her boss. It didn't matter. It couldn't stand.

It had been a long time ago and hadn't ended well, but I'd been a cop once. I'd had a few run-ins with bold drunks and fearless gang-bangers. I'd been bruised and bloodied, but the fights never ended until I threw the last punch. Or kick. You had to be tough to take someone's best shot, but you earned respect by beating a man down.

Or woman, I guess.

I looked down at Miranda and the part of me that hadn't been a cop realized I'd just hit a woman. I squatted down and slowly put my arms under Miranda's armpits. She tensed.

"I just want to get you over to the couch. No more punches. I promise."

She relaxed a bit and let me help her to her feet. She stepped out of her lone flip-flop, and I eased her over and down onto the couch. I checked the pockets of her sweat top and pulled out a cell phone.

I looked down at her. Her face was still flush with pain and fear clouded her eyes. My gut turned over. I wasn't a street cop anymore. I didn't want to be feared. At least, not by a woman.

I went into the kitchen, put my gun and Miranda's cell phone on top of the refrigerator, and pulled an ice pack from the freezer. Miranda hadn't moved since I went into the kitchen. Midnight had. He now sat in front of Miranda, leaning his back against her legs. Either he'd seen more good in her than I had or had read my body language in helping her to the couch. Miranda had one hand pressed to her side where I'd hit her and the other scratched Midnight behind the ear.

Maybe she was more than just a hired thug. I handed her the ice pack and sat in the recliner perpendicular to the couch that Moretti had soiled with his cologne last night. She put the ice pack under her sweat top and pressed it against her side.

"Why does Rankin have you tailing me?"

"I don't know. I just do what I'm told." She'd regained her breath, but her face still hued pink.

"Okay. Then tell me exactly what Rankin told you to do."

"Follow you and call him and tell him wherever you went and whoever you saw." She moved the ice pack and winced. "I didn't even know you weren't home until you pulled up. I thought your car was in the garage."

"Did you call Rankin when I came home?"

"Yes."

"Did you mention that I'd run inside and left the car door open?"

"Yes."

Shit. Rankin would be expecting a call about where I'd driven off to when I came back out of the house. I could have Miranda make a dummy call to him right now, but it wouldn't get me much. When she left today, she'd go right back to Rankin and tell him what really happened. That's if she didn't go to the police first. I needed a better plan.

"How long have you worked for Rankin?"

"About a year."

"After you kicked me in the face, twice, why did you tell me it wasn't personal?"

"Because I felt bad about it." She dropped her brown eyes. "I didn't want to hurt you, but I get paid to do what Alan says. I am sorry I had to do that. Is your nose broken?"

"I don't know."

"You haven't gone to a doctor?"

"No." Probably should, though. Still couldn't breath through it.

"Sorry."

"Don't be sorry, dammit. I just kidney punched you from behind. You'll probably piss blood for days."

"It's okay. I know you were just trying to protect yourself. It wasn't personal." She smiled and I couldn't help but laugh.

"How did you get caught up with Rankin, Miranda? You can do much better."

"I owe him." She shifted position and winced again. A pang of guilt ran down my spine. "Are you going to keep me here against my will or am I free to go?"

"Of course you're free to go." Now I was more worried about her going to the cops than back to Alan Rankin. "Where are you going?"

"You don't have to worry about the police." She scooted forward on the couch and gasped. "They're not an option. Besides, this makes us even."

"Maybe I should take you to a doctor. You're still obviously in a lot of pain. Sorry." I really was.

"I don't need a doctor. I've been kicked in the kidneys before in the ring." She stood up, groaned, and then sat down hard like she'd been punched again.

"Either stay there or I'm taking you to a doctor." What if I'd really hurt her? I punched a woman and put her in the hospital. Something to put on my agency's webpage.

"No doctors."

"Then lie down." I gently lifted Miranda's legs onto the couch as she shifted to horizontal.

"I'm supposed to call Alan."

I went into the kitchen and pulled Miranda's cell phone from the top of the refrigerator. Seeing the Ruger .357 I'd put up there reminded me of what a stupid idea it had been to confront Miranda, force her into my house at gunpoint, and then punch her. No, the FBI file Special Agent Richmond had didn't contain everything stupid or illegal I'd done. Or had yet to do.

I walked over to the couch and handed Miranda her phone.

"What do you want me to say?" Miranda asked.

"Say whatever you want." I wouldn't feel guilty about hurting whoever Rankin sent next.

Miranda tapped the phone's screen and put it up to her ear. "It's me. He went to the grocery store. I don't know. Do you want me to follow him home? Okay."

"You didn't have to do that on my account."

"I didn't. It was on my own account." She looked worried. That made me worried.

I pulled a blanket out of a closet in the hallway and draped it over Miranda.

"Thanks."

I went into the kitchen and grabbed a couple waters from the fridge, returned, and gave one to Miranda.

"It's been a while since a man took care of me." Miranda smiled. This one a dazzler with a lot of teeth.

"How long since a man personally put you in the situation that required care?"

"About the same amount of time."

"Oh." The fact that I wasn't her first abuser made me feel worse, not better. "Rankin?"

"No." She looked at me and tilted her head like she was deciding if she wanted to say more. "He actually got me out of an abusive relationship and into MMA."

"So Rankin got you into MMA and you kicked your boyfriend's ass and moved on?"

"No, I just moved on. From a lot of things." She pulled her hair up and turned to show me the back of her neck. "Ever heard of them?"

A tattoo of a sunglassed Velociraptor in a leather jacket grinned at me from the back of Miranda's neck. A chill spiraled down my spine.

"Yeah. I've heard of them." And had felt their wrath.

"I figured you would since you know Alan."

"I don't know either that well and don't want to."

"I understand why with the Raptors. I used to be a member until Alan got me out of the life." She looked at the floor. "I owe him."

"How are you paying off that debt?" I grimaced when I pictured Rankin, over twice Miranda's age, pawing at her.

"Not that way." Miranda read my face. "He's gay."

"Then what's it take to pay off the debt?" I leaned toward her and waited for her to look at me. "How much longer do you have to do Rankin's dirty work before you can walk away? There are a lot of other things you could do, Miranda."

"You think you know me, but you don't." Tears welled in Miranda's smoky brown eyes. "I shouldn't have told you any of this. I don't even know you."

"You're right. And I can't help you unless you want me to."

"Why do you want to?"

A good question.

"Maybe I think I can redeem myself for past sins if I help you. Maybe I know what happens when you keep stacking bad decisions on top of one another. Or, maybe you're beautiful and I think I'll get something out of helping you."

"Probably that last one." She gave me the big smile again.

"Probably." I smiled back. "I'm only in it for myself. So maybe you can help me figure out why all of a sudden Rankin cares about where I go and who I see."

"I don't know. He called me at home this morning and told me to follow you and report back to him. That's all I know."

"How long are you supposed to be on me?"

"Until six tonight."

"Who's the night watch?"

"I don't know if there is one."

I studied her. No facial tics or body movements. She may have been telling the truth. Didn't matter. Rankin had to be sending a tail. If he wanted me followed during the day, he'd want the same at night. And it probably wouldn't be someone as bad at it as Miranda.

I'd be ready.

CHAPTER TWENTY-FIVE

MIRANDA SPENT THE next hour on my couch. I warmed up some stir-fry Orange Chicken for lunch that I'd made last night. Miranda was able to walk to the butcher block island and sit down without my help. Progress. She ate like a fighter in training. Fast. But she seemed to enjoy the food and looked disappointed that there wasn't any left over for seconds.

As much as I enjoyed spending time with an attractive woman who liked my cooking, I still owed Brianne the rest of the day and all of tomorrow to work her husband's case. Even if I had to send her the results via email.

"How are you doing?"

"Better. You do pack a powerful punch, though." Miranda smiled like it was a compliment from one fighter to another.

"Yeah, I'm pretty dangerous when your back's to me." I got off the barstool and backed away from the butcher block island. "Miranda, I'm working a case that has nothing to do with Rankin. I promise. Whatever he wants to learn about me, it has nothing to do with this case. I need to get back to work, but I can't have you shadowing me."

"Are you asking me to leave?"

"Yes. If you're up to it. If you're not, then I have to take you to a doctor or the emergency room."

"I don't need a doctor."

"Then it's time to go. I need to get back to work on a case that has nothing to do with Rankin or you."

"I understand." A micro-frown. "I'll leave your house, but I can't promise I won't still spy on you."

"Look, Miranda—"

The house phone rang, interrupting me. I walked over to the kitchen counter and checked the incoming number. Unknown. Good, at least it wasn't the bank. Unless the loan officer had suddenly gotten smart and called me from his cell phone. I took the risk and answered.

"Rick Cahill?" Male voice that I didn't recognize.

"Yes."

"This is Special Agent Mallon from the FBI. I understand you wanted to talk to me."

"What's your badge number, Agent Mallon?" I'd gotten regulations runaround and veiled threats from the Special Agent in Charge of the San Diego field office earlier today. Now a voice over the phone wanted to volunteer what I needed. How did I get so lucky all of a sudden?

The voice gave me a badge number, easy like he knew it by heart. Didn't mean he hadn't made it up, but I had no way of checking. I didn't have connections with any law enforcement agency that could verify the number. I'd left a wildfire of burned bridges behind me over the years. I'd asked for the badge number to try to get a read on the man's voice. Seventy-five percent he was telling the truth. I owed it to Brianne to go with the odds.

"Who told you I wanted to talk to you?"

"Do you want to talk to me or play games?"

I looked over at Miranda who pretended she wasn't listening. "I want to talk."

An exhale of breath. "If Jim Colton hadn't been a SEAL, I wouldn't even be talking to you, much less meeting with you."

"You were a SEAL?"

"This isn't about me, Cahill, but I served in the Navy. Wasn't good enough to be a SEAL. Colton deserved better. Any SEAL would. I'm jammed up until about nine o'clock tonight. We can't meet here. Meet me at 4838 Sorrento Valley Boulevard at nine fifteen. It's a friend's auto body shop. Park in the back. If anybody sees me with you, I'm . . . Just don't be late." He hung up.

I wrote the address and time down on a notepad I kept on the counter. I had eight hours to kill before I potentially found something out that could turn the Colton case upside down.

Miranda looked at me over her water bottle. I ripped the page from the notepad and put it in my pocket.

"Time to go, Miranda." I walked over to her at the butcher block. "Sorry about everything."

"It's okay."

She stood up and I jammed my hand into her sweat top pocket and ripped out her car keys, then took a couple steps back out of her kicking zone. "I need a promise. Take the rest of the day off. Go to a movie and tell Rankin I stayed home all day."

"Give me the keys." She stood up from the stool.

"I need you to promise me, Miranda, or I'm borrowing your car for the rest of the day."

"Rick, give me back my keys." She took a step toward me.

I backed up into the foyer, then hustled to the front door out of Miranda's view and opened it. Miranda stayed in the kitchen out of my sight. Shit. She'd called my bluff and now I really had to use her car. I took a step outside, then remembered the gun I'd left on top of the refrigerator. I rushed back into the kitchen. Miranda walked along the kitchen counter in my direction. Hands empty. Her face flushed pink when she saw me. I glanced at the top of the fridge. The gun was still there.

"You win, Rick. This isn't worth it. Give me my keys, and I'll leave for the rest of the day." She glanced at me, then avoided my eyes.

I didn't trust the sudden change of mind but didn't want to challenge her on it. I'd test her when she left. I took the gun off the top of the refrigerator and gave her keys to her.

"I'll follow you out."

"You don't have to do that." She smiled.

"Yes, I do." I smiled back.

I walked her outside to her car. She moved more fluidly than she had before, and I felt relieved. Hopefully, I hadn't done any lasting damage. Miranda turned toward me when she reached her car.

"Thanks for lunch." Her lips curved up into a closed-mouthed smile and her eyes widened. She gave me a hug like we'd been on a date instead of me kidnapping her at gunpoint. We'd only spent a couple hours together. Not long enough for her to form the Stockholm Syndrome. I hugged her back.

All I could think to say was, "Sorry."

"Don't be. Bye." She got into her car.

I got into mine and punched the garage door opener. The door began its rise just before Miranda backed out of the driveway. I turned on the ignition and rolled the car into the garage. I wanted Miranda or the night shift to think that the car was in the garage when one of them came by to tail me.

I got out of the car and hustled down the street and peeked around the corner. Miranda's black Camaro was already a quarter mile up the hill and soon left my sight. She looked to be true to her word, but I had a plan if she wasn't.

I ran back to the garage and pulled out my car. I drove down to the street below mine and parked it in front of a house with no cars in the driveway. Hopefully, Miranda would report to Rankin that I'd parked my car in the garage. When the night shift came by tonight, they'd see lights on inside my house and think I was home while I met with Special Agent Mallon in Sorrento Valley.

And I'd finally learn the truth about one of the mysteries in the Colton case.

CHAPTER TWENTY-SIX

PAULIE'S AUTO BODY Repair was located in Sorrento Valley, just a few blocks from the FBI San Diego field office. It sat under an off ramp from Interstate 5 in the middle of a business park, a couple blocks from FBI headquarters. I arrived twenty minutes early and circled the block. I didn't spot anything suspicious. Just dimly lit office buildings not open for business until tomorrow morning. Special Agent Mallon was still only a voice on the phone. He came across as legit to me, but I couldn't take any chances. My Ruger .357 Magnum sat in my coat pocket, and I had my conceal carry license in my wallet.

I was out of LJPD's jurisdiction and wasn't concerned about a violent "misunderstanding." At least not with them. I'd still be wary tonight until I saw an FBI badge and official ID.

Paulie's had a fenced-in parking lot on its left side that swung around to the back. I pulled my Mustang slowly into the parking lot and parked in an empty spot in the back. The only other cars in the lot were a rusting pickup in the far corner, a late model Lexus with a crushed front fender, a black Range Rover with tinted windows that didn't look like it needed any work done, and a van with Paulie's Auto Body Repair stenciled across its side parked two slots away from me.

I exited my car and scanned the parking lot. No movement. I waited. A minute later a metallic rattle snapped my head to a

corrugated steel door in the middle of the back wall. Someone inside was cranking it open. I slid my hand into my coat pocket and
felt the handle of the Ruger. More reflex than conscious movement.
Dim light crept out of the door with each pull of the chain lifting
the door. Not enough to get a good look at the figure that stood
at the edge of the opening when the door finally raised all the way
up. My eyes battled a spotlight mounted above the door pointed
toward the parking lot. All I could make out was the outline of a
man. A large man.

"Rick Cahill?" The voice on the phone. "It's Special Agent Mallon.
Is that you?"

I released my grip on the gun. "Yes."

I took a step forward. Footsteps quick behind me. I turned too
late and a prick stung the back of my neck. I spun around. The night
dimmed. My head kept spinning. Then everything stopped.

* * *

Dark. Metallic whiff of solvent tickled my nostrils. I opened my
eyes. Blurry. An outline of a man. Tall. Wide. Dangerous. The image
slowly came into view. Black. Everything from boots to gloves to ski
mask. A canvas bag lay on a table in front of the man. I didn't want
to find out what was in the bag. I jerked my legs to run, but couldn't
move. My arms, the same. I was tied to a chair.

"You're not going anywhere, pal." The voice came out of the ski-
masked man. It sounded like the voice on the phone, but different.
Raw. Venemous. Malevolent.

"You must have me mistaken for someone else. I'm here to see
Special Agent Mallon from the FBI."

I knew there was no Agent Mallon, or if there was, he hadn't been
the man I'd spoken to on the phone. I talked now to see if I could

get back any information that could help me. It was a Hail Mary, but all I had. There was some hope of survival, however. The man wore a mask, meaning he didn't want me to be able to identify him. Meaning he didn't plan to kill me.

At least, not yet.

"Why did you go to the FBI today?"

"To try to get some information about a case I'm working on."

The man in black looked at something over my shoulder. Possibly the person who stuck the needle in my neck when I arrived. Then he punched me in the solar plexus, and all the air spat out of my lungs. I gasped, fighting for air. I tried to pull some oxygen back into my lungs. I finally grabbed enough to breathe.

"Why did you go to the FBI today?"

My cases were my clients' business and mine. Nobody else's. But I couldn't breathe without air in my lungs. And I thought Brianne would understand.

"I'm investigating a suspicious death. The victim called the FBI and talked to someone for seventeen minutes a few days before he died. I'm trying to find out who he spoke with and what about." I twisted my head over my shoulder, trying to get a glimpse of the other man.

A fist exploded in my gut and all the precious air I'd saved whoomped out of me.

"Why did you go to the FBI today?"

I couldn't answer. I couldn't breathe. I couldn't escape.

Finally, I sucked in enough air to speak. I kept my eyes pinned on Ski Mask. This time I'd at least see the punch coming and tighten my abs. Maybe that would save me one gulp of air. "Look, I'm telling you the truth. Ask me something specific, and I'll tell you what I know."

I braced for Ski Mask's punch. It didn't come. I could see his eyes staring at me through the mask's slits. Blue eyes full of evil.

He picked up the canvas bag off the table and my breath left me on its own. I braced for brass knuckles, pliers, a blowtorch. He pulled out a plastic water pitcher and a towel. Nothing else. He tossed the pitcher and the towel over my head and I heard someone catch them, then the sound of water from a tap filling the pitcher. The partner who didn't want to be seen even in a ski mask or heard at all.

Someone I knew or had seen or heard speak before? Maybe.

Ski Mask shook the canvas bag upside down to show me nothing else was in it. Then he shoved the bag over my head. I tried to calm my breathing. I figured I'd need as much air as possible. Suddenly my head fell backwards and changed positions with my feet. Ski Mask had tilted my chair back like an astronaut ready for blastoff on a trip I didn't want to take.

"Just tell me what you want to know!" Futile, but it was all I had.

Someone whipped the bag off my head, and for a second, I thought I'd gotten a reprieve. Then Ski Mask put the towel over my face. It was soaked and water started to drip into my swollen nose. Hands grabbed my head from behind and held it in place so I couldn't shake off the towel. I opened my mouth wide to breathe but just sucked in more water. Then someone poured water over the towel. I couldn't breathe and tried to hold my breath but there was no air to hold. My heart pounded a thousand miles an hour. I gasped and water rushed into my mouth in the place of air. Panic. I squirmed against the ropes tying me to the chair, but strong hands held me down. Water filled my nasal passages.

No air. No escape.

Suddenly someone whipped off the towel and pushed the chair upright so I was vertical. I coughed out water and gasped for air. My throat made noises I'd never heard before and my whole body shook.

"Why did you go to the FBI today?"

I caught my breath and my heartbeat regulated. I already told the truth. What did I have left?

"I told you! I wanted to find out who Jim Colton talked to before he died."

Ski Mask grabbed my chair and tilted it back.

"I'm telling you the truth!"

He put the towel over my face and the water started again. Terror.

They whipped me back upright just when I thought I'd drown again. I fought the battle for air.

"What did Special Agent in Charge Richmond tell you?"

I spat out everything I could remember from my unpleasant conversation with Richmond. Verbatim.

The chair went back and the water came down again.

When it was over, "Tell us what Brianne knows."

"What do you mean? Knows about what?"

The chair went back. The towel. The water.

Ski Mask asked me the same questions again and again and waterboarded me again and again.

After the sixth or seventh time, Ski Mask said, "He doesn't know anything."

He shoved the canvas bag over my face. My body shook. Now from the November chill in the warehouse against my soaked clothes and skin.

Faint footsteps walking away. Then a hushed conversation. The whispers didn't reveal a voice I recognized and I could only make out an occasional word: "Here." "I can't be here when . . ." ". . . the van . . . the beach . . . salt water."

Then I heard the metal door being cranked open. Ski Mask's voice, "Craigslist when it's done."

"Help!" I shouted as loud as I could through the canvas sack. A punch to my stomach stole the air from my shout.

A car door slammed shut, then another right on top of it. Or maybe just the first's one's echo. A car engine hummed. Could they both be leaving?

The sack was ripped off my head. Ski Mask stared down at me then punched me in the stomach. I tried to breathe. He punched me again. I gasped for air and he stuffed the sack in my mouth. I tried to inhale through my broken nose and nothing came through. Ski Mask grabbed a rag off a workbench and tied it around my head to secure the bag in my mouth. I inhaled with chest and shoulders and all I could get was a tiny thread of air navigating my bent nose. I hyperventilated. Not enough air was getting through. I was going to suffocate in this chair after almost drowning for the last thirty minutes.

Ski Mask walked outside, and I heard a van door slide open. He came back in with a five-gallon water jug and a five-gallon plastic bucket. The jug was full of water. He set the jug and bucket down next to me. I fought harder for air and rocked the chair back and forth. Ski Mask laughed and let me rock until the chair fell over onto its side on the concrete floor. Now what could I do?

Ski Mask pulled a syringe out of his pocket. He uncapped it and stuck the needle into my neck at the base of my skull. Just like the silent partner had when he snuck up behind me in the parking lot. Panic. Spinning. The night fell on me.

"Just go to sleep, bub. It'll make it easier for both of us."

The last thing I remembered was Ski Mask pouring water from the jug into the plastic bucket.

CHAPTER TWENTY-SEVEN

SALT. NO AIR. Calm.

Pressure on my chest. Again and again. No air. Panic. Salt water gushing up my throat. I coughed and vomited out the sea. More coughs. More water. I sucked in a wedge of oxygen. Coughed and gasped.

And breathed.

I opened my eyes expecting to see the black ski mask above me. Instead I saw a drop of blood fall from a yellow halo and splash down on my left eyeball. I blinked and someone grabbed me under my arms from behind and sat me upright. The air came easier now, in long deep woofs. Two snips and my hands were free from their bonds. The hands disappeared and Miranda stepped from behind me. Blood trickled down her forehead from a gash along her hairline, giving her pink streaked hair like an alt-band groupie. Her right eye looked like a razor-slit plum. Her face, the color of the cement floor. She smiled, then her mouth went slack. Her knees buckled and she sat down hard and her back, then head, slammed against the cement.

I scrambled to my feet and lurched toward Miranda. Too late to soften her landing. I felt for the carotid artery in her neck with my finger and hovered my cheek over her mouth. Breath on my cheek. She was alive.

I whirled around expecting a charge from Ski Mask, but the garage was empty. Miranda must have somehow fought him off by herself.

"Miranda. Miranda. Wake up." My voice raspy. My throat sore. I gently pushed open her left eyelid with my finger. White. The bottom of her iris just visible at the top of the eye socket. I put my hand under her head and felt for a lump. There was a small soft one on the lower part of her skull, probably from landing on the cement. She needed medical help.

Fast.

A 911 call would take time and an explanation. It might take the paramedics ten or fifteen minutes to arrive. Scripps Memorial Hospital was a five-minute drive from the auto body shop. I'd beat the paramedics under any scenarios. Besides, a 911 call would bring the police. A crime had been committed and they'd investigate. I'd either have to lie or tell the cops about the fake FBI agent and the assault on me. That would get the FBI involved and probably LJPD as I had been investigating the death of one of their own. That would bring Moretti, who might have been behind the attack tonight.

He could have even been the silent partner.

I wrapped my arms under Miranda's armpits from behind and lifted her up to a standing position. Except she couldn't stand. One hundred forty pounds of dead weight. I backpedaled her to a Mercedes CLS550 awaiting a paint job. Her heels dragged along the cement like a dead person's. No shoes. She'd probably kicked off her flip-flops to use her best weapons when she battled Ski Mask.

And saved my life.

The cement scraped at her heels. A fireman's hold over my shoulder would put her head below her heart and pump blood into her injured areas. I bent my knees and swooped under her like a groom carrying his bride over the threshold. When I straightened up I caught a glimpse of something black in the shadow of the wheel well of the Mercedes. No time to check what it was. Her head lolled back like a broken puppet's. I scrambled to my car and was able to open the passenger door with my hand under her knees. I slid her into the seat as gently as I could and buckled the seat belt.

I ran around the car, jumped in, and gunned it out of the parking lot. The Paulie's Auto Body van was gone. So was the Range Rover. No doubt used by Ski Mask in his escape. I fumbled my phone out of my pocket and punched Brianne's number. No answer. Shit. I had to warn her about Ski Mask and his partner. They'd asked me what she knew. They'd go after her next.

If they hadn't already gotten her.

I hit the number again. No answer. Again. And again. And again. Finally, a click.

"We weren't going to talk on the phone anymore. Remember?" Angry.

"Get out of your house now. Go stay with a friend. Or at a hotel. Anywhere. Just make sure you park the Mustang in a garage out of sight."

"Why? What's going on? What's wrong with your voice?" Panic. "You're scaring me."

"Do what I say and you'll be fine, but go now. I'll call you back soon. Pick up when I call."

"Rick?"

"Go. Now!" I hung up.

I blew down Sorrento Valley Boulevard and made a quick jog onto a side street that dumped me on I-5 South. I glanced at Miranda. Chin on chest, she would have flopped onto the dashboard if she weren't strapped in by her seat belt.

"Miranda. Wake up!"

Nothing.

I whipped off the freeway onto Genesee and bolted up the slight hill to the hospital. I locked up the brakes and skidded to a stop in front of the emergency room entrance. Miranda was dead weight and a tough lift up out of the passenger seat, but I managed to threshold hoist her into the emergency room.

"I need a doctor!"

Waiting room patients' heads turned toward me, and the admitting nurse behind the counter eyed me with cold eyes. I carried Miranda over to the counter and an orderly appeared from behind a curtain pushing a gurney. He helped me ease Miranda onto the gurney and pushed her behind the curtain.

The admitting nurse pushed a clipboard with forms on it at me. She looked to be in her fifties and filled up her chair with extra hanging over the sides. Her eyes had seen a lot and right now they saw a domestic abuser. I didn't bother to explain.

"Fill out that form and return it to me when you're done." She nodded over to the few empty chairs in the waiting area.

I stayed where I was and studied the form. The only lines I'd be able to fill in would be Miranda's first name and that she'd passed out and banged her head. The rest I didn't know. Last name. Age. Residence. Phone number. Her insurer. Whether or not she even had insurance.

"I don't really know her. I can't fill this out."

"You just found her lying unconscious somewhere and brought her in because you're a Good Samaritan?" She doled out the sarcasm like Ski Mask had the water onto my face and eyed my swollen nose and the faded rainbows around my eyes.

"Her first name's Miranda. That's all I know. Someone must have attacked her, and she passed out right in front of me. Her head banged the ground pretty hard and there's a small lump on the back of her head."

I could have told her that Miranda had gotten hurt saving my life but I doubted she'd believe that any more than she believed I hadn't been the one to put Miranda in her present condition. I could have also told her that Miranda worked for Alan Rankin and given her his phone number. But I wanted to see him as much as I wanted to see the police.

The nurse pulled the top form off the clipboard and handed the board back to me. "Fill out your personal information and return the form to me when you're finished." She nodded to the waiting area. "Have a seat in the waiting area. The doctor will want to talk to you."

I fought the urge to bolt out of the hospital and jump into my car and go find Brianne.

She was in danger and still my responsibility. But she hadn't saved my life. And put her own life in jeopardy doing it. I owed it to Miranda to stick around. I needed to know that she'd be okay.

I sat down and leaned against the wall that was painted a shade of green I'd only ever seen in hospitals. Sort of lime green mixed with gray. Or death. I looked down at the form. The bad guys already knew who I was. Hopefully, Miranda would recover, but when she did, she'd tell Alan Rankin what had happened tonight. If the cops questioned her, she'd either tell them about rescuing me or she wouldn't. I wasn't going to file a complaint with the police. This was my puzzle to solve, not theirs. I pulled the pen from behind the clasp and wrote John Doe on the form. Nothing else.

It had only been about ten minutes since I'd called Brianne. I'd give her more time to settle in somewhere before I called and found out where that somewhere was. I wanted her full attention on getting the hell away from her house.

I took a deep breath, a luxury I hadn't had in the last couple hours, and immediately was reminded of Ski Mask's punches to my solar-plexus and the salt water I'd swallowed. I swallowed the pain and tried to relax so I could think.

The night didn't add up. Somebody knew that Brianne and I

had gone to the FBI today. How? I'd kept my eyes in the side view mirror on the drive to FBI Headquarters and we hadn't been followed. That meant someone at the FBI had told Ski Mask and his silent partner that we'd been there. But not why we'd been there. Couldn't have been Special Agent in Charge Richmond. Ski Mask had asked me what Richmond had told me. He also asked why I'd been there. Brianne and I had repeatedly asked both SAC Richmond and Special Agent Singh to talk to the agent who had spoken with Jim Colton on the phone before he died. That knocked out Singh, too.

Which left Agent Blanton, the guy who led us into Richmond's office, and a few agents who came and went while Brianne and I waited in the lobby. Blanton seemed more like an ass sniffer than someone in league with the men who put Miranda in the hospital and tried to kill me. That left all the agents who walked by who I didn't even pay attention to.

And Miranda.

How had she tracked me to the auto body shop? Thank God she did, but I'd made sure I wasn't followed. The only way she could have tailed me was by hiding a GPS tracker on my car and following the little red ball on a tablet or smart phone. Didn't happen. I never left her alone near my car. In fact, the only time she was out of my sight had been when I went outside and bluffed her into promising me she wouldn't follow me. That only lasted about ten seconds.

Shit. When I came back in, Miranda was walking away from the counter. Where I'd written the time and address of my meeting with Fake Agent Mallon on a notepad. I'm worrying about GPS trackers and Miranda probably just pocketed the notepad page under the one I'd written on. She just had to do the pencil trick over the indentation of my writing when she had a minute to herself. She didn't have to follow me. She knew where I'd be. Who was the rookie now?

I pulled out my phone and called Brianne. It had been almost a half hour since the first call.

"What's going on?" A wisp of panic in her voice.

"Where are you?"

"The Marriott on La Jolla Village Drive."

Only a few minutes away. Good. "What room?"

"Room 715. What's going on?"

"Somebody ambushed me tonight and they wanted to know why we went to the FBI. I don't want to take any chances in case they decide to look for you." I didn't want to tell her the thugs had asked me what she knew. Not when she was all alone.

"Did you call the police?"

"No."

"Why not?"

I didn't have a good answer to that question yet. Not even for myself. Instinct and experience were guiding me now. Okay for me, but probably not for Brianne. "We'll talk about it when I get to the hotel."

"When?"

"I'm not sure yet." I couldn't leave the hospital not knowing Miranda's condition.

"Where are you?"

"The hospital."

"Are you okay?" The concern in her voice touched me.

"Yes. I'll explain when I get there. Don't open the door for anybody. Just me. Check the peephole."

"Okay. Hurry."

I hung up in time to greet the doctor who'd walked over to me from behind the curtain that led to the examination rooms.

Actually, more curtained-off enclosures than rooms. I remembered. I'd been to this very emergency room less than a year ago. Another instance when I'd relied on instinct and experience. Maybe it was time to listen to something else.

"I'm Doctor Patel." Young, dark, and thin. He had an understandable Indian accent.

"Are you the person who brought in Miss Jennings?"

"Miranda?"

"Yes." They must have found a wallet on her. "Your name, sir?"

"John." For now. "Has she regained consciousness?"

"What is your relationship to Miss Jennings?" Matter of fact. Clinical, not accusatory.

"I just met her. How is she doing? Is she awake?"

"She has not yet regained consciousness. Can you explain how she incurred her injuries?"

Just the bruise on her kidney and the bump on her head. "No. I found her on the street. She looked like she'd been attacked. She was bleeding from her scalp and her eye was swollen shut. She fainted right in front of me, and I couldn't catch her before her head hit the ground. Is she going to be okay?"

"She has an epidural hematoma, which is a concern."

"What's that?"

"In layman's terms it's bleeding on the brain."

Shit.

"From the fall onto the ground?" If only I'd been quicker.

"No. That caused a minor hematoma at the base of the skull. The epidural hematoma is between the skull and the frontal lobe. It's a very serious injury. And you are not aware how she incurred these injuries?" He looked down at my hands, no doubt looking for bruised knuckles.

"No. Like I said, she must have been attacked."

Dr. Patel stared at me through poker eyes. Finally, "Please wait for the police. They'll want to hear your story."

I nodded. It was the same as saying "Okay" but at least I didn't have to hear myself lie out loud.

CHAPTER TWENTY-EIGHT

I EXITED THE hospital parking lot just as the police cruiser entered. Another minute talking to the doctor and I'd now be talking to the police. LJPD. Scripps Hospital was in La Jolla. Even if the cops believed my story, their boss wouldn't. And even if he did, it wouldn't stop him from squeezing me in place of other crimes I'd committed. And he'd know I'd gone to the FBI, if he didn't already. Moretti may have been the reason Jim Colton talked to the FBI in the first place. Things hadn't turned out too well for him.

When Moretti had his say, they'd be just as bad for me.

The hotel where Brianne had a room was less than a mile away, down a couple city streets. My house, five miles in the other direction. Ski Mask had taken my gun after the silent partner had stuck a needle in my neck and drugged me. I had a backup at home. For the next time we met.

I got onto I-5 and headed south.

I took out my phone and pulled up the number I'd hoped never to call. Alan Rankin's. He was an enemy. And a coconspirator. But none of that mattered right now. I tapped the number. No answer. I left a message that Miranda was seriously injured and under the care of Scripps Memorial Hospital.

My phone rang a minute later. I answered.

"What did you do to her, you son of a bitch?"

"I didn't do anything to her. She saved my life. Get your wallet up to Scripps and take care of her."

"Who hurt her?" I could almost hear his teeth clench.

"I don't know. All I know is that they're very dangerous. Even for you and your friends."

"I need descriptions. Of their physical appearance, their vehicles, clothes. Everything you can remember."

"They drugged and blindfolded me. And damn near drowned me. I don't have any of that information." Mostly true. I could have given some useful information, but I didn't want Rankin and his killers blowing up my investigation. "If I need your help when I track them down, I'll let you know."

"Not good enough, Rick."

"It's all I got right now. Just make sure Miranda gets the care she needs."

"You have this arrangement backwards, Cahill. You take orders from me. Not the other way around."

"We don't have an arrangement. Good-bye, Ran—"

"Moretti contact you?"

Out of the blue and too close to home.

"No. Why?" If I told him the truth it might be the last time I told anything to anyone.

"Just following up on our little chat the other night."

Coincidence? Did he know Moretti had come by last night or was he just fishing? Either way, I definitely needed that backup gun.

"Just take care of Miranda." I hung up.

I parked on the street below my house like I had earlier that day, in case Rankin's men were watching my home. Or Moretti's. Or Ski Mask. Midnight barked once from inside the house when I leapt over the fence into the backyard, then he recognized me. Even in the dark. He sniffed me all over when I came inside. A pup sniffing his father when he returned to the den. He must have smelled the salt water that I'd almost drowned in, the man in the mask who'd tried to kill me, Miranda who'd saved my life, and the fear that I'd felt while in that auto body warehouse.

I went upstairs with Midnight on my heels and, with the light off, peeked out the window of the guest room. I scanned the street to see if any of my enemies had the house staked out. I didn't see any cars that didn't belong, but I couldn't see all the way down the street. That was fine. I wouldn't be home for long.

I went into the closet in my bedroom and punched in the combination on the stand-up gun safe I kept there. The safe weighed over 250 pounds. It had taken all the friends I had to get the thing upstairs after I bought it. Both of them. I opened the safe door. Standing up on their butts was a Mossberg 590A1 Pump-Action Tactical Shotgun and Bushmaster XM-15 Semiautomatic Rifle. The top shelf held a case with a Smith & Wesson .357 Magnum revolver. I grabbed the case, a box of magnum ammo and a shoulder holster, and started to shut the safe door. I stopped and pulled out the Mossberg and a box of shells. After tonight at the auto body shop, a single handgun didn't seem like enough.

After I lost my job as a cop, I'd lost my interest in firearms, too. I got rid of anything that reminded me of being a police officer. Then my life changed and I needed a gun. It changed again and I needed more guns.

The Smith & Wesson was more accurate at distance than the short-barreled Ruger that Ski Mask had taken off me, but with a five-inch barrel it was bulky and hard to conceal. The Ruger had fit in my bomber jacket pocket and the UnderTech t-shirt. The Smith & Wesson was too big for those.

I took off my jacket and put on the leather shoulder holster, which had straps that went over both shoulders like the skeleton of a vest. The holster sleeve that held the gun dangled down about eight inches below my left armpit. The right side had a pouch full of extra bullets. I pulled the .357 out of its case and checked the six-shot cylinder. Full. I slid the gun into the holster, put my jacket back on, and zipped it up. There was a slight bulge from the handle of the .357, but probably only noticeable to those who knew what to look for.

I tossed an extra change of clothes, the box of shotgun shells and .357 Magnums into a backpack, grabbed the Mossberg, and went downstairs. Midnight went to the sliding glass door, and I let him outside. He read me better than any dog I'd ever owned and must have sensed he'd be spending the night alone. He went out to empty his bladder and bowels.

It was too late to call my next-door neighbor, so I texted her to ask if Micalah could come over and feed Midnight before school in the morning, in case I didn't make it back before then.

I let Midnight back inside, exited with my mini arsenal, and descended the hill below my house to my car. I tossed the backpack in the trunk and put the shotgun in a rack I'd mounted on the inside of the lid back when I went a little gun crazy. I only used it when I went to an outdoor shooting range, which wasn't very often. Ammunition was expensive.

And right now, I might need all the ammo I had for moving targets.

CHAPTER TWENTY-NINE

I PARKED IN the multi-level garage attached to the Marriott, grabbed the backpack, and entered the hotel. The lobby had a high ceiling and was grand in a modern sort of way. I went up the elevator to Brianne's room and knocked on her door. A bark from inside. George, her Boxer. I'd forgotten about him. I stood back to give her a good view through the peephole. The door opened within five seconds.

I walked inside and George sniffed me and wagged his tail. Brianne shooed him away and hugged me. Longer and tighter than a normal greeting. The backpack I wore forced her to hug me around the neck. Intimate. There had been no hugs when I left her house this morning. Just a brusque good-bye with an admonition that all further communication should be through email. Danger can do that. Break down superficial walls and get to life's essence. I felt guilty about it. She'd made a reasoned judgment about me earlier and now fear and survival had taken the place of reason. I was the beneficiary, but at least the danger hadn't come from my preexisting demons.

"You're carrying a gun?" Brianne stepped back and looked at the bulge in my coat. Years of living with a soldier-turned-cop. Her eyes went wider than normal. "Please tell me what's going on."

She grabbed my wrist and walked me away from the door over to the bed and sat down. George followed and jumped onto the bed and laid down next to his mama. I took off my backpack, put it on a mini desk, and sat down in the desk chair opposite the bed and spun it around.

"We struck a nerve with someone by going to the FBI today. And whoever it is struck back." I told her about the call from "Special Agent Mallon" and my interrogation at the auto body shop.

"That's horrible." Her eyes, soft blue pools. "I'm so sorry."

"Some good came of it. I'm sure these men killed Jim and I think I know how they incapacitated him before they stuck a noose around his neck."

"My God." She put her hand to her cheek. "How?"

"One of them snuck up behind me when I arrived at the body shop and stuck a needle in my neck. Whatever was in that needle knocked me unconscious in just a few seconds. I don't know how long I was under, but I don't think it was very long. They did the same thing before they tried to drown me. They must use some fast-acting drug that is hard to detect or leaves your system quickly. I think we need to have another autopsy performed. Looking for this drug and needle marks around the hairline at the back of the neck."

"That's impossible. Jim's parents, Cash, and I all agreed it was time to lay Jim to rest after the autopsy. We had him cremated per his wishes."

"Shit." Almost dying and Miranda fighting for her life was a lot to barter against new evidence that couldn't be verified. "We still need to take a look at the autopsy reports. Maybe there's something in them that we missed which hints at the drug and needle marks. But whatever we find or don't find, the needle in the neck tells us something else. Jim was murdered by someone he knew. He let his murderers in the house, and they got close enough to stick a needle in his neck without leaving any bruises, abrasions, or defensive wounds. A stranger couldn't get that close without a fight."

"Who do you think did it?" Wide eyes.

"You tell me. From what I've learned, your husband didn't have a lot of close friends. Just old SEAL buddies and a few friends on LJPD."

"You're right."

"Well, at least we know what suspect pools we're drawing from."

"Are you okay?" She reached across and touched my hand. "I can't imagine what you've gone through tonight."

"I'm fine."

"How did you get away?"

How did I get away? Now we were onto my demons that had nothing to do with her and her late husband. I couldn't tell her the whole truth, but I needed to tell her some of it. "I've made some enemies in my life, as you found out this morning from Agent Richmond at the FBI. You already know about LJPD Police Chief Moretti. There are more. One of them had me followed tonight and the person who followed me, the same person who did this to me a few nights ago"—I pointed to my face—"saved my life."

"How?"

"I'm not really sure. I was unconscious and probably drowning in a bucket of salt water. She must have fought off the guy with the ski mask."

"She?"

"Yes. She's a former MMA fighter who works for someone who doesn't like me very much. She saved my life and risked her own and now she's in the hospital and in bad shape." I told her what Dr. Patel had said about Miranda's condition.

"Why would she do that when she's working for someone who hates you?"

"I don't know."

I didn't know. Miranda and I had formed a strange quasi-Stockholm Syndrome bond earlier that day, but it couldn't explain what she did. She was strong, well trained, and nails-tough, but the man she took on had her by close to a hundred pounds and was probably better trained than Miranda. And he was a killer. I knew that the instant I saw his eyes through the slits of his ski mask. Miranda had to know she'd be risking her life to save mine. She could have called the police and left the scene knowing I'd die but she'd be safe. The only way to save me was to take action immediately, no matter the risk. Somehow she fought Ski Mask off even after he'd beaten her so badly she might die.

"Is she going to live?"

"I don't know." Another life left shattered in my wake. I prayed for her, but didn't know if I believed in God anymore. Or if He believed in me. He'd never answered my prayers, but maybe that was His test. Maybe He had to beat me down until I had nowhere to go but back to Him. But that made all the people who'd died or had been broken because of my actions mere pawns in my tragedy.

I wasn't that important. If there was a god, I was a sideshow. God's will, karma, it didn't matter. I'd made my life, I had to deal with it.

"Who is this person that had you followed?" Brianne peered at me with her big blue eyes, challenging me not to lie.

"It's better that you don't know." Certainly true.

"Why did he have you followed?"

"I can't tell you that."

"You have to start telling me something, Rick."

"Brianne, I promise you none of this other stuff has anything to do with Jim's case. The danger we're in tonight does. I'm a believer now. Jim was murdered. Why else would someone kidnap and interrogate me about our visit to the FBI? Then, when they got what little they could out of me, try to kill me? But listen, they asked me what you knew. They're not going to stop with me."

"Then wouldn't the safest thing be to call the police?"

"What if Chief Moretti is behind all of this? What if Jim called the FBI about him before he died? We go down to LJPD and tell our story, I might have a fatal car accident on the way home and you might commit suicide just like your husband."

"Why do you think it could be Moretti? Jim didn't trust him, but I don't think he thought he was a murderer. Are you sure you're not just basing your theory on your personal history with Moretti?"

"Maybe." A fair question. "But that doesn't change the fact that Moretti was running an extortion racket out of LJPD through asset forfeiture arrests and Jim was thinking about quitting the force because of it."

"What?"

I told her what CIT Sergeant Ruiz had told me about the asset forfeiture arrests Moretti had ordered them to make and Jim Colton's disgust with them.

"Jim never mentioned any of this to me," Brianne said.

"I think the bulk of them occurred after you two separated." I leaned forward in my chair. "You still want me to go to the police?"

"No." She got off the bed and walked over to the nightstand and opened the drawer. Her back was to me, and I couldn't see what she pulled out until she turned around. She held a Sig Sauer P229 pistol at her side, finger on the trigger guard. "And no one's going to find me in my garage hanging by a rope."

The Sig P229 was the service weapon of choice of LJPD. I'd looked down the wrong end of the barrel of enough of them to recognize it.

"You know how to use that?" But the way she held it easy in her hand told me she did.

The P229 wasn't a typical choice for a woman. It fired .357 Magnums, which gave off a nasty recoil. Most women didn't like that much of a kick. A lot of men didn't, either.

"I went to the range with Jim every once in a while." She ejected the magazine into her hand, checked to see if it was loaded, and snapped it back in place. She already knew it was loaded. That was just a show of her proficiency. I enjoyed the show. "I know how to pull the trigger."

Brianne wasn't like most women. I already knew that.

Still. "It's different than the range when you're pointing it at a live person who's pointing back." A lesson I learned the hard way.

"If it's them or me." She sat back down on the bed across from me. "I'll pull the trigger."

"Good. Keep that thing with you at all times until we get this mess straightened out."

"What do you mean 'until we get this mess straightened out?' I thought tomorrow was your last day."

Her eyes seemed to sparkle now and had the look they'd had when she'd come over to my house a few nights ago. But she wasn't high now. She parted her lips.

"I thought we were supposed to only communicate through email now."

"Things have changed."

She leaned in and so did I. Our lips touched and a warm buzz rushed out to all my extremities. She was right. Things had changed. I lived by just a few rules that shaped my life. Sometimes they were hard to obey, but they were the only skeleton of morality I had. I never broke any of them.

Until tonight.

CHAPTER THIRTY

"I NEED A shower." The stink of fear left behind seeped from my pores. I didn't want that to be the memory scent of our first time together.

"So do I."

Brianne stood up, took my hand, and led me into the small, stark hotel bathroom. We kissed again, pressed against each other. Hard. Like our lives depended on each other's contact.

She stepped back and unzipped my jacket and took it off, tossing it against the bathroom door. I unslung my shoulder holster and set it on the sink. Brianne took over again and grasped my t-shirt from the bottom, and I lifted my hands over my head so she could remove it. Next my pants. Unzipped and slowly pulled one leg off at a time. My shoes, socks. Underwear. Naked before her and to the wrath that would come down on me for breaking my own rules.

Brianne's eyes lolled to piercing blue half-moons and she lifted her arms over her head. I pulled her shirt up and off. Black bra against pale, smooth skin dotted by freckles like beauty marks across her shoulders. Flat porcelain belly. I unzipped her jeans and eased them down while she swooshed her hips in concert. Long athletic legs of a tennis player against a black thong. I unhooked her bra, loosing round breasts that only hinted at gravity's pull. She stepped out of the thong, took hold of me where I wanted her to, and led me into the cozy stand-up shower.

Warm water matched the heat of our bodies. Brianne lathered me with soap, slow languid movements, giving special attention to the parts of me that needed it most. She rinsed me off and I repaid the gift. I made it as far as her breasts before she pushed away the soap and enveloped me. We were one pulsing being, split like an atom and joined back together.

When we were done, my legs wobbled and my skin, pruned. The punches, waterboarding, and the drowning had all been washed away. Contentedly spent and clean, except for the stain from the rule I'd just broken. I lazed above it, serene in the warm blanket of post-lovemaking. Fooling myself for the moment, that I could break the rule and be free of consequences. But down deep, just out of sight, I could sense the edges of dark shadows creeping in from their corners.

George met us at the door when we left the bathroom. His eyes looked E.T. big and he sniffed at our naked bodies, sensing the change in chemistry. Brianne shooed him away and had him lie at the foot of the bed.

"He's used to sleeping on the bed ever since Jim and I split up."

I looked at George and his uncropped Boxer ears perked up. "One of us is sleeping on the floor tonight. Your mom will have to decide."

Brianne pulled back the sheets on the left side of the bed, then put her hand to her chin. "Hmm, let's see. George does a really good job of keeping my feet warm. But he snores and his morning breath is just as bad as his nighttime breath."

"Well." I looked back at George then at Brianne. "Sounds like a draw."

Brianne got into bed and pulled back the covers from the right side of the bed. "I think George will understand since you're our guest."

I slid under the covers and George immediately jumped up on the end of the bed.

"George, down," Brianne said.

George looked sadder than his alien face should have been able to convey and slinked off the bed.

Brianne turned off the light and swam over to me in the dark. Her head found my shoulder, her hand my chest as I lay on my back. I slid my arm around her waist. Natural, like we'd been in this position together many times before. Her hair, slightly damp against my cheek. She smelled of autumn. Earthy and spicy at once. I stroked her hair and breathed her in.

"You know, as scary and disruptive as this night has been for you, it's been the same for George. He can sense your anxiety, but he can't ask you what's wrong."

"So along with being a gigolo, you're a dog whisperer?"

"You think I'm a gigolo?"

"No." She sighed. "But if I call you that I can try to convince myself this wasn't my idea."

I thought of Kyle Bates's story of Brianne coming on to him at a beach party, but let it pass.

"And all the time I thought it was mine."

"Gigolo." Her head left my shoulder. "George, up."

Soft double pad and then a flop on the bottom right of the king bed followed by a long sigh.

"Happy?" Brianne's head returned to its spot.

"Si."

"Jackass."

Brianne nuzzled me and I let out a sigh that rivaled George's. Content amidst the chaos. I'd known Brianne less than a week. Her life was a mess. So was mine. She was a couple days removed from the man she'd left her husband for and despised by her son because of it. I was a year past not stopping a woman I loved from moving in with her second choice whom she'd since married. And ten years beyond failing my wife on the last night of her life.

We were a good match.

And somewhere out in the night, hiding behind ski masks and shadows, were two men who wanted to kill us.

CHAPTER THIRTY-ONE

"Ski mask." My eyes snapped open, wide awake.

"Huh?" Brianne's sleepy voice floated in the dark.

We'd separated during a sleep that we both desperately needed. But mine was over for now. I looked at the clock: 3:17 a.m. in red block letters.

"Go back to sleep," I whispered. "I have to run an errand. I'll be back in less than an hour."

"What?" Movement. The bedside light flicked on. Brianne rolled over and faced me. "It's three o'clock in the morning. What kind of an errand do you have to run now?"

"I just have to go check on something." If I told her where, she'd worry and try to stop me. "I won't be long."

"Where?" She sat up in bed and my vagueness had accomplished the opposite of my intention.

I wanted to tell her I had to go check on Midnight. But now, through our actions tonight and the actions of my captors earlier, we were in this together.

"I have to go by the auto body shop and check on something."

"Are you crazy?" She sat up. "What if they came back?"

"Even if they did, they won't still be there now." I got out of bed. "I'll be fine."

"What is that?" She stared at my stomach.

I looked down. A large blue bruise mushroomed across my

stomach below my breastplate. The sight of it reminded me that it hurt.

"That's from the guy with the ski mask."

"That looks horrible. It wasn't there when we were in the shower." Her cheeks pinched upward. "Does it hurt?"

"Must have taken a while to form. It doesn't hurt much." Except when I took a deep breath.

"Did it hurt when I rubbed soap on you?"

"Nothing hurt then." I smiled.

"Rick, you can't go back there."

"Don't worry. I'll be careful and I'll be armed."

"You were armed the last time you went there."

"I'll be ready this time." I walked over to the desk and grabbed a shirt and pair of underwear out of my backpack and put them on. My stomach ached with each movement, but at least Brianne wouldn't have to look at my bruises anymore.

"What do you have to check on?" She folded her arms across her chest like a parent questioning a teenager on a Friday night.

"Miranda must have knocked the ski mask off the guy who tried to kill me. I think I saw it on the ground when I rushed her to the hospital."

"So what?"

"His DNA will be on it. If we go to the police, they might be able to get an ID on the guy if he's in the criminal database. If not, we might be able to send it to a private lab." That would take money I didn't have. Brianne might not either. Didn't matter. The ski mask was evidence and I had to grab it before someone else did.

"I'm coming with you." Brianne got out of bed and opened a suitcase lying on the floor.

"Stay here with George and try to get some sleep. I'll be back in less than an hour." I walked around the bed and put my hands on her shoulders. "I won't take any chances. If I even think someone's there, I'll turn around and come right back."

"You're the only person who believes me about Jim's death." She took my hands off her shoulders and held them in her own and looked up at me with big eyes. "You're the only person left I can trust. I can't do this without you."

"You won't have to." I kissed her. "I'll be back soon."

"Call me when you get to the auto body shop."

"I'll text, in case you're asleep."

"I won't be able to sleep until you get back here. If I don't hear from you in a half hour, I'm calling the police."

"Make it forty-five minutes."

I finished dressing, put on the loaded shoulder holster, then my coat, and left the hotel room. Fatigue pulled at my body, but my senses were hyper-alert. I scanned the empty hallway and walked in the opposite direction of the elevators. Brianne's room was on the seventh floor. A lot of stairs to ground level, but I couldn't risk an elevator. You never know who'll be staring at you when the doors open. I found the staircase at the end of the hall and scooted down the seven flights.

I got to my car without seeing another soul. Good. I didn't want to see anyone for the rest of the night. And a few days on top of that. Except for Brianne, my broken rule.

I made it back to Paulie's Auto Body Repair in less than five minutes. I circled the block twice looking for the black Range Rover and the company van that had been in the parking lot when I'd arrived earlier. Nothing.

I parked across the street from Paulie's and entered the dimly lit parking lot on foot. I pulled the Smith & Wesson from the holster and formed a shooting platform keeping my upper body still and duck walked with my knees bent along the fence. The only cover

I had was the night. I went slowly, letting my breathing steady and my eyes adjust to the deepening night as I moved away from the one light on the side parking lot. I made it around the back and was relieved that neither the black Range Rover nor the van were parked there.

The relief was short-lived when I saw that the corrugated metal door to the body shop was closed. No light seeped out beneath it. Shit. Someone had come back and cleaned up the scene. I checked the lock that secured the door to a steel ring in the foundation. Combination. Damn. I found a conventional door with a knob just north of the car entry. I pulled out my lock pick set I kept in the trunk and went to work. A minute later, I got the doorknob unlocked, but the door wouldn't open. Dead bolted from the inside.

Probably didn't matter anyway. Ski Mask or his partner had come back and scooped up any evidence left behind. Including the black ski mask that Miranda had pulled off my attacker's face. No DNA left behind. No way to ID him . . . except.

I whipped out my phone and ran to my car. I punched Alan Rankin's number on the way. No answer. I jumped in the car, fired the ignition, and burned rubber onto Sorrento Valley Boulevard and punched the number again.

"What the hell do you want, Cahill? It's three forty-five in the morning."

"Is Miranda still in the emergency room?"

"Why the hell do you care?"

"Because she can ID the man who attacked her, and he won't let her live to do that."

"They moved her into a hospital room an hour ago. I just got home. I'll get men up there."

"Is she in the ICU?"

"No. She's stabilized. They just put her in a normal room."

"What number? I'm two minutes away."

"Hold on. I wrote it down." Clunk of the phone being set down on a table. Finally, "Room 432. I'll have a couple men up there in twenty minutes."

"Tell them what I look like. I don't want them to see me in Miranda's room and think I'm the bad guy and start shooting."

"They know what you look like." He hung up.

Rankin's henchmen knowing what I looked like suddenly didn't seem like such a good thing. He was already worried about me connecting him to Randall Eddington's disappearance. Making me disappear would solve that problem. I took a hand off the steering wheel and slid it into my jacket and touched the handle of the Smith & Wesson in the shoulder holster. I knew it was there, but the feel of the gun was reassuring.

The lights of the red brick and concrete hospital shone in the left corner of my windshield. I turned into the parking lot and parked on the second floor of the parking structure behind the hospital. I called Brianne on my way down the stairs.

"Change of plans. I'm at the hospital guarding Miranda's room until backup arrives. I'll check in again in an hour if I don't get relieved by then."

"What? Why does she have to be guarded?" Hot sizzle of anxiety.

"She can ID the guy who put her in the hospital because she pulled off his ski mask."

"The same man who tried to kill you? Maybe it's time to call the police, Rick."

She might have been right, but I doubted Alan Rankin would agree. Nor did I. If Miranda wanted to talk to the cops, fine. But until she did, I wasn't going to volunteer.

"I'll call you in an hour. Bye."

I exited the parking structure and went into the hospital. The staircase had an emergency latch on it so I'd have to take the elevator. I pushed the button and looked down at the bulge in my jacket. I wish I still had the Ruger, which I could easily conceal in the pocket of my bomber jacket.

The elevator door opened, and no one stepped out. Empty. I got in and pushed the fourth-floor button. The doors opened with a ding into a small foyer. Empty. Two for two so far. I turned left out of the foyer into a main hall and wasn't so lucky this time. A doctor or orderly in green scrubs and face mask walked down the hall in my direction. We avoided each other's eyes. He passed and I saw a desk in a hallway to my left manned by a woman. I kept walking.

"Excuse me. May I help you?" She looked at the bulge in my coat.

I stopped and saw that the scrub-clad man I'd passed had done the same. With his head, nose, and mouth covered, all I could see were his eyes.

Dead. The eyes of a killer. Ski Mask.

CHAPTER THIRTY-TWO

SKI MASK BOLTED down the hall of the hospital. I chased after him.

"Hey!" The woman at the desk.

"Check on room 432!" I shouted over my shoulder as I ran. "Call the police."

Fast and agile, Ski Mask flew down the hall and had me by five yards when he hit the latch on the door to the stairwell. It banged open. No alarm. The door slammed shut just as I got to it. I pulled out my gun and pushed low through the door to the stairwell.

Clear. Just footsteps hammering down stairs below me. I sped down the stairs, but he'd increased his lead on me, and I couldn't see him. Just heard his feet peppering the stairs. I hit the second-floor landing and heard a door slam open against the wall and then slam shut. Down the next flight.

I jammed through the exit door low again. A piece of concrete exploded off the wall next to the door where my head would have been if I hadn't come out low. I dove behind a planter box and wood splintered above my head. My nerve synapses fired all at once and my breath pogoed. Someone out in the night with a high-powered rifle with a suppressor had me pinned down. It couldn't have been Ski Mask. I'd only been five seconds behind him. There was someone else out there laying down cover so Ski Mask could escape.

The silent partner.

I stayed smeared to the ground behind the wooden planter. I had no other move. Playing hero would get me killed. The parking structure was about fifty yards away. The man with the rifle must have been up there somewhere waiting for Ski Mask to make it to their escape vehicle or for me to pop my head up.

Snap, snap, snap. Three more splinters of wood. Probably a last volley to make me stay put before they ran for their car and got away. Probably was too much of a gamble to risk my life. I could have raised up exposing myself and fired blindly into the parking structure and maybe gotten lucky. Or a doctor or nurse going to their cars after the late shift could have been unlucky and gotten hit by a stray. I stayed still and tried to listen past my rushing breath.

Thud, thud. Gentle rumble. Soft, but echoing from the parking garage. Two car doors slamming shut and the car driving away. Was there a third man driving? I pushed off the ground and sprinted around the planter toward the garage. Zigging and juking as if I were running with a football through a defense avoiding tacklers. Only this defense had a gun and bullets instead of tacklers. Fifty yards. Forty. Now thirty yards away from the garage and no invisible whistles streamed by me or pinged off the concrete around me.

Twenty yards from the garage, I saw the Range Rover emerge. I'd never be able to get to my car and follow it, but I might be able to get a look at the license plate. The backseat passenger window came down and I caught a glimpse of something round and steel about the size of a soda can.

A suppressor for a rifle.

I cut hard right and a sizzle whispered by my ear. I sprinted toward the back of the garage to block the shooter's angle. Safe. For now. I hit the door to the staircase and kept running up to the second floor. Adrenaline pushed me. I'd never catch up to the Range Rover, and it would be safer not to. But I couldn't stop. Anger pushed past fear. The people in the SUV had killed Jim Colton and tried to kill me. Twice.

That couldn't stand.

The SUV had to be almost to the booth by now, almost out of the hospital parking lot.

The tollbooth.

They'd have to stop and stick their ticket into the machine and then stick in money or a credit card to lift the gate. I yanked my keys out of my pocket and hit the trunk button on the key fob. The trunk popped open just as I reached my car. I lifted the lid and saw the shotgun in the rack. Not now. That was for close quarters when killing was the only option. I grabbed the surveillance binoculars I kept in the trunk, slammed the lid, and jumped behind the wheel and gunned the Mustang out of the parking structure.

I didn't want to get close enough for the rifle to come out of the Range Rover again. Just close enough to see the license plate through the binoculars. I sped around the soft curve in the road and caught a glimpse of the back of the Range Rover just as it approached the tollbooth. I snapped the binoculars up to my eyes. 6ZUB573. I repeated the numbers aloud, again and again.

I dropped the binoculars and saw that the SUV was already through the tollbooth gate. What was left of it. The wooden arm lay on the ground twenty feet from the booth off the left. The SUV's taillights disappeared below a slight hill just as I reached the tollbooth. I sped through but lost sight of the SUV.

Down the hill to the stop sign that opened onto Genesee Ave., I looked left toward the freeway and right toward the Golden Triangle. No taillights in either direction. Then I heard it. The whir of a police siren coming from the direction of the freeway. I guess the hospital staff had heeded my directive. I hung a right and punched it up the hill and around the slight bend. The siren grew louder, and I made it around the bend without seeing the rainbow lights. And without the cops seeing me.

I hadn't done anything wrong, but they were LJPD and I was me. Fire and ice. Unsworn enemies. Talking to them would just give Moretti one more look. One more angle. One more avenue to put me away.

I got back to the hotel in a couple minutes. I parked in the garage and pulled out a pen and notepad from the center console and wrote down the license plate number of the black Range Rover. Then I pulled out my phone and called Rankin. No answer. I called again. The same. I left him a message to call me right away.

This time I took the elevator. Too tired for the stairs. All the adrenaline that had coursed through my body tonight had sucked out any energy I might have had in reserve and left a vacuum. If the elevator stopped and the doors opened up to enemies, I'd just shoot them in the face. I unzipped my jacket and unsnapped the leather strap that secured the Smith & Wesson in the holster. I put my hand on the handle, watched the elevator lights climb, and readied for an Old West showdown.

The doors opened on the seventh floor, and no one shouted draw. My phone rang before I made it to Brianne's door. Rankin's number.

"You called."

"Are your men at the hospital yet? Is Miranda okay?"

"She's okay. My guys got there about the same time the police did. What the hell happened up there?"

I told him all of it. "Are you sure she's okay? These guys are big on needles."

"Apparently, the thug hadn't made it to her room yet. Seems you arrived just in time."

"Thank God."

"Don't hold your breath waiting for a thank-you."

"I just wanted to make sure Miranda was okay. The less I talk with you, the better."

"Couldn't agree more. Unfortunately, we do have to talk. Come by the house tomorrow. Damn. It's already tomorrow. Get here at ten this morning."

"We can talk on the phone, but not now."

"Come by the house, Cahill. Too many phone calls."

"I'll think about it. In the meantime, if you put someone on my house again, I'll shoot up their car. Just for starters." Of course, if he hadn't sent Miranda to watch my house we wouldn't be talking right now. I'd be lying facedown in the sand in the shoreline of some beach as an accidental drowning victim.

Too bad. My days as a victim were over.

CHAPTER THIRTY-THREE

I WOKE UP not knowing where I was and barely knowing who I was. I felt Brianne's shoulder under my chin and George's back against my legs. Now I remembered. My new life.

I slipped out of bed without waking up Brianne. George followed me and plopped onto the floor.

"Wah?" Brianne, sleep groggy.

"Taking George out to poop," I whispered. "Back to sleep."

George heard his name, figured out the plan, and snuffled up against me. I got dressed, grabbed the plastic bag out of the complimentary ice bucket, and led George out of the room on his leash. We took the elevator down. Looking at George made me think of Midnight and I hoped my neighbor had gotten my text about feeding him. I wondered how Midnight would like having a new buddy to occasionally chase around. Like me, he was a loner. But even loners could use a friend to chase around sometimes.

I led George through the lobby outside, looking for something green that he could leave something brown on. We went across the street to a large mirrored office building that had a lush lawn around it. Perfect for deposits.

It was about seven forty-five, so the building's parking lot had just a smattering of cars. George found a nice hedge to lift a leg against, then sniffed around for the perfect landing site. He found one and left a package, which I wrapped up in the ice bucket plastic bag and tossed into a trash can. Dogs must think their poop is a valuable commodity as the people who follow them around on a leash are always there ready to wrap it up and deposit it in a special container. Maybe that's why dogs seem to save them up. With urine, they're more cavalier.

I was tired but figured George needed the exercise after being cooped up in a strange hotel room all night. Besides, I had work to do and I wanted to let Brianne sleep. We headed west toward Scripps Hospital and the highway. Fog sealed in the morning and the air was nippy enough for my coat, which made concealing the shoulder holster easy.

No more victim.

I pulled out my phone and called a number I couldn't live without, but rarely used.

"Hello?" Loud and jolting like a pissed-off rooster beating the sunrise. But he was a she.

"Moira, it's Rick."

Moira MacFarlane was a private investigator like me. Well, not quite like me. She had relationships with LJPD and the San Diego Police Department. I had a relationship with LJPD but wished I didn't. The only cooperation I'd get from them was an open door to a six-by-eight-foot jail cell. SDPD wouldn't let me near enough to share any information. When I needed something that only a cop could get, I called Moira.

"Who else would it be?" Staccato, like a machine gun.

"Sorry to wake you."

"I didn't say you woke me, Cahill." Being asleep probably signified weakness in her mind. She'd never admit to it any time of day or night. "What part of your job do you want me to do for you today pro bono?"

"I need a plate run."

"Of course you do. You always need something. Just once, I wish you'd call me without begging for something that makes your life easier and mine harder."

"So we could just talk?"

A snort that would have made George proud rattled my ear. "God, no. You have a point. Give me the number."

I read her the plate number of the Range Rover off my notepad. "I'd really appreciate it if you could hurry this one."

"That's a surprise. What have you got for me?"

"What do you need?"

"Steady work."

"Sorry."

"You suck. I'll call you back." She hung up.

George and I walked to the hospital, then up a few blocks going north. When we circled back toward the hotel, I took out my phone and checked the time: 8:22 a.m. Good. Time to take a flyer. I called the FBI.

"FBI, can I help you?" An officious female voice. Luckily not the one I'd talked to before when I'd called the FBI.

"Hi, this is Detective Broderick Macdonald out of San Diego." Broderick was my given name and Macdonald, my middle. Easy to see why I went by Rick. "I need to talk to Special Agent Mallon."

I didn't expect to hear the voice I'd heard last night, but was pretty confident there was a real Special Agent Mallon. The person who called me yesterday would have figured I'd check to see if there really was an Agent Mallon. Better late than never.

"In regard to what matter?" Bingo. There was a real Special Agent Mallon.

"It's about an investigation, but it's for his ears only."

A click and a long pause then someone picked up. "Special Agent Mallon."

Not Ski Mask's voice.

"We need to talk, Agent Mallon."

"Isn't that why you called, Detective Macdonald? I don't have any open cases with San Diego PD, so this must be new."

"Someone posing as you tried to kill me last night."

"What? Is this a joke? You're not with SDPD are you?" Irritated, like my almost dying was a nuisance. My calling was a mistake.

"No and you're not a killer, are you, Agent Mallon?"

"Did you file a police report on this, ah, attempted murder?" He didn't believe a word I'd said.

"No."

"Well, I suggest you do that, then I'm sure the police will contact me and the FBI can become officially involved."

"I can't do that."

"Why not?" A lot of air. Irritated.

"Because the police might be involved. I know you don't believe me, Agent Mallon, so I'll make you a deal. If you were in FBI Headquarters yesterday around one p.m., I'll hang up now and never bother you again. If you were out of the office, let's meet somewhere and talk."

His silence told me I'd been right. That didn't mean he'd agree to meet me, but at least I was making headway.

I let the silence lie a couple seconds but didn't wait for an answer. "The reason I know you were out of the office then was because that's when someone posing as you called me to set up a meet last night where he and his partner tried to kill me."

"If you really think the police were involved, come in and we'll start an investigation." No irritation now.

"I can't do that either. At least, not now. Someone saw me in your office. That's why they tried to kill me."

"So now you're saying someone from the Bureau teamed up with someone at SDPD to try to kill you?" The disbelief crept back in.

"Not SDPD, but it doesn't matter. I know it sounds crazy. But only someone on the inside would know I'd been there yesterday morning. And only someone on the inside would know that you were out of the office at one so if I called I'd learn there really was an Agent Mallon, but I wouldn't be able to talk to him. They only needed to fool me long enough to get me to meet them. After that, it wouldn't matter because I'd be dead."

More silence. Good.

Finally, "What is it you want from me, whatever your real name is?"

"I want to meet somewhere and talk about this. Try to figure it out. You'll find out who I am when we meet."

"Whoever you are, your life seems to be full of conspiracies. Why trust me?"

"Because you were out of the office yesterday around one." I took a deep breath and let it out. "And there's no one else to trust."

I called my neighbor and asked if she'd mind having Midnight stay at her house for a day or two. She agreed to send her daughter over and pick him up. I didn't know how long I'd be chasing shadows or running from them. I didn't want Midnight to be home alone if my attackers tried a home invasion with guns blazing.

Moira MacFarlane called me back just as George and I reached the Marriott driveway.

"You have to buy me dinner, Cahill."

"Sure. Hopefully, I'll be free in a week or so."

"Oooh." She sounded like a valley girl half her age. "Not with me. I had to agree to take a cop to dinner to get you your damn plate."

"Do you like him?"

"Asshole." Almost a laugh in her voice.

"Me or him?"

"Asshole."

"Me." I still had it.

"Yes. I'll send you a bill, jerk."

"What'd you find out?"

"The plate was reported stolen this morning off a brand-new Lexus IS owned by, ah, Transcope Technologies." Sounded like she was reading from notes.

"Where was the car when the plate was stolen?"

"In a parking garage at their office building at 600 West Broadway in downtown San Diego."

"This plate was on a late model Range Rover last night. You sure it was reported stolen this morning?" Ski Mask and his pal must have stolen the plate last night and no one noticed until this morning. Pretty early this morning.

"That's what the police officer told me. You just asked me to have the plate run. I didn't think it meant cross-examining the cop who was risking his job giving me the information."

"I guess the car could have been parked there a few days and no one noticed the plate missing until today. So there was no person attached to the ownership, just this Transcope Technologies?"

"Again with the cross-examination?" Sincere irritation now. "The car is a company car owned by Transcope. That's all I know. Next time, you develop a source in a police department and then you can ask him twenty questions. They love that."

"Thank you, Moira. I really do appreciate this. Send me a bill for dinner."

"Asshole." She hung up.

So my attackers stole a license plate from a late model Lexus and put it on the late model Range Rover they probably stole. These guys had a sense of style. But something about the plate and where they stole it bothered me.

A downtown parking garage of an office building seemed like an odd place to steal a plate. Too much of a chance to be interrupted or seen by someone going to their car. The men who assaulted me were pros. They'd intended to kill me from the start last night, but still wouldn't let me see their faces just in case I escaped.

It had taken a miracle in the form of a kick-ass woman who risked her life to save me, but I did escape. Their precautions had been wise. They could have probably killed me in the hospital parking lot, but might have exposed themselves to witnesses to do so. They were cautious. That's why stealing the license plate in the garage seemed like a mistake. Out of character. Why? If I could figure that out, I just might find out who killed Jim Colton.

CHAPTER THIRTY-FOUR

ALAN RANKIN LIVED on La Jolla Farms Road. I don't know if there'd ever been real farms up there, but there were plenty of estates that could fit small working farms in their backyards. Rankin's was no exception. I'd been to his home once about a year ago as an uninvited guest.

I pushed the intercom button on the stacked stone arch that anchored a wrought-iron gate. A closed-circuit camera stared down at me and the gate opened. I drove down fifty yards of flagstone pavers surrounded by palm trees and a manicured lawn dotted by olive trees and stopped in front of a sunrise-colored Tuscan villa.

A slab of meat in light blue sweats stood on the porch with its arms folded. Bald and buff. We'd met before. Briefly. I parked in the circular drive and got out of the car. The Smith & Wesson .357 heavy and reassuring holstered under my arm.

Buff invaded my space once I hit the porch. He had three inches and forty pounds on me, plus bad memories from the last time we met. I had a gun inside my jacket.

"Arms and legs out wide, Cahill." Hot gusts of sour protein shake splashed my face. "No cheap shots with a black jack this time. Maybe after Mr. Rankin is done with you we can see what would happen in a fair fight."

"If I want a fair fight, I'll join a boxing gym." I kept my arms at my side and my legs together. "Besides, the HGH you flavor your protein shakes with and the needle packed with juice you stick in your leg hardly makes things fair. Step back and go tell Mr. Rankin I'm strapped with a Smith &Wesson .357. It stays with me or I turn around and go home."

Buff's eyes went big, and I could see the hamster running on the wheel behind them. He was weighing making a move and possibly getting shot against telling his boss he hadn't disarmed me.

"Wait here." He said it like he was still in control, then hurried into the house.

A few minutes later, Buff opened the door, the hangdog look on his face erasing all pretense of being in control. "Follow me."

I stepped inside quickly and angled to the right in case someone had been hiding behind the door. Clear. Apparently, Rankin was playing it clean. Buff led me through the foyer and a massive open kitchen with high-end appliances that made the cook in me envious. We exited a door to a long walkway in the backyard that ended in a courtyard with a magnificent view of the Pacific Ocean wallowing up against the horizon, La Jolla Shores to the south, and Black's Beach directly below.

Rankin, in full lawyer suit and tie, sat in a wicker chair and stared out at the ocean. He nodded at Buff and the slab of meat exited, leaving just the two of us.

"Sit down, Cahill." Rankin was short and thin. Somewhat birdlike, back when birds were still transitioning from dinosaurs. He gestured to a matching chair on his right next to a side table that held a bottle of eighteen-year-old Glenlivet single malt scotch and two glasses.

"Tell me about the men who put Miranda in the hospital."

"They're professional. Dangerous. Violent. That's all I know."

"I need more than that. Names. Addresses."

"I don't know who they are or even what they look like. But they're my problem, not yours. I'll handle them." Somehow.

"Yes, and you've done a fine job so far. When they laid their filthy hands on Miranda, they became my problem." He squinted out at the ocean rolled out under a pewter haze. Possibly to clamp down on a rare human emotion he felt for Miranda. "I want you to contact me when you find out who these animals are."

"If I need your help, I'll let you know. How's Miranda?"

"She's improved. Conscious and able to speak."

"Has she talked to the police?" If she talked to LJPD and Moretti sent the men who tried to kill me and put Miranda in the hospital, both our lives could be in danger.

"Yes. She doesn't remember anything."

"That's the truth or what she told the police?"

"As far as you're concerned, there's no difference." Rankin poured two fingers of scotch into a glass and raised it toward me.

"No thanks. A little early for me."

He took a sip of scotch and gazed back out at the ocean for what seemed like minutes. Then he looked over my shoulder back at his mansion.

"Is there something else you wanted to talk to me about or are we done?" I asked.

"You know the market value of this property, Cahill?" Rankin panoramaed an arm that didn't come close to encompassing his estate.

"Twenty mil?"

"Twenty-seven."

"Congrats, but you didn't ask me here to discuss real estate values."

"It's important that you know what this property is worth because you need to know that I'm not a frivolous man." An ocean breeze lifted a wisp of Rankin's remaining hair off his head. "I've worked hard to accumulate this kind of wealth. I've made tough decisions and sacrifices to get where I am."

"You're a smart, powerful man. I knew that before I got here." I lightly pressed my left arm against the gun inside my jacket. Still there.

"That's right, and I'm not going to give up any of this because some low-rent private dick wants to be a do-gooder and salvage his pathetic life."

"I guess that would be me. Tell me what you think it is that I should already know."

"Don't play stupid with me, Cahill."

"This isn't an act."

Rankin eyed me with reptilian eyes left over from the pre-evolutionary period. "You are a pretty convincing idiot."

"Thank you."

"You think this is all a joke?"

"I think you asked me to come here for a reason, but you're wasting my time instead of getting to the point."

"Stand up." He stood up and looked down at me.

"You challenging me to a duel, Rankin?" I stood up and towered over him.

"I'm going to pat you down since you wouldn't let Buck do it." He took a step toward me and touched my chest. I twisted his wrist off me, hard enough to hurt but not injure him.

"I already told your boy, I'm armed."

"I'm checking for a wire." He rubbed his wrist. "I don't care about the gun. If I wanted you dead, someone would already be planning your funeral."

I took off my jacket and laid it on the chair, then pulled out the .357 and held it at my side. "Go ahead."

Rankin ran his hands down my sides, my front and back and my legs. His hand lingered in the crotch area, but not long enough for me to punch him in the head. He sat back down. I holstered my gun, put on my jacket, and sat down.

"You are a loose end, Cahill." He took a sip of his expensive scotch. "And my clients taught me a long time ago that loose ends need to be clipped."

"But I'm still breathing."

"That's mainly because you probably saved Miranda's life in the hospital last night, even though you're the reason she's there in the first place."

"Still don't know why I'm here. Am I supposed to thank you for not having me killed?" I stood up. "I don't have time for this bullshit."

"Chief Moretti paid me a visit yesterday."

I sat down.

"He told me he talked to you the night before last." Rankin looked at me like he expected me to confess to something. I stayed silent. "I asked you last night if you'd talked to Chief Moretti and you told me you hadn't. Why is that?"

"'Cause it's none of your damn business."

"It sure as hell is my business when he's trying to implicate me in a murder that you committed."

"Get up." I stood up and looked down at Rankin. "My turn to check for a wire."

"Don't be ridiculous."

"Get up." My lips moved over clenched teeth.

Rankin stood up. I pulled off his jacket and checked for listening devices then patted him down. Clean. We both returned to our chairs.

"You've now twice treated me with disrespect in my home, Cahill." He gave me the predator eyes. "There won't be a third."

He was right about that. If I made it out alive today, I'd make sure never to come back. "What did Moretti tell you?"

"That he's come across new evidence and that your arrest is

imminent." He studied me like I was on the wrong end of a microscope. "And that you're prepared to implicate me once you're arrested."

I didn't know what game Rankin was playing or if he was telling the truth. I looked into the lizard eyes and saw cold practicality devoid of emotion. When I no longer fit into his equation, when I become more threat than ally, I'd be erased.

"Moretti's lying. He doesn't have anything. He located the Eddingtons' Volvo that disappeared with Randall. If the rest of your men are more competent than your manservant in the blue sweats, there's nothing to worry about."

I grabbed the scotch and poured some into a glass. It was sipping whiskey, but I needed a jolt. I threw it back. A warm catch in my throat put a glow in my face, but not my attitude. "Moretti's fishing and it sounds like you took the bait. If he had anything legitimate, one or both of us would already be in jail."

"What did he say about the Volvo?"

"That it was found in Reno and that they were running forensic tests on evidence collected from it."

Rankin spat out a laugh and his eyes looked human for a microsecond.

"What's so funny?" I asked.

"Strictly hypothetical, but I believe it's somewhat difficult to collect DNA evidence from bleach."

"Doesn't matter to me either way. As I told Moretti, I never came into contact with the Volvo."

"He's still a loose end, just like you. Two loose ends might get tied together. One has to be clipped." Rankin made a scissoring gesture with two fingers.

"Are you asking me to kill the La Jolla Chief of Police?"

"I'm not *asking* anything. I'm merely stating a fact."

"What are you going to do, kill the whole department? Moretti or not, the case will still be investigated."

"Maybe not." He took a sip of scotch and smiled. This time no signs of humanity entered his eyes.

"What's that supposed to mean?"

"Moretti is currently undertaking the investigation into Randall Eddington's disappearance on his own."

"What? How do you know that? What about his very public statement in the *La Jolla Lantern*?"

"The *Lantern* statement was primarily to get my attention." He tapped his chest. "It also served to make the public think that he's a bulldog who never gives up. His department no doubt took it solely as a PR move with no teeth as there is no active investigation. Moretti may be a police chief now, but he's a very political animal. Every move he makes, every public utterance is calculated toward a personal goal. Take it as gospel, Moretti is conducting a secret investigation."

I didn't know whether or not to believe Rankin, but I knew I couldn't trust him. However, Moretti's last words from the other night came back to me. "Your secret's safe with me." Could Moretti really be conducting a secret investigation? Why?

"He doesn't have anything prosecutable on either one of us. We're both safe." Except Randall Eddington's phone, but maybe Rankin didn't know about that.

"For now, Cahill. Are you willing to wait until he has enough evidence and goes public with his investigation by arresting you? Sooner or later, it's going to come down to you or him. In your gut, you know I'm right."

He finished the rest of his drink and stood up. "Now it's time for you to go. *Better Homes and Gardens* will be here soon to do a cover story. Wouldn't want them to think I do business with unsavory characters."

When I got to the front door, Buff was there to open it wearing a dress shirt, slacks, and loafers. Another façade in a mansion full of them. I got into my car, turned on the ignition, and gunned the gas as I let out the clutch. The tires spun in place before they grabbed flagstone and left a black smear as I sped up the driveway.

At least there'd be one stain that would be hard to erase.

CHAPTER THIRTY-FIVE

THE COASTAL MARINE layer hung low over the morning, compressing the sky. Out of habit grinded into necessity, I constantly scanned the car mirrors, the road, and everything surrounding it for trouble. Once, LJPD was my only worry; now I radared for trained killers, too.

If Rankin had told me the truth about Moretti, something was missing from the story. Why would Moretti run a secret investigation on Randall Eddington's disappearance and not use the full resources of his department? I didn't doubt Rankin's contention that Moretti only took action that would personally benefit him. But wouldn't an arrest for Randall Eddington's supposed murder do just that? And putting all his detectives on the case would only enhance that possibility. It wasn't as if they had other murders to investigate. People in La Jolla died of old age and heart attacks, not murder.

No, something was missing from the equation. Moretti wanted something from Rankin. Why else would he lie about me implicating Rankin? Money? Something as crass as blackmail? I knew Moretti to be corrupt, but only in abusing his power. Maybe after years of policing for the wealthy, he wanted to take a shortcut to become one of them. To me, it was still a stretch.

Whatever it was to Rankin, he wanted Moretti dead. And he wanted me to pull the trigger.

Now I had to watch out for Rankin, too.

* * *

Special Agent Mallon had agreed to meet me at the Del Mar Plaza.
Theoretically, neither one of us knew what the other looked like,
but I figured I could spot a Fed in the wealthy, yet laid-back beach
town.

Del Mar hugs the coast ten miles up the road from La Jolla.
Much smaller, it's like a condensed version of La Jolla. Cooked
down so the fat has been rendered and all that's left is succulent
protein. Expensive protein. Its tiny downtown maintains a village
charm, but the homes on the hills with ocean views would stretch
even La Jollans' pocketbooks. Unless you're in the Alan Rankin tax
bracket. The riffraff is tolerated in the summer when they come to
the annual fair and then the horse races. Other than that, Del Mar
is mostly populated by One Percenters vacationing in second or
third homes and young upwardly mobile couples vying to get into
single-digit percentages.

I chose Del Mar because it was out of Moretti's jurisdiction and a
short drive for both Agent Mallon and me. Just enough sun poked
through the clouds to make my sunglasses appropriate. I'd traded
my jacket in for a sweatshirt and ball cap. The sweatshirt was a
better blend with the casual locals than the bomber jacket. Even
though I had a conceal carry license, I left my gun in the car. This
was to be a friendly meeting, and I didn't want a gun bulge to make
Mallon nervous.

We'd scheduled our meet for one at Enoteca Del Fornaio, an
outdoor café version of its big brother, Il Fornaio, across the way.
I arrived a half hour early and took a seat on the patio outside
the restaurant area that afforded me a view of the street and the

two entrances up to the third level. I nursed a beer and watched the wealthy and the wannabe wealthies dressed in casual wear like me. Except my clothes came from JC Penney, theirs from Neiman Marcus. We all drank the same beer.

Special Agent Mallon arrived at the front of the restaurant at exactly 1:00 p.m. Blue suit with a neutral tie, perfectly coiffed brown hair, aviator sunglasses. Right out of an FBI catalog. I checked the entrances and the crowd for a partner in a matching blue suit or someone dressed like me paying too much interest to Mallon or to everybody else. No partner. Nobody working undercover.

Mallon stood outside the parade fenced-in area that made up the café outdoor dining area and scanned the lunch crowd inside. Not seeing a single male alone, he expanded his search to the full deck area. His sunglasses locked on mine, and I gave him an inch nod of my head and took a sip of beer. He strode over to my table. Chin up, chest high.

"Buy you a beer, Special Agent Mallon?"

"Not while I'm on the clock. Thanks."

We had that in common, except that my clock never stopped now. Finding Jim Colton's killer and staying alive had become my twenty-four-hour job. So I broke my own rule to ease the pressure.

"The tables are a bit close together at the café." I nodded to the restaurant. "What do you say we skip lunch?"

"Fine by me." Mallon sat in the high-back chair opposite me. "In fact, unless you show me a valid ID, we're going to skip the whole thing."

I pulled out my wallet and slid it across the table to him. He picked it up and looked at my driver's license inside. "Jesus Christ."

"Not even close."

"You don't have a stellar reputation in the law enforcement community, Mr. Cahill."

I didn't know if the "mister" was in deference to the three or four years I had on him or to keep me and my story at a distance. I'd bet on the latter.

"Some of it's earned. The rest, myth. Either way, it has nothing to do with the fact that someone impersonating you tried to kill me last night."

"I really think you should go through the proper channels and report this to the police department." Monotone and mechanical behind his aviators. A bureaucratic automaton. "You're a civilian. There's nothing federal about this."

"Except that an FBI agent or someone posing as one tried to kill me. That sounds federal to me."

"I can't make the call on my own, Mr. Cahill." He sounded like he just didn't want to. "Follow me back to headquarters and I'll arrange a meeting with the Special Agent in Charge and we'll see what he thinks."

"I talked to SAC Richmond yesterday on another matter. He doesn't like me very much."

"What did you talk to him about?"

I gave Agent Mallon the whole Colton case: Colton's suspicious death, his call to the FBI, Brianne's and my meeting with SAC Richmond, the phone call from someone impersonating Agent Mallon to set up the meet, the ambush at Paulie's Auto Body Repair, the waterboarding, the drowning, Miranda saving me, Ski Mask at the hospital, the gunfire, and the stolen license plate.

Mallon didn't say a word or take notes during my recap. He didn't even move. Just pointed sunglasses at me and all I could see was my own reflection. When I finished, he took off his sunglasses and rubbed his eyes. Now I knew why he favored the shades. His brown eyes were doe-like and made him look like he was a high school senior.

"Look, Mr. Cahill, this kind of thing isn't my expertise." He put his sunglasses back on, but he lost the authority in his voice. "I investigate financial crimes. Up until five years ago, I was an accountant. Let me take this to the SAC, and he'll assign more qualified agents to investigate."

"Call me Rick. Why did you join the FBI, Special Agent Mallon?"

"Ah, you can call me John. But I don't see why I joined the Bureau has anything to do with any of what you just told me."

"I became a police officer because I wanted to help people. Thought it was my duty because my father had been a bent cop. I wanted to erase the stain he'd left behind. I failed miserably. Got my wife killed. There's no making up for that, no matter how hard I try." I took off my sunglasses and stared into Mallon's. "Why'd you join the FBI, John?"

He tilted his head down at the table and stayed silent for a few seconds, then lifted his head back up. "My brother was a Marine. He died over in Iraq. An Iraqi soldier who my brother had trained for three months turned his gun on Jack and four other Marines. He was an insurgent who shared meals with my brother, took pictures with him and other soldiers. He waited three months for the right opportunity to murder men who thought of him as a friend. I joined the FBI to cut off the money to the people behind that insurgent and track them down."

"I can't help you with that. But like you, I'm trying to do the right thing in my own way. Jim Colton was a Navy SEAL and, like your brother, he served in Iraq. He came back alive, but somebody murdered him and made it look like suicide. They left him hanging in his garage so his son could find him. I want to bring those people to justice, but I need your help. You, and you alone."

"I wish I could help you, Rick, but I can't by myself." He stood up. "I'll be happy to take this to the SAC and let him decide how to handle it, but I can't run some rogue investigation for you."

"Ten or so people saw me at your office yesterday. Only someone there could have known when you were out of the office and called me to set up a trap. I can't trust anyone there. You're the only person who can help me. Sometimes you have to do what's right even when all the rules say it's wrong. I need your help, John."

"Sorry." He started to walk away. Chest not so high, chin down.

"At least find out if there's an FBI connection to Paulie's Auto Body Repair. The man posing as you had a key to get in."

He didn't say anything and kept walking. I let him go. I'd put my faith in a by-the-book glorified apparatchik, and he wasn't willing to look anywhere but between the lines. And if he followed those lines back to his boss and told him about our meeting, the people trying to kill me might learn everything that I knew about them.

CHAPTER THIRTY-SIX

I WALKED DOWN to the parking garage and called Dr. Lin at the Medical Examiner's Office. The screener wouldn't put me through to her so I left my number on the 1 percent chance that she'd call me back. I found my car and pulled out onto Camino Del Mar, the thoroughfare that served as main street for downtown Del Mar. There wasn't a whole lot to it, but most of the buildings had a cool Tudor influence and the restaurants served good food.

My phone rang after I exited Camino Del Mar and headed up and over the hill to get onto I-5. I answered it.

"This is Doctor Lin. What can I do for you now, Mr. Cahill? And please be brief. I'm very busy."

"Did you check for needle marks along the hairline at the base of Jim Colton's skull?"

"This is why you called me?" Loud and high pitched.

"It's not an accusation. I have good reason to ask the question. Please."

"I doubt it. I'd have to look at the report, but it's not an area I'd typically examine in a death by hanging."

"Understood. Could an injection there be effective?"

"What do you mean by effective?"

"Would the needle be able to deliver the drug without banging into bone?"

"Sure? Why do you ask?"

"One more question and then, I promise, I'll tell you. Can you think of a drug that could knock someone unconscious in less than ten seconds but would wear off quickly and would not typically be searched for in a suicide tox screen?"

"So we're back to this?"

"Humor me and I'll leave you alone."

"Fentanyl would seem like a likely choice. It's very fast acting."

"Fentanyl? Isn't that the drug Kristin Rossum used to kill her husband in the American Beauty murder? It's lethal, isn't it?"

"Yes, that's it. Almost any drug can be lethal at a high enough dosage." Loud exhale like educating me was a chore. "Although fentanyl is trickier than most. There is less room for error. An improper dose could cause cessation of breathing very quickly."

"So it's not a street drug and you would have to have some medical background to administer it without killing the person?"

"Most likely."

"But you say it's the most logical drug to use under the scenario I described. Works rapidly and wears off quickly as well?"

"Yes."

"Thanks, Doc."

"Okay. You've piqued my curiosity." Another loud exhale like she was mad at herself for admitting interest. "Have you found new evidence in James Colton's murder?"

"I can't connect all the dots yet, but someone contacted me on the pretense of discussing the case and then ambushed me when I showed up. They stuck a needle in my hairline at the base of my skull, and I was unconscious in seconds. I don't know exactly how long I stayed unconscious, but I think it was less than ten minutes."

"My God. Really?" Genuine concern. "Did you call the police? Can you identify your attackers?"

"No. To both."

"Why haven't you contacted the police?"

"I wish I could. My life would be a lot easier."

"What does that mean?"

"Doesn't matter. Thanks."

"Wait. With this new information, I'd be willing to perform a second autopsy on my own and look for needle marks at the base of the skull, as well as run another toxicology scan looking specifically for fentanyl or other opioids. The likelihood of finding it isn't good, but if there are needle marks, I'll find them."

"I wish you could. The body was cremated."

CHAPTER THIRTY-SEVEN

I WENT BACK to the hotel room and found a note from Brianne telling me her phone had died and she went home with George to retrieve the charger she'd forgotten to pack. Shit! She could be walking into an ambush. I hurried back down to my car and sped out of the parking garage. If Brianne only left a few minutes ago and went through La Jolla, I might have a chance to catch her. I took La Jolla Village to Interstate 5 and raced to Brianne's house through La Jolla's back door. I'd get there quicker and avoid any possible encounter with LJPD until I exited Pacific Beach via Soledad Mountain Road.

No LJPD cruisers, black Range Rovers, or any sign of Brianne's 1965 cherry-red Mustang on her street. A canopy of Torrey pines surrounded Brianne's house, blocking any view of the driveway until you were perpendicular to it. I rolled past and glanced in. Empty.

I'd either beaten Brianne to her house or she'd already come and gone. Or she was captive or worse inside and someone had put her car in the garage or driven off in it. I parked the car a house away, took the Smith & Wesson from the trunk, and hustled back to the house.

I peeked through the crack between the garage door and its frame and saw the back of Jim Colton's pickup truck but no vintage red Mustang.

The gate to the front courtyard that separated the house from

the driveway stood open. I entered and tried the knob on the front
door. Unlocked. I eased the door open and squatted low with gun
extended. Clear. I listened before I entered, trying to separate the
noise of a passing car on the street from the silence of the house.
Quiet.

I entered the house and stopped in the foyer and scanned the
open kitchen and living room. Clear. I listened before I moved
again. Silence. I slow-motioned a step into the hallway and stopped.
Sound coming from Jim Colton's den. A drawer opening and shuffled papers?

Possibly. Didn't matter. All that mattered was that someone was
in Colton's den.

And that I had a gun.

I advanced down the hall. Gun extended. Finger on the trigger
guard. Take a step. Stop. Listen. Take a step. Stop. Listen. I finally
made it to within a yard of the den's door. A massive back leaned
over Colton's desk.

Adrenaline jolted muscle memory through my body all the way
back from my days as a street cop. A quick step and I was opposite
the doorway. "Don't move."

The man froze.

"Hands over your head and turn around slowly or I'll shoot you."
I kept the gun trained on center mass as the man turned.

Oak Rollins stared at me. Fear in his eyes dissolved into anger.
"What the hell are you doing?"

"You stole my question." I motioned the Smith & Wesson toward the wall behind Colton's desk. "Against it and spread 'em."

"You're making a mistake, Cahill." Rollins still had his hands
raised, but I kept my distance. "Put the gun down and we can talk."

"We'll talk, alright." I aimed the gun at his knee. "Grab the wall
or learn to walk with a limp."

Rollins eyeballed me for a two count, then turned and pressed his hands against the wall and spread his legs. He must have read in me what I'd determined after cheating death last night. I made my own rules now.

I immediately saw the bulge on Rollins's hip. I pressed the barrel of my .357 Magnum firmly against his back with my left hand. He stiffened.

"Don't move." I slid my hand under his polyester jacket and removed a Glock 9mm pistol from a pancake holster on his belt. I stuffed the gun behind the waistband of my pants above my butt. I patted the rest of him down just as I had Alan Rankin earlier today. Only it took longer. There was a lot more of him. I emptied the contents of his pockets onto the desk next to Jim Colton's Navy SEAL paperweight. Keys, wallet, cell phone. The usual stuff. Other than a Swiss Army knife in his front pants pocket, he was clean. I pocketed the knife and the cell phone. "Sit down on your hands in the chair."

Rollins did as told. I backpedaled to the doorway, a solid six feet away from him, and dropped my armed hand to my side. He tried to play hero, I'd still have enough time to put two slugs in his chest. Even as big as he was, he couldn't outmuscle lead.

"You never answered your own question," I said. "What the hell are you doing?"

"Following up on a favor to a friend."

"What's the favor?"

"Making sure she keeps paying for Cash's education and doesn't spend the money on herself." Rollins looked me straight in the eyes. Could have been telling me the truth. Could have been lying. I'd learned not to trust my instincts lately.

"She has a name."

"Not to me."

"So you thought breaking into the one without a name's house and rifling through your dead best friend's desk was the best way to make sure Cash was still in school?" I tilted my head and one-eyed him. "Ever occur to you to call Cash or check with UCLA?"

"I didn't break in. Jacks gave me a key when I stayed here for a few weeks a couple years back. I knocked and no one answered, so I let myself in." He nodded at the keyring. "I was looking for Jacks's will. He had a provision in it that set aside a certain amount of money for Cash's college tuition."

"I know you live in Nevada, but here in California you can't let yourself into someone's house without their permission just because you have a key." I smiled. "That's unlawful entry. And just to look at a will, huh? What are you really looking for?"

"The will."

"Two and a half months after your buddy dies you finally decide to follow up on a favor." I dropped the smile and thought of the sound of a second car door closing last night at the auto body shop when the silent partner left. I'd taken it as an echo last night, but now realized it could have been someone else getting into the car at the same time. "Where were you last night?"

"In a hotel in Bishop." His eyes held steady. "It's a long drive from Lake Tahoe."

"It's an hour and a half flight from Reno for a couple hundred bucks. But I guess it's not easy to fly with guns anymore, so it makes sense to drive if you're bringing some."

Rollins continued to look at me and stayed silent.

"But what doesn't make sense is why you felt the need to bring a gun when all you'd planned to do was make sure Cash's education was paid for."

"I work security. I have a conceal carry permit. I carry a gun all the time."

"You have one for California? Each state has their own."

"You want to talk lawbreaking, Cahill. You're holding me against my will while brandishing a weapon. Kidnapping. At least. Even a couldn't-make-it-ex-cop like yourself knows that."

"I know I'm holding the gun and you're lying to me. Got a receipt from that hotel in Bishop?"

"Not on me. It's back at my hotel here in town. Why don't we head over there and I'll show you?" He lifted up from the chair.

I zeroed the gun on his chest. "Back down or you can add murder to my list of offenses."

He sat back down.

"Hands." I pointed the gun at his hands that were now in his lap. He shook his head and slid them under his rear end.

"Made any calls lately, Rollins?" I pulled his cell phone from my pocket. "Who's going to answer when I start dialing recently called numbers?"

"My wife."

I clicked into his phone log and saw a list of numbers. He'd made two this morning. Both to 775 area codes. Northern Nevada. Probably was his wife. I scanned the rest of the numbers. There was a call either to or from a number with a 619 area code placed yesterday at 10:24 in the morning. San Diego. The number looked vaguely familiar. I tapped it with my thumb and put the phone to my ear. The expression on Rollins's face didn't change. Either he was unconcerned or he'd picked up a dynamite poker face from his years working in a casino.

"Oak, when you getting to town? We still on for Friday night at the cabin?" Pretty sure it was the voice of Kyle Bates, the former SEAL who served with Jim Colton and Rollins overseas and now lived in Coronado. I ended the call.

"When Bates calls back, tell him it was a butt dial," I said.

The phone rang. I pointed the gun at Rollins, tapped the answer button, then the speaker button, and walked over to the desk where Rollins sat and set the phone down, never taking the gun off him.

"Oak? Oak? You there? Why'd you hang up?" Kyle's voice over the speaker.

"Accidental dial, bro. Sorry. I'm in the middle of something. I'll see you Friday night."

"Roger." The phone went dead.

I kept the gun on Rollins and picked up the phone.

"What's Friday night?" I asked.

"We're having dinner."

"A couple of old friends."

"Yeah."

"Yet, he didn't even know you were already in town. Didn't know you were over at the house of your dead SEAL buddy going through his desk."

"Jacks's request was just between the two of us. KB, or anybody else, doesn't need to know about it." The poker face finally broke into a flinty glare.

"Were you ever a medic in the SEALs, Rollins?"

"No." Poker face.

"Know anything about fentanyl?"

"What's this all about, Cahill?"

"A lot of things." I lifted the gun from my side to remind him who was in charge. "Fentanyl?"

"It's some sort of painkilling drug, I think."

"What time you hit the road yesterday?"

"Five p.m."

"Your wife verify that?"

"I left from the casino."

"So someone there will be able to confirm that?"

"Maybe not the exact time. I don't report to anybody or have a clock in my position, Cahill. I'm head of security and come and go as I please."

"I know. You're very important." I looked at the call log on his phone, scanning for calls with the 775 area code that were different than the first two on the list. "So let's see if I can find the work number or do you want to tell me?"

"You seem to be having a good time playing detective. Figure it out."

"Rick?" Brianne's voice startled me from the front of the house.

My head shot toward her voice. Movement from Rollins. I whipped my head toward him and sprang the gun up from my side. A dark blur exploded against my head.

CHAPTER THIRTY-EIGHT

"Rick?" A voice floating down from heaven. "Rick?"

My eyes fluttered open. A blurry face hovered above me.

"Are you okay?" The voice seemed disembodied from the face above me.

I blinked a few times and the face came into focus. Big round eyes. Short square snout. George the Boxer peered down at me with concerned eyes. Or surprised eyes. Or just big eyes. I moved my head to the left and it screamed from inside. Thumping pain.

Brianne's face materialized through the wall of pain. Blue eyes, amber hair pulled back behind her ears, freckled button nose.

"Are you okay?" She held my face in her hand.

"Where's Rollins?" I lifted up and wished I hadn't.

"Stay down." She gently guided my head back to the floor. "Odell was here? He did this to you?"

"Yes. How long have I been out?"

"Not very long. I heard a crash after I called your name and froze. Then I heard the den door to the backyard slam against the wall and I came back here." She lowered her chin. "Sorry I didn't come right away."

"Wouldn't have made a difference, but we have to find him." I pushed off the floor to a sitting position and ate the pain.

"He's already gone."

"Help me up."

"We should call 911."

"Help me up!" I rolled over to all fours and pushed off the floor.

Brianne put her shoulder under my arm and lifted. She powered me to my feet, and George took a couple steps backward.

"Where's the phone?" I scanned the floor and saw my gun against the wall by the doorjamb and the brass paperweight that Rollins smashed into my temple at my feet, but no phone.

"I think it's in your pocket. I can feel it against my leg."

"Not mine. His."

"I don't see it. He must have taken it."

I shoved my hand down the back of my pants while Brianne held me steady. No gun. Rollins had taken his gun and phone and left me alive. Why? No time to put a bullet in my head after he yanked his gun from my waistband? It takes less than a second to point and shoot. Concerned about Brianne seeing him? Why not put her down, too? Whatever his reasons, I should have just been grateful that I was still alive, but his actions didn't fit. Maybe I'd figure it out when my head wasn't jackhammering pain and we weren't exposed.

"We have to get out of here in case he comes back with his friends." I bent down to pick up my gun, and Brianne bent with me steadying my body. "I saw your note. What took you so long to get here?"

"I took George for a walk at the beach first." She studied my eyes. Something must not have looked right. "I think we need to take you to the emergency room."

"I'm okay." I disengaged from her and saw the large stand-up gun safe in the far corner of the office. "Do you know the combination to the gun safe?"

"Yes."

"Open it up."

Brianne raised her eyebrows at me, but walked over to the safe with me right behind. She punched numbers into the digital key-pad, spun the sprocketed handle, and pulled open the safe door

with both hands. She stepped back to allow me to look inside. Jim
Colton sure did like his guns. Inside was a Mauser M 12 bolt-action
hunting rifle, a Colt M4 assault rifle, a Mossberg 5901A1 tactical
shotgun, and a mint-condition Winchester 30-30 lever action rifle.

The upper shelves held handguns. A Smith & Wesson .357 revolver like mine, a Sig Sauer 9mm, a Colt .45, and a Bonds Arms Texas
Defender two-shot derringer. There was also a KA-BAR tactical
knife in its sheath. I grabbed the knife and stuck it in my back pocket.
I checked the derringer. Loaded. I stuck it in my front pants pocket
and put a box of .357 shells in the front pocket of my sweatshirt.

Brianne closed and locked the den door to the backyard.

"Let's get the hell out of here." I stiff-legged toward the door. My
head swirled around the room and vibrated pain. Each step was another piece pulled from a Jenga set. I didn't know how many I had
left before I went tumbling down.

A picture on the wall of the office caught my eye, and I stopped to
look at it. The one with the four Musketeer SEAL buddies kneeling
in front of the pot of gold. I grabbed it off the wall. "I'm taking this
with us."

"Why?"

"For a lineup. I'll explain later." I teetered into the hallway.

Brianne followed behind with George. "I'll meet you outside. I
just need to get my phone charger and some dog food for George."

"Where's the dog food?"

"In the pantry in the kitchen."

I tightroped into the kitchen and the walk-in pantry and grabbed
a half-full thirty-five-pound bag of dog food. The good stuff, like I
fed Midnight. I also grabbed a bag of Oreos. The bad stuff, like I
sometimes fed myself.

Brianne was already on the front porch when I went outside. She
held George's leash in one hand and a guitar case in the other. She
saw me looking at the case.

"I don't know how long I'll be gone. I can't be without Brad for very long."

"Brad?"

"Paisley."

"Of course."

"Stressful times can be very inspiring." She smiled and I laughed. "Let's hope you don't have to write too many songs."

* * *

I let Brianne drive me back to the hotel and left my car on the street near her house. I lay down on the hotel room bed and Brianne pressed ice wrapped in a plastic bag against the lump on my left temple. The ice didn't help the pain. But I didn't want the lump to get any bigger. We'd stopped at a store on the way to the hotel and bought some Motrin. Six tablets—1200 milligrams—hadn't eased my throbbing headache, yet. Under normal circumstances, I might have let Brianne drive me to the emergency room. But the circumstances had been abnormal over the last couple days. Hospitals drew cops, and I didn't want to bump into any. Years of butting heads with LJPD had made me paranoid. The last couple days dealing with Chief Moretti and the FBI metastasized that paranoia.

Brianne's blue eyes looked at me with affection clouded by concern. So different from the angry eyes I'd seen after we left the FBI meeting yesterday morning. I welcomed the change and the new intimate aspect of our relationship, but was leery. Not of her intentions, but of repercussions from my decisions.

I'd ordered my life around a handful of rules. Not gleaned from societal norms or self-help gurus or even the Good Book. They had been forged through the fire of my own life experiences. And those experiences had taught me not to get involved with a "client." But even beyond the rules, I'd lost confidence in my instincts and judgment. With Brianne so close, mistakes I made now wouldn't only hurt me, they could get her killed. I'd already lost people in my life because of errors in judgment. I couldn't risk doing it again.

"I think you should get on a plane and fly back home to Brooksville until I get this thing settled." I put my hand on top of hers, holding the ice to my head. "Take George with you, leave him with a friend, or put him in a kennel for a while. I could even find a short-term home for him, but you need to get out of town."

"Do you think Cash is in danger?" Eyes wide.

"No, but it wouldn't hurt to alert him to be aware of his surroundings."

"I already did." She laced a strand of hair behind her ear. "Rick, the only way I'm leaving is if you're with me. I'm the one who got you involved in this. Half of me wished I hadn't and the selfish half is glad I did or I wouldn't have gotten to know you."

"I don't have any regrets about taking the case, but we have to be clear-eyed about this. These men are killers and they're not going to stop until they eliminate all possible threats to themselves and whatever they're protecting. They went after Miranda because she may have gotten a glimpse of one of them. They tried to kill me even after they knew I didn't know anything and that I couldn't physically identify them. Just by being Jim's wife, you're a threat. They'll come for you if they haven't already."

"What do you mean, if they haven't already?"

"Odell Rollins. I think he may have been one of my attackers last night. And today he shows up at your house and searches Jim's desk. What if his original mission was to kill you? If you'd been home when he came by, you would have invited him in. If you had, you'd probably be dead."

"Odell would never hurt me." She replaced her hand with mine on the ice bag and sat up straight. "He doesn't like me anymore, but he used to love me like a sister because Jim was like a brother. He'd never hurt either one of us."

"Brothers kill each other every day. It's not even news anymore."

"The only two things I'm sure of about Jim's death is that he was murdered and Odell had nothing to do with it. They had a bond that I'd never seen between two men and rarely between two women." Brianne leaned down and kissed me on the forehead. "You're giving your heart and soul to finding Jim's killer, and I can't even express how much it means to me. Maybe someday I will in a song. But you have to trust me on this. Odell would never hurt Jim or let anyone else hurt him."

"Okay, then why did he enter your home uninvited and rifle Jim's desk with a gun strapped to his hip?"

"A lot of ex-military carry guns. With what's going on in the world today, I'm glad they do. Maybe Odell really was making sure that I was paying for Cash's education." I'd already told her about the bullshit story Rollins had given me. "Or maybe he was looking for something that might have led to Jim's murder."

"When I saw him in Lake Tahoe, he almost had me convinced that he believed Jim killed himself."

"I doubt he really believes that. He probably didn't want to give you too much information. It's still name, rank, and serial number with those guys. They look after each other and clean up their own messes."

"That's pretty stupid if I'm the only person trying to find Jim's killer."

"Maybe Odell's trying to take care of it on his own." She scratched George, who'd planted himself next to her, behind the ear. "Maybe that's why he came down here."

"Why now? Your husband's been dead for three months."

"I don't know."

"He's supposed to meet Kyle Bates for dinner Friday night and Bates doesn't even know he's already in town."

"That doesn't prove anything." She straightened up.

"It proves he got here earlier than expected and doesn't rule out that he could have been one of the men who attacked me last night."

"If that's true, why didn't he kill you today when he had the chance?"

"I don't know. I haven't figured that out yet." I opened my hands. "But he did knock me unconscious. Still convinced that Rollins had nothing to do with Jim's death?"

"I don't know." Her eyes circled in uncertainty and fear. She looked like she'd just been told that all the truths she knew about life were lies. I'd never felt worse about winning a point in my life. "But why would he kill Jim?"

"I don't know. Maybe it had to do with something that happened overseas."

"They've both been in the States for four years. Why do you think it has something to do with their time overseas?"

"I don't have an answer yet. It's all speculation right now. The best I can do is look at the facts we know and try to draw reasonable conclusions."

"What if you're wrong?"

"If I'm wrong then I keep working until I'm right. But right or wrong, you need to leave town. It's too dangerous here right now. If you stay here, I'll have one more thing to worry about. I need all my attention pointed in one direction."

"I'm not a child, Rick. I'm forty years old. I've raised a son, and somebody killed his father. A man who I once loved and will always admire. This is my fight. I'm going to stay here with you, and we're going to find out who killed Jim."

I was lying on my back with an ice pack shoved against my head, had my nose broken by a woman, been knocked unconscious, drugged, had a gun taken away from me, been water boarded, and saved from certain death by a woman who endured a beating that almost killed her just so I'd live.

"Okay." I needed all the help I could get. "You can stay unless it gets hairier."

"Good. I've got enough Marriott rewards points for three more free nights here. After that, we'll have to stay somewhere cheaper."

I just hoped we'd live that long.

CHAPTER THIRTY-NINE

I TOOK A cab back to my car in La Jolla and drove over to the hospital at 7:00 p.m. I left Brianne back at the hotel with George, her Sig Sauer, and a box of .357 Magnum shells.

Miranda was still in room 432, but now she had a Rankin side of beef standing sentinel outside her door. This one made Buff back at the mansion look like a bantamweight.

"Call your boss and tell him Rick Cahill is here to see Miranda."

"No visitors." His voice sounded like it came out of the bottom of a well.

"Call your boss." I was glad he was there but tired of no. "We're on the same team."

"No visitors." He stuck a hand out that I could have sat in.

"Rick?" Miranda's voice floated through the open door. "Sebastian, it's okay. You can let him in."

Sebastian? At least his parents had a sense of humor.

"Mr. Rankin said no visitors." But his voice had lost its echo. Miranda held sway over him. If those two ever walked down a dark alley together, I'd feel sorry for the alley.

"He didn't mean Rick. He saved my life."

She had it backwards, but I let it lie. Sebastian dropped his hand, and I went into the room. Miranda pushed a button on a square controller and rose with the bed into a sitting position. She had two black eyes, one almost swollen shut, and a hematoma on the left side of her head that gave me lump envy. Her whole face was a half size too big.

Yet she smiled when she saw me, which warmed me and made me feel guilty all at once.

"How are you feeling?" I set down the flower arrangement I bought at the gift shop on the table next to her bed.

"Better. I still have a pretty bad headache, but they ran a CAT scan and some other tests and everything looked okay. I should be out of the hospital in a couple days. Thanks so much for the flowers. They're beautiful."

"That's the least I could do." I sat in a chair next to the bed. "You saved my life, Miranda. Twice, really. You stopped the guy in the ski mask from finishing the job and then you brought me back from the dead. I don't know how I . . . I don't know . . ."

My eyes welled and my throat tightened around the words. The emotion snuck up on me, pulling at me from a part of me I tried to ignore. I wasn't tearing up for myself. I'd cheated death before. Not that it was old hat, and I wasn't grateful to be alive. I treasured life and still hoped to find true happiness in mine before I died. But I knew death was out there in the shadows, stalking me. And more and more, I felt it wouldn't wait for old age.

No, I wasn't teary-eyed for my own mortality. I was humbled that someone would risk their life to save a wretch like me.

"It's okay, Rick." Miranda took my hand in hers and stroked it. "You would have done the same thing for me."

This former MMA fighter, who had nearly died in the last twenty-four hours and who I'd really only known for one afternoon, could read my mind.

"Why did you do that?" The emotion gone, I was now a scientist trying to understand the human condition. "Why didn't you just call the police and get the hell out of there?"

"I didn't want you to die."

"You barely knew me. You risked your life to save me when ninety-nine percent of people would have run and then maybe called the police."

"I don't want anyone to die. Unless they deserve it. But I especially don't want you to die." She smiled through her broken face. "I guess I'm that one in a hundred."

"At least." I didn't want to get into a conversation about why I was special to her. My life was complicated enough and I didn't have those kinds of feelings for Miranda. But I knew I could without trying very hard.

"And we're even anyway. You probably saved my life by rushing me to the hospital and again when you stopped that guy from getting into my room. We're definitely even." She gave me the beautiful gargoyle smile again. "At least."

"Okay. Even." I held up my hands. "But how did you stop the man from killing both of us? Why did he leave? I know you can fight, but he almost killed you. Why didn't he finish the job?"

"He almost did. He had me down and was on top of me and kept punching my head. I got a hand up and tried to gouge his eyes, but could only rip off his ski mask." Her eyes glistened with moisture. "The garage started to go dark on me. I knew I was going to die. Then he shifted his body, and with strength that must have come from God, I jammed my knee into his testicles. I hurt him and he rolled off me. Then we heard a siren, and he ran out of the garage and drove off. The siren faded out like it was up on the freeway. Somebody didn't want us to die last night, Rick."

"I guess so." I held her hand and squeezed it. Lucky to be alive, but my situation hadn't changed. "Rankin told me you told the police you couldn't remember anything about how you got hurt. Do you think they believed you?"

"I'm not sure, but they won't do anything unless I suddenly re-member something and call them."

"Why didn't you just tell them the truth?"

"Where I grew up, you didn't talk to the police. Alan wouldn't have approved, either."

"Okay." Nothing had been easy in this woman's life, but she wouldn't play victim. "Did you get a look at the guy's face? I know you pulled his ski mask off at some point."

"Yes."

I took the photo from Jim Colton's wall out of the backpack I'd brought with me and put it in Miranda's lap.

"Is he in this picture?" Jim Colton and Doug McCafferty were dead. Odell Rollins was black. That left Kyle Bates. I was 99 percent sure the man in the ski mask hadn't been Bates. All the SEALS I'd seen from Colton's unit were built about the same. V frames, mus-cular without being musclebound. Rollins was the thicker outlier. Bates looked to be slightly leaner than Ski Mask and his voice didn't match. But he could have altered his voice, and my perception of the man in the mask was skewed because I only saw him while I was sitting or nearly upside down and under duress and briefly in the hospital before the chase.

Miranda intently studied the photograph. Finally, she handed it back to me. "No. He's not in there."

She kept staring at the photo as I held it in my lap.

"What is it?" I asked.

She held out her hand, and I gave her back the picture frame. She studied it again for a few seconds, then put her finger on one of the men in the photo and tilted it toward me. "This isn't the guy, but there's a resemblance. Could be this guy's brother, maybe. Something about his eyes."

Miranda's finger was on Doug McCafferty. I didn't know if

McCafferty had a brother, I just knew he was dead. I studied his eyes and tried to picture them surrounded by a black ski mask. They were blue and hard. The man's eyes at the body shop had been blue and hard also, but colder. Remorseless.

Although there were some similarities in the eyes between Doug McCafferty and the man in the mask, I wasn't convinced there was a familial resemblance. I put the photo back in my backpack again, then noticed the dry erase board hanging on the wall. Hospitals use them to put up patient information like emergency phone numbers and to keep track of nurses' schedules.

I went over to the board and grabbed the black marker on the board's mantel. I sat back down and retrieved the photo from the backpack.

"Are you going to draw on a beard?" Miranda craned from her bed to see what I was doing. "He didn't have one."

"No. A ski mask." I colored McCafferty's face black except the eyes. A chill froze along my spine. I showed the altered photo to Miranda.

"Yep. Those are the same eyes, but the rest of his face is different. Weird. Who is he?"

"A dead soldier."

CHAPTER FORTY

BRIANNE AND GEORGE both greeted me at the hotel room door. A honey-I'm-home moment in our new makeshift relationship. We walked over to the bed and sat down, and I told Brianne about my visit with Miranda and the eyes of Doug McCafferty.

"Do you know if he had a brother?" I asked her.

"I only met him a few times. Back when they all completed SEAL training and a couple family barbeques when they returned home from deployment. Doug had a different girl on his arm each time I saw him. I don't remember him or Jim mentioning a brother."

Brianne's computer tablet sat on the desk across from the bed.

"Do you mind if I use your tablet?" I stood up.

"Hold on!" She leapt up and punched a couple keys on the Bluetooth keyboard. She turned back to me, a little red in the face. "Sorry."

"Diary?" I sat down at the desk.

"In a way. I'm writing a new song and I don't want you to see it until I'm ready to play it for you."

"Wow. Can't wait. I'm honored." Nobody had ever sung a song to me. My wife used to read me her poems. Back in the early days before everything turned to shit and she died.

"Wait until you hear it before you go and feel honored."

"Uh-oh."

"Well, I am a country singer, after all. It's not all rainbows and unicorns."

"Nope. Pickup trucks, cheating hearts, and whiskey."

"And cowboy boots."

"Oh, yeah." I tapped on the Bluetooth keyboard and brought up a free data-mining website. "Do you know where McCafferty lived before he died?"

"Oceanside. I think."

"How old was he when he died?"

"Oh." She put her hands on her hips and looked down at the carpet. "Probably about thirty-five or -six."

I punched in what I knew about McCafferty into the website. I searched through page after page, but didn't find anyone who matched our guy. Free sites can only take you so far. I pulled a credit card out of my wallet and looked up a pay site I often used.

"Use mine." Brianne grabbed her purse and searched for her wallet.

"That's okay. This one's on the house. Perks for writing a song that I may or may not be honored to hear."

I punched in the credit card info and then McCafferty's information. A list of Doug McCaffertys popped up. Bingo. Douglas Scott McCafferty, 1970–2006. There were a number of residences, the last one being in Vista, California, which was just east of Oceanside. His military history was listed, including that he'd been a SEAL. His parents were both deceased, but he did have a brother, Dwight Edward McCafferty, age thirty-seven. Current residence, Boise, Idaho.

Brianne read the information over my shoulder. "You think he could have been the guy who tried to kill you?"

"I don't know. Let's find out."

I paid for a search on the brother. He was married with two

young children. He'd followed his older brother into the Navy but only served four years. He'd been a sales rep for a sporting goods company for the last three years, but before that had been in pharmaceutical sales. Double bingo. I wondered how many samples he'd kept and if one of them was fentanyl. I told Brianne about my talk with the coroner and her guess that it could have been fentanyl that had been used on me and her husband to knock us unconscious.

"Oh, my Lord, and he used to be a pharmaceutical rep." She lifted her head and pinched her lips. "I'm not sure if pharmaceutical reps have access to an opioid like fentanyl."

"What?" I blinked. "How the hell would you know something like that?"

"Our bass player's sister is a rep."

"Whether McCafferty sold it or not, he might know how to get hold of some or another drug like it."

"You're probably right." She put her hands on my shoulders. "How do we find out if he was here last night and when Jim was killed?"

"For the night Jim died, we'd need to get some law enforcement agency involved or I'll have to impersonate a cop. I have a ruse to find out about last night, but it will only work if I talk to his wife and not him."

I used the hotel phone to dial the number the data-mining website had for Dwight McCafferty. Brianne would have to eat the cost for this one. The websites rarely had cell phone numbers and usually provided landlines. I hoped that was the case tonight.

"Hello?" A woman's voice. So far, so good.

"Mrs. McCafferty?"

"Yes."

"Sorry to bother you. My name's Dave Belton and I'm an old SEAL buddy of Dwight's brother, Doug, God bless his soul. I'm in Boise for a couple days and was supposed to meet Dwight last night to toast the memory of his brother. Unfortunately, he didn't show, and I lost his cell phone number. Is he home tonight? Maybe I got the nights mixed up." I held my breath and hoped McCafferty wasn't there.

"Oh. Maybe Dwight was the one who mixed up the nights. He's out of town on business, but he'll be back tomorrow. Why don't you give me your number, and I'll make sure he calls you back. I'm sorry."

"Okay, here's my cell." I gave her a made-up number with a San Diego area code. "I must have gotten the dates all messed up. He was out of town last night, too?"

"Yes. He has to travel a lot for his job. He has a big sales territory."

I thanked her and hung up, then relayed Mrs. McCafferty's side of the conversation to Brianne.

"Oh, my God." She slumped down onto the bed. "This guy really could be Jim's killer. What do we do now?"

I Googled Dwight McCafferty, Boise sporting goods sales rep, and listings came up for him in a Boise State charity function. I clicked on the hyperlink and a picture of McCafferty with the Boise State baseball coach came up. It was small and in low res. I spread my fingers on the tablet's screen and enlarged the photo. A little blurry, but his eyes were blue, just like the man's in the ski mask.

I couldn't tell if they were the eyes of a killer.

I looked him up on social media and didn't find any Dwight McCaffertys who were a match for Doug's brother. But when I punched in his wife's name, I found him. She had a lot of photos on her page, mostly of their children. There were a few with Dwight in them, but he was always smiling with the kids. Hard to match the joy in his eyes with the cold stare of the killer's I'd seen last night. But I couldn't rule him out. Not by a long shot.

* * *

Brianne and I made love again an hour later. Her passion pulled me in and I got lost in it for a while. I didn't want to find my way back to my real life. Once we finished, I couldn't avoid it. Dwight McCafferty, Oak Rollins, Alan Rankin, and Tony Moretti all whirl-pooled around in my head. But on the perimeter of the swirling eddy was a life preserver. Brianne. She was a part of my life now. The good in the bad.

Was she the broken rule that could save me?

CHAPTER FORTY-ONE

I WOKE UP and looked at the clock: 8:27 a.m. Holy crap. I couldn't remember the last time I'd slept past seven thirty. My head reminded me that it still had a lump on it. Despite sleeping in, I hadn't had a restful sleep. I rolled over to an empty space next to me.

"Good morning." Brianne sat at the desk in a t-shirt and a thong, her head turned toward me. Hotel life on the run wasn't so bad.

"Looks that way." I smiled, but the itch that had turned my sleep restless still nibbled at me. "We need to talk."

"That doesn't sound good." She stood up and took a step toward the bed.

"No." I held up my hand. "Stay there. Please. I don't want having you next to me influence me or vice versa."

She sat back down in the chair and pursed her lips. "Now you have me really worried, Rick. What's going on?"

I sat up in bed. "I think it's time for you to go to the police."

"Why now?"

"I don't think Police Chief Moretti or LJPD had anything to do with Jim's death. It looks like this Dwight McCafferty dude and someone else killed Jim. I don't see a connection with Moretti."

"Okay, Rick. I have confidence in your judgment. But you said it was time for me to go to the police. Don't you mean *we*?"

"No." I wasn't sure how to say what I needed to without scaring Brianne away. But maybe that was the only fair thing to do. "A couple days ago Agent Richmond told you some things about me you didn't know. There's more. When Police Chief Moretti gets together enough evidence, he's going to arrest me for murder."

"What?" Brianne's eyes circled in fear. "Who does he think you killed?"

"Randall Eddington."

"The man you helped free from prison who went missing?" Her eyebrows rose.

"Yes."

"Why does he think you killed him?"

"He has his reasons."

She studied my face. I held her eyes letting her search inside me. Finally she spoke, "When we went to the FBI, I'd only known you for a few days, but I felt like I knew you well. Knew the person you were. When Agent Richmond told me those things about you, I wasn't only upset with you, I was upset with myself. I was mad because I'd fallen for this person I hardly knew and who I'd already created a whole persona around."

"I don't blame you."

"But darlin', I was right in the first place. The last two days have shown me that. Yes, we've only known each other a week, but that week has had more adversity than most people will ever have to endure in a lifetime. I don't care about some FBI file that has ten-year-old information. I know who you are now."

"Randall Eddington wasn't ten years ago." I had to give her an out. She was the rule I'd broken. I didn't want to be the mistake she'd made.

"I don't have to know what happened to Randall Eddington. I know who you are. That's all I have to know. If you think *we* should go to the police, let's go right now. If you only think that *I* should go, I'll wait until you're ready for *we*."

"Look, Brianne, going to the police might be the only way you can stay alive." I looked down at the bed, then back at Brianne. "I've been putting my freedom ahead of this case. I've made decisions because I didn't want to get arrested, not because I thought they'd help the case. I might be some of the man you think I am, but I also know the other half."

"I know that other half, too. It's a survivor." She walked over to the bed, knelt down, and took my hand in hers. "And I'm going to hold onto that half as hard as I hold onto the rest of you because I know all of you will help keep me safe. You've already risked your life for me. It would have been easy for you to walk away from this case, but you didn't. We are where we are because you tried to help me. There's no way I'm going to walk away from you now."

She kissed me. I pulled her onto the bed and delayed the start of the day another hour.

We finished in each other's arms. We stayed there, silent, staring into each other's eyes for what seemed like minutes. Brianne's blue eyes, both piercing and inviting at once. My broken rule. What would be the repercussion?

"Kyle Bates told me a story about a beach party the other day." I studied her eyes. They closed and she let out a breath through her nose. Her eyes opened at half-mast.

"What did he say?"

"That you came on to him."

"Well, he's right." She frowned.

"I'm listening." I waited for the broken rule's whiplash.

"Kyle always flirted with me whenever we were alone. I always thought it was an act and macho bullshit." She sat up and held her pillow in front of her. "We were at this beach party and I got tired of listening to the boys tell war stories by the bonfire so I took a walk down the beach. Kyle slipped off and caught up to me and started in with the flirting, so I called his bluff thinking he'd back off and stop flirting all the time. That was a mistake. He thought I was serious and tried to kiss me."

"What happened?"

"I had to use all my strength to push him off. He finally let go and walked back to the bonfire."

"Did you ever tell Jim?"

"No. Jim and I weren't getting along anyway and I felt kind of guilty for leading him on." She shook her head. "I shouldn't have. Kyle is a jerk who doesn't understand boundaries. He thinks he can take whatever he wants."

"Do you think he could have had something to do with Jim's death?"

"No. Not really. He's a jerk, but I don't think he's a killer. He kind of held Jim in awe."

My phone groaned on the nightstand. Unknown number. Another one. Nothing good had come from unknown phone numbers. I answered anyway.

"Rick? This is Special Agent Mallon." Hushed voice.

I sat up in bed. "Yes, Agent Mallon."

Brianne's eyes and mouth formed O's.

"Can we meet?" Clipped.

"Sure. When and where?"

"There's a restaurant called Leilani's Café on Cass Street in Pacific Beach. Can you meet me there at noon?"

"I know the restaurant. I'll be there."

CHAPTER FORTY-TWO

LEILANI'S LOOKED LIKE it belonged on the beach even though it sat a few blocks inland. Weather-worn wood shingle structure that had seating for about twelve inside and three times that on its two wooden decks outside. It also had the best Hawaiian food in San Diego. And maybe the forty-eight contiguous states.

I beat Mallon to the restaurant and ordered at the window inside. The tan-even-in-November Polynesian woman behind the counter handed me a little table stand with a number on it.

The noon sky had turned leaden, brewing up some El Nino rain. Unfortunately, inside was taken so I sat at a table in the corner of the deck and waited for Special Agent Mallon, my food, and the rain.

My food arrived at 12:10. No Mallon. No rain. Darker skies.

At 12:15, I wondered if Special Agent Mallon had stood me up. Or if the FBI and LJPD had formed a joint task force and were about to roll up with sirens blazing and arrest me. Or if Mallon was dead and Ski Mask was behind a parked car on the street with a rifle lining up a bull's-eye on my head.

Too much free time.

Mallon arrived five minutes later. Alive and alone. Without his sunglasses under the dark skies, he again looked like a kid in high school. A kid nervous before a test he hadn't studied for.

"Sorry I'm late."

"That's okay. Everything alright?"

"I have people looking over my shoulder." He looked around the deck as if those people might be among the other diners. "I can lose my job for giving you information without going through the proper channels. You have to promise me that you won't tell anyone where you got the information."

"I promise." I meant it. Mallon was going way out on a limb for me. I didn't know why, but I wasn't going to saw it off behind him.

Mallon pulled a file out of his briefcase and opened it. "Take notes. I can't give you the file. I'm destroying the paper trail after we talk."

"What about the digital trail you left behind?"

"I have freedom to follow tips on potential financial crimes. I'm covered there, but I can't have you walking around with an FBI file."

"Got it." I pulled out a notepad and pen.

"Paulie's Auto Body Repair is owned by a Swiss holding company named Wiedergeboren Holdings." Special Agent Mallon read from the report. "Founded by Jurgen Bjorn Wilander and Benjamin Charles Townsend in 2009."

"Really?" I wrote down the information. "Is it normal for a Swiss holding company to own an auto body shop in the States?"

"Not really. Holding companies own all sorts of assets, such as stocks, bonds, private equity funds, hedge funds, real estate. Usually those types of entities. I'd never heard of one owning an auto body shop before. It's, ah, highly unusual."

"Unusual, as in a possible criminal enterprise?"

"I won't go that far, but a number of car repair businesses have been caught laundering money gained through illicit means."

"What else does the company own?"

"It's a small entity, though somewhat diversified. It owns stock in Amway, some S&P 500 stocks, a Swiss watch company, City

Textiles in Los Angeles, and Elite Automobiles and Ultraclean Janitorial Supplies, both in San Diego. The American holdings are managed by a subsidiary called Phoenix Holdings."

"So the American office is in Phoenix?"

"No." He ran a finger down the report. "It's here in San Diego at One America Plaza downtown. It must be named for the other Phoenix from Latin mythology. Benjamin Townsend runs things from there. A unique person to be a partner in a holding company."

"How so?"

"He's had a varied career that doesn't point to founder of a holding company." Mallon looked back at the report. "By the time he was fifty, he'd sold used cars in Trenton, New Jersey, dealt blackjack in Atlantic City and, later, Las Vegas, sold Herbalife in Los Angeles, started a Police Charitable Organization in Santa Ana, sold Amway in Bakersfield, and been an investment banker in San Diego. He'd been a hedge fund manager of BCT Capital in San Diego, which he founded, from 2006–2009, until he sold the business for a couple hundred thousand and started Wiedergeboren Holding Company with Swiss banker Jurgen Wilander."

"Every job he's had until the holding company has the potential to be on the shady side of the law."

"I agree. Also, I haven't been able to find the money trail that would lead him to be able to come up with the three million he used to capitalize his half of Wiedergeboren Holdings."

"Did you find any connection with the FBI or other law enforcement agencies?" I watched his eyes for a tell.

"No." He shook his head and looked straight at me.

"How do you think the men who tried to kill me came up with your name and knew you were out of the office the other day when they called me?"

"I don't know." Mallon looked at me, then squinted, pursed his lips, and seemed to be looking past me.

"What is it, Special Agent Mallon? You just thought of something."

"I went to my son's play at his school that afternoon. Everyone in the office knew about it."

"Anyone else know you were going?" I asked.

"Just some friends and parents in the neighborhood and at school."

The man in the ski mask who tried to kill me at the auto body shop was probably Dwight McCafferty. The potential suspects who might be the silent partner who abetted him just grew to almost anyone Special Agent Mallon knew.

Mallon left without ordering anything, which was fine with me since I was paying the bill.

* * *

I looked up Phoenix Holdings online. A photo of Ben Townsend took up about a third of the page. Townsend looked to be in his early sixties trying desperately to look like he was in his early forties. Dark tan, slicked-back hair too black to be natural, tight eyes, sport coat around an open-chested shirt revealing a gold chain and gray chest hair.

I guess he ran out of Grecian Formula.

Not the staid, conservative look I'd expected to see from a founder of a holding company. But what did I know? I'd just learned what a holding company was twenty minutes ago. Besides, the former Swiss banker probably held down the conservative end of the partnership. Townsend had the look of a wheeler dealer. Or a used car salesman.

The address at the bottom of the webpage stuck out to me. I flipped back in my notepad to find the address Moira MacFarlane had given me of the company that reported the stolen license plate found on the Range Rover. It was the same as Phoenix Holdings. Both companies were located at One America Plaza.

The stolen Lexus license plate on the Range Rover driven by my attackers. One America Plaza where the license plate had been stolen. The auto body shop where I'd been ambushed. All the dots were connecting in a straight line to Phoenix Holdings.

Ben Townsend and I needed to talk. Today.

CHAPTER FORTY-THREE

My phone rang as I turned on the ignition of my car. Scott Buehler, the reporter from *The Reader*. I turned off the ignition.

"I'm sure you know that Congressman Peterson of the 52nd district is gravely ill." Buehler started in without a hello.

"Sort of. Is he the one with pancreatic cancer who won't resign his seat?"

"That's him. Unless there's a miracle, he won't make it to Christmas. When he dies, there will be a special election in a few months."

"This is fascinating stuff, Buehler, but what does it have to do with Chief Moretti and asset forfeiture arrests?" I tried to hide the irritation in my voice. Buehler was still an asset.

"Well, the word is that the chief is going to throw his hat into the ring for the seat."

"It would be nice to get Morreti out of San Diego, but I'll repeat my question, what does it have to do with asset forfeiture arrests?"

"Hear me out. You'll find this interesting." He paused, I guess to build the suspense. "What I've found so far in the three forfeiture arrests is that the charges were dropped in all of them and the assets returned."

"You're right, now I'm interested. What does it all mean?"

"Time to scratch my back, Rick."

"An image now indelibly etched in my mind, Buehler. What do you want?"

"An interview."

"No."

"It's not going to be a hit piece. You know my reporting on you has always been fair, Rick."

"True, but I never gave you or anyone else an interview and that's not going to change now. Besides, I'm old news." At least until Moretti arrested me for murder.

"When Chief Moretti announces his run for the House, a lot of powerful people in San Diego are going to line up to sing his praises. All I ask is for our readers to hear a voice from the other side. You are the voice of our readership, Rick. Alternative culture, antiestablishment, occupy—"

I cut him off before he could rhapsodize further. "Just because the establishment doesn't like me, doesn't mean I'm antiestablishment. And I'm probably as alternative to *The Reader*'s culture as I am to any other."

"Still, our readers would want to know what you had to say about the police chief who could be our next Congressman."

"You want me to call out Moretti in the newspaper?" Buehler was asking me to paint the target Moretti had put on my back in glow-in-the-dark paint and outline it in neon. "Pass."

"I never took you for scared, Rick."

"No, but apparently you took me for stupid. If you don't want to tell me what you discovered about the asset forfeiture arrests, this phone call is over."

"You know Jack Hunt of Jack Hunt Mile of Cars?"

"I've seen his ads." Biggest car dealer in San Diego County.

"He and his wife threw a big party in the summer and LJPD showed up even though no one complained about the noise. Apparently, Hunt and his wife like to have a good time and there were drugs at the party. A lot of them. So the cops arrested Hunt. If you could call it that."

"What do you mean?"

"Hunt was taken from his home down to LJPD, but he wasn't handcuffed. The so-called arresting officers deposited him in Moretti's office instead of an interview room or a cell."

"That just sounds like typical intimidation tactics by Moretti." Memories. "He brings you in, threatens you, veiled or otherwise, gets what he wants, and then lets you go. He's not exactly a by-the-book cop."

"Maybe, but Sergeant Colton went into Moretti's office after Hunt was let go, and the two of them got into a loud argument."

"What was it about?"

"My source didn't hear all of it, but he distinctly heard Colton say, 'Your own private police force.'"

"What was the date of Hunt's arrest?"

"I know where you're going and I already went there." A smug lilt in Buehler's voice. "August third. Three and a half weeks before Jim Colton's death."

I'd all but eliminated Moretti as a suspect in Colton's death. Now I had to reconsider. Could Moretti somehow be connected with Dwight McCafferty, or whoever was in the ski mask, and his partner? Or was he the silent partner?

"Did your source make the same correlation? Does he think Moretti could have anything to do with Jim Colton's death?" I asked.

"He didn't connect any dots, and I don't think he thought there were any to connect."

"Back to Hunt. What assets were seized?"

"The house. LJPD had a US Marshall there before they even took

Hunt to the station." Buehler was excited now. His voice had lost its usual monotone. "He sealed up the house with seizure stickers. The whole deal."

"They seize the house and then Hunt has a talk with Moretti and voila, no more arrest and he gets his house back?"

"Exactly."

"And there's no record of this arrest?" I asked.

"None that I could find."

"And the other two arrests were similar?"

"That's what my source says."

"What does he say is Moretti's real reason for these so-called arrests?" Although I'd already developed my own theory.

"My guy is a Dragnet kind of cop. Just the facts. He doesn't impute motive or look for conspiracies. He just sees Moretti's actions as wrong and wants something done about them."

"Then why didn't he go to the state attorney general with it instead of waiting around for a reporter to get a whiff before he did anything?"

"He may be an idealist, but he wants to keep his job. If he reported to the AG, then he'd have to come out of the shadows and take sides. If Moretti prevailed, this guy's career as a cop in La Jolla, or probably anywhere else, would be over."

"When does this story hit the streets?"

"Maybe never. Without someone willing to go on the record, my editor may not even allow it in print. I've been trying to get an interview with Hunt and the other two, but they're ignoring me."

"Do you have a theory on what Moretti's up to?" See if it matched mine.

"Yes, but I won't write about it until I can verify its accuracy. I know you have good reason to hate Chief Moretti, but you can't use what I tell you to get even with him."

"I won't use what you tell me to get even with Moretti."

I didn't care about even. I cared about survival. And I'd use whatever I needed to against Moretti to stay out of prison for the rest of my life.

"Okay." He sounded relieved. I felt badly that I might betray his trust. But not badly enough to spend the rest of my life in prison. "From what I can tell, Moretti formed an under-the-radar exploratory committee to run for Congress about seven or eight months ago. Obviously, he can't go public until Congressman Peterson dies or finally retires. So this committee is probably lining up money men and women behind the scenes right away. The 52nd district is highly competitive. Both parties will pour a lot of money into it."

"So you think Moretti is using the arrests that weren't arrests to set up a quid pro quo down the line when it comes time to grease the campaign skids?"

"Exactly."

"Call me again when this all shakes out." If I'm not in prison. "I'll give you your quote."

Ben Townsend was still out there on my horizon. But I needed to make another stop first.

CHAPTER FORTY-FOUR

RAIN PELTED MY windshield. A rare occurrence in San Diego. When it does rain, however, it's usually the big drop variety, not a Seattle steady mist. The windshield wipers fumpped back and forth turning the rain into a cellophane smear. The rain lifted the months-old grease and soot off the road into a hydroplaning oil slick. The first rain always brought a slew of fender-benders and one or two jackknifed big rigs on San Diego freeways.

I had to park about a quarter mile away from my destination in La Jolla. The rain torpedoing down from the granite sky soaked through my ball cap, jeans, and shoes. My leather bomber jacket protected my torso, but when your feet are wet it doesn't matter what's dry.

Miranda had been replaced by a more conventional assistant behind the receptionist desk in Alan Rankin's office. Stunningly beautiful, but I doubted her kick could raise a welt.

"I need to see Rankin."

"Do you have an appointment?" She looked at me as if I'd just crawled out of a dumpster and asked for a table at George's At The Cove. "He's very busy."

"Tell him Rick Cahill's here. He'll see me."

She picked up the phone handset. I walked toward the door of Rankin's office.

"Sir!"

I smiled back at her and opened the door.

Rankin looked up from papers on his desk, startled. "Cahill? Shut the damn door."

I did as told, then walked over and planted my soaked rear end down onto one of his thousand-dollar leather chairs. "We need to talk."

"We talk when I say we do and where I say we do." His face flashed crimson and a vein I'd never seen before pulsed from his forehead. "You can't just saunter into my office whenever you like!"

"Why? Afraid Moretti will catch wind of it and change his mind?"

"What?" He gave me courtroom-feigned ignorance, but some of the red sucked out of his face. "I don't know what you're talking about."

"Yes, you do. Moretti is shaking you down for your money and your influence when he runs for Congress after Congressman Peterson dies. That is, unless you have Moretti killed first."

"What are you trying to pull? I don't know what you're talking about."

"I get it." I stood up and took off my jacket, revealing my holstered gun, and pulled up my t-shirt with one hand. "You'll have to take my word on my legs and crotch. I'm not letting you fondle me this time. No wire. You can cut the bullshit now. You know exactly what I'm talking about."

"Moretti tell you this?"

"No. I figured it out for myself and I'm keeping it to myself." I sat back down. "I don't care about your agreement. I just need to know what evidence Moretti has about Randall Eddington and if he plans on making an arrest soon."

Rankin gave me a poker stare, but I knew his mind was whirling behind it. What could he tell me that would push me in the direction he wanted me to go? I had to try to glean the truth from whatever lie he told me.

"They found DNA on Eddington's phone which was recovered at Windansea Beach. It just came back from the lab. Unknown donor."

My stomach sank, but I held my own poker face. Unknown would exonerate me if my DNA was already in the system. But it wasn't. I'd been arrested for my wife's murder ten years ago in Santa Barbara, but SBPD never took my DNA. I spent a week in jail and then the charges were dropped. The DNA might be mine and Moretti could show up at my house with a warrant for a sample any day.

But something didn't ring true.

"He couldn't have gotten DNA back in a week. The state lab is always backlogged for months. He's lying to you."

"He didn't send it to the state lab. He sent it to a private laboratory. Remember, as of now, Moretti is still running this investigation on his own in the dark."

"When did he tell you about the DNA?"

"The other day when he invaded this office." He double blinked.

A lie. This was new information. Moretti must have just told him. Why? To keep Rankin in line and let him know I was going down soon and he could either go down with me or play ball and stay out of jail?

"What's his next move?"

"You're smart. You've already figured that out."

"He'll get a warrant for my DNA." I said it to myself as much as Rankin.

"There's still time." Rankin leaned across the desk and his eyes went dark reptilian. "Not much of it, but enough for you to put an end to this whole matter. Once he requests a warrant from a judge, it's out in the open and out of your hands."

"I'm not going to murder anybody, Rankin. Not for me and, certainly, not for you."

"Worst case for me, Rick, is I stay in Moretti's pocket. Worst case for you is you go to prison for life. Hell, maybe even get the death penalty." He smiled. A raptor showing his teeth before an attack. "And you'll have a hard time implicating me if I'm in Moretti's pocket. I'll have his protection."

The timing may have been a lie, but the information was the truth. Moretti was coming for me. It was no longer just a possibility out in the ether. It was as certain as death. The only question was when and the only answer was soon.

"If you're safe either way, why do you want Moretti dead?"

"You take me for a handkerchief, Rick? Only removed from the owner's pocket to wipe up snot?" Cold-blooded reptilian glint returned to his eyes. "Congressman Peterson's condition has taken a turn for the worse. You'd better hope he lives long enough for you to figure things out."

The wind spit rain in my face on the way back to my car. A chill that wrapped around my bones and bled into my muscles. I wouldn't feel the rain in prison. I wouldn't feel anything, except a clock ticking away on time unspent until I died.

Moretti's clock was ticking. As soon as Congressman Peterson died, the alarm would go off and Moretti would arrest me for a splashy send-off to his congressional campaign.

CHAPTER FORTY-FIVE

THE RAIN SHROUDED the day in limited visibility, but did nothing to camouflage my drive home. If someone was sitting still in the wet gray watching my house, they'd see me before I saw them when I pulled into my garage. The fact that I didn't spot anyone didn't mean they weren't there. I didn't use my backdoor approach from the street below this time because the rain slicked the hill I'd have to climb, and I couldn't afford to tumble down it on my exit and muddy the clothes I needed to wear to get into Ben Townsend's office.

I grabbed the garage door remote from the windshield visor, got out of the car, and exited the garage without closing the door. I went around the right side of my house, pulled the Magnum from the shoulder holster, then finally closed the garage door with the remote. I went through the gate into the backyard and tucked up against the side of the house as I made my way along the wall. The rain hushed the day and sucked all other sound into it. I peeked through the kitchen window between the curtains. No movement or changing shadows through the sliver of a view into my house.

If there was someone inside and they heard the garage door close, they'd be focused on the door leading into the house from the garage. I gently slid the key into the lock of the kitchen door, took a deep breath, then whipped open the door and rushed in low, gun out. Nobody pointed a gun back. Downstairs was empty. I carefully climbed the stairs and cleared the three bedrooms upstairs. Empty again. If anyone had staked out my house, they didn't do it from the inside.

Safe. For now. And Midnight was safe next door.

I went back into the master bedroom, pulled off my soaked clothing, and changed into slacks, dress shirt, and a tie. I put the shoulder holster and gun back on and covered them with the only sports coat I owned. I went into the bathroom and looked in the mirror. It said cop, except for the black eyes. I opened the women's concealer I'd bought on the way home and smoothed it into the skin under my eyes. It hid the yellow-purple tint remaining from Miranda's kick to my nose. Luckily, I'd found a shade that matched my skin tone. Irish pale, but they called it something else. I studied my artwork in the mirror after the last dab. Passable. Nothing I could do about my swollen nose.

Maybe my convincer would help. I went into my bedroom and opened my sock drawer and rummaged around until I found a small, hand-carved wooden box.

The box contained the only thing my father had left me in his will. Really, the only thing of value that remained after he'd drunk himself to death. But the item in the box didn't hold any intrinsic value. I opened the box and took out the La Jolla Police Department badge. The value of any badge was only as worthy as the person wearing it. My father had left the badge worthless. Tainted. Such that he wasn't allowed to keep it when he'd been forced into a pensionless early retirement. The only reason my father had possession of the badge was because his ex-partner used up some favors to get it and give it back to him.

I'd only kept the badge because my father had wanted me to have it after he died. He hadn't much cared about what I had or did during the last years of his life. The badge meant nothing to me and thus remained in a box in a drawer. But death wishes had to be honored. I kept the badge.

I hadn't kept my own badge when I'd been pushed off the force in Santa Barbara. I didn't even know if keeping it had been an option. I didn't care. I didn't want it. And I didn't have an ex-partner who cared enough to use up favors to get it back for me.

I slid the badge onto my belt just inside the hip. Now it might have just enough value to get me to pass for a cop.

I put a clean pair of jeans, some underwear, socks, and a couple t-shirts into a duffel bag and took them, along with my bomber jacket, downstairs and placed them into the trunk of the car. I got into the car and slid back out onto the street under the curtain of rain.

CHAPTER FORTY-SIX

THE ADDRESS MOIRA MacFarlane had given me for the Lexus stolen license plate was the home of One America Plaza. At the center of San Diego's business district, the building vibed power and
wealth. The tallest building in San Diego, it stands as a giant obelisk
that screws into the sky with a Phillips-head roof and towers over
the waterfront on West Broadway in downtown San Diego. The
upper floors have million-dollar views of San Diego Harbor and
the USS *Midway* aircraft carrier, one of America's largest maritime
museums.

I parked in the underground garage where the license plate had
been stolen from a Lexus and put on the Range Rover that held
the men who tried to kill me two nights ago. Ben Townsend and
Phoenix Holdings were on the fourth floor, but I had another stop
to make first.

I took the elevator up to the twenty-seventh of the building's
thirty-four floors. Transcope Technologies, the business that
reported the stolen plate, took up the entire floor. A suit-and-tie-
dressed male receptionist wearing a wireless headset smiled at me as
I approached the counter.

Time to skirt, if not completely break, the law.

"Hi, I'm Detective Broderick Macdonald." Partial truth. Those
were the first two names on my California private investigator's license. "I need to talk to the person who reported the license plate
stolen from a Lexus yesterday."

I was 90 percent certain the SDPD had more important crimes to follow up on than a stolen license plate. Hopefully, I was the first "cop" to contact Transcope since the plate had been reported stolen.

I opened the right side of my sports coat to reveal the La Jolla Police Department badge clipped to my belt. Just long enough for the receptionist to get a glimpse of the badge, but not long enough to notice it wasn't a detective's badge or from San Diego PD, which would have jurisdiction on the case. But the gesture alone was enough to get me a year in the county jail and a fine.

"I haven't heard anything about a stolen license plate. Oh, dear." He grimaced like it was a major crime. "If you'll give me the name of the person who called the police, I'll let them know you're here."

"This is kind of embarrassing and why I'm here." I shrugged my shoulders, tilted my head, and raised my eyebrows. "The dispatcher who took the call is new, I guess, and she didn't write down the caller's name." I pulled out a notepad and looked at it. "I know the car was a 2016 Lexus IS. Maybe if you could just let me talk to the person in charge of purchasing your company cars, we could get this squared away."

"Sure." He punched in a few numbers on a phone keyboard. "Mr. Duerson, there's a detective from the San Diego Police Department here investigating a stolen license plate from one of our cars."

"Mr. Duerson will be right with you, Detective," the receptionist said. "You can have a seat while you wait, if you like."

I eschewed a seat and went over to a large window that looked out on the waterfront below. Even grayed by the rain, the beauty of the waterfront cut through. Waterfront Park's dark blue wading pool sprayed by white water from fountains, the turquoise kids play areas, and the Star of India, the world's oldest sailing ship, with its white sails docked just beyond the park.

"Detective?" The receptionist's voice pulled me away from the view. "This is Mr. Duerson."

I turned to see a man in a gray silk suit that put my sports coat to shame. He looked to be my age and wore black horned-rim glasses. He put out a hand. "Adam Duerson. CFO. How can I help you, Detective?"

"Broderick Macdonald." I shook his hand. "I'm following up on the reported theft of a license plate from a late model Lexus IS owned by your company."

"Really? I don't believe we've had a license plate stolen off one of our cars." Duerson scratched his head. "Let's go into my office and we can discuss this there."

He led me down a hall of glass offices full of people busy at work. Duerson's office was in the back right corner of the floor and had a panoramic view of the waterfront and the business district.

"Have a seat." He sat behind his immaculate glass desk and pointed to a chair opposite him. "Now you say someone here reported a stolen license plate off a Lexus?"

"Yes." I read him the license plate number from the Range Rover that had come back from SDPD as stolen from a Lexus.

He punched something into his computer. "Hmm. We just leased a fleet of Lexus ISs from a car dealer a week ago, but the system shows that we have yet to receive the license plates. Who reported the license plate stolen?"

"That's the problem. The dispatcher didn't take down their name." I shook my head. "Who usually sends you the plates when you lease a fleet? The DMV or the dealer?"

"The dealer. At least for all the leases I've purchased. I don't think anyone here could have reported the license plate stolen since we're still waiting for them. Maybe the dealer received them from the DMV already and somehow had one stolen."

"What's the name of the dealer who leased you these Lexuses?"

"Elite Automobiles." He frowned. "I've leased cars from them for the past four or five years. Have they done something wrong?"

Bingo. Elite Automobiles was one of Phoenix Holdings' companies.

"Probably not, but we have to connect all the dots." I gave him a weary "just doing my job" smile. "I've never heard of Elite Automobiles. Do they come highly recommended? Why did you choose them?"

"One of the tenants here at One America suggested them to me. We've never had a problem before."

"And what's the name of the person who recommended them?"

"Ben Townsend from Phoenix Holdings."

CHAPTER FORTY-SEVEN

Phoenix Holdings didn't have the aerie view Transcope Technologies had up on the twenty-seventh floor. It was on the fourth floor facing away from the waterfront with a view of the old YMCA building across from it.

A woman in her late twenties sitting behind the reception desk greeted me when I walked into the office. Straight blond hair, casual blouse showing just enough cleavage to let your mind wander. Naturally beautiful. She looked like she'd just come from a shower after a morning surf as opposed to have just gotten her hair done at a salon.

"I'm Susan. How can I help you?"

"I'm Detective Macdonald and I need to speak to Benjamin Townsend." I gave her the badge burlesque I'd given the kid upstairs.

"And what police department are you with?" Intelligent, slightly suspicious eyes. Like she'd seen that the badge said La Jolla Police on it and not San Diego or she'd greeted enough cops at the office to be suspicious.

"La Jolla."

"Isn't this out of your jurisdiction, Detective?"

"Are you Mr. Townsend's lawyer?" I set my jaw hard. "Tell Mr. Townsend I need to speak to him about one of his holdings or we can do this the hard way."

Her not playing ball was the hard way for me. I didn't have any other ways. Any harder and she'd call LJPD to check up on me.

Susan played tough for another few seconds then picked up a phone and pushed the number one on the keypad. A big operation. "Benny, there's some cop here to see you."

Susan and I played a game of blink while I waited for Townsend. He arrived in the lobby before either of us could declare victory. He wore a Hawaiian shirt under a blue sport coat over tan slacks. The used car salesman must have still been in his blood.

"Detective?" Townsend said it like the title was in question.

"Macdonald." I held out my hand.

"Ben Townsend." He shook my hand like we were old friends even though his eyes said the opposite. "We can talk in my office."

I'd come to One America Plaza without a real plan. I thought I'd flash my badge at Townsend, get him alone, and try to make him nervous. After the info I'd gotten about the license plate at Transcope, I had a real agenda.

Turns out I didn't need one. He hadn't even asked why I was there. A "cop" shows up and is immediately shuttled down the hall out of sight. Most people don't know what to do when the police arrive. They're surprised and almost always want to know what the police could possibly want with them right away. Not Townsend. He seemed to have a plan already in place. Like the police showing up was just a normal part of doing business.

I followed Townsend down a short hall into his office. The only other rooms in the hallway were a bathroom and a small break room. As best I could tell, Phoenix Holdings consisted of Townsend and my pal Susan at reception. Townsend's office walls were covered with pictures of him playing golf, captaining a speedboat, toasting with champagne, and lounging shirtless on beaches. Chest hair and a gold chain were prominent in every shot except for a couple of him playing golf in cold weather conditions.

This guy liked his leisure time and he liked gold chains and chest hair. The last two figured prominently above an opened shirt button today.

Townsend sat down behind a cluttered desk, and I caught him eyeballing me like I was a counterfeit twenty. "Now, what can I do for you, Detective?"

He still said detective like he didn't mean it. He might have recognized me from my years-ago TV and newspaper time. Even if he had, I was all in on the bluff and wouldn't show my cards until I got a peek at his hole card.

I picked up a box of files from a wooden chair, dropped them onto the floor, and sat down. "I'm following up on a reported theft of a license plate from a car that Elite Automobiles leased to Transcope Technologies right here at One America Plaza."

"I'd like to help but I don't have anything to do with Elite Automobiles."

"So, you're not familiar with the company?"

Townsend held my eyes and didn't blink. Maybe debating whether to tell a big lie or a small one. "They're one of Phoenix Holdings' properties, but I don't know anything about car leases or license plates. I can give you the name of the sales manager and you can talk to him, if you like."

I didn't buy his plea of ignorance about car leases. He'd recommended Elite to the CFO of Transcope. Almost all of Phoenix Holdings' holdings were similar to industries Townsend had worked in on his way up. Townsend didn't look to me to be a numbers guy, unless the word "racket" was attached to them. He'd somehow convinced his Swiss partner to purchase businesses he knew something about. From what FBI Special Agent Mallon told me, Phoenix Holdings owned unusual properties for a holding company. I bet Townsend not only knew about the fleet lease to Transcope, but his fingerprints were all over it.

"Sure, you can give me the sales manager's information before I leave." I pushed my feet against the side of the desk and leaned back in the chair. "But you spent a few years selling cars, so you must know a little bit about leases. Especially ones in which cars were leased to a company right here at One America Plaza per your recommendation."

"Of course, I'll do anything I can to increase the value of one of our holdings." Cool. Friendly voice, but eyes still hard. "I recommend Elite to anyone looking for a luxury vehicle."

"So you know a little more about Elite Automobiles than you were willing to admit a minute ago."

Townsend smiled. "Semantics. I don't know the specifics of the lease, but I know of it."

"Okay. I'll try to ask more specific questions, so we can avoid semantical misunderstandings." I smiled back. "Do you know why license plate number 6ZUB573 that is registered to a Lexus IS Elite Automobiles leased to Transcope Technologies was on a late model Range Rover, also owned by Elite, that was involved in a shooting two nights ago?"

I'd guessed on the ownership of the Range Rover, but struck home. Townsend's face lost some of its tan, and he blinked three or four times.

"A shooting? I don't know anything about a shooting."

I believed him, but the realization that whatever he was involved in was now dangerous and out of his control spread across his face.

"How do you explain that the license plate that was stolen was never sent to Transcope, yet someone claiming to work for them reported it stolen?"

"I told you, I don't know anything about license plates." He still looked stunned. "Was anyone injured in the shooting? Have you made any arrests?"

Arrests. Not arrest. I never mentioned that there was more than one person. Townsend knew the people who attacked me. Would my father's badge be enough to make him tell me who they were?

"That's confidential, but I can tell you that Phoenix Holdings has been implicated and I suggest you tell me all you know about the men in the Range Rover before they try to pin this thing on you."

"What thing? I don't know what you're talking about."

"Yes, you do, and unless you speak up now, you'll be arrested as an accessory to murder."

All in on the bluff.

"Murder? Who was murdered?" All the color drained from his face leaving it the same shade as the tuft of chest hair poking out of his shirt.

"James Colton."

"Who's that? I've never heard of him." He looked sincere.

Townsend was dirty. Of that, I was certain. If I'd had a real badge of my own and a handful of warrants, I'd find out just how deep the dirt ran in Phoenix Holdings. But I also believed he didn't know anything about the violent side of the people operating behind the cover of Phoenix Holdings.

"He was a sergeant on La Jolla PD."

"A cop? When was he murdered?"

"A few months ago."

Townsend put me back under the magnifying glass. "I remember now. It was in the news . . . I thought he committed suicide."

"The case has been reopened."

"You came in here asking me about a stolen license plate in San Diego and now you're talking about a murder in La Jolla." He smiled and the color returned to his face. My bluff was about to be called. "Do you work for San Diego PD or La Jolla? Or are you really a cop at all?"

"La Jolla." I stood up and did a quick coat flip to give him a glimpse of my father's tarnished badge. "The cases are connected."

I sat back down and gave him my best cop stone face.

"I'd like to get a better look at that badge, Detective. One can't be too careful."

I pulled the badge off my belt and flipped it onto his desk as I would a poker hand of cards that had just been called. Townsend picked up the badge, looked at it, and then gave me a smile with a lot of teeth.

"This isn't even a gold shield. You're not a detective and probably not even a cop."

"I'm in training." I reached across the desk and grabbed the badge from Townsend's hand. "And I'm just a bit ahead of the police, but I'm helping them get caught up."

"Really? By impersonating a police officer? That can get you time in county jail." He stood up and his chest and the hair on it puffed out. He put his hand over his office phone. "Maybe I'll give your friends at LJPD a call and let them know what you're up to. You think you can come in to my office and run a con on me? Who the hell do you think you are?"

"I'm someone who'll rip the lid off this con you're running if you call the police. Go ahead."

"Get the hell out of my office." He thrust a hand at the door.

"I'm the best shot you've got at not going to jail, Townsend." I stayed seated. "I think it just dawned on you how dangerous the men you're hooked up with are. Who do you think is going to be made the fall guy? Or worse. Let's go talk to the police. Get out in front of this thing while you still can before your partners see you as the weak link."

"Wait a second." Townsend pointed a bouncing finger at me. "I know who you are. It's been itching at me ever since you walked in here with your phony badge. You're the son of a bitch ex-cop who murdered his wife up in Santa Barbara and got away with it. Something Cahill. What the hell kind of scam you trying to pull now?"

"I conned your assistant with the badge to get in here, but everything else is the truth." I zeroed in on Townsend's eyes to make sure he saw the truth in mine. "The men you're connected with are killers. They killed James Colton and they tried to kill me. Give me their names and get out from under this thing. If you testify, I'm sure you won't do time."

"You're the only killer I've ever met, Cahill. Now get the hell out of my office."

"Give me their names, Townsend."

"Get out!" He picked up the phone receiver and pressed a number on the keypad. "Sue, get building security up here."

I stood up and walked to the door. I'd gotten as much as I could and, hopefully, rattled him enough to call his partners after I left. No need to get into a scuffle with security. Townsend might not call the cops on me for impersonating one of them, but security sure as hell would.

A picture on the wall next to the door caught my eye. I wasn't sure why until I stopped and examined it. The photo featured Townsend, shirtless, at the helm of a boat. He looked to be maybe twenty years younger when the color of the black hair on his head was natural. But he hadn't been what caught my eye. It was a woman sitting behind him. A teenager really. Dark hair, deep tan, very fit. Twenty years later, she hadn't changed much. I pulled the picture off the wall and turned back to Townsend.

"Your daughter?" I pointed at the teenager in the photo.

"You threatening my family, you son of a bitch?" He rushed around the desk and grabbed at the picture. I pushed him off.

"Nope. Just figuring out who all the players are." I took one last look at the twenty-year-old photo of Alyssa Bates, wife of Jim Colton's old SEAL buddy, Kyle Bates. I handed the photo back to Townsend. "The police are a lot smarter than I am, Townsend. Once they get a whiff of this, they'll connect the dots a lot faster than I did."

I walked out of his office and left the door open.

CHAPTER FORTY-EIGHT

BRIANNE STOOD NEXT to the elevator down the hall from Phoenix Holdings' office. Dressed in slacks and a jacket, she could pass for an executive about to take the elevator down to the parking garage. I'd called her from my car on the way over to One America Plaza and told her to Google a photo of Benjamin Charles Townsend and then get down to the building and stake out the elevator on the fourth floor.

"Townsend is probably on the phone right now calling the men in the Range Rover or he'll soon be heading down to his car."

"So, he believed you were a police detective?"

"No, but I found another way to rattle him." The elevator door opened, and I pressed my hand against it. "Give him twenty minutes to head for his car. If he's coming, I think it will be much sooner. If not, at least we tried."

I kissed her on the forehead and went inside the elevator.

I sat in my car for twenty minutes. No call from Brianne, yet. I'd give her another five minutes and then shut it down. Maybe I hadn't rattled Townsend as deeply as I thought. Maybe I was wrong about everything.

My phone rang, pulling me out of my head or the other end of me. I'd been right after all. I turned on the ignition and checked my phone expecting to see Brianne's name on the screen. Wrong. Unknown. I turned off the ignition and answered the phone.

"Gloomy day, huh, Cahill?"

The phone number was unknown, but the voice wasn't.

"You can skip the weather report, Moretti." My voice held steady, but my gut didn't. It wrapped around itself and squeezed. "I'm in the middle of something."

"You certainly are." A chuckle. "I'm hoping you can help me with a missing persons case that's looking like a homicide."

"Just get to it, Moretti." My time was running out.

"I'd like to eliminate you as a suspect in the Randall Eddington investigation. DNA has been recovered from Randall's phone. All I need is a buccal swab from you, and if your DNA doesn't match the sample, we can just about eliminate you."

"Don't you need a warrant for that?" Congressman Peterson must not have made it through the day.

"Only if you're uncooperative. I thought you'd jump at the chance to clear yourself."

"That DNA came back pretty fast. That has to be a record for the state lab."

"Yes, things are moving quickly now, Cahill. Why don't you head down to the station now and ask for me when you get here?"

"Shouldn't I ask for Detective Denton? She's your top homicide dick, isn't she?"

"You get my personal touch."

"Like I said, I'm in the middle of something. Maybe tomorrow."

"You're running out of tomorrows, Cahill."

"Why were you so quick to rule Jim Colton's death a suicide, Moretti?" He was right about my tomorrows. Offense was the only defense if I hoped to have many more. Moretti was no longer on my suspect list for Jim Colton's murder, but I still had some leverage. "He was about to blow the whistle on your asset forfeiture scam and suddenly ended up dead. You work on getting your warrant, and I'll work with the California Department of Justice on getting Colton's death investigated. Along with any surrounding corruption."

"You're playing a dangerous game, Cahill." His voice pushed through clenched teeth. "The ME made the determination of death by suicide, not me."

"With your rubber stamp. You wanted the Colton investigation closed down as soon as possible. A homicide investigation might uncover everybody's dirty little secrets, so you made sure it was tagged a suicide."

"The wife just wants the insurance money. She's playing you like one of her guitars. You're a fool, Cahill."

"I'm just following the evidence, Moretti. Something you should have done in the first place."

"I am following the evidence, Cahill. And we both know where it leads." His voice a hoarse snarl. "Don't leave town."

Click.

I'd stunned Moretti with the asset forfeiture and Department of Justice remarks, but he was still coming for me. I couldn't stop him unless I chose Alan Rankin's way out. Rankin wouldn't kill Moretti on his own or pay someone else to do it. He wanted distance and a fall guy. That was me. And even if the police never suspected me, Rankin would have leverage over me. A crowbar to wield whenever he wanted me to perform some black bag operation.

Moretti lived and he was coming. I needed to find another way out of prison besides murder. But unless I dealt with the men trying to kill me, I might already be in a coffin when Moretti knocked on my door with an arrest warrant.

CHAPTER FORTY-NINE

I CHECKED THE clock in the dash. It had been a half hour since I left Townsend's office. My ploy hadn't worked and I was running out of options. I didn't have enough to take to the Department of Justice. Rankin wouldn't let Miranda back up my story on Ski Mask and his partner. DOJ would just send me back to LJPD. The head of the local FBI office had already turned me down. FBI Agent Mallon was too scared of his own shadow to take it up the chain.

I called Brianne to tell her to shut it down.

"Hello, Mr. Taylor." A hint of excitement in her voice. "I'll be back in your office in twenty minutes."

The game was still on. Townsend must have finally taken the elevator, with Brianne in it, down to the parking garage. I hung up and waited for her call. Twenty seconds later my phone rang. "He's driving a new red Cadillac ATS-V Coupe. He just backed out of his space on the first floor."

"Great job. Go back to the hotel." I sped out of my parking space toward the exit sign. I was a floor lower than Townsend and needed to catch up or I'd lose him.

"I just got to my car. We can do a two-team tail."

"This isn't a game or a movie, Brianne. It could be dangerous." A car backed out of a space in front of me forcing me to hit my brakes. I'd just made the first floor but couldn't see the exit. "Shit!"

"What?"

"Some jerk just cut me off. I may not catch Townsend."

"That's okay. He just left the garage, but I'm twenty yards behind him. He's turning right on Kettner."

"How'd you get ahead of me?"

"I lucked into a spot on the first floor when I got here." A hint of glee tickled her voice. She enjoyed the chase. "He just turned right on A Street."

"Okay." I finally made it to the exit. "Stay with him until I catch up."

"Will do, partner." A pause. I thought she'd put the phone down. Then, "He did something a little strange before he left the garage."

"What?"

"He was carrying two briefcases when he left the office and he put one in the trunk of his car and the other in the front seat with him."

"Hmm. That is strange. Just stay on him, and we'll figure out the rest later."

The rain still pounded down and it pulled the night down on top of it. Late fall and the rain blurred the night's visibility. Rush-hour traffic and the wet turned the streets into slo-mo brake light conga lines. Without Brianne, I would have lost Townsend. But I still had a hunch about where he'd end up.

"He just got onto 5 South."

"Okay. When he takes 75 to get onto the Coronado Bridge, you can turn around and head back to the hotel. I know where he's going." To see Kyle Bates, his son-in-law, who was connected with Oak Rollins and probably Dwight McCafferty. At least one of whom, maybe all, had killed Jim and tried to kill me.

"He got onto the 94, going east."

"You sure? Maybe you lost him and are following the wrong car."

"Not a chance. I've been behind him the whole way. Here's his license plate number." She gave it to me.

Maybe Townsend was headed home, wherever that was, and he'd meet Dwight McCafferty and Odell Rollins there. I finally made it onto 5 South. The traffic was worse going north. I hit the 94 in a couple minutes.

"Brianne, you still on him?"

"Yes. He just passed the 15. Still heading east."

I weaved through traffic and sped up. The exit to Interstate 15 whizzed by. The further east I went, the more the traffic thinned. I saw running lights ahead that could belong to a '65 Mustang. It got off on 125 North.

"He just took 125 North."

"I think I'm right behind you. Put on your right turn signal." The right turn signal flashed on the car ahead of me. "Got you. How far ahead is Townsend?"

"About a hundred yards in my lane."

"Okay. Get in the right lane and I'll pass you." Brianne moved over and I passed her. I think I saw her wave. "That him straight ahead?"

"Yes."

"Okay. I got it from here. You can head back to the hotel. Thanks. You saved my butt."

"I think we should tag-team him. We can switch places every so often so he doesn't see the same headlight configuration behind him all the time."

She was right, but who knows where Townsend was leading us? Maybe he knew we were tailing him. I'd already walked into one ambush in the last week. I didn't want to lead Brianne into another one. But my gut told me that Townsend was running scared and had no idea we were following.

"Okay. If he doesn't get off the freeway soon, I'll move over and you can take the lead. We'll change every few minutes." I'd send her back to the hotel as soon as Townsend finally made it to his destination. "Get behind me."

"Roger. Red Stallion out." She didn't hang up.

"Stay on the line."

"Roger."

Townsend took 8 East and the minutes ran by. I'd been on his tail for over half an hour. I feared he might be driving to Phoenix or until his car ran out of gas. My Mustang started the day with a full gas tank, but I was sure the Caddy had a much bigger tank. Brianne and I stayed a hundred yards or so behind Townsend and took turns taking the lead.

About forty-five minutes into the tail, Townsend exited the freeway onto Pine Valley Road. I followed but gave him a lot of slack. He drove through the tiny town of Pine Valley in the foothills of the Laguna Mountains.

There weren't many cars on the road, so I faded back as far as I dared without losing him. Townsend went all the way through the town, which wasn't very far, and turned up a residential street. I made the turn well after Townsend and thought I'd lost him. The street forked, and I didn't see any taillights. I gambled and went to the right up a winding hill. Brianne's headlights disappeared behind me. Homes sat scattered on huge lots along the hill, shadows on the unlit street. I rounded a bend and got a glimpse of red. Taillights.

The car turned into a twisting driveway up to a house on a butte overlooking the valley below. I killed my lights, pulled over, and picked up my phone.

"Brianne, I got him from here. Go back to the hotel and call me when you get there."

"You sure?"

"Yes. Go."

I checked the rearview mirror for headlights, ready to dive down if any approached, figuring they could be Townsend's partners. Clear. I looked up the driveway and could just see the top of the car and caught a flash of white, then darkness. Must have been the dome light of the Caddy turning on when Townsend opened the door and then off when he closed it.

The rain tattooed the roof and windshield of my car and squeezed down the night's visibility. I could barely see the top of the front door and windows along the front of the darkened house. The front door opened into darkness, and I caught the top of someone's head entering. The door closed. An orange spark lit up the front window then vanished, like Townsend had lit a cigarette.

I waited for lights to go on in the house.

Dark.

I looked for the glow of a lit cigarette through the window.

Dark.

A minute. Two. Three.

Dark.

Headlights behind me. I slid my torso down to the right onto the empty passenger seat. A hole exploded through the windshield. My left arm burned. The headlights passed. Another hole punch through the windshield thudded into the seat above me. Gunshots! Silenced.

I shoved the passenger seat release back, dove into the feet well below the seat, my legs stretched along the console tangled against the stick shift. The night now silent except for the sound of my heart and my pistoning breath. Warm blood trickled down my left arm, fright sweat rolled off my body.

The gunshots hadn't come from the car that passed by me. At least not the first gunshot. It had been fired through the windshield while the car's headlights were still behind me. My guess was both shots came from the area around the house up on the hill where Townsend had parked his car and gone inside. I hadn't taken Townsend for a killer, but maybe I'd been wrong.

Then I remembered the silencer on the muzzle of the rifle sticking out of the Range Rover the other night in the hospital parking lot. Townsend wasn't alone. At least one of his partners was up on the hill with a rifle.

Whoever it was, McCafferty, Bates, or Rollins, hadn't been able to kill me in two tries. I couldn't give him a third. Maybe one of them had been in the car that passed by me. Locked and loaded and coming to finish the job. I'd left my Smith & Wesson in the trunk with the shotgun, fearing a vehicle stop by a nervous cop who might see the bulge in my jacket and go SWAT on me before I could show him my conceal permit.

A decision to save my life now might cost me it.

If I stayed in the car, I'd die. A fish floating belly up in a barrel. I had to get to the trunk.

I angled my arm up across the dashboard below the view of the windshield and pulled the keys from the ignition. The dome light. If it went on when I opened the door, I'd die. I reached up around my head, opened the glove compartment, and searched blindly for the Maglite flashlight I kept there with my good hand. Got it. I held the black Maglite by the bulb end and slowly raised it toward the switch for the dome light. Shit. I stopped. I couldn't remember if the "Off" side of the toggle switch was to the left or right. I held my breath and pushed the handle of the flashlight onto the left side of the toggle switch. The night stayed black.

Maybe I'd survive.

I started to count to three in my head.

The passenger door whipped open on two.

Oak Rollins, gun in hand, stared in at me eye to eye.

CHAPTER FIFTY

I LUNGED FOR the gun, but Rollins grabbed my arm with his free hand.

"Crawl out." He yanked me out of the car from a squatting position, as easily as a father pulling his son from a car seat. He held the gun at his side in his other hand. "Stay low. Somebody's got a rifle up there."

Rollins was saving my life, not ending it. At least for now.

I knelt on the wet sidewalk, head below the bottom of the car's window, and grabbed my left bicep with my right hand. Blood leaked through a slash in my coat, matched by one in my arm. I clamped my hand across the wound. It hurt, but I'd live. The bullet had nicked me, leaving behind a gouge but no lead.

Rollins leaned his back against the side of the car, head low. Dressed all in black. Black watch cap on his head.

"You hit?" Rollins looked at my hand clamped to my arm.

The sky pelted down rain on us.

"Flesh wound." I looked down the street beyond the Mustang. "What happened to the car that came up behind me?"

"Up the hill around the bend."

"Those headlights saved my life. Where the hell did you come from?" Rollins had appeared out of rain-soaked midair. How? Why? Maybe he and the shooter were on the same team. Maybe this was some sort of ploy to get close to me and find out what I knew. Maybe waterboarding hadn't been enough.

"That's not important now. If you live through the night, I'll tell you." Rollins rolled down onto his stomach and army crawled to the back of the Mustang. He peeked around it up at the house on the hill. He crawled back to me. "Stay here. I'm going to take out the shooter."

"Are you out of your damn mind?" I grabbed his arm. "He's on higher ground with a rifle. Plus, there may be more than one up there. Townsend's in there and I doubt he's the one with the rifle."

"One shooter. It's not Townsend."

"How can you be so sure?"

"Townsend's not a killer. The man with the rifle is."

"Who is he? Bates?"

"I'm not sure," Rollins said.

I didn't believe him.

"I'll call the police." I pulled my phone from my pocket. "Let them get SWAT up here and take down the shooter."

"This is an unincorporated area. It will take the San Diego Sheriff's Department a half hour to get out here."

"What's the rush? We lay low and live."

"He won't wait. He'll either come for you now or run and kill you later. We gotta move." Rollins crawled back to the rear of the Mustang. "He may already be on his way down here."

"I've got a gun in the trunk."

"How's the arm?"

"Workable."

"You open that trunk and the inside light will go on and you'll be dead before you get the gun out." Rollins pulled something out of his pocket. "We need a diversion. I'm going thirty yards down the hill. Keep your eyes on the front door of the house without popping your head up as a target. As soon as you see a beam of light hit the front door, pop the trunk, and get the weapon out."

Rollins crawled over the sidewalk to the brush that ate up most of the distance between the large plots of land. The nearest house was a hundred yards down the street. Lights blared from the gate opening to the driveway, but their illumination only spread thirty or so feet. The area around my car and the distance between it and the house on the hill was charred black and the rain's sizzle was the only sound.

I strained my eyes to follow Rollins through the brush, but lost him after ten or fifteen seconds. Good. If I couldn't see him, hopefully the shooter couldn't either. I crawled to the back of the Mustang and peeked around it up at the house. If the shooter had a night-vision scope, I was presenting a target. I changed my angle every ten seconds.

A circle of light hit the front door. I pushed the trunk button on the key fob. The trunk popped open. I bolted up and grabbed the shoulder holster with the .357 and dove back behind the car.

The night stayed silent except for the hush of rain.

I gripped the Smith & Wesson in my right hand and crawled to the front of the Mustang. I peeked around the front tire up at the house. The oval of light still shined on the front door. I strained to hear footsteps through the rain, anything. Nothing but the constant hiss.

"Cahill." Rollins's voice.

He jogged toward me on the sidewalk. Upright. An easy target if the shooter was still up there.

"Get down!"

"He's gone. He either thought he killed you or didn't want to risk sticking around to make sure."

"How can you be so certain?" I felt the Magnum heavy and ready in my hand.

"He didn't shoot at the light and you're still alive."

"What about Townsend?"

"Let's go up and take a look."

"What if he has a gun?"

"We'll have two."

Rollins's certainty bothered me. He knew much more than he was willing to tell me. Because he knew the players? Or because he was on their team? My life might depend on me finding out.

I grabbed some duct tape from a duffel bag I kept in the Mustang's trunk and wrapped some around the gash in my jacket. The blood flow had eased to a gentle weep. The pressure from the tape over the wound stung me into hyper-alert.

I followed Rollins down the hill to retrieve his flashlight, which he'd mounted on some rocks and aimed at the door to the house that Townsend had entered. He crossed the street and headed up the long winding driveway up to the house. Rollins was sure we were out of danger. I wasn't. So I walked directly behind him up the hill, keeping his massive body between me and the house the whole way up. I figured it'd take a pretty damn big caliber bullet to go through him to get to me.

I didn't feel the least bit cowardly, either.

Rollins finally took some precautions when we crested the hill. We each circled around the back and looked through windows into bedrooms. Too dark to see anything, but no human shadows. Rollins checked a sliding glass door to the back patio. Unlocked. Instead of entering, he shined his flashlight around the patio and then beyond it. A lawn, then a ring of trees stretched out behind the house sloping up a hill to a wooden fence at least fifty yards away.

"That's the way the shooter left." Rollins pinned the light on the faraway fence. "He probably had a vehicle parked up on the hill back there where the street loops around."

Rollins opened the slider, and we both entered. I kept my gun in front of me. Rollins kept his holstered. He led us through a kitchen in a darkened house with the flashlight. We made it to the foyer. Ben Townsend lay next to the front door. The left corner of his head was missing above staring eyes. The blood around his head had already stopped pooling.

The orange flash when he entered the house. A silenced pistol. Someone knew Townsend was coming and had laid in wait. Because I'd rattled him and he made a phone call.

I fought back bile rising in my throat. I'd seen death before. Too much of it. People I'd killed. People I cared about who died because of mistakes I made. People in between. Still, I never got used to it.

Thank God.

Rollins stared down at Townsend. Darkness hid his expression, but he didn't seem surprised. He didn't seem anything. Except that he'd grown used to the sight of death.

"Who killed him, Rollins?"

"I don't know."

"Yes, you do."

"Let's clear the house then get out of here, Cahill."

He started down the hallway. I followed. We checked each bedroom, using only the beam from his flashlight. They'd all been ransacked. Dresser drawers hanging open and clothing strewn on the floor.

"Staged," Rollins said after the last. "This was murder made to look like a burglary gone wrong."

That was the first thing he'd said that I believed 100 percent. We went back to the kitchen where we'd entered through the sliding glass door.

"Let's get the hell out of here."

"You touch anything?" He grabbed a dishtowel off the counter.

"No." I hoped none of my blood had eased out under the duct tape and dropped onto the floor.

We exited through the sliding glass door and Rollins wiped down the handle with the dishtowel. We hustled back to my car and got in out of the rain. I pulled out my cell phone.

"What are you doing?"

"Calling the police."

"What will that accomplish?"

"Oh, I don't know, catch whoever killed Townsend. We both know Bates is involved. We'll bring the whole damn thing down."

"Maybe. Maybe not. Bates will have an alibi and Townsend's death will be ruled a murder in the commission of a robbery. You'll have put yourself in the area after you followed Townsend here fifty miles from his office and some of the blood from your wound probably dripped onto the floor. You really want to take your chances with the police?"

"What's your game, Rollins?" I held my gun in my lap. Rollins's was in a holster on his hip.

"No game. Just practicality. What if we let this thing play out? See if Bates or his wife report her father missing."

"I don't like it. We'll be withholding information in a murder investigation."

"There is no investigation, yet." Rollins's face blending in with the night. I could only make out the whites of his eyes. They told me nothing. "Let's talk to Brianne and see what she thinks before you call the police. I'll meet you back at the hotel."

"What hotel?"

"The Marriott in La Jolla. I followed Brianne there from her house after I had to give you a nap."

"Why?"

"Because I know they'll come for her. When they do, I'll be waiting."

"You've been using her as bait?"

"No. I've been protecting her. Just like I promised Jim I would."

CHAPTER FIFTY-ONE

WATER SPLASHED INSIDE the car through the two bullet holes in the windshield. The wipers made it worse with steady deposits. Every third wipe water would splash off my chin. Spiderwebs spiraled out from the holes about an inch or so. I could see where I was going, even at sixty-five miles per hour in the rain, but I doubted any cop who saw my car would believe me.

I called Brianne.

"Are you still out in Pine Valley?" She sounded worried. "Did Townsend meet with anyone?"

"I'm on my way back to the hotel. Are you there yet?"

"No. I'll probably be there in ten minutes. Is everything okay?"

"Yes. How well do you know Oak Rollins?"

"I used to know him pretty well. We used to go on vacations with him and his wife. Why?"

"I need your help with something. I should be back to the hotel in about forty minutes. Take George out for a walk or a drive and wait for me to call you and tell you when to go back to the room. Don't go back to the room unless I call. Okay?"

"Rick, what's going on? I don't like this."

"Oak's coming to the hotel. I need to know if you think he's telling the truth or lying."

"What? Why?"

"I just need your help. I'll explain later."

"Why can't I be there when he gets there?"

"I'm not sure it will be safe."

"What's going on, Rick? What happened out at Pine Valley?"

"I ran into Oak. He might be on our side. He might be on theirs. I need your help to find out."

* * *

I'd dropped Rollins at his SUV, which had been parked down the street from the death house. He said he had to stop by his hotel before he met me at the Marriott. Maybe to meet with his partners, McCafferty and Bates. Or, maybe I was just paranoid. I'd earned it. Either way, I'd be ready when one or all of them knocked on the hotel room door.

I parked in the hotel garage and pulled something from a duffel bag in the trunk and then hustled up to the room.

George greeted me at the door when I went inside. He was supposed to be with Brianne on a walk.

"Brianne?" I stuck my head in the bathroom. "Brianne?" Empty.

I walked over to the window and pulled the curtains back to check the patio. She wasn't there either. My stomach turned over and sweat beaded my hairline. I called her phone. It went straight to voicemail.

"It's Rick." My mouth sucked dry. The words came out raw. "Where are you? Call me."

I scanned the room for anything missing or out of place. I didn't know what I expected to see, but nothing stuck out. Brianne hadn't made it back to the hotel. At least not up to the room.

Rollins had admitted he'd tailed Brianne. Claimed he'd done it to protect her.

She wasn't protected now.

Had Bates and Dwight McCafferty gotten to her? Kidnapped her or worse? If they had, Rollins might be the only hope I had of getting Brianne back alive if he wasn't with them right now. But why was I still alive? Rollins could have killed me when he opened the door to my car and plenty of times after that.

Something didn't fit.

I called Brianne again. Voicemail. I paced the room. George matched my strides. He looked worried, too. I called the number I had for Bates. Voicemail. Did he have Brianne? Is he on the way over with Rollins to finish the job? All I could do now was wait.

Twenty minutes later, someone double knocked on the door. George barked and shot his hackles. I quieted him and put him in the bathroom, then checked the peephole.

Rollins.

I studied Rollins through the hole. Blank face. Calm. He looked down both ends of the hall. He didn't look to be ready for battle.

I was.

Rollins held a small duffel bag in his right hand. The other hand, relaxed at his side. I opened the door and stood back from it to let Rollins's massive frame pass by me. I let the door close and stuck the barrel of my Smith & Wesson in the middle of his back. He stopped mid-stride.

"Drop the bag."

He did. I kicked it against the wall. I kept the barrel against his back but switched to my left hand. Pain shot along the gouge in my arm all the way up my neck. I reached under Rollins's jacket and pulled the Glock 9mm from the holster on his hip and shoved it into the waistline of my pants behind my back. I patted Rollins down. Clean.

"Hands behind your back. Kneel down."

"You're making a mistake, Cahill."

"Not my first." I pushed the barrel harder into his back. "Kneel down."

He knelt. I pulled a pair of steel handcuffs from my coat pocket that I'd grabbed from the duffel bag in the trunk of my car. If a cop ever went through the bag on a vehicle stop, I'd go downtown for having a rape kit. There were also Flex-Cuffs and duct tape in the bag along with a lock pick set and a black jack. I feared Rollins might be able to snap the plastic cuffs, so he got steel. No duct tape or black jack. I needed him conscious and talking.

"Raise your arms up behind you, wrists together."

"You're wasting time with this bullshit, Cahill. I'm on your side."

"Hands or it ends here."

He raised his hands as high as his bulky muscles would allow. I snapped a cuff around his right wrist and cinched it down, then clasped the other around his left. I walked around him and pointed the gun at his forehead.

"Where's Brianne?"

"I thought she was supposed to be here." He swiveled his head as if looking for her. "How long has she been gone?"

"I don't know." I couldn't read him for sincere or lying. "Why didn't you follow her when she left Pine Valley? I thought you were supposed to be protecting her."

"I knew there had to be a reason the two of you followed Townsend out to Bates's cabin in Pine Valley. I figured I needed to stick with you if I was going to find the men who killed Jacks."

"But you were supposed to keep Brianne safe. Or so you say."

"The best way to do that is to put them all down." His mouth pulled tight.

"Who are *they*?"

"Bates and McCafferty."

"How does Dwight McCafferty fit in? He wasn't even in your unit."

"Dwight?" Rollins grimaced. "I'm talking about Doug. Dwight's got nothing to do with this."

"Doug's dead." I lowered the gun as if on reflex.

"He's alive." Rollins shifted from one knee to another.

"I thought he was killed overseas." I pulled my head back. "That's the one thing in this whole mess that everyone agrees on."

Rollins stood up. I aimed the gun at his head.

"Kneel back down."

"You've pulled a gun on me twice, and I've sat on my hands and allowed you to handcuff me—"

"Allowed me?"

"Yes." He nodded his head and sneered at me. "Allowed you so you could ask your questions and we could then get on with nailing the traitors who killed Jacks. I've had four surgeries on my knees. I need to be mobile tonight. If I keep kneeling, that's not going to happen. I'm not kneeling anymore. I'm going to sit in that damn chair and answer your questions." He nodded to the chair by the desk.

"You're going to stand right where you are. Why the hell should I believe anything you say?"

"Look inside that bag." He nodded to the duffel bag he'd brought with him.

"What's in it?"

"A first aid kit in case you're stupid enough not to go to a doctor."

"Sit in the chair."

He did as told and I walked over to the duffel and picked it up, never taking my eyes or the gun off Rollins. I sat down and unzipped the bag with my left hand. I didn't look inside, but dumped the contents onto the floor and quickly glanced at it. Gauze, scissors, bandages, surgical tape, Q-tips, suture needle and thread, tweezers, hemostat, Neosporin, saline solution, Betadine, and a vial of pills.

"Take these cuffs off and let me patch you up."

"I asked you yesterday if you'd been a medic in the SEALs and you said no."

"I wasn't. Bates was our corpsman, but I learned how to sew a few stitches. Hell, everybody in the unit knew how to do that."

Bates. Fentanyl. The silent partner who stuck a needle in my neck from behind at the auto body shop.

The first aid kit could have been a ploy to gain my trust. But to what effect? He'd already had a chance to kill me. If he and the others were playing a game, I couldn't figure out what it was.

"Stand up." I walked over to Rollins's chair. He stood. "Turn around."

He did as told and I unlocked the handcuffs and removed them from his wrists. He turned to face me and held out his hand. "The Glock."

If I gave Rollins the gun, I'd be all in. I trusted him or I didn't. I wanted to because I couldn't do what needed to be done without him. If I was wrong, I'd be dead and so would Brianne.

I put my gun in my coat pocket, reached behind my back, and took the Glock 9mm from my waistband.

All in.

I put the gun in Rollins's hand. He slowly closed his fingers around the handle, then snapped the gun up under my chin.

CHAPTER FIFTY-TWO

ROLLINS PUSHED HIS face close to mine. Coal eyes squeezed down. I let out a long breath. I wasn't ready to die, but at that moment, I wasn't afraid to either. My instincts, wrong too often, had finally gotten me killed.

"You've pulled a gun on me twice, Cahill. Nobody else has ever done it once and lived. Do it again and you better pull the trigger." Rollins yanked the gun down and placed it in his holster. "Let's go into the bathroom and patch up that arm."

My instincts were making a comeback.

He scooped up the first aid supplies into the duffel. I let George out of the bathroom, and Rollins followed me inside. He used the scissors to cut through the duct tape that I'd used as a tourniquet/bandage on my arm in Pine Valley. I took off the sports coat and shirt and looked at the wound. A four-inch gouge traced along the outside of my left bicep. A thin black scab had started to form, but the wound still wept small tears of blood. The gouge ended six inches from the scar on my shoulder.

"How'd you get the other one?" Rollins nodded at my shoulder and grabbed a washcloth from the nook under the sink.

"In a shootout with a bad man."

"When you were a cop?"

"After."

"What happened?"

"I got the last shot."

Rollins gently grabbed my arm and looked at the wound. "It's not too late to go to the emergency room."

"We don't have time."

"Then I have to open the wound and clean it to make sure it doesn't become infected."

"Okay."

"Lean over the sink." Rollins dampened a washcloth and then poured some Betadine on it. "This is going to hurt."

I held my arm over the sink. "I'm ready."

Rollins held my arm with his left hand and then scrubbed the wound with the washcloth with his right. Pain seared along my arm all the way into my stomach. Sweat poured off my forehead and down my sides. I gritted my teeth and groaned. Blood seeped from the wound.

Rollins then pulled the plastic bottle of saline solution out of the duffel bag. He poured the solution along the wound until the bottle was empty. Then he squirted the Betadine into the wound, up and down. He padded the wound with a dry towel and then applied Neosporin with a Q-tip.

"Now comes the painful part." He handed me another wash-cloth. "You might want to bite down on this."

I could take pain, but cleaning the wound hadn't exactly been a soothing massage.

Rollins clasped the small curved suture needle with the hemostat and pulled it from its thin plastic case. He looked at me and raised his eyebrows. "Ready?"

I let go a breath. "Go."

Rollins stuck the needle into my skin behind the wound. I bit the washcloth. Sweat boiled out of my forehead. He twisted his wrist and the needle poked through my skin on the other side of the wound. More endurable pain. He tied off a knot, then three or four more. He clipped off the ends of the suture. One stitch done. How many more to close the wound?

Stab. Twist. Knot. Ten stitches? Fifteen? I lost count. I just wanted Rollins to stop. When he finally did, the pain burned on afterward. Smoke from a still burning fire. Rollins put a couple large bandages over the wound and then taped gauze around it.

Then he popped open a small vial of pills, took one out, and held his hand up to me. "Percocet. This will help with the residual pain."

I shook my head. "I need to be alert until this is over." I wished it was already over. "Tell me how a dead man came back to life."

CHAPTER FIFTY-THREE

"McCafferty and Bates were hunting a sniper and looking for weapons caches in Haditha during Operation Red Bull in 2006. McCafferty opened a cabinet and an IED blew off his head and upper chest. The only identifiers were his dog tags and his uniform." Rollins blew out a loud breath. "At least that's the official story."

"Where were you and Colton? I thought you were all in the same unit."

"We had rotated out stateside for some R and R."

"Was anyone else hurt?"

"No." Rollins shook his head. "The two of them went off on their own one night following up on intel from a known source. According to Bates, they were given the location of the home belonging to an Al-Qaeda sniper who'd been responsible for three US KIAs in the area. Bates claimed that he and Dirt had just cleared the last room of the house without finding the sniper or any weapons caches. Bates exited the house, not realizing Dirt was still inside until he heard the explosion."

"That doesn't sound like standard operating procedure."

"Not much they did that night was, but McCafferty was an action junkie with a hero complex. He was always trying to get the rest of us to break protocol or ROE."

"ROE?"

"Rules of Engagement. We had our hands tied behind our

backs half the time over there." Rollins stared at me, but his eyes looked by me into the past. "Sometimes it felt like the brass cared more about political correctness than Americans coming home in body bags. But we were SEALs. Trained to follow orders and that's what we did. Dirt was a little different. Blurred the lines when he could. Jacks always worried about Dirt when we rotated out for R and R. Thought he'd do something reckless and pull Bates along with him while we were gone. Seemed like he was right."

"Did Bates leave the military after that?"

"Not until two years later when his hitch was up."

"So, a year after McCafferty supposedly is blown up and a year before Bates retires from the military, his father-in-law, a guy who never held the same job for more than a couple years, starts up a multimillion-dollar international holding company with a Swiss banker. Coincidence?"

"It all fits." Rollins stood up and paced back and forth across the room like a caged big cat. "There was an investigation into missing gold bullion confiscated from Iraqi warlords about six months before McCafferty's death. Nothing ever came of it and the missing gold was kept under wraps. The brass kept a lid on anything that could be perceived as negative to the war effort."

"So you think McCafferty and Bates stole the gold and then faked McCafferty's death so he could escape Iraq with the gold and launder it through the holding company that Bates's father-in-law suddenly founded?"

"Yep."

"How much gold went missing?" I asked.

"I don't know the exact amount, but it was rumored to be about two million dollars."

"Hmm." I stroked the stubble on my chin. "McCafferty and Bates would have to cut in Townsend and probably the Swiss banker plus pay for McCafferty's plastic surgery and new identity. Two million is a lot of money to me, but split four ways the reward doesn't fit the risk."

"Like I said, I don't know the exact total. It could have been more."

Wiedergeboren Holding Company had been capitalized with six million dollars. Three million of which came from Ben Townsend, Kyle Bates's father in-law, who, according to Special Agent Mallon only had a couple hundred thousand in assets of his own when he cofounded Wiedergeboren. That left him eight hundred thousand short if he used the stolen gold and his own money.

The money didn't add up, but not much did in this case.

"What were you looking for at the Colton house yesterday?" Speaking of things that didn't add up.

"His cell phone."

"Why?"

"He left me a message the day he died that he had a picture of the man he'd seen at the harbor and was now sure that it was McCafferty. I wanted to get a look at the man who I had to track down."

"Why didn't Jim email or text it to you back in August?"

"He wasn't big on technology and hadn't spent much time on how to use all the properties of his cell phone. He didn't know how to attach images. He was a bit of a dinosaur in a lot of ways." Rollins's eyes went soft. "In a lot of good ways. I didn't have the chance to call him back the day he died and walk him through it."

"If you never saw the photo, what convinced you that the man Colton saw is McCafferty?"

"The way Dirt died always bothered me. He could be reckless in his personal life and in his decision making, but never on a mission.

He was as skilled a SEAL as I ever knew, and Bates would never lose track of his partner. Certainly, not if they weren't under fire."

"Why didn't you tell me any of this when I questioned you in Lake Tahoe or the other day at Colton's house?"

"Team guys take care of our own, and I wasn't a hundred percent sure Jim had been murdered when you questioned me at the casino. I was ninety-nine percent certain when Bates called me out of the blue a couple days after you came to Tahoe and invited me to come down for a reunion out at the cabin."

"The cabin? You mean the house out in Pine Valley where Townsend was murdered tonight?"

"Yeah. He'd had a reunion out there once before about three years ago. Jacks and I couldn't figure out at the time how Bates could afford two mortgages. Now I know."

"Why did his invite make you suspicious?"

"He and I were never really friends. In fact, we didn't like each other. Jacks was the connection between us. The only time I'd ever see Bates off the battlefield was back in the States when someone would have a party for the whole unit. After he invited me down here, I checked with a couple of guys from our unit and none of them had been invited. The suspicions that had been percolating in my head went to a full boil. Bates had killed Jacks and invited me down to kill me and tie up the last loose end."

"Does Bates know you're already here?"

"No. I told him I was flying in tomorrow. Even bought a plane ticket in case he checked up on me. I rented a car and left my truck in the casino parking lot."

"That's smart, but won't matter if Bates or McCafferty saw you in Pine Valley tonight."

"There was only one man up there and I'm sure it was Dirt. I think that's where he's been hiding out since he's been down here.

There were empty cans of beans and chili in the kitchen trash, and the bed in one of the guest rooms had hospital corners. None of the other beds in the house did. Someone who'd spent time in the military had been staying there."

"You're pretty damn good at this. Brianne should have hired you instead of me."

"I knew what to look for."

"How can you be sure that he didn't see you?"

"I can't be one hundred percent. Dirt was there to kill Townsend. Probably because you shook him up and he must have called Bates. Bates probably told him to meet him out at the cabin. Dirt and Bates couldn't trust him anymore so he had to go. I don't think they expected you to follow Townsend. Dirt might have thought he killed you with the first shot, but couldn't risk checking to make sure in case he didn't and you called the police or someone saw you get shot."

"I can't wait any longer." I whipped out my phone and called Kyle Bates. The call went to voicemail. I spoke after the beep went off. "Bates? You and Doug McCafferty let Brianne call me right now or I go to the police, the FBI, the state attorney general, and the media."

I hung up.

"What the hell was that?" Rollins's eyes went wide.

"Brianne should be here. She won't answer her phone. I think they grabbed her. Either they want her as leverage to get to me or she's already..." I looked at Rollins but couldn't say the word. "I had to make sure they know I'm still alive. That they still need Brianne as leverage."

"Give me until tomorrow before you call the police."

"I'm not calling the police unless I somehow get Brianne back without getting her or me killed."

"You're not going to get her back." Rollins's eyes softened like they did when he thought of Jacks Colton. "She's already dead or she will be if you try to play hero and exchange yourself for her."

"I can't let her die."

My phone rang. I looked at the screen. Brianne. "Hello?"

"Here she is." Ski Mask's voice. My insides turned over.

"Rick?" Brianne. Scared. My guts flipped again.

"Are you okay?"

"Yes." Voice bloated with emotion. "They're going to kill me if you don't do what they say."

"Stay strong. I'm coming for you."

"Good to know." The man's voice again. He laughed. The devil's cackle. "You have what we want, we have what you want. We'll make an exchange when the time is right. Sit still for now. Call this phone at exactly ten o'clock. A minute late, she dies."

The line went dead.

"Where and when?" Rollins asked.

"And what?"

"What do you mean?"

"They think I have something that they want to trade Brianne for." I pushed my good hand through my hair.

"What the hell is it?"

"I don't know, but I'm not going to let them know that."

"What time is the meet?"

"I don't know yet." I walked toward the bathroom.

"Where are you going?"

"For a shave first. Then Coronado." I pointed to the duffel. "The surgical tape still in there?"

"Yes. Why the hell do you need to shave now?"

I went into the bathroom and shaved where I needed to.

CHAPTER FIFTY-FOUR

THE SKY, ALL bled out of rain, pushed a gray haze against the black night. Rollins and I drove separately to Coronado. Rollins agreed with me that Bates would want to set up the meet on terrain he knew. Coronado.

I parked two houses down from Bates's house and Rollins pulled in behind me. Streetlights sat far apart leaving pockets of dark between some homes. I sat in my car in a pocket. Rollins tapped on the passenger side window wearing a ski mask. My heart double tapped and I flashed back to the night in the auto body shop. I settled and scanned the street. A scattering of parked cars, but no humans. No cars in the Bates driveway or on the curb out front. A porch light lit up the front of the house.

I got out of my car and opened the trunk. Rollins stood next to me. His Glock 9mm in his hand. I grabbed a ski mask from my duffel in the trunk and put it on. Only my eyes and mouth were exposed to the cool November air. I unracked the Mossberg 590A1 Pump-Action Tactical shotgun from the rack on the inside of the trunk lid, then gently closed the trunk.

It was 9:05 p.m. Thirty-five minutes since the call on Brianne's phone. Still fifty-five minutes until I had to make the call. If we were lucky, Bates was in his house with Brianne and McCafferty, waiting to head out to wherever they planned to walk me into an ambush. I hadn't been lucky yet on this case. Unless you counted only taking a flesh wound instead of a bullet to the head. I wasn't sure whether or not I wanted my luck to change.

Rollins edged up next to a hedge in the shadows of Bates's neighbor. I gave him fifteen feet, then followed behind. Rollins dashed across the neighbor's driveway lit by a spotlight then disappeared back into the darkness next to Bates's backyard fence. I caught up to him.

Rollins nodded and opened the gate into the backyard. A dark shadow sprang out past his legs and dashed into the neighbor's bushes. My heart double clutched and instinct zeroed the Mossberg on the bushes until my brain caught up with my eyes and I realized it was just a cat. I knew Bates didn't have a dog. Didn't know about the cat.

Rollins stepped through the gate. I followed. The cat kick-started my heart and it stayed redlined as I followed Rollins. I'd gone up against killers in the dark before, but they hadn't been trained by our government to kill silently and quickly.

The backyard was dark. Grass under our feet, we crept along the side of the house until we hit a wooden deck. A wood-framed glass door connected the deck to the house. Diffused light from deep in the house bled through the glass.

Rollins stopped at the door, looked through the glass, then tried the knob. Locked. He stepped back, took a shooters stance, and scanned the yard. I knelt in front of the door and looked inside. The kitchen, dark except for light coming from another room. I took out my lock pick set and went to work. A few tweaks with the rack and tension bar and I had the door open in less than a minute. No alarm went off. At least not one we could hear. No noise at all. No conversation. No TV. Not even the hum of a refrigerator.

I stepped back and Rollins advanced through the door. He swept the Glock along the left side of the room. I pushed in behind him and traced the Mossberg along the right. Kitchen, clear. Living room, clear. We slowly, silently, worked our way down the hall and checked the rest of the house. All clear.

Our gambit hadn't worked. The adrenaline slowly backed off from life or death down to full ready. We searched the house, looking for some residue of Brianne or a clue to where she and her captors were. Nothing. Except in the quiet, still air, I felt more than smelled the scent of Brianne. A gossamer trace or just my imagination, but I knew she'd been in the house tonight. I had to get to her before the killers ended her life or all I'd have left of her was the memory of a scent I couldn't smell.

We exited the house the way we entered and retreated to our cars. I drove down the street a half dozen houses in the opposite direction I thought Bates would exit the main drag and parked. Rollins parked his rented SUV opposite me on the other side of the street. I spied the street and waited until it was time to make the call.

A couple cars pulled into driveways and homeowners entered their houses. No sign of Bates and the other killer, McCafferty.

I stared at my phone from nine fifty-five until ten o'clock. The longest five minutes of my life. I tapped Brianne's number at the same time a one and three zeros appeared on the screen.

The phone rang four times. No answer. My mouth sand-papered dry by the fifth ring.

The call connected, but no one spoke.

"Let me talk to Brianne." I tried to stay calm, but my voice, tight in my throat, betrayed me.

"Right on time. You're being a good little soldier, Rick." The same devil voice.

"Put Brianne on right now or I go to the police."

"We both know you're not going to the police, Rick. Not with the life-changing wealth you stumbled across."

Silence. Finally, "Rick. Thank God!" Brittle.

"Stay strong, Brianne. I'm coming for you."

"They're going to—"

"How about a steak, Rick?" The devil.

"Let's get this over with. I give you what you want, you give me Brianne. That's the deal."

"I decide what the deal is." Silence to let his command of the situation sink in. "Back to your old haunts. The phone in Muldoon's Steak House is going to ring at exactly ten thirty. Anybody but you answers, she dies."

Click.

I peeled out down Bates's street, slammed a left, and sped up toward Orange Avenue. Muldoon's was about twenty miles away up in La Jolla. Twenty-seven minutes to go. Traffic should be limited this time of night. I could make it in time. If nothing got in my way.

My phone rang. Rollins. I picked up.

"They're running me. I have to make it to Muldoon's Steak House at 1250 Prospect Street in La Jolla by ten thirty. I used to work there. They have music in the bar tonight. There will be too many people to make an exchange there." I made a right onto Orange Avenue. "They're going to call the restaurant, and I have to answer. They think I found some money or something valuable and they're expecting me to bring it."

"Maybe they had something stashed at the house in Pine Valley and McCafferty fled without it."

"Or maybe Townsend brought something up to the house. Brianne followed him from his office to his car in the parking garage. She said he had two briefcases and he put one in the trunk and the other in the front seat with him."

"That must be it. They think you took whatever was in the other briefcase."

"Whatever it was in exchange for Brianne."

"Maybe, but don't rule out them killing you on sight. They may be luring you to a familiar place so you feel safe and shoot you as soon as you get out of your car."

"What about whatever was in the briefcase?"

"They grab it while you bleed out. Don't get out of the car until I can give you cover."

"I don't think that's a good idea. I think they're running me to take the time to get set up at the real drop location." I turned right onto Fourth Street and headed toward the massive bent horseshoe bridge that connected Coronado to San Diego. "Maybe there's a lookout in La Jolla to see if I bring the cops or anyone else."

"That would mean there's a third man. They will need at least two people at the drop. One high up with a sniper rifle, one on the ground to make the fake exchange."

I thought about the echoed door slam at the auto body shop and the quick getaway from the hospital parking garage. A third man? Had he always been there outside the periphery? Within reach, but out of sight?

"Who could the third person be? Someone from your old unit?"

"I don't know. I don't think so. Bates and Dirt were as tight as anyone in the unit. I don't see them letting anyone else in on the scam. Must be someone else. Someone on the money end who came in later."

The Coronado Bridge rose up out of the water, banking softly to the left as it climbed to its two-hundred-foot summit. The water dark and dangerous below. The skyline lit up and welcoming off to the left. The twisting span of steel and cement hovering in between.

The gateway to paradise. And all the shadows hidden beneath.

Rollins hung in my rearview mirror as I exited the bridge onto Interstate 5 North. I checked the clock on the dashboard: 10:11.

Nineteen minutes. Doable. I pushed the Mustang up to seventy-five and scanned the road for cops. A pull-over now could get Brianne killed. A car chase speeding into La Jolla could do the same to me. Traffic was light. I'd make it with a couple minutes to spare.

Then I saw the brake lights on the smattering of cars up ahead and beyond them a California Highway Patrol car slowly swerving across all lanes, light bar lit up. Shit! He was slowing traffic for some obstruction ahead. Could be a quick shutdown of a couple lanes with traffic still moving. Could be a complete shut down for a jackknifed big rig. I couldn't gamble on Brianne's life.

I swerved around the slowing cars out to the far left lane and then back hard all the way to the right lane before I caught up to the CHP. I flew onto the Grand/Garnet exit and just held four wheels on the ground under the bridge on-ramp. A red light stopped me at the busy Balboa and Mission Bay Drive intersection. Rollins pulled up behind me. Seconds ticked by. A minute.

Green.

I fishtailed into the left-hand turn and had to make a decision as I approached the next light. Continue on Balboa and then onto Mission Boulevard and its stoplights or over the mountain with fewer lights but greater distance? I slid through the right turn onto Soledad Mountain Road and sped up the hill. Rollins mirrored me in the rearview. Stoplight ahead. Good visibility and no traffic. I slammed the gas instead of the brakes. I checked the time at the top of the hill next to the French American school across from the Presbyterian church.

Six minutes left.

Red light at La Jolla Scenic. I stopped, scanned traffic, then slammed the gas and ran the red onto the Nautilus extension long downhill S turn. Race-carred into the opposite lane around a dawdling SUV. Blew through the light at West Muirlands and made it to Fay Street and the high school with three minutes to go. I gunned a straight line to Prospect.

Genter cross street. Mercedes. Brakes. I snapped the wheel to the left and the world spun around me. Smoke peeled up from my tires and burnt rubber stink filled the car. My car stopped perpendicular to the road. A car horn stuck on anger blared through the night. I hit the gas and whipped the steering wheel left. More rubber. A fisted middle finger from the Mercedes in my rearview mirror disappeared behind Rollins in the SUV.

Green through Pearl. One minute. Hard right onto Prospect. Cars stopped three ways at the T intersection of Prospect and Girard. I jumped on the horn and swerved around a Beemer in the intersection.

10:30 p.m.

Muldoon's three hundred yards up on the left. Gas. I whipped a left turn in front of a braking Tesla into the valet parking spot chasing a red-coated valet onto the sidewalk. If there was a sniper out there, now was his chance. I jumped out of the car and raced across the sidewalk. No gunshots, loud or silenced. No projectiles into my body.

"What's your problem, asshole?" the valet shouted at me as I ran by.

I leapt over the stairs down eight feet onto the patio, tumbled onto the ground, tucked and rolled back up to my feet and through the door into the restaurant. A cocktail waitress held the phone to her ear at the hostess stand. I charged her and snatched the phone from her hand.

"Hello? Hello? It's Rick."

The waitress gaped at me with wild, frightened eyes that probably matched my own. She rushed into the bar.

The phone went dead. I hung it back up, whipped out my cell, and hit Brianne's number.

Ring. Another. More until voicemail stopped them.

"That was an employee who answered Muldoon's phone. I just got here. Traffic. Call back. Please!" I ended the call. And waited.

"Rick? What's going on?" A minute later, Pat the bartender marched toward me from the bar. "You scared the crap out of Jessica."

The restaurant phone rang. I grabbed it off the hook. "Hello?"

"What the hell are you doing?" Pat reached for the phone.

I pushed his arm away and held up a finger.

"You like to make things interesting, don't you, Rick?"

"I got here as soon as I could. Traffic."

"Coronado Beach. Lifeguard hut 3C in front of Hotel Del. Get there by eleven or she dies."

"I need more ti—"

Click.

I dashed out of Muldoon's with Pat's voice trailing after me. Three leaps up the twelve-step staircase and I was on the sidewalk. I ran to my car and spotted Rollins double-parked across the street with his window rolled down.

I shouted, "Back to Coronado," and jumped into my car. I keyed the ignition and saw Rollins peel away through my rearview mirror. Then a large SUV blocked the view. I waited for it to move past. It didn't. I honked the horn. The SUV didn't move. I leapt out of the car and bounded to the SUV. The passenger side window rolled down and the valet who called me an asshole smiled at me from behind the wheel.

"Move this fucking thing now!"

"You almost killed me and parked illegally in the valet spot. The cops are on the way."

I flung open my coat so the kid could see the handle of my Smith & Wesson in my shoulder holster. "Move the fucking car!"

The SUV sped out of the way. I jumped back into my car, slammed it in reverse, and whipped a turn, out of the parking space, almost hitting an Escalade on the other side of the street. I caught red at the light onto Torrey Pines Road. 10:36 p.m. Twenty-four minutes left.

Green. I burned down the four-laner and out the back door of La Jolla onto I-5 South.

10:38 p.m.

My phone rang a couple minutes later. Rollins.

"Where are you? I never saw you get onto the freeway."

"I'll catch up." I told him the when and where for the exchange.

"McCafferty's going to be somewhere up high. He's the better shot."

"Hotel Del Coronado has a tall turret on top of the Grand Ballroom on the left side that overlooks the beach."

"I went there a couple times when I was stationed at The Center in Coronado. I remember the turret. It has a kind of bird's nest look out on top, right?"

"Yes."

"That's where McCafferty will be. He'll have a view of the street to see if the police are coming and he'll have a view of you on the beach through his crosshairs. Wait until I take him out before you walk onto the beach. I'll back you up, and we'll get that son of a bitch Bates."

"We don't have time. I'll be lucky to make the beach in time as it is. They won't try to kill me until after the exchange."

"You're taking too big a chance."

"I can't risk being late." I checked the clock as I sped down I-5 past Mission Bay. 10:41 p.m. I pushed it up to eighty miles per hour. "They'll kill Brianne."

"They're going to kill her anyway if she isn't already dead. And then they'll kill you, too."

"This is the only shot we've got. If we call the police, they'll kill Brianne when the cops show."

"I don't want the police. I'll take care of this myself. You can walk now. And you probably should."

"I can't."

"I don't get you, Cahill. You're not too smart, but you don't seem stupid. Why are you risking your life for someone you just met? You couldn't have fallen in love that fast."

"She's my responsibility." I scanned the horizon and mirrors for cops. Clear. "Just like she's yours."

"I'm keeping a promise to a friend. This is about Jacks, not Brianne."

"Let's not fail either one of them."

We put together a plan for Coronado and ended the call. I put my phone's ringer on vibrate and prayed I'd get a vibration before I did a bullet in my head.

CHAPTER FIFTY-FIVE

I BLEW PAST the Interstate 8 merge. 10:43 p.m. Old Town exit flew by. Then Washington Street and a view of the airport and the San Diego skyline lit up beyond. Civic Center/Front Street exit then the slight drop and the rolling right-hand turn down to the 75 connection to the Coronado Bridge.

10:49 p.m.

The speed limit for the bridge was fifty. I hit it at seventy-five and slid toward the concrete divider on the climbing right-hand turn. I pulled off the gas, death-gripped the wheel, and rode it out inches from the wall. Sweat boiled out of me. My heart shotgunned in my chest. The Mustang held the road, but when I straightened out, I had to brake hard to keep from rear-ending a Toyota Prius out sightseeing. I swerved behind an Audi doing the speed limit.

10:50 p.m.

I rode the Audi's bumper until it cleared the Prius and swerved into the other lane and pushed it up to seventy-five. Both the Audi and the Toyota stood on their horns. They disappeared in my rearview mirror as I crested the summit and started the rolling right-hand turn down onto the island.

10:51 p.m.

Adrenaline pumped sweat and thumped my heart. I wouldn't make it on time. I pushed through the sharp S on 4th Street and gunned past a couple cars to catch a green light onto Orange Avenue.

10:53 p.m.

Orange Avenue hockey-sticked to Hotel Del, but stubborn lights always halted traffic. Only a few cars on the road tonight, but I caught red at the first light. A police cruiser sat diagonally to me going the other way. I waited. My stomach vacuumed in on me turning my guts into a black hole.

Green. I eased away from the light and watched the cop do the same in my rearview mirror. Red on light number two.

10:55 p.m.

No cross traffic. The cop disappeared from my view. I punched it through the light and caught green on the last. Coronado Beach didn't have a parking lot. You had to park on the streets around the hotel and walk a quarter of a mile or so to reach the beach.

I slammed into an open spot about fifty yards from the entrance into the hotel grounds. 10:58 p.m. I flew out of the car, popped the trunk, grabbed my duffel bag, and sprinted toward the hotel. A handful of couples strolled the grounds. The hotel turret, lit from below, looked like the top of a giant merry-go-round. The bird's nest on top. I glanced up as I sped below it down the hotel's walkway. No sign of a shooter. Maybe Rollins was wrong about where the sniper was hiding.

I cleared the hotel grounds and hit the beach. The rain had firmed the top layer of sand, but the sand underneath gave way with each stride. The night swallowed up more and more residual light from the hotel grounds with each stride deeper into the beach. Twenty yards in, the scythe half-moon and pinhole stars provided the only light.

Coronado Beach has a massive swath of sand before you hit the ocean. I could hear a gentle shore break but couldn't yet see the water. Or lifeguard hut C3. Or another human. I was an easy target for a sniper with an infrared scope. I hoped Rollins was back there somewhere with a bead on the man who had a bead on me.

Fifty yards. I saw shore break whitewater dance atop slick sand. Then a hulking shadow to my right. Another five strides, the shadow turned into a self-composed lifeguard stand. I pulled out my cell phone, tapped the flashlight app, and pointed it at the structure. A large "3C" was painted in black on the back of the powder blue stand.

I swung my head around. No Brianne. No Bates. No one.

I dropped the duffel bag and hunched over, hands on my hips. The adrenaline that had powered me from my car, past the hotel, and through the sand drained out of me. I gasped for breath and sweat rolled down my face. The night squeezed in on me. I pulled out my phone and checked the time.

11:01 p.m.

Late, but not by much. Bates couldn't have been waiting here a minute ago and then disappeared off the beach. Maybe this was just the second leg in a multi-leg runaround. Tire me out so I couldn't think or act quickly when my life depended on it. I punched Brianne's number on my phone. Straight to voicemail.

"You're late."

I whipped around, saw a shadow against the night twenty feet away. It stood next to a much larger mounded shadow. A sand dune.

"Where's Brianne?" My words, raw energy.

"You bring what I wanted?" Kyle Bates, still just a shadow, took a step toward me. Former Navy SEAL, present-day murderer. His arm outstretched with something in it pointed at me. Long and cylindrical. A pistol with a silencer attached to the barrel.

Bates's partner, Doug McCafferty, overlooking us from a hidden vantage spot, was cover.

Bates could handle any killing up close. If I went for my gun now, I'd end up dead and Brianne with me. If she wasn't there already. I had to rely on my wits and an ex-Navy SEAL, who up until a couple hours ago I thought was an enemy, somewhere out there in the dark.

"Where's Brianne?"

"She's here." The shadow nodded toward the sand dune.

"I need to see her."

Another nod. Another shadow emerged from behind the dune. Arms together in front. Bates kept the gun on me, but grabbed the shadow with his free hand. He took a couple steps toward me, and I could make him out.

And Brianne.

Her hands were cuffed together in front of her in plastic restraints. Duct tape covered her mouth. Her face was mostly shadow, but I could still see the whites of her eyes. Desperate.

Anger pushed inside me.

"Let her go and you'll get what you want." I spit the words out jagged between my teeth.

Bates pulled Brianne a couple steps forward to within ten feet of me.

"Brianne, kneel down and lie on your back." He tugged her arm and she did as commanded.

The clock was running out.

"You killed Jim Colton over money?" I watched his eyes. "You fought together for God and country and killed him because of money? He saw the new McCafferty at Seaport Village one day and realized it was the old McCafferty, then figured out you two faked his death after you stole the Iraqi gold and started up the fake holding company. Couldn't you just have fled the country and let him live?"

"I'm impressed, Cahill. But not too much." He took another step toward me. "Hands behind your head and walk slowly towards me."

"I just hoped it was something more important than money." I didn't move and kept my hands at my side. "An old grudge, a woman, honor."

"Hands up!"

"Okay!" I snapped my hands into the air and took a step toward Bates.

"Stop."

I did.

"Back up. Pick up the bag, then slowly walk toward me."

I did as told.

"Stop. Drop the bag."

I stopped a yard in front of Bates and dropped the duffel bag.

"Both hands behind your head." He approached me and stuck the gun under my chin.

I froze. Cold steel against my skin. Fear pushed the anger out of my blood for the first time on the beach.

Bates patted down my jacket with his free hand. He stopped when his hand pressed against the handle of the .357 in my shoulder holster.

"Were you planning on using this?" He smiled at me as he unzipped my jacket and shoved his hand in to retrieve my gun. He put it in the waistband of his pants behind his back.

Next he felt around my waist, then bent down and searched my legs inside and out. He yanked off the KA-BAR knife I'd taped to my calf.

"You were going to stab me, too?" He stood all the way up and looked me in the eye, then threw the knife, blade first, into the sand. It stuck. "To answer your earlier question, yeah, it was just for the money, Cahill. Only the money."

"Was it worth it?"

Bates's eyes softened. He pulled the gun from under my chin, but kept it aimed at my chest.

"When Jacks figured everything out, we went over to his house to talk to him. He was sitting in his den looking at old photos of us in Iraq. Like that all still mattered. We gave him the option to come in with us. But he hadn't changed at all since the war. We didn't have a choice. He wanted us to turn everything in. To who?" Bates's voice rose. "Back to the Iraqi businessmen who were funding terrorists? The US government? So they could spend more on fucking bureaucrats and send us out to fight their wars with our hands tied behind our backs? Fuck that. We did our time. We lost friends. We killed for the bureaucrats. We just wanted our piece."

"So you and McCafferty drugged him and hung him in his garage where his son would find him."

"Story time's over." Bates put his free hand in his pants pocket and pulled out a ten-inch cylinder and snapped his wrist. The middle of the cylinder expanded out. A metal nightstick. He slammed it against my right kneecap before I could twist away. Pain exploded along my knee, and I crumbled to the ground. Brianne moaned behind the duct tape. I writhed in the sand on my back and grabbed my knee.

Bates picked up the duffel bag and unzipped it. He shoved his hand inside and shuffled it around. Finally, he turned the duffel upside down and dumped out its contents. My burglary tools fell into the sand. Bates slammed the bag onto the ground and zeroed his gun on me.

"Where are the bonds, asshole?"

"What bonds?" I honestly didn't know what he was talking about. The duffel bag was a prop. Something to make Bates think I'd brought what he wanted to give Oak Rollins time to sight him in the crosshairs of a rifle scope. Time was up. I stared at the gun and prayed that my phone would vibrate. That Oak was out there somewhere with Bates in his crosshairs.

"You really going to play dumb now?" Bates stood over me and aimed the gun at my face. "The bearer bonds. Where are they?"

"I've got them hidden away." Ignorance wouldn't keep me alive. Lying might. For a while. "You'll get them when no one's pointing a gun at anyone."

"You just killed your girlfriend."

Bates swung the gun toward Brianne. I shoved my hand down my pants and grabbed Jim Colton's derringer taped above my crotch. I thumbed the hammer back blind and yanked the gun out. I pulled the trigger. A loud snap jerked Bates to the right just as his gun fired. Bates grabbed the side of his neck and spun toward me. I cocked the hammer and fired at center mass. Bates tumbled to the ground, eyes wide.

A rifle shot echoed through the night. I whipped my head toward the bird's nest in the hotel's turret. Something dark tumbled down the lit merry-go-round roof. A body. I didn't know whose. Doug McCafferty or Oak Rollins.

I dropped the empty derringer and lunged at Bates. My knee screamed under the adrenaline. Bates lay on his back, one leg bent at a wrong angle beneath him. His gun in the sand inches from his hand. I grabbed it and pointed it at him. A damp spot grew on his chest and blood gurgled in his throat. Then stopped. His eyes stared at nothing.

"Brianne!" I tried to stand up, but fell down. I fought the urge to burrow into the sand to hide from another rifle shot fired by the wrong man.

Brianne rolled over and stood up. Her mouth covered by duct tape, she nodded and ran toward me. My phone vibrated in my pocket. I pulled it out.

"You okay?" Rollins.

"Yeah." I blew out a breath that I held for the whole night.

"Brianne?"

"She's fine."

"Bates?"

"Dead. McCafferty?"

"Dead. Let's get the hell out of here."

"I'm not sure I can walk."

"You hit?"

"No. Busted knee."

"I'm on the way."

Brianne grabbed the KA-BAR knife from the sand with her bound hands and dropped to her knees next to me. She pushed the knife toward me, her eyes frantic. I grabbed the knife and then pulled the duct tape from her mouth as gently as I could.

"Cut these off." She thrust her bound hands toward me. "We have to catch her!"

CHAPTER FIFTY-SIX

"Who?" I carefully slipped the knife between her wrists and sawed at the Flex-Cuffs.

"Alyssa." Brianne's body vibrated.

Alyssa. Wife to Kyle Bates and daughter to Ben Townsend. Was she the third person? The second car door at the auto body shop. The driver of the SUV at the hospital. The connection between Bates and McCafferty to Townsend. It made sense. I just hadn't seen it before.

"She was here?"

"Yes. She was holding me behind the sand dune. She's getting away!"

"No she won't. The police will catch up to her. We can't avoid getting them involved now."

The knife gave and Brianne's wrists flew apart, each with a plastic loop still around it. She bounced to her feet.

"We have to go after her. Can you run?" She bent down and slid her head under my arm and her arm around my back and lifted up.

"Why?" I hopped up on one leg and tried to put weight on the other. Pain shot through me and my leg buckled. I fell and Brianne went down with me. Bates's gun tumbled down into the sand. The police would be on the scene any minute. Someone must have heard the gunshots and called them in. Coronado was a small island. The police wouldn't have far to go.

"I have to stop her." Brianne stood up and held out her hand. "I need your keys."

"The police will take care of her. She's their problem now."

"Please!" More anger than sadness.

I pulled out my keys and tossed them to her. "The Mustang's fifty yards north of the hotel on the same side of the street. How do you know where she's going?"

Brianne didn't respond. She bent down and picked up Bates's gun from the sand.

"What are you doing?"

Brianne sprinted up the beach, gun in hand. She yelled over her shoulder, "I'm going to find her."

"Where?" I shouted after her.

She didn't answer and disappeared into the night. I sat crumpled in the sand, Brianne's void already hollowing out my insides.

CHAPTER FIFTY-SEVEN

ROLLINS TOOK MOST of my weight as we three-legged toward his SUV. He carried a plastic case, slightly larger than a briefcase, in his free hand. The rifle he used to kill McCafferty before McCafferty could kill me was dismantled inside the case.

We cleared the hotel grounds. The SUV stood twenty-five yards away. A siren. We crouched behind a parked car. My knee bent. I ate the pain. The siren screamed louder and rainbow lights danced in the night. A cop car pulled into the hotel's private parking lot thirty yards away. Then another. Car doors clicked open and slammed shut out of sight.

"We give ourselves up now, we've got a long night of interrogation," Rollins whispered. "You might be able to explain shooting Bates, but shooting McCafferty will be a tougher sell."

"I can't spend all night in a square white room and leave Brianne out there on her own."

Rollins hoisted me up and we shuffled to his SUV. He pulled quietly away from the curb without his lights on and U-turned away from Hotel Del Coronado.

"Where to?" Rollins asked.

"Brianne took off after Alyssa. Head over to Bates's house. Maybe she's there."

"Roger."

The scene at the beach rushed back up at me. Brianne and I would be dead if Rollins hadn't taken out Doug McCafferty.

"I didn't see McCafferty in the bird's nest when I ran through the hotel grounds," I said as I tried to arrange my leg in a comfortable position. "Why were you sure he'd be up there?"

"It's the highest vantage point in the area. It was the only place he could be, unless he was on the beach with Bates." Rollins clicked on the car lights as we did the speed limit down Orange Avenue. "I had to enter the beach way south of the hotel to stay out of his line of vision. I got a bead on McCafferty just as the gunshots went off between you and Bates."

"What if McCafferty had been on the beach?" I pulled out my phone and hit Brianne's number.

"You'd be dead."

Brianne's voicemail message sounded in my ear.

"Shit."

"What?"

"Brianne must not have her phone with her. Bates or his wife probably have it." The night's high-throttle energy evaporated and my insides ached along with my knee. "She's all alone, and I have no way of finding her."

"Police?" Rollins looked over at me. Blank face.

"You think they'll put out a BOLO for my car just on my word?"

"No. Not until they have us under the hot lights for a while and sort out the dead bodies back at the hotel and on the beach. We need to get our story straight before we talk to them." He took a deep breath and let it out. "If we talk to them at all."

We drove by Bates's house. No one home. My heart sank deeper.

We didn't speak again until we were off Coronado Island and clear of the bridge.

"Hospital?" Rollins asked.

"No. Back to the hotel. Thanks."

"Why do you think Brianne went after Alyssa by herself?"

"I don't know. She was almost crazed. Maybe they did something horrible to her and she won't let it stand."

Whatever the reason, I was scared I'd never see her again. At least, not alive.

* * *

Rollins did his hero routine and crutched me up to my room at the Marriott. George greeted us whining at the door.

"Damn. He needs to go out. He's been stuck in the room all night," I said as Rollins lowered me onto the bed.

"I'll do it." Rollins leashed up George and took him outside.

Alone, concern for Brianne swallowed me. Why had I given her my keys? So what if Alyssa got away? Did Alyssa have a gun? Probably. She wasn't at the house. Wherever she was, Brianne might be walking into a trap.

I took out my phone and willed it to ring. It did.

Rankin. My dreams never came true.

"You see the news tonight?"

12:10 a.m. The local news had been over for over a half hour. No way they could have had a story on the Coronado shootings. Even so, Rankin wouldn't have any way to know I was connected.

"No."

"Congressman Peterson died."

I didn't say anything.

"Chief Moretti is looking for one more high-profile arrest before he declares for Peterson's seat. Fight or flight, Rick."

Click.

CHAPTER FIFTY-EIGHT

GEORGE'S BARK WOKE me from my zombie sleep. Dead, but still semi-conscious, clothed on top of the bed. Rollins had returned him to the room and left around 12:30 a.m. I could hear him scratch the door, trying to get outside. 2:43 a.m. on the bedside clock. I'd been asleep maybe thirty minutes. A soft knock on the door. George barked again, then whined.

I grabbed the Smith & Wesson off the nightstand and gimped to the door in the dark. I leaned over George and looked through the peephole.

I was wrong about dreams coming true.

I whipped open the door and George beat me into Brianne's arms. Only fair. They'd been together longer. Brianne stepped around George and hugged me so hard I almost lost my balance. We kissed long enough for George to whine, then backed into the hotel room.

Brianne walked me over to the bed and we both sat down. I didn't notice until we got there that she had a canvas grocery bag hanging over her shoulder.

"What happened? Did you find her?"

"Yes." She smiled. Biggest smile I'd ever seen on her. She kissed me again.

"Well, what happened?" Something was off. Brianne was too happy. Bloodlust? "Did you call the police?"

"Rick, hear me out." She carefully pulled the canvas bag off her shoulder and set it down onto the floor. "Do you believe in karma?"

"Where's Alyssa?" The adrenaline from earlier that night reloaded. All nerves. "Did you do something to her?"

"No. Yes. Not really."

"What happened?"

"You think I killed her?" She pulled her head back, then laughed. "She fine. But this isn't about her. It's about us."

"What do you mean?" I was still worried. Brianne was almost manic. This was a side of her I'd never seen. I wasn't ready to like it, yet.

"You know better than anyone that life is unfair and hard and cruel." She held my hand. The warmth massaged my nerves. "So when it gives you a gift you have to take it, right?"

"What gift?" My head swirled, on tilt.

She leaned over, picked up the canvas bag, and hugged it against her chest. "This is our gift, Rick. This is life trying to even things out."

She flipped the bag over and emptied its contents onto the bed between us. About a dozen papers tumbled out. They were roughly the size of notebook paper. Watermarked and the color of US currency. US treasury bonds. Eleven in all.

Each had a million-dollar value listed across the top. I picked one up. My hand shook.

"They're bearer bonds. They come due on December first of this year. Three weeks from now." Excitement pitched her voice high.

"Where did you get them?" But I was pretty sure I already knew the answer.

"Alyssa had them."

"How did you find her?"

"I heard Kyle and Doug talk about them at Kyle's house after he kidnapped me. I guess Doug shot Townsend at the house in Pine Valley and took his briefcase. But it only had a few of the bonds in it. Then I remembered the other briefcase I saw Townsend put in the trunk of his car."

"How did Bates kidnap you?"

"He followed me back to the hotel from Pine Valley and pulled a gun on me in the hotel parking structure."

"How could he have done that? You left before the shooting started."

"I think he got to Pine Valley just as I turned around to head back and he recognized my car." Liquid gathered in the bottom of her eyes. "I thought you were dead. Doug said he shot you."

"So, when you took off from the beach to follow Alyssa, you really went up to Pine Valley to get the other suitcase?"

"I knew that's where she'd go."

"But you went there to get the treasury bonds."

"I went there to make sure she didn't get them."

"Well, I guess it worked."

"She still has the first suitcase." She put her arms around my neck. "But none of that matters. We can start a new life. You and me."

"That money has blood on it." I put my hands on her wrists and gently pulled her arms from around my neck. "Four people died because of it."

"Yes, and one of them was my husband."

"Who you were going to divorce."

"You can be cruel when you want to be, Rick." She stood up, face tight, and grabbed the canvas bag off the floor. She stuffed the million-dollar bonds into the bag one by one. "They killed my husband and left me and my son with nothing. I'm not going to be the good little martyr and live my life off someone else's idea of a clean conscience."

"You can live your life however you want to. I don't know anything about clean consciences." But I knew sooner or later, I'd need a high-priced lawyer. Trying to beat a murder didn't come cheaply. A million or so dollars would give me a chance.

"I'm not going to keep all of this for myself, Rick. I'm going to give some to charity. A lot. Something good can come from this. I can help people who really need it. I can help Cash and the people in my life I care about." Her face went soft and her eyes glistened an impossible blue. "I care about you, Rick."

Just like that, my life could change. Brianne's already had. In her mind, she'd washed the blood off the bearer bonds and made them clean. And justified her decision. I couldn't make that decision so easily.

And I didn't know if I could love someone who could.

CHAPTER FIFTY-NINE

I GOT OUT of the bed Brianne and I shared at seven thirty the next morning. Or later that same morning. Or the morning after the night that never ended. I'd gotten maybe two hours more of zombie sleep after Brianne's revelation. She'd slept like a baby. Was still asleep.

George followed me as I limped around the hotel room quietly collecting weapons and dirty clothes and stuffing them into my duffel bag. I got dressed into my last clean t-shirt and underwear. I pulled the jeans I'd worn last night off a pile of clothes on the floor and struggled into them. My knee yelled when I bent it, but I stayed silent. The empty shoulder holster lay on top of my bomber jacket on the floor. I placed the holster in the duffel bag and put on the jacket that now had a bullet hole in the left arm

Something didn't feel right. A piece was missing. I took off the jacket, reached back into the duffel bag, pulled out the holster, and put it on. I took the Smith & Wesson .357 out of the duffel and slipped it into the holster, then put the jacket back on. Better. I felt whole now. The threat to my life had ended last night, but I still craved the security of a firearm strapped to my body. How long would that need last?

Would I be wearing it when Police Chief Tony Moretti knocked on my door? What would I do to stay free?

I had a lot to figure out beyond even my freedom. Brianne's offer hung over me like an albatross and an angel. Enough money to ensure my freedom on a faraway island. No Randall Eddington. No Tony Moretti. Just my demons. I doubted there was enough money anywhere to chase them away. Could I live with myself for making the same decision I might never forgive Brianne for making?

I didn't have any answers. At least not the right ones, yet.

I left a note on the hotel notepad telling Brianne I'd call her later that afternoon. Maybe I'd have answers by then. Maybe even the right ones.

George tilted his head into a question when I left him behind and exited the hotel room.

The morning sky held more gray than light as I drove home. I found a local news station on the car radio and braced for what I knew I'd hear. The death of Congressman Peterson and the shootout in Coronado split time dominating the news coverage. I was a part of the news again, even if the news didn't know it yet. I couldn't stay hidden forever.

Nothing so far about Ben Townsend in Pine Valley. Sooner or later, someone would notice the car hadn't moved in the driveway for a while and investigate and then call the police when they whiffed the stink of death.

Kyle Bates had been identified and the reporter was already calling him an ex-Navy SEAL. It wouldn't take long for the police to find out that he and recently deceased LJPD Sergeant Jim Colton had served together and were friends. Maybe the exposure would force Moretti to open up Colton's suicide investigation. Maybe Brianne would finally get that insurance money, now that she didn't need it.

I called Rollins and we coordinated our story about Coronado. We'd only use it if the cops came calling. No volunteering. I already had one supposed murder hanging over my head. I wasn't going to show up at Coronado PD and try to explain one more.

I made it home and parked in my driveway, left the duffel bag in the car, and limp-hustled next door to pick up Midnight. He jumped up and licked me in the face and bounced all the way home. I felt the same way. I just couldn't bounce. We went inside and I turned to shut the door and saw a car pull up across the street. A Crown Victoria. Local law enforcement choice for plain-wrap cop cars. I braced for Moretti to get out of the car and feared my reunion with Midnight might be the last I'd ever have.

The car door opened, but it wasn't Moretti who got out. FBI Special Agent Blanton. Special Agent in Charge Richmond's toady who escorted Brianne and me into the SAC's office. He wore an overcoat over his blue suit like a real live G-Man. I'd expected law enforcement, just not the FBI. I held the door ajar and waited for him to approach.

"Mr. Cahill." Blanton gave me his bureaucratic smile.

Midnight stuck his head between me and the door and growled. Low. Menacing. Determined.

"Quiet." I snapped my finger and he quieted, but his hackles stayed at full spike.

"Oh, dear." Blanton inched back away from the door. "I was wondering if I could have a moment of your time."

"Can this wait, Agent Blanton? It's been a long week."

"It's really rather urgent and involves the conversations you had with Special Agent Mallon."

"Then why didn't he come?"

"He's currently under suspension." Blanton dropped the smile. "We'd like to get your side of the story before we take further disciplinary action."

Mallon had helped me out and had gotten into a jackpot because of it. More ruin in my wake. He'd helped me crack the case. The least I could do was stick up for him.

"Come on in." I swung the door open. Midnight showed Blanton his teeth.

"I was mauled as a child." Blanton looked at Midnight and then back at me. "Would you mind securing your dog?"

"He only bites people who want to hurt me. But sure." I limped over to the back door and let Midnight outside.

"What happened to your leg?" Blanton had the front door closed and was already standing near the couch in the living room.

"Old football injury." I headed back into the living room.

"Have a seat, Mr. Cahill." He pointed to the couch. "Do you need a hand?"

"I'll manage." I finally made it to the couch and sat down. It would have felt good to sit, except that I had an FBI Special Agent standing over me in my own house.

"Why did you contact Special Agent Mallon?"

If I told him the truth, I didn't know where it would end. Maybe on Coronado Beach kneeling over the dead body of Kyle Bates. I couldn't lead him down that path. Not yet. Hopefully never.

"It involves a case I'm working on and it's confidential." Mostly true. "I'm sure you understand. The FBI is big on confidentiality."

"How'd you like to be indicted as Special Agent Mallon's coconspirator?" His smile pinched flat and his small eyes went hard. "Should we talk here or back at the field office?"

Protecting Special Agent Mallon suddenly lost its righteousness. I'd been fearing Moretti putting me behind bars; now the FBI wanted to jump ahead in line.

"Coconspirator to what?" My mouth cottoned up.

"Why did you contact Special Agent Mallon?"

"After I talked with SAC Richmond at your headquarters, someone called me claiming to be Mallon. He agreed to meet me that night and give me information about the phone call Jim Colton made to the FBI before he died. I went to the meet and someone tried to kill me. I called the real Special Agent Mallon the next day and told him what had happened."

I'd taken the first step along the path that led to two dead bodies on Coronado Beach. They'd died trying to kill me and Brianne. Open and shut self-defense. Except I'd always had a hard time making law enforcement believe me.

"What about Paulie's Auto Body Repair, Ben Townsend, and Phoenix Holdings?"

I couldn't tell him what I knew without mentioning Doug McCafferty and Kyle Bates. I'd be back at the FBI field office as soon as the conversation was over. Or the Coronado Police Station.

"I don't know what you mean." I wasn't under oath. Yet.

"I know from Special Agent Mallon's computer searches that he collected information about Paulie's, Mr. Townsend, and Phoenix Holdings and passed it on to you." Blanton peered down at me, hands on his hips. "Who besides you and Brianne Colton know about them?"

An odd question for someone trying to learn the truth.

"Know what about them?" The hair on the back of my neck rose up.

"Maybe you should look at this." Blanton smiled and reached his hand inside his coat. He pulled out a gun and pointed it at my face.

CHAPTER SIXTY

I FROZE. THE air left my body. My pulse spiked.

Special Agent Blanton.

The third partner. The inside man at the FBI. Brianne's interaction with Alyssa Bates had convinced me that Alyssa had been the silent partner. I'd forgotten that there had to have been someone inside or very close to the FBI.

My carelessness might get me killed.

"Stand up. Hands behind your head."

I stood up and Blanton pressed the Glock 9mm against my chest. A black metal cylinder was screwed into the barrel. A silencer. Like Kyle Bates had used last night on the beach. Cold. Quiet. Deadly. The tool of an assassin. He patted me down with the hand not holding the gun pointed at my chest. He pulled the revolver from my shoulder holster and put it in the pocket of his trench coat.

Midnight howled and slammed against the sliding glass door from the outside.

"You were the person Colton talked to when he called the FBI a few days before he died."

"Gold star." He waved the Glock at me. "Sit down."

No weapon in range. No Oak Rollins to bail me out. No way to get to Blanton before a bullet stopped me. I sat down.

"I don't get it. Colton calls you with his suspicions about Bates and McCafferty and they suddenly decide to make you a partner?"

"I'm taking your gold star away." He smiled. A mask he probably wore his whole life to get close to people he could use. Even now when he held the upper hand. "We served together in Iraq. Well, served at the same time. But we did drink together, sometimes. I was in the logistics chain on the ground in Haditha. I was responsible for getting needed supplies into the war zone. But I also knew how to get things out. Like gold bullion, currency, and the last bearer bonds ever issued by the US Treasury in 1986 and sold exclusively overseas that some Al-Qaeda sympathizer ended up with. Until they were seized by a couple of enterprising SEALs."

"So why join the FBI when you were a millionaire?" Time. Luck. A mistake. The only things that could keep me alive.

"A millionaire's not what it used to be." He laughed. A mirthless bark. "I had two years left on my hitch in the Army. Bates and McCafferty the same in the Navy. We needed someone to get the little bit of gold we stole out of Iraq. McCafferty volunteered to die for the team and be born anew while Bates and I did our time for the USofA. We used the gold and sold a few bonds for fifty cents on the dollar to set up the holding company and then waited for the bonds to mature. Fifteen million split three ways is a much better lifestyle than a million apiece."

"But why join the FBI?"

"No better place to be to keep an eye open for any investigations into missing Iraqi war booty. Took me five years to get transferred to San Diego where I could also keep an eye on Bates. We were almost home, too. Then McCafferty gets spotted while he's in town by Colton who couldn't let things go. Such an anal sense of duty to a country that held him in as high regard as used toilet paper."

"So you had to kill him."

"Not me. Although I would have if needed." His dead eyes told me a stopwatch had just started ticking on my life. "I left that to his brother SEALs, McCafferty and Bates. The ones you somehow killed in Coronado last night. I guess I should thank you for increasing my share."

"Where did they get the fentanyl they used to incapacitate Colton before they hung him?"

"Good guess. You aren't as stupid as you look." The smile. I wanted to punch it off his face. "You'd be amazed at the things you can find in an FBI evidence locker."

"Someone's going to figure out your involvement, Blanton. Killing me just leaves more evidence to track."

"You're a problem, Mr. Cahill. You involved Special Agent Mallon. He started connecting dots and asking questions. Fortunately, he asked them of me thinking I'd take them to that politician SAC Richmond. But, you're right, sooner or later word will get to Richmond and he'll start an investigation. Now tell me where my bearer bonds are and maybe you can live."

We both knew he was lying about the living part, but all I could do was play along and try to stretch the clock. "I don't know where they are. Alyssa Bates probably has them. She was there on the beach last night and took off after her husband died. I didn't even know about—"

Someone knocked on my front door. Pounded the door.

Blanton put a finger to his lips and pointed the gun at my head.

Midnight howled and threw himself against the sliding glass door.

More knocks.

"Cahill, let's get this over with!" La Jolla Police Chief Tony Moretti shouted through the door.

"He won't go away," I whispered and prayed I was right.

"Get up." Blanton looked surprisingly calm.

He stepped forward and shoved the gun against my head and

used his other hand to help me off the couch. He walked me to the door.

"Any movement and you die." He stuck the gun in my side and glanced through the peephole. Then he stepped behind me with the gun still in my side. "Answer it and get rid of him."

I opened the door. Moretti stood on the porch in a suit, brown lunch bag in his hand at his side. Alone.

"You want to do the buccal swap here or downtown?" He smirked and lifted the paper bag. "The time has come, Cahill."

The gun pushed harder into my right side hidden by the door.

"You have a warrant?"

"Hardball. Always hardball with you, Cahill. I thought you'd jump at an opportunity to exonerate yourself, but if you want a warrant, I'll get you one."

"Downtown. I'll go downtown with you, Moretti." I blurted the words out. Maybe jail could save my life.

"Chief Moretti. So nice to see you again." Blanton stepped from behind me in front of the door with open angles on both Moretti and me. His gun hand hidden behind his right leg. "Come in and we can discuss who has jurisdiction to arrest Mr. Cahill."

"Special Agent Blanton?" Moretti scrunched his face. "What the hell are you doing here?"

"You're not the only agency investigating Mr. Cahill." The smile. "Come in and we can compare notes."

Moretti stepped inside, his face frozen in a squint. Blanton pushed the door closed.

"I'm ready, Chief. Downtown." I took a step. "Let's go."

"We can all figure this out down at the station." Moretti turned the doorknob.

Blanton swung the gun up at Moretti.

"Look out!" I lunged at Blanton. Flames came out of the silencer with a soft "pift." Burnt gunpowder stained the air. I hit Blanton in the side with my shoulder and grabbed for the gun. I heard Moretti's body hit the ground just before Blanton and I landed on the floor. Blanton slid on his back and angled the gun at me. I grabbed his jacket but couldn't reach his arm.

The sliding glass door exploded into shatterproof pellets. Midnight tumbled along the hardwood floor. Blanton twisted and swung the gun at Midnight. My hand found his coat pocket. And my .357 Magnum. The pift of Blanton's silencer. The magnum's trigger. Six explosions. Empty.

Blanton still. Midnight, unhit, stood over his body, growling. I staggered over to Moretti. A hole in his chest. Shirt soaked red. He blinked and held up a hand. Then our eyes met and reality crystallized between us. No warrant. His investigation was still off the books.

If he died, I went free.

EPILOGUE

I FOUGHT BACK tears the first time I heard Brianne's number-one hit on the radio, "California Cowboy." The song she'd written for me, but never sang out loud. Now it came from a studio two thousand miles away in Nashville. She moved there shortly after December 1. She hired the best studio musicians in Music City and cut a demo that went platinum. I still get a $5,000 check in the mail from Nashville at the beginning of every month.

I haven't cashed one yet. I never will.

Rollins and I turned ourselves in to Coronado PD the day the ambulances arrived at my house. After the San Diego Police Department questioned me for three hours about the blood-bath in my home. It took many more hours under the hot lights in Coronado and corroboration from Brianne, but Rollins and I weren't arrested. In fact, we were hailed as heroes on the news. Jim Colton's death was finally ruled a homicide with the help of the new La Jolla Chief of Police.

I've suffered tragedies in my life and been unlucky in love. But in the end, life finally tried to even things out. I've been shot a couple times, but survived. Had bones broken and bent, but can still walk. My dog's been poisoned and shot at, but is still alive and healthy. I have a job I like and I still own a home. There's even a number-one country song about me on the radio, sung by a woman I could have loved.

And I have a brand-new Congressman named Tony Moretti, who, legend and the official record say, saved my life. Not the other way around, which is fine by me. Hailed a hero, Moretti left my city for Washington D.C.

And he's finally decided to let the past stay dead.

And buried.